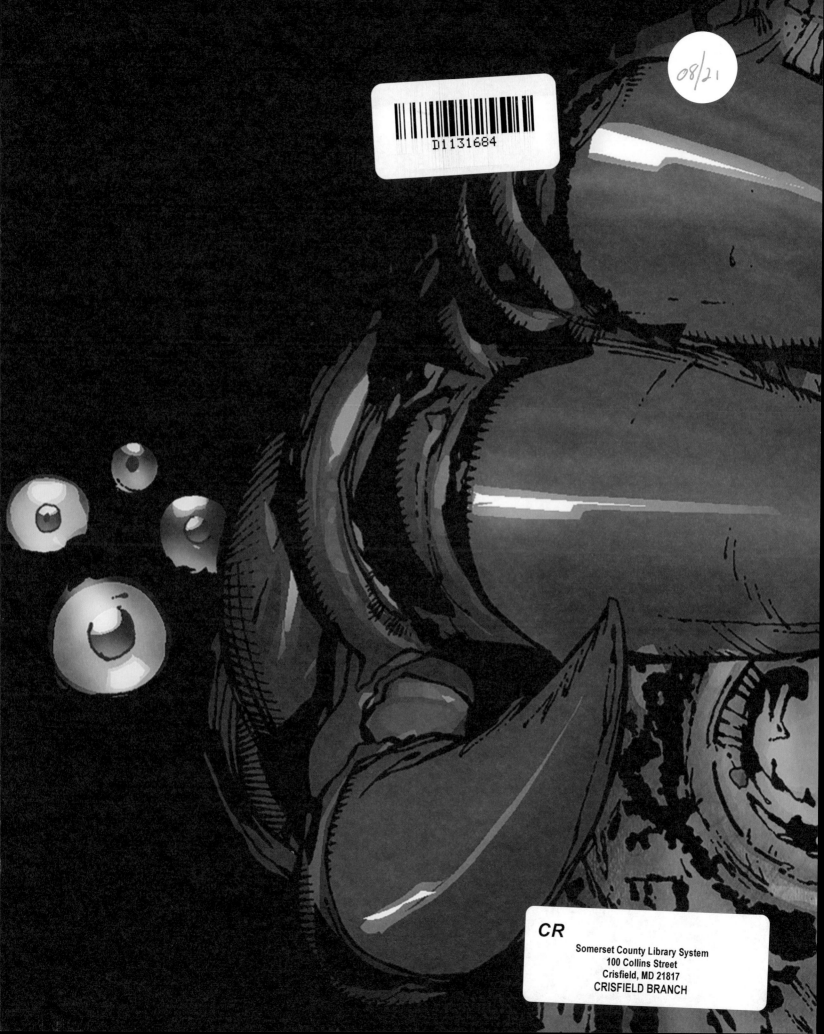

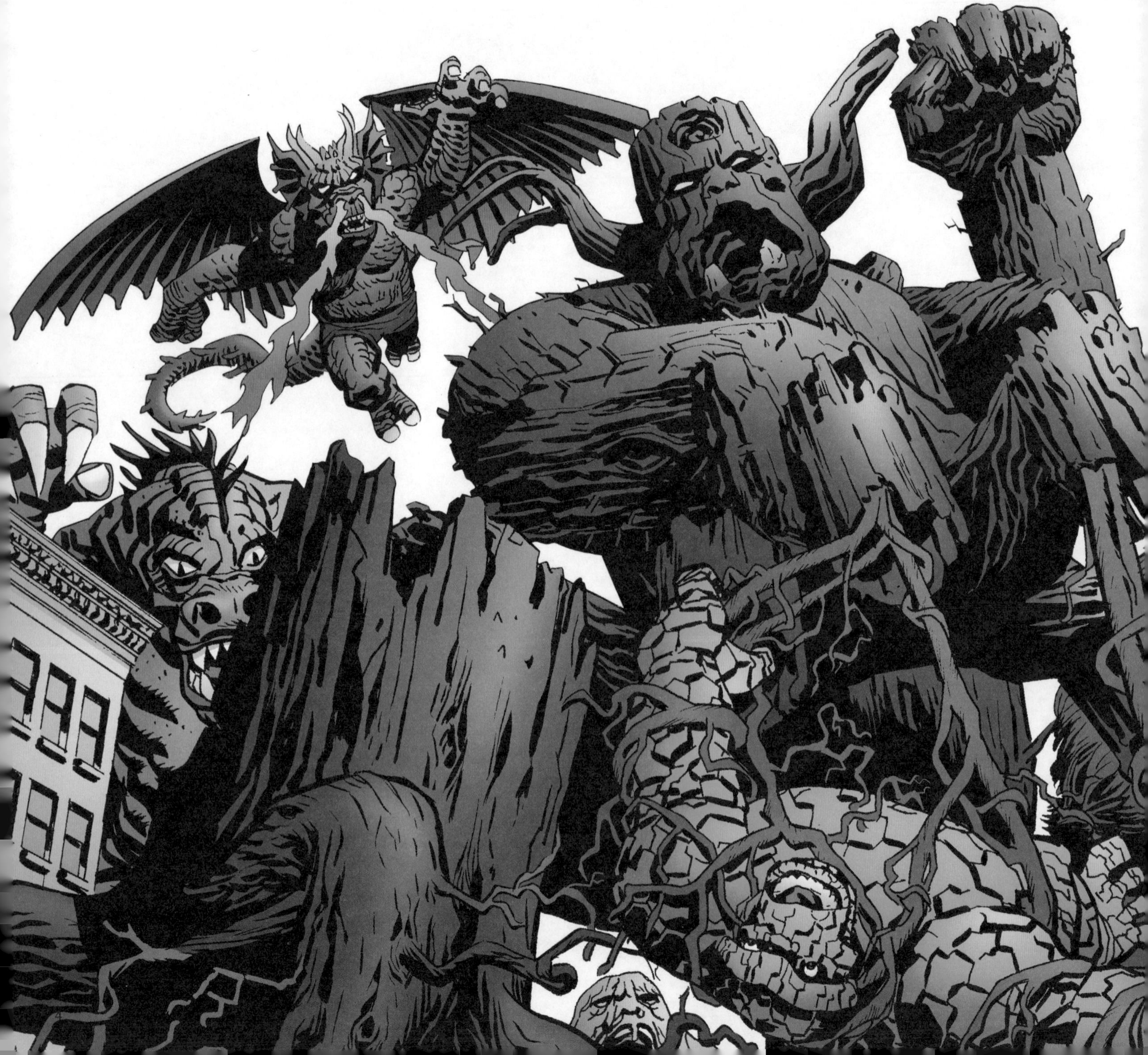

MARVEL

MONSTERS

CREATURES OF THE MARVEL UNIVERSE EXPLORED

WRITTEN BY KELLY KNOX

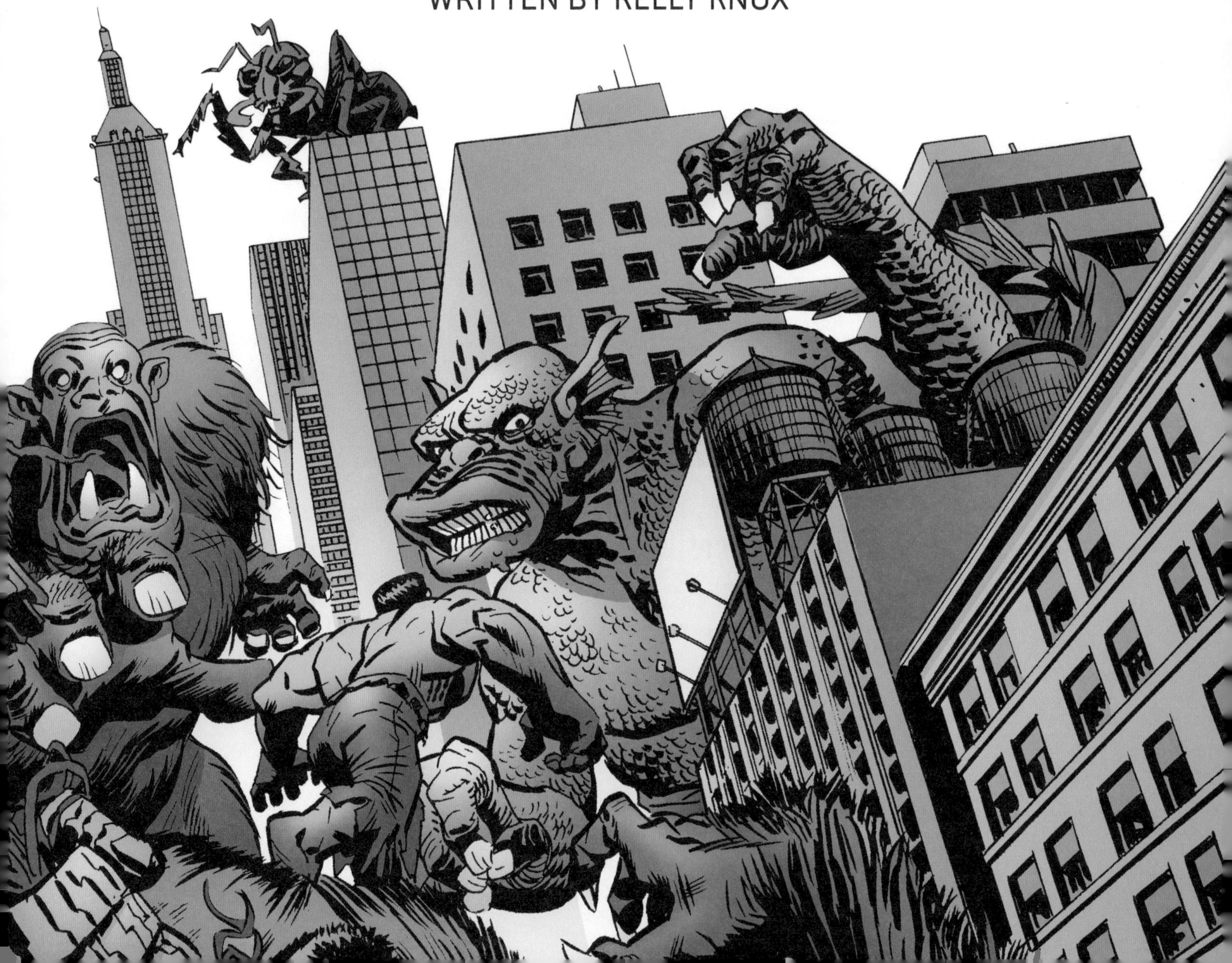

Contents

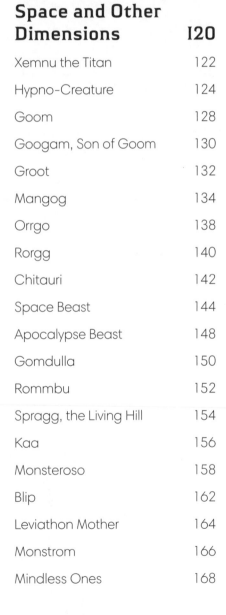

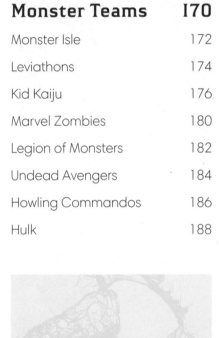

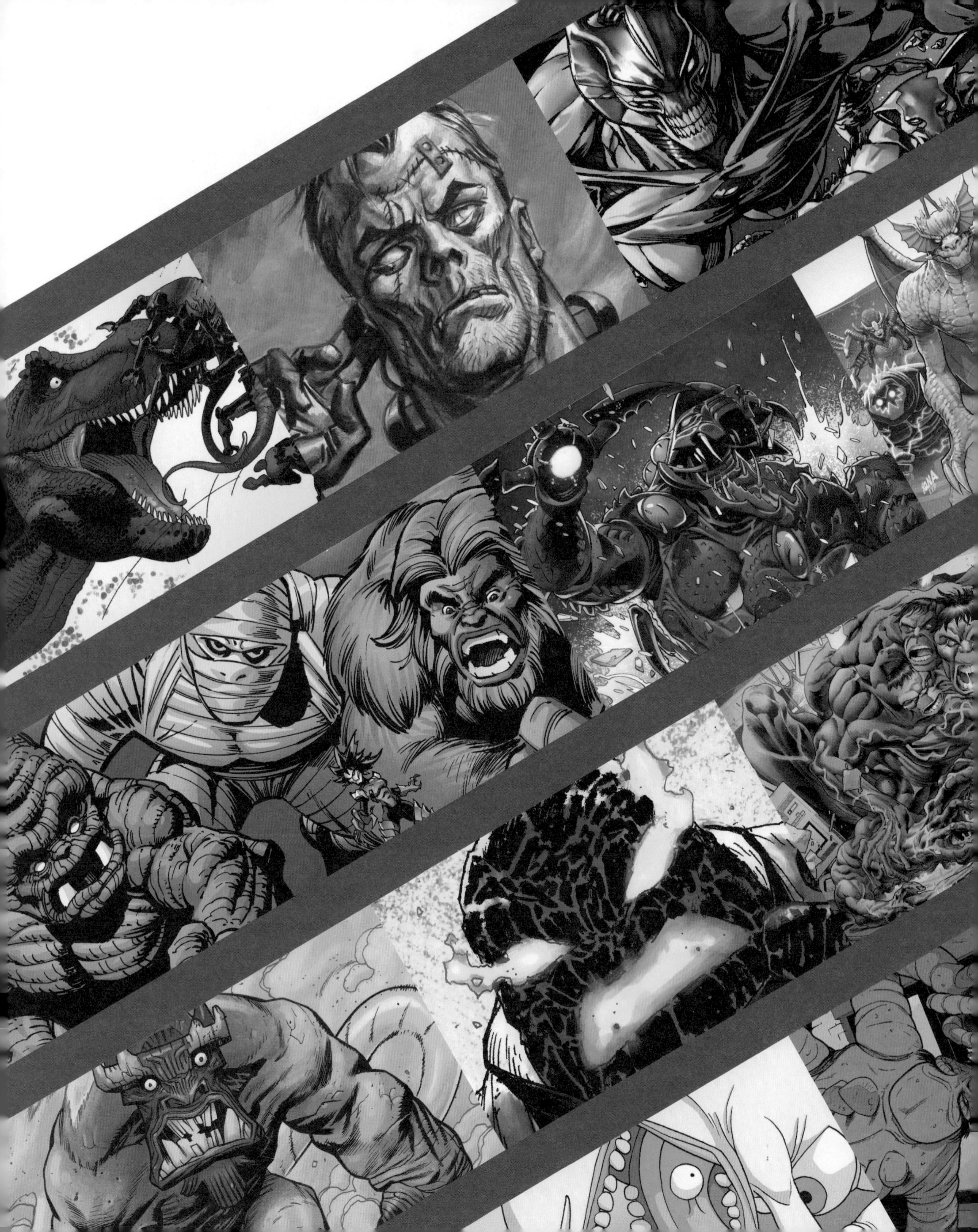

Introduction

"My monsters were lovable monsters. I gave them names—some were evil and some were good."

– JACK KIRBY

What makes a monster?

Before masters of the medium Stan Lee and Jack Kirby created some of the world's greatest Super Heroes, they made monsters. Their creations rampaged and bellowed across the colorful pages of 10 cent comics found in newsstands across the country. Lee and Kirby's strange and astonishing tales tended to reflect the fears and hopes of the 1960s. Monsters were born from radioactive accidents against the backdrop of the Cold War, and conquerors from the stars declared the Earth for their own as the Space Race marched on.

In later years, more Marvel creators would shape their creatures as signs of the times. During the 1970s and 1980s, legends like werewolves and vampires were transformed into modern monsters such as the Werewolf By Night and Morbius the Living Vampire. Monsters also became contemplative and complicated anti-heroes, including the Hulk. As the 20th century came to a close, the end of the world took hold in the collective consciousness, and, in the next millennium, monsters that could bring about Armageddon were born. Apocalypse Beast, Marvel Zombies, and the Leviathon Mother were almost the end of it all until brave and brilliant heroes banded together to stop them.

No matter the era, Marvel's monsters highlight the courage of characters, both average and extraordinary, who stood in their way. This collection is a peek back through time where voices of everyday people often told larger-than-life stories of extra-sized extraterrestrials, glowering giants, and mysterious misfits.

In a world filled with beings that defy belief, monsters stand out from the crowd, and not just because of their size. A monster is a creature we don't understand yet. Why is it here? What does it want? Answering those questions are just the first steps in turning monsters from "it" to "them."

Let's meet some monsters.

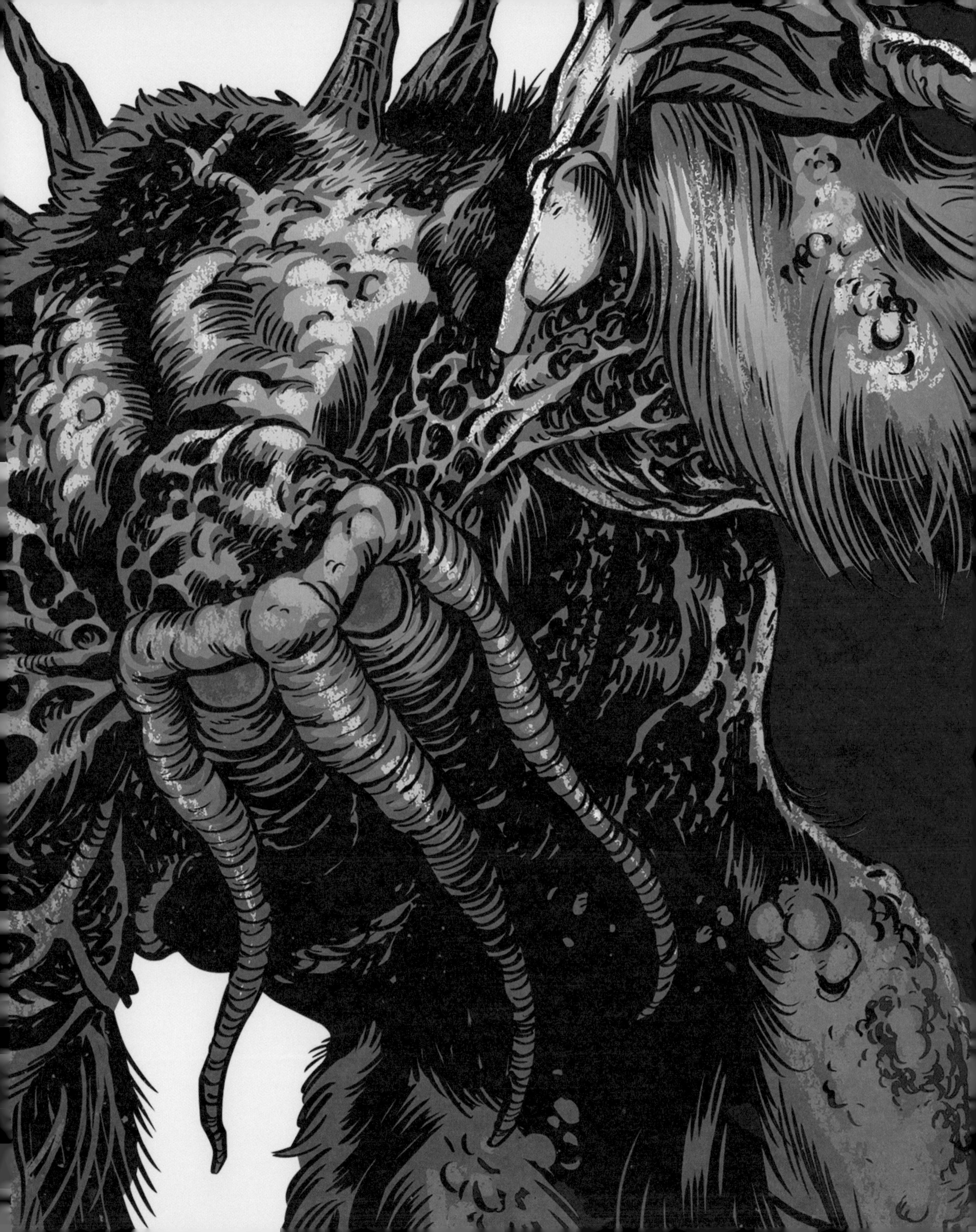

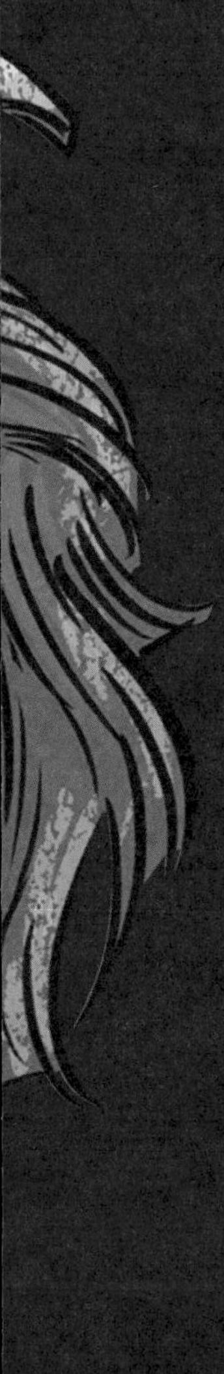

AQUATIC

The pitch-black ocean floor, frozen regions, murky marshlands, the frothing waves on a coastline: The water is home to some of planet Earth's most fearsome monsters.

Add radioactivity that has gone awry, mystical magic, bizarre chemicals, or ancient science into the mix, and there is a recipe for some of the most threatening and strange terrors to rise up from the watery depths.

Giant sea creatures such as Monstro and Titano, plants and humans merged into organic ogres like Man-Thing and Glob, and other denizens of secret sea kingdoms emerge from their watery abodes. Perhaps equipped with webbed fingers and toes, or internal organs specially adapted to breathing in water, these monsters have physiologies well suited to aquatic environments.

Let's dive into a swell of monsters from the sea and swamp.

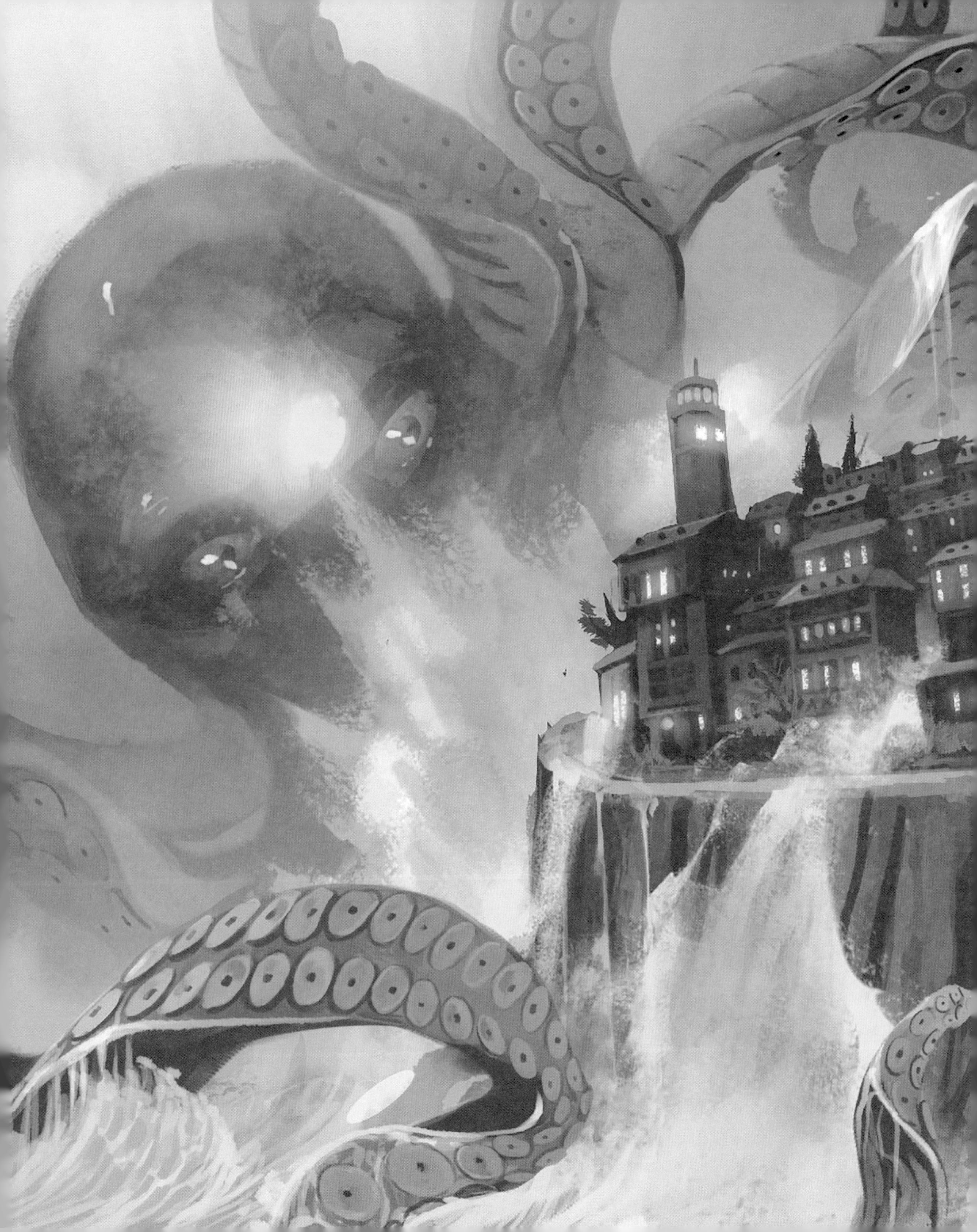

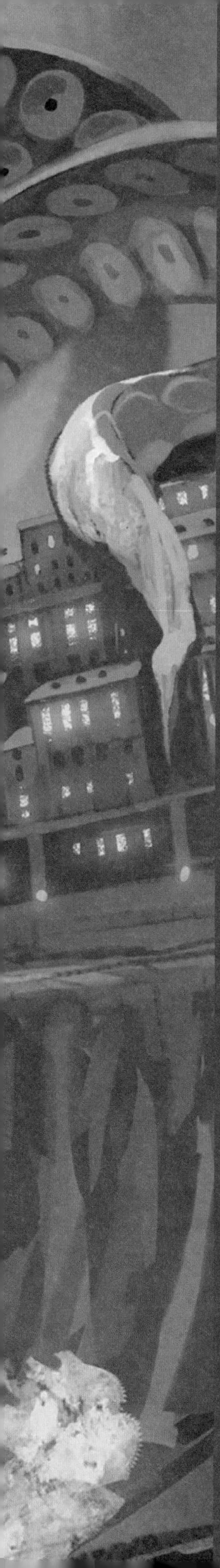

Height: 328ft (100m) **Weight:** 30,000 tons **Origin:** Unknown **Powers:** Massive size, strength, and durability

Monstro

Rising up out of the sea, a giant octopus of unfathomable size draws up its tentacles and smashes them down on the building below. A Soviet coastal town becomes the first target for this marine monster—Monstro, the Menace from the Murky Depths.

This gargantuan, orange cephalopod has two massive, unblinking eyes. At his first known sighting he remained in the ocean water where he surfaced, near an Eastern European coastal city. The monster appeared unwilling to leave the area and soon proved himself to be a menace: upturning boats, destroying buildings, and smashing the pier with his tentacles. The shaken citizens dubbed him Monstro, and fled. Declaring the situation to be a national emergency, the desperate authorities contacted a top American scientist for help. The marine biologist traveled to their country to see the eight-legged threat for himself.

Donning scuba-diving gear, the scientist rowed a boat out to the creature as it languished in the city's harbor. Despite the obvious danger, he dived in to examine Monstro. After running a test on the mighty octopus, he advised the authorities to simply leave Monstro alone for the next 24 hours. When pressed by the mistrustful officials, the scientist refused to elaborate. Later, spotting a lynch mob outside his hotel window, the man secretly fled back to the US.

Twenty-four hours later, true to the scientist's word, Monstro reverted to his regular size. The sea monster was originally an ordinary octopus, the scientist later explained to a colleague. Undisclosed atomic testing and radioactivity had mutated the cephalopod; the scientist hadn't wanted to reveal that he had learned this secret, fearing the authorities would destroy Monstro in an attempt to hide the evidence of their meddling.

That was not the last of Monstro, however. He was later spotted in his giant form in the US West Coast city of San Diego.

First Appearance: *Tales of Suspense* #8 (1960) by Stan Lee, Larry Lieber, and Jack Kirby

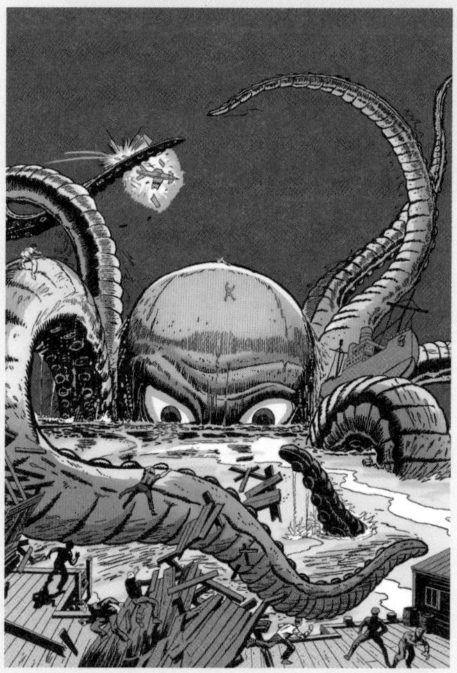

Eye contact
Like a regular octopus, Monstro possesses two eyes, but they are irregularly the size of small boats.

Monstro Anatomy

Three hearts, nine brains, and eight tentacles sound like a body only a monster could have, but that's typical for even the most ordinary octopus in the ocean. As a mutated member of the species, Monstro displays all these—just on a much larger scale.

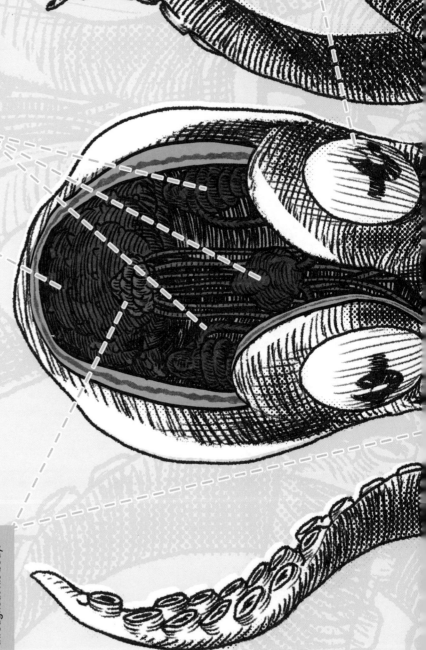

Tentacle touch
Each tentacle is capable of searching for enemies and prey thanks to its sensitive suckers and abundant nerve cells.

Super vision
Two large eyes can see even in the darkest, murkiest seawater.

Poison sac
Radioactive chemicals are stored in an enormous pouch.

Heartbreaker
Monstro has one main heart and two branchial hearts to pump blood throughout his body.

Nine brains
Like all octopuses, even the non-mutated ones, Monstro has nine brains located throughout his body.

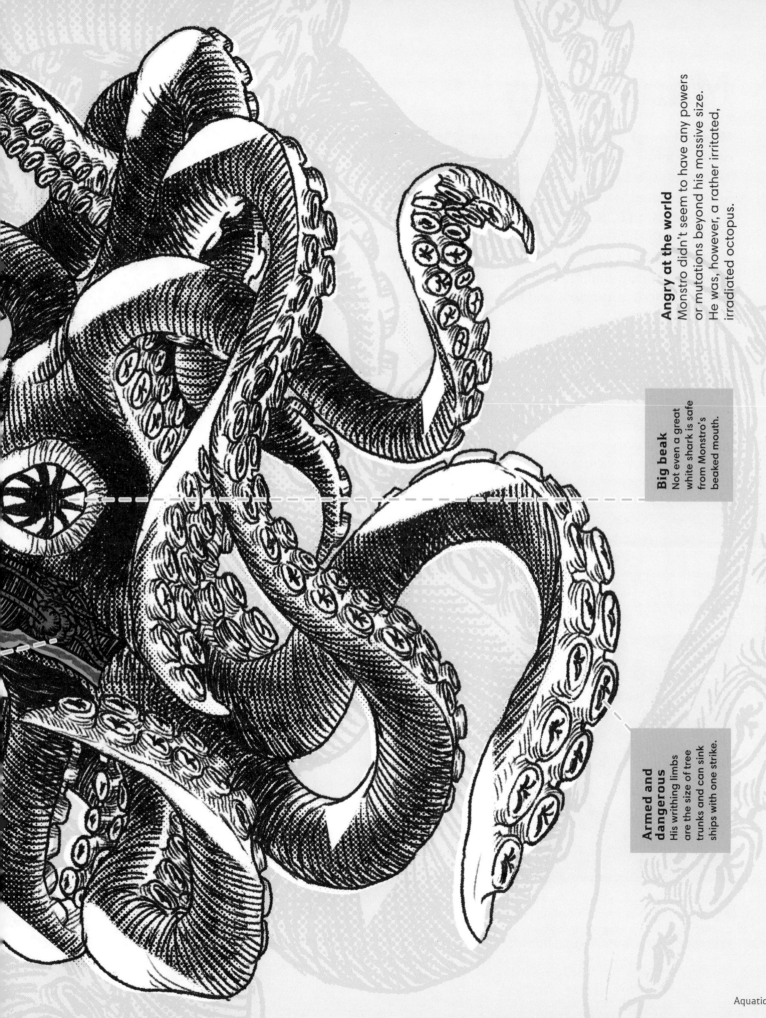

Angry at the world

Monstro didn't seem to have any powers or mutations beyond his massive size. He was, however, a rather irritated, irradiated octopus.

Big beak
Not even a great white shark is safe from Monstro's beaked mouth.

Armed and dangerous
His writhing limbs are the size of tree trunks and can sink ships with one strike.

Man-Thing

Man or beast? Plant or animal? Hero or villain? Man-Thing almost defies definition. He was once the brilliant Theodore "Ted" Sallis, a biochemical researcher working on the next Super-Soldier formula. Attacked by rivals hoping to get their hands on it, Sallis fled. In desperation, he injected himself with the experimental serum and, in the same moment, his car plunged off a bridge into the swamp beneath. Mutagenic chemicals mingled with the murky water of the Everglades, and the scientist was transformed.

The boggy soil Sallis fell into was no ordinary muck. Sallis had merged with a part of the swamp that serves as a nexus of mystic dimensions. Newly resembling the dense marshes, Sallis became a beast that would be named "Man-Thing" by the terrified humans he encountered. Forced to make his home there, he became the guardian of the Nexus of Reality. A creature of both science and magic, Man-Thing has crossed paths with some of the most mysterious beings in the universe, from demons like D'Spayre to notable heroes such as Doctor Strange and Howard the Duck.

Driven by his powerful empathic ability, negative emotions cause Man-Thing physical and psychic pain. Above all, it seems Man-Thing abhors fear the most and mindlessly attacks the source of it, whether friend or foe. Anything that knows fear burns when touched by him. Man-Thing is an unthinking creature, acting on instinct to save the innocent and protect his watery home, without knowing why.

Following this instinct he has teamed up with Spider-Man and Thor, been a member of the Legion of Monsters alongside Ghost Rider and Morbius, and withstood punches from Hulk, The Thing, and She-Hulk. The seven-foot-tall Man-Thing is more than a match for these other behemoths with his own super-strength and regenerative abilities granted by mystical energy sourced in the muddy swamp waters.

Beast vs. beast
Anything—human, animal, dinosaur, or even synthezoid—that feels fear will drive the mindless Man-Thing to attack.

First Appearance: *Savage Tales* #1 (1971) by Stan Lee, Roy Thomas, Gerry Conway, and Gray Morrow **Further reading:** *Adventure Into Fear* #10 (1970), *Man-Thing* #1 (1974), *Marvel Team-Up* #68 (1972), *Champions* #23 (2016)

Height: 7ft (2.13m) **Weight:** 500 lbs (227kg) **Origin:** Florida **Powers:** Super-strength; empathy; regeneration; burning touch; mystical abilities

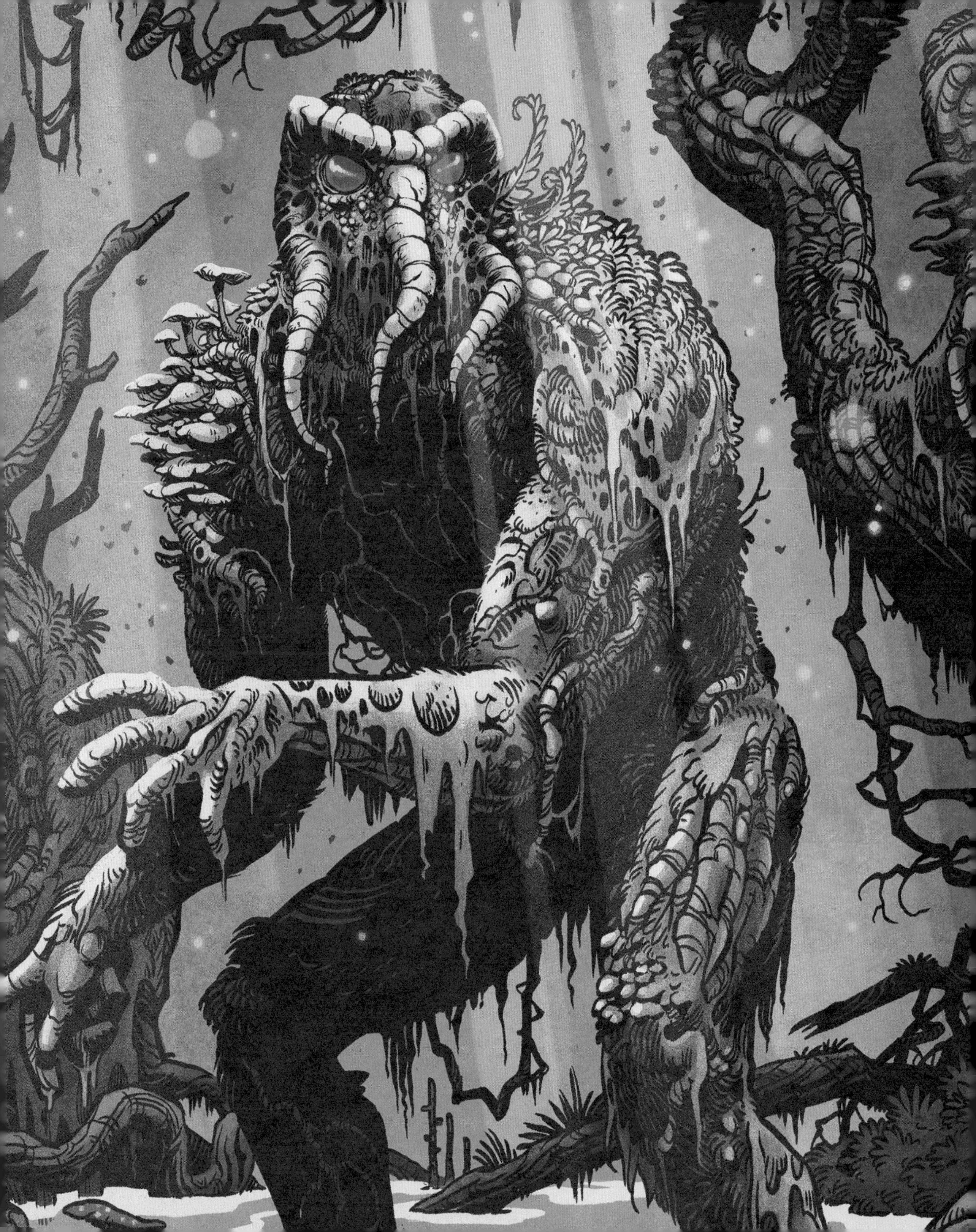

Man-Thing Anatomy

Since his mutation into Man-Thing, Sallis has become a being of pure emotion and instinctual reactions, no longer guided by conscious thought or reasoning. Only a sliver of his original humanity remains—buried deep inside his massive, marshy frame. As a consequence of the transformation, the Everglades swamp is now his life source as well as his refuge—if he leaves the waters for too long, he risks growing dormant.

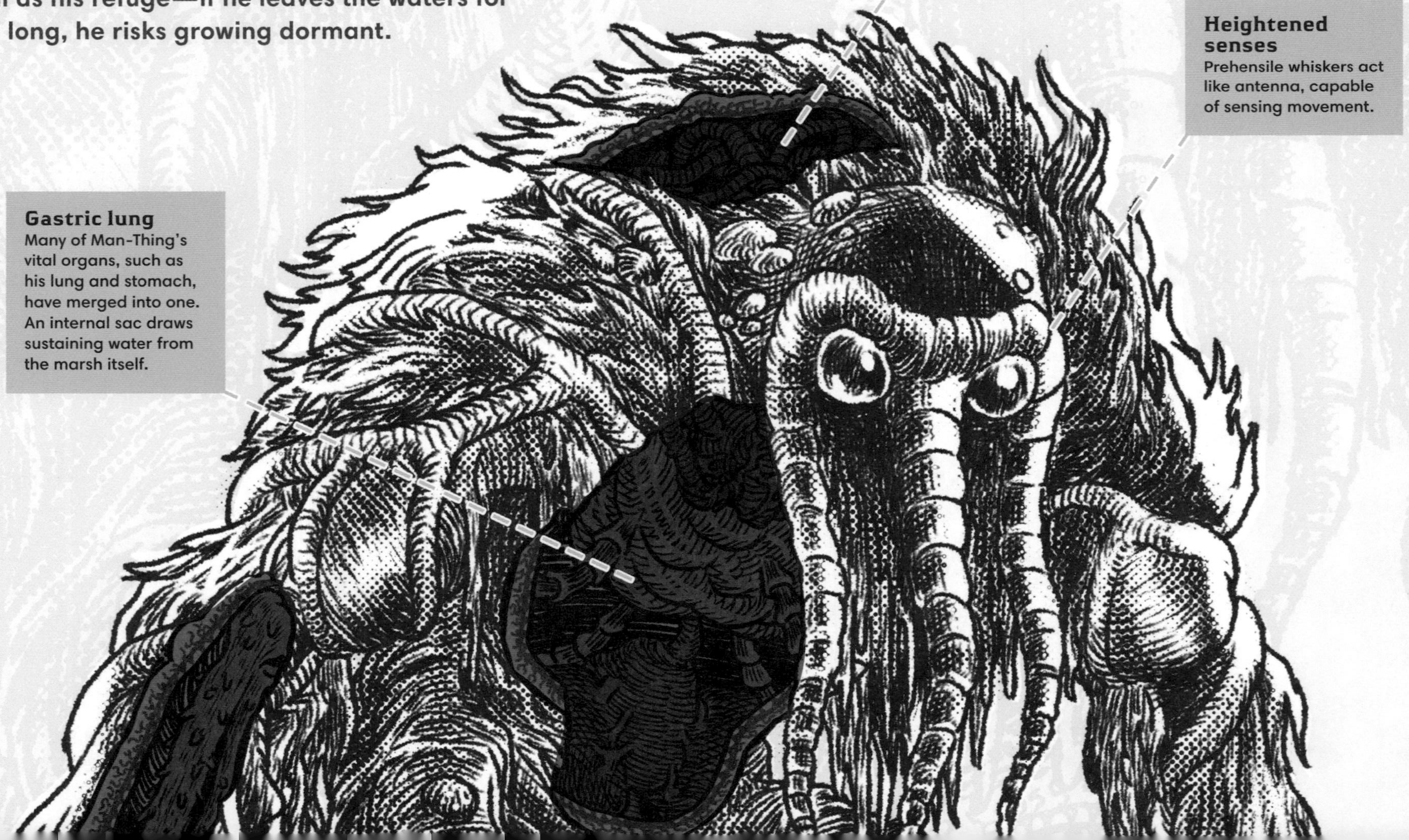
Swamp inside
Roots, ooze, and slime make up the inside of the murk-monster. His veins are filled with highly acidic blood.
Heightened senses
Prehensile whiskers act like antenna, capable of sensing movement.
Gastric lung
Many of Man-Thing's vital organs, such as his lung and stomach, have merged into one. An internal sac draws sustaining water from the marsh itself.

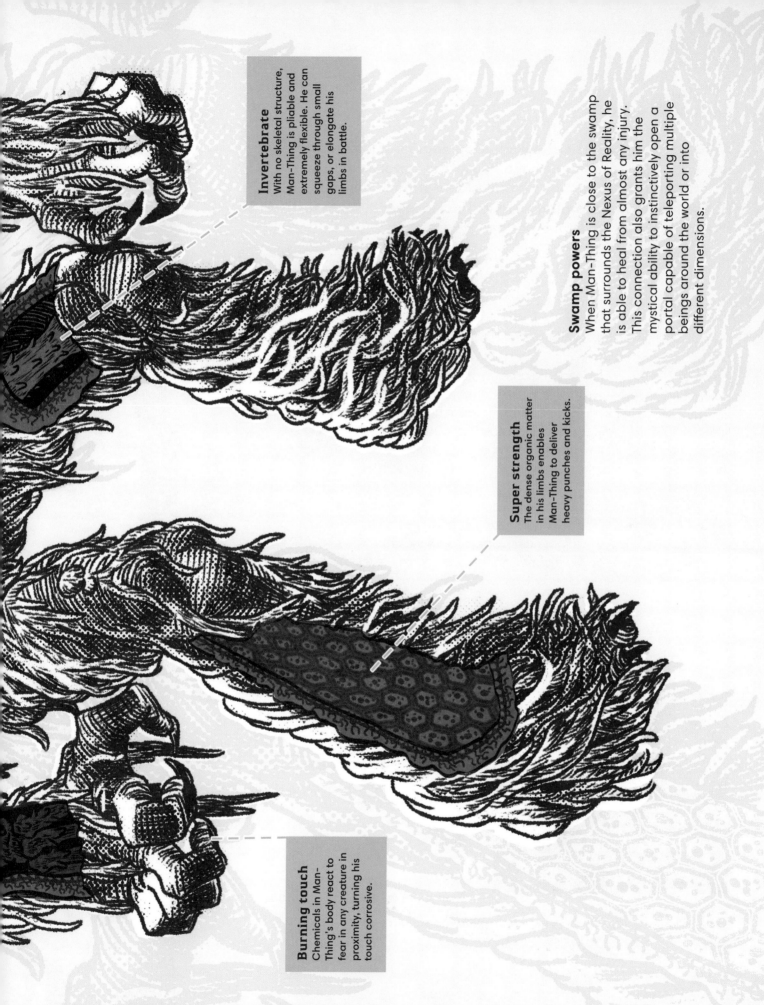

Invertebrate
With no skeletal structure, Man-Thing is pliable and extremely flexible. He can squeeze through small gaps, or elongate his limbs in battle.

Swamp powers
When Man-Thing is close to the swamp that surrounds the Nexus of Reality, he is able to heal from almost any injury. This connection also grants him the mystical ability to instinctively open a portal capable of teleporting multiple beings around the world or into different dimensions.

Super strength
The dense organic matter in his limbs enables Man-Thing to deliver heavy punches and kicks.

Burning touch
Chemicals in Man-Thing's body react to fear in any creature in proximity, turning his touch corrosive.

Titano

With grasping pincers capable of snapping a warship in two and each giant eye the size of a house, this supersized sea monster terrorizes the oceans and islands around the world. He is Titano and according to South Pacific legend, when he rises from the deep, let the world beware.

The quiet calm of a sunny day in the South Pacific was shattered when Titano first rose from the ocean depths. Once considered a creature of local legend, Titano proved to be all too real as his massive, crab-like body created tidal waves on the coastlines of Japan and Alaska. He attacked anyone who dared to get too close. The US Navy was dispatched in a last-ditch effort to stop the enormous crustacean.

US Navy Commander Hartnell came up with a cunning plan. He ordered a crew of volunteers to cover a submarine in quick-drying, luminous paint. Tracking the behemoth to where he was last sighted, Hartnell gave the order to head north east. Acting as a lure, the glowing submarine attracted the attention of Titano. The submarine sped through the ocean depths into the freezing waters of the Arctic, with the monstrous menace in pursuit. Hartnell commanded his crew to head straight toward an iceberg, changing course by 90° at the very last minute. It was too late for the monster to stop, and it became trapped in the vast Arctic ice. The threat was at an end—for the time being.

Titano is said to be so big that no one has ever seen more than a fragment of him. Even whales are dwarfed by his enormous size. He appears to act only on instinct as he lashes out in reaction to other creatures and is mesmerized by the glowing colors of a submarine. Like a crab, Titano has a thick protective shell and two gigantic snapping claws. He is also agile and quick enough to keep pace with a speeding atomic-powered submarine. As he moves, his sheer bulk creates tidal waves.

There have been no further reports of Titano, so presumably he remains frozen in the Arctic ice.

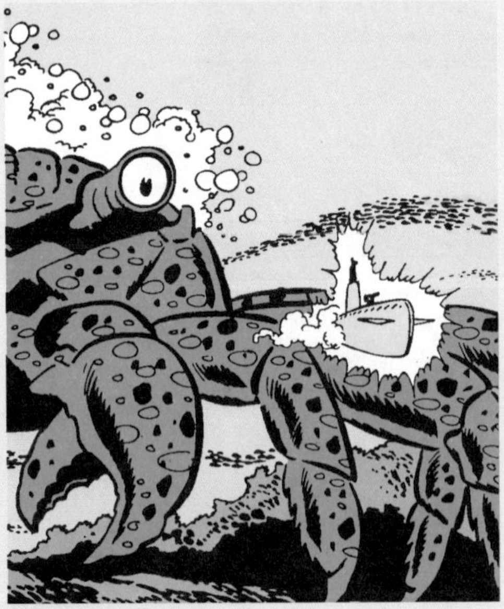

Pincers of power
The crab's unbelievably big claws are capable of snapping the reinforced metal hull of a warship or submarine in two.

First Appearance: *Tales to Astonish* #10 (1960) by Stan Lee, Larry Lieber, and Jack Kirby

Height: Unknown **Weight:** Unknown **Origin:** Pacific Ocean **Powers:** Behemoth size; massive super-strong claws; capable of creating tidal waves

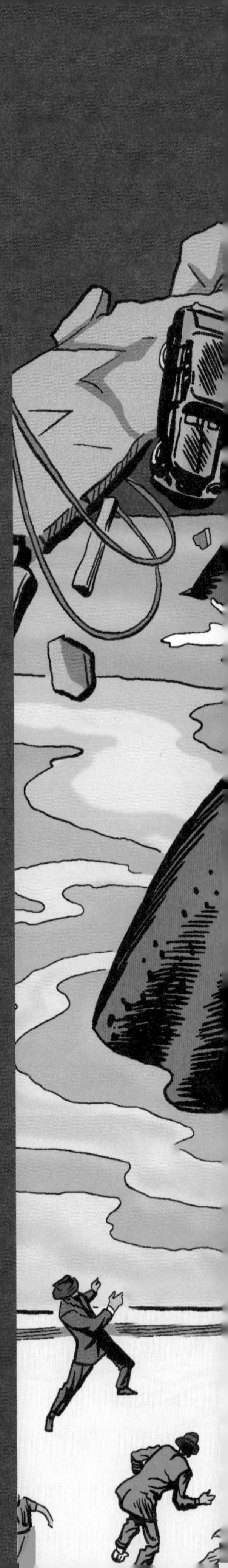

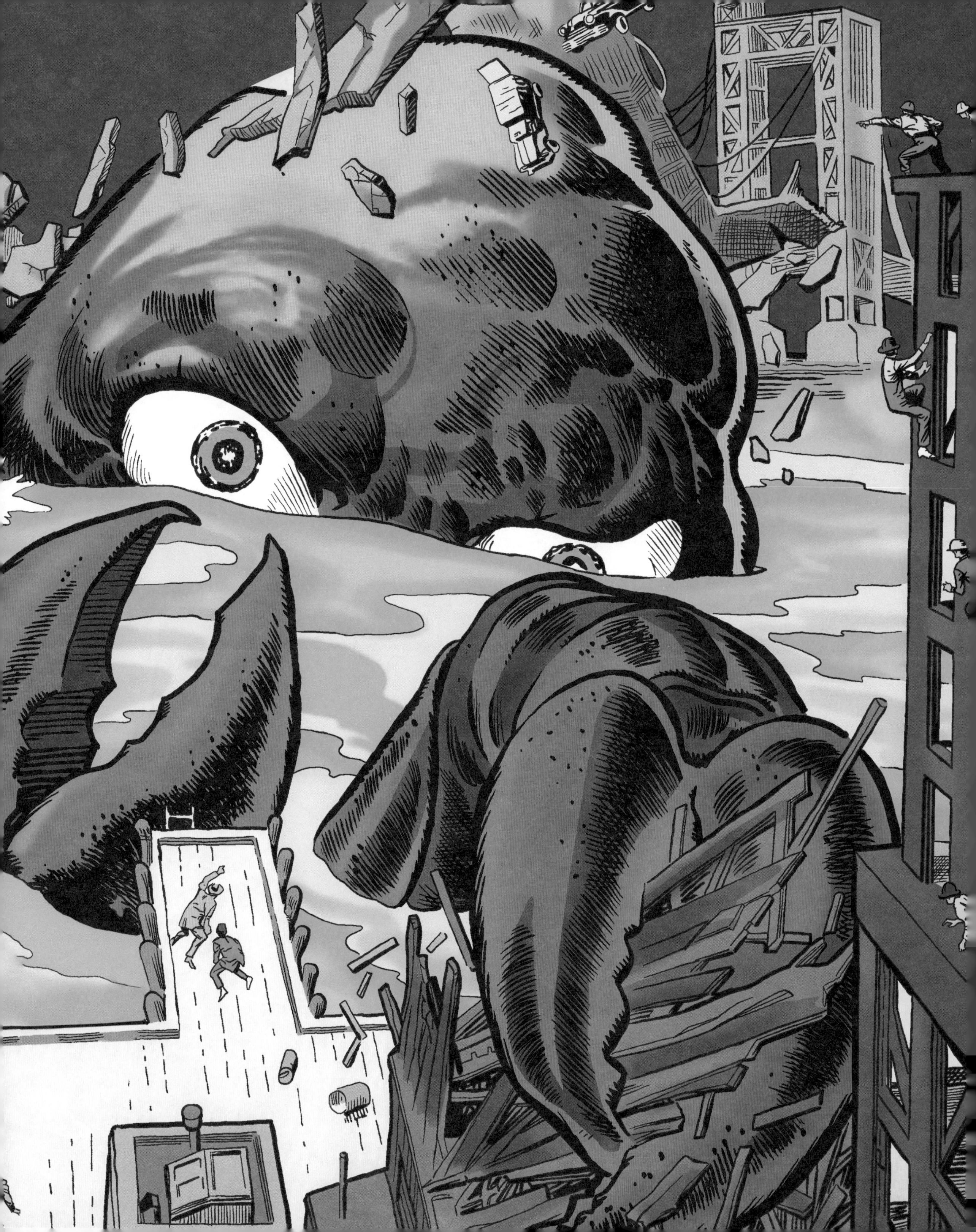

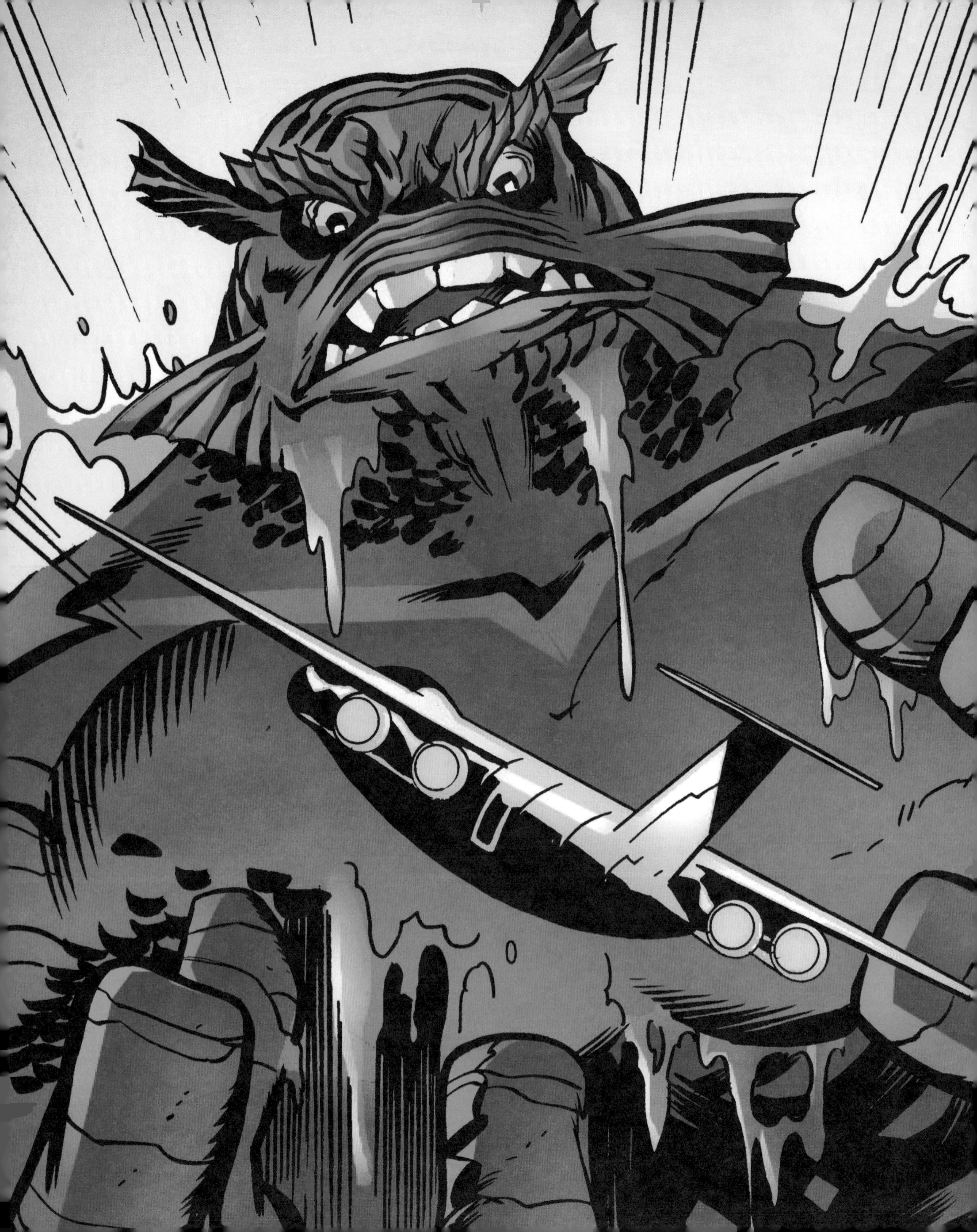

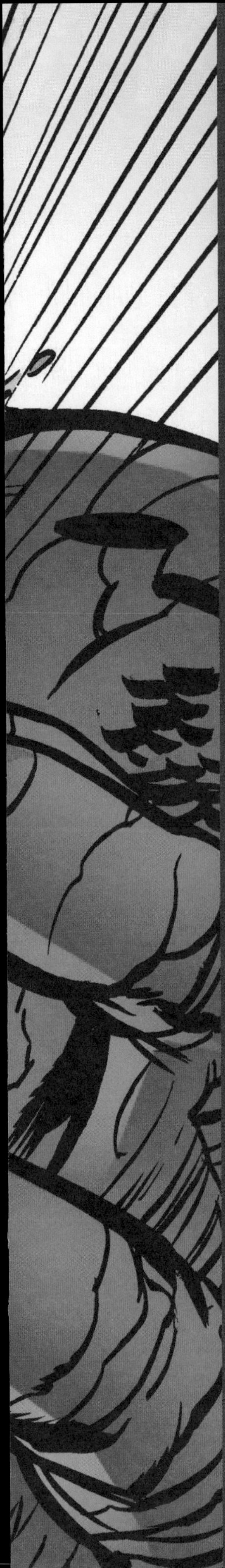

Height: 500ft (152.4m) **Weight:** 146,000 tons **Origin:** Mu **Powers:** Superhuman size, strength, and durability; amphibious breathing

Gigantus

When a monster big enough to topple ships and generate tsunamis emerges from the watery depths of the Atlantic Ocean, he is dubbed Gigantus, the Monster that Walks Like a Man. Laying claim to the surface world, his very presence sends Earth's inhabitants fleeing for the hills.

This amphibious behemoth surfaced from his underwater home of Mu at the behest of his ruler. He was commanded to explore Earth's surface and prepare the humans for his kind to arrive and rule them. Gigantus' colossal steps through the ocean created tidal waves that threatened to overturn seagoing vessels and demolish coastline cities. At the request of the land dwellers, Gigantus agreed to let them evacuate to the mountains before he set his webbed feet upon the land.

Free to scout the terrain unopposed, Gigantus determined humanity posed no threat—deeming people to be too small to be concerned about. As he prepared to return to the deep to report his findings, Gigantus came face to face with a being more than twice his size. The creature called himself Ulvar, and laid claim to the planet for his own invasion. Daunted by the extraterrestrial's massive size, Gigantus abandoned his plans and asked for Ulvar to allow him to retreat to the safety of the sea. He fled, never to return, unaware that Ulvar was an enormous model figure built by a cunning advertising man hiding inside. Earth's people had decided that the only way to defeat a monster of such size was to create something even larger—a bold tactic that worked.

Eventually, Gigantus would take up residence on Monster Isle as one of Mole Man's loyal companions. He was dedicated to their leader and defended the island's shores whenever he was called upon.

This orange-scaled, oceanic ogre is a Deviant Mutate—a result of experimentation by the advanced Deviants race that preceded humanity. Resembling a giant, walking, humanoid fish, Gigantus has webbed fingers and toes, as well as an enormous dorsal fin. He is amphibious, while dwelling underwater, he can also survive on Earth's surface for some time.

First Appearance: *Journey Into Mystery* #63 (1960) by Stan Lee, Larry Lieber, and Jack Kirby **Further Reading:** *Journey Into Mystery* #649 (2013)

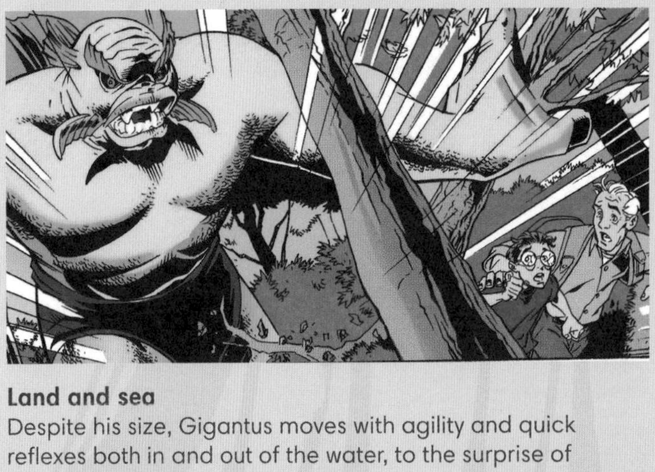

Land and sea
Despite his size, Gigantus moves with agility and quick reflexes both in and out of the water, to the surprise of any humans who encounter him.

Gigantus Anatomy

The monster from Mu is a literal fish out of water, capable of walking with an amphibious anatomy. His fascinating physiology is strongly suited to swimming, walking, and defending himself. One poke from his venomous fins could completely incapacitate an attacker.

Massive muscles
Gigantus, like the others of his aquatic kind, has enormous strength capable of breaking a ship in two.

Poisonous points
His fins not only help him navigate smoothly through water, but some contain toxic liquid as well.

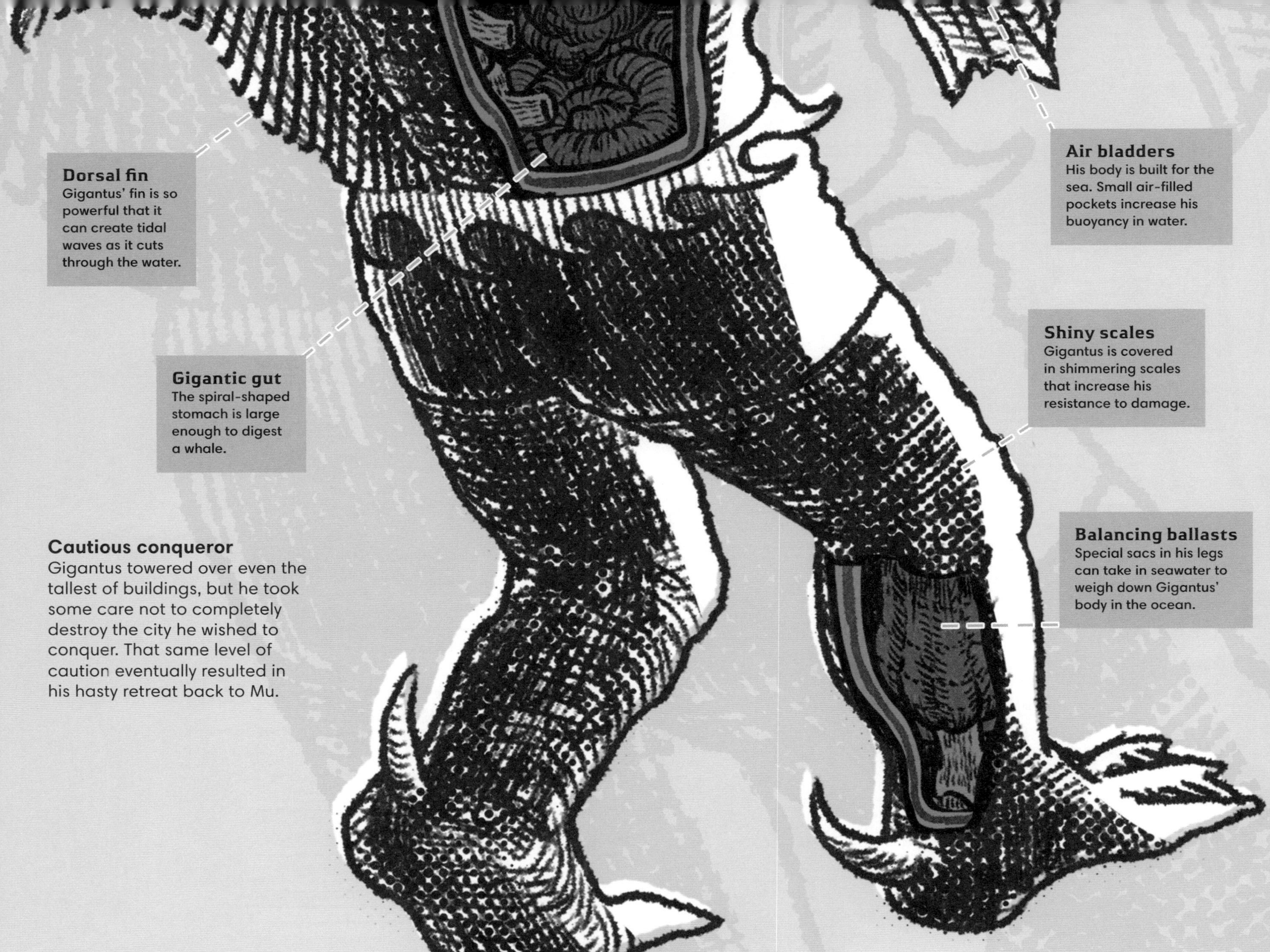
Dorsal fin
Gigantus' fin is so powerful that it can create tidal waves as it cuts through the water.
Gigantic gut
The spiral-shaped stomach is large enough to digest a whale.
Air bladders
His body is built for the sea. Small air-filled pockets increase his buoyancy in water.
Shiny scales
Gigantus is covered in shimmering scales that increase his resistance to damage.
Balancing ballasts
Special sacs in his legs can take in seawater to weigh down Gigantus' body in the ocean.

Cautious conqueror

Gigantus towered over even the tallest of buildings, but he took some care not to completely destroy the city he wished to conquer. That same level of caution eventually resulted in his hasty retreat back to Mu.

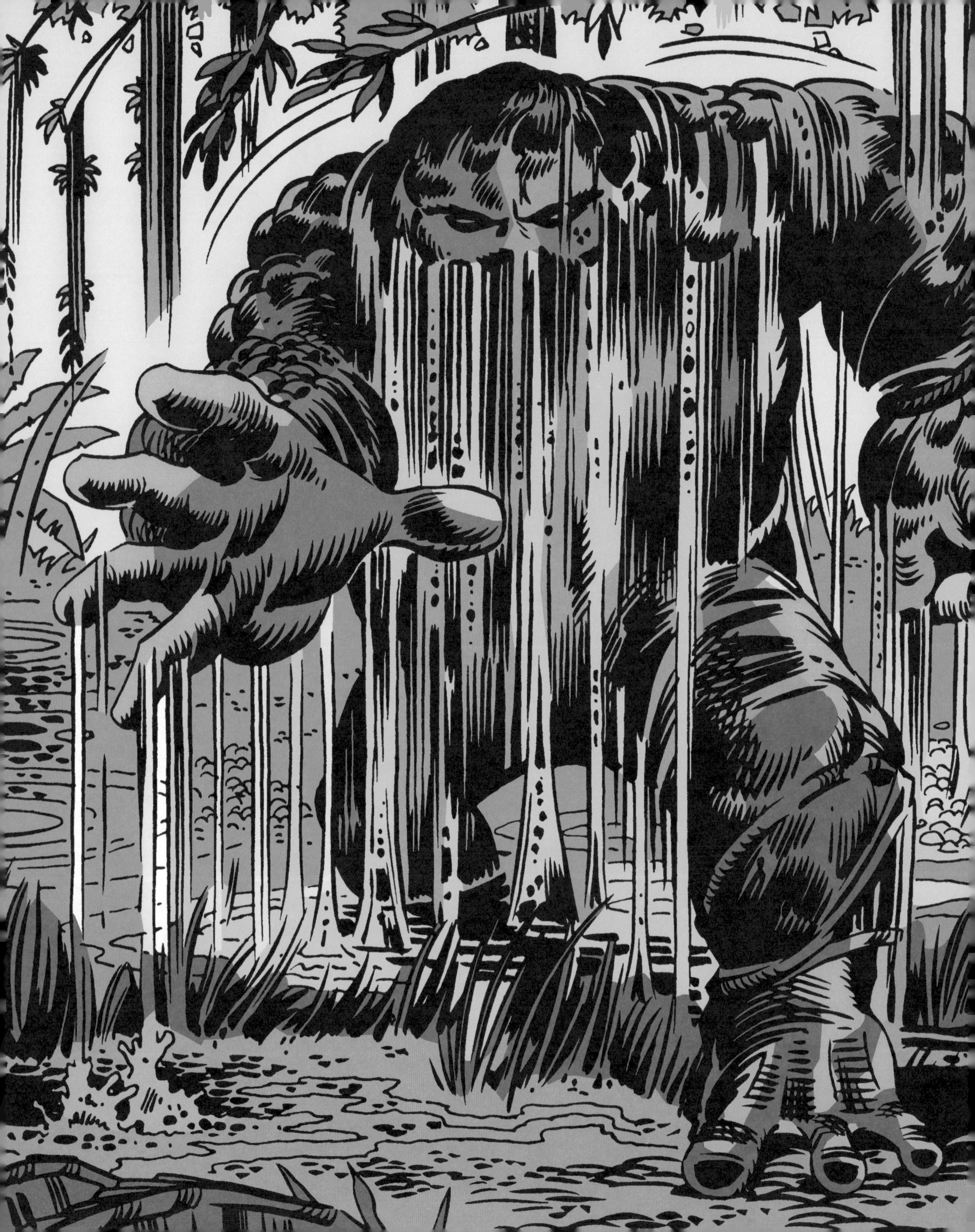

Height: 6ft 6in (1.9m) **Weight:** 900 lbs (408kg) **Origin:** The Everglades, Florida **Powers:** Superhuman strength and durability; regeneration

Glob

Shaped by swamp slime and radioactive waste, the monster aptly named Glob dwells among the Florida Everglades. Despite his limited intellect, Glob's exceptional strength, stamina, and durability mean that he can hold his own against any adversary—even the mighty Hulk.

This boggy beast was once a man named Joe Timms on the run through the Everglades. Timms had escaped from a nearby jail to find the love of his life before an untimely death claimed her. As Joe splashed through the dark of night, the bog pulled him down into its dank depths. Decades later, during a rage-filled tantrum, the Hulk hurled radioactive waste into the muddy water close to the spot where Joe had disappeared. The unstable chemicals transformed Joe's long-dead body into a creature made of muck: Glob. Rising from the swamp, Glob kidnapped Betty Ross, the daughter of an Air Force general, mistaking her for his long-lost love. The Hulk accosted the marshy monster and the two traded blows, each using all of their strength, until Glob seemingly dissolved back into the murky depths, leaving Betty with Hulk.

Former chemical-plant-worker-turned-villain the Leader later resurrected the Glob to attack his nemesis, the Hulk. In the process, Glob was smashed into pieces, but he gradually reconstituted himself, for a time into a more clay-like form. Glob was then captured by the Collector and exhibited in a staged swamp environment, before being rescued by Hulk and Man-Thing. After a period of service with Nick Fury's Howling Commandos, Glob was last seen in the custody of S.H.I.E.L.D.

Glob's lidless, dark eyes don't have an intelligence behind them. The swamp monster is often driven by instinct and the broken remnants of his memories as a human. His strength is equal to—or might even exceed—that of Hulk, who considers Glob something of a kindred spirit. Mud, vegetation, and gunk make up his body, which can absorb any impact. Virtually indestructible and capable of reforming himself, Glob is a formidable foe.

First Appearance: *Incredible Hulk* #121 (1969) by Roy Thomas and Herb Trimpe **Further Reading:** *Incredible Hulk* #129 (1970) *Giant-Size Man-Thing* #1 (1974)

Clay upgrade
For a short time, the reanimated Glob was a creature of clay. In one battle of muck versus mire, the Man-Thing was victorious over Glob.

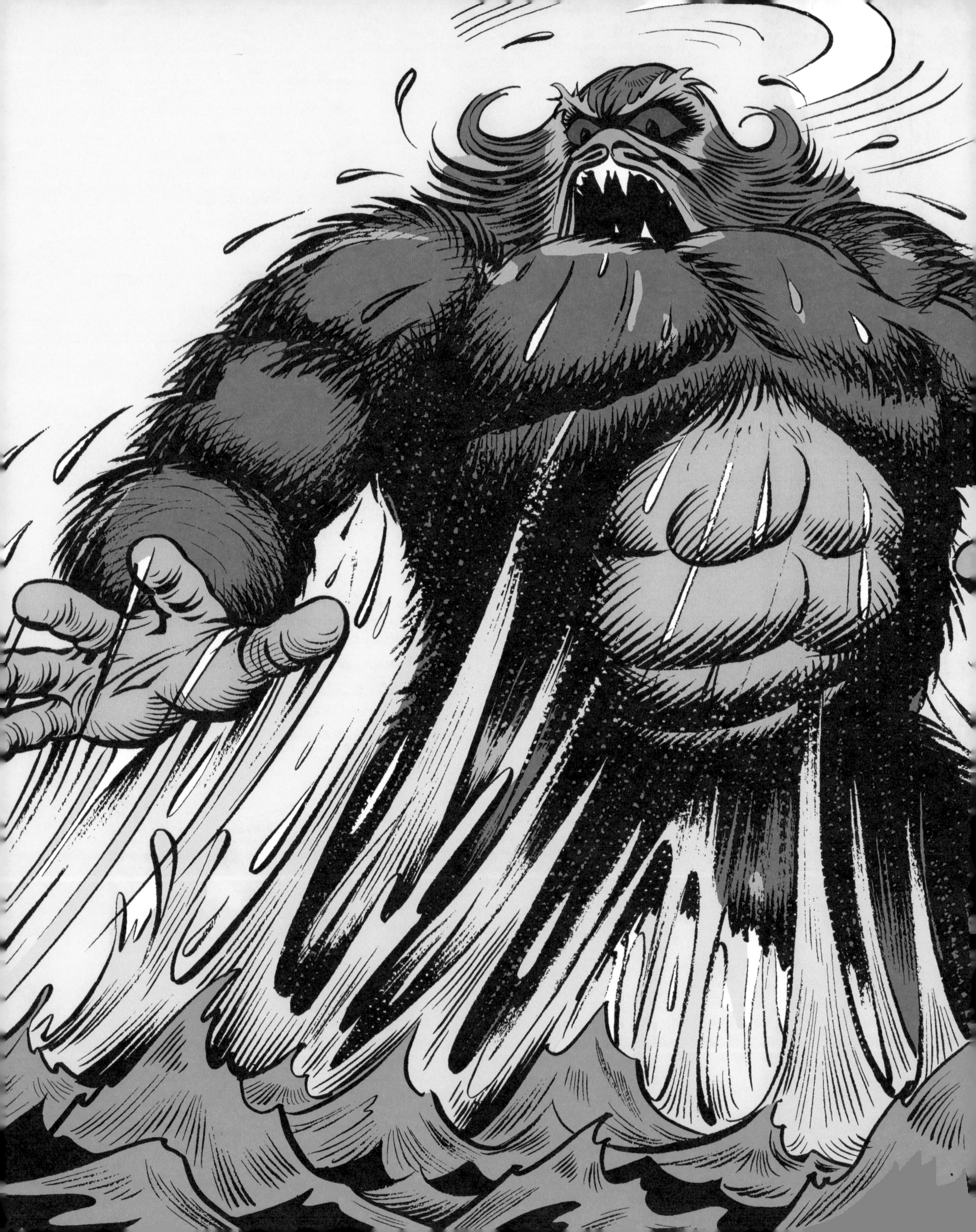

Height: Unknown Weight: Unknown Origin: Unknown Powers: Behemoth size and strength; impervious hide; command over sea life

Torg, the Abominable Snow-King

One creature that dared to claim dominion over Atlantis and the ruler of the oceans, Namor, the Sub-Mariner, was the immense Torg, the Abominable Snow-King. Strong enough to trade punches with Namor, and able to mentally command sea creatures to do his bidding, this enormous, green-haired primate rose up out of the ocean without warning.

The first known sighting of giant apelike creature Torg was in the Antarctic Ocean, where he was found stealing valuable cargo from ocean-going vessels. Torg was able to telepathically control some sea lions to make them capsize unsuspecting ships and bring their cargo to his underground cave. When Namor investigated the shipwrecks, the Atlantean prince quickly found himself facing off against the self-titled Abominable Snow-King. The Sub-Mariner couldn't help being curious about the wily behemoth and his devious actions.

Torg's origins are a mystery. Namor speculated that the sea-dwelling creature was a mutant of some kind, but the Abominable Snow-King would only reveal that no one knew where he came from. The two battled until Namor toppled an iceberg onto him, trapping Torg beneath.

This supersized monster is covered in shaggy green and yellow fur that protects him from the extreme polar temperatures. He has glaring red eyes and he bares sharp fangs when provoked. Bullets bounce off Torg's thick hide as if it were armor. The primate's large size grants him considerable strength and durability. Torg was able to withstand Namor's powerful punches, and later resisted a coordinated attack from the Avengers when he was freed from the iceberg.

The Abominable Snow-King was last seen retreating into the icy ocean after battling the Avengers. Could this Antarctic abomination return to claim the sea for his own?

First Appearance: *Sub-Mariner* #55 (1972) by Bill Everett **Further Reading:** *Avengers* #43 (2001)

Big mouth
Torg likes to talk and make his feelings known, even in the middle of a fight. When antagonized, he is just as likely to sling insults as he is to swing punches.

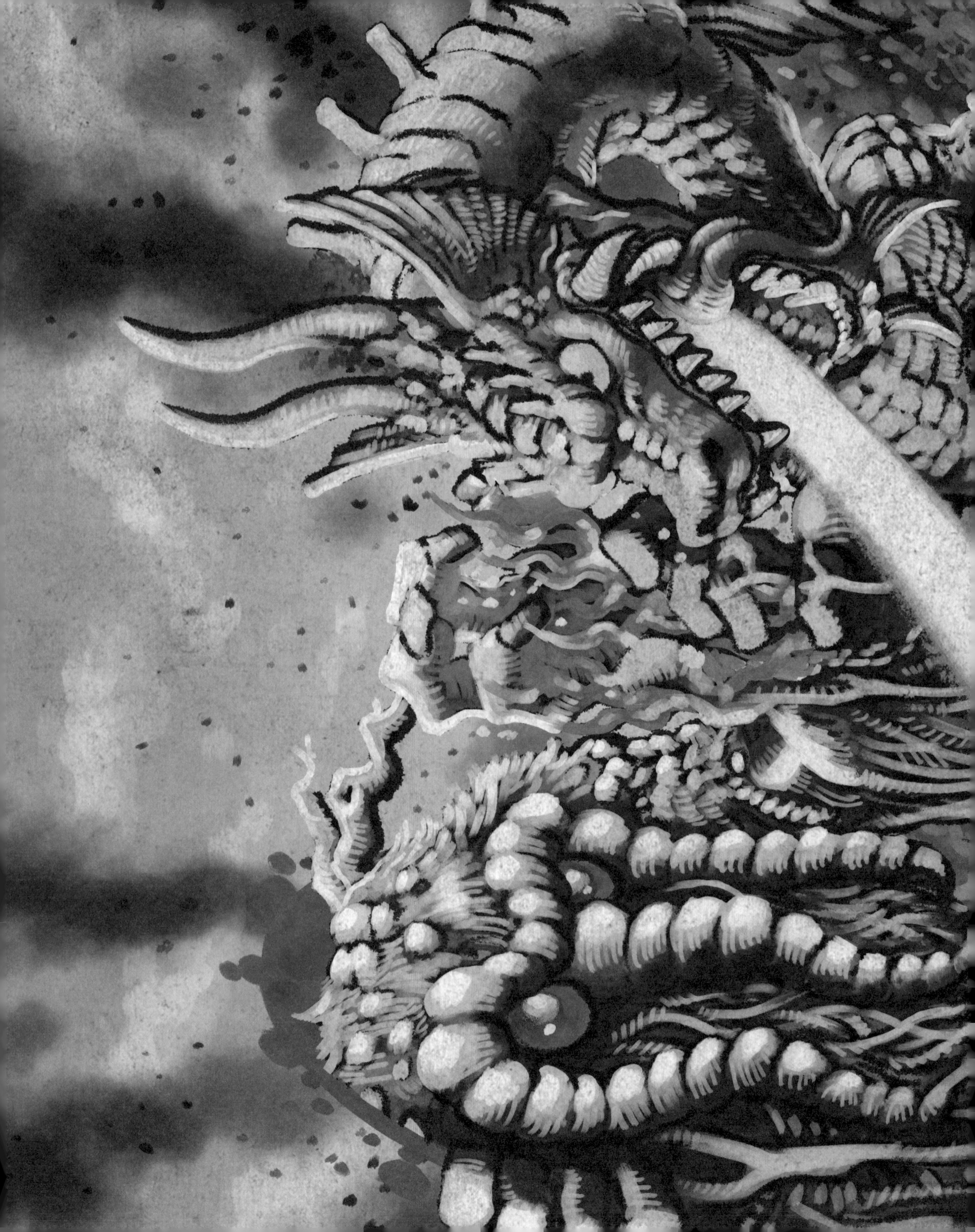

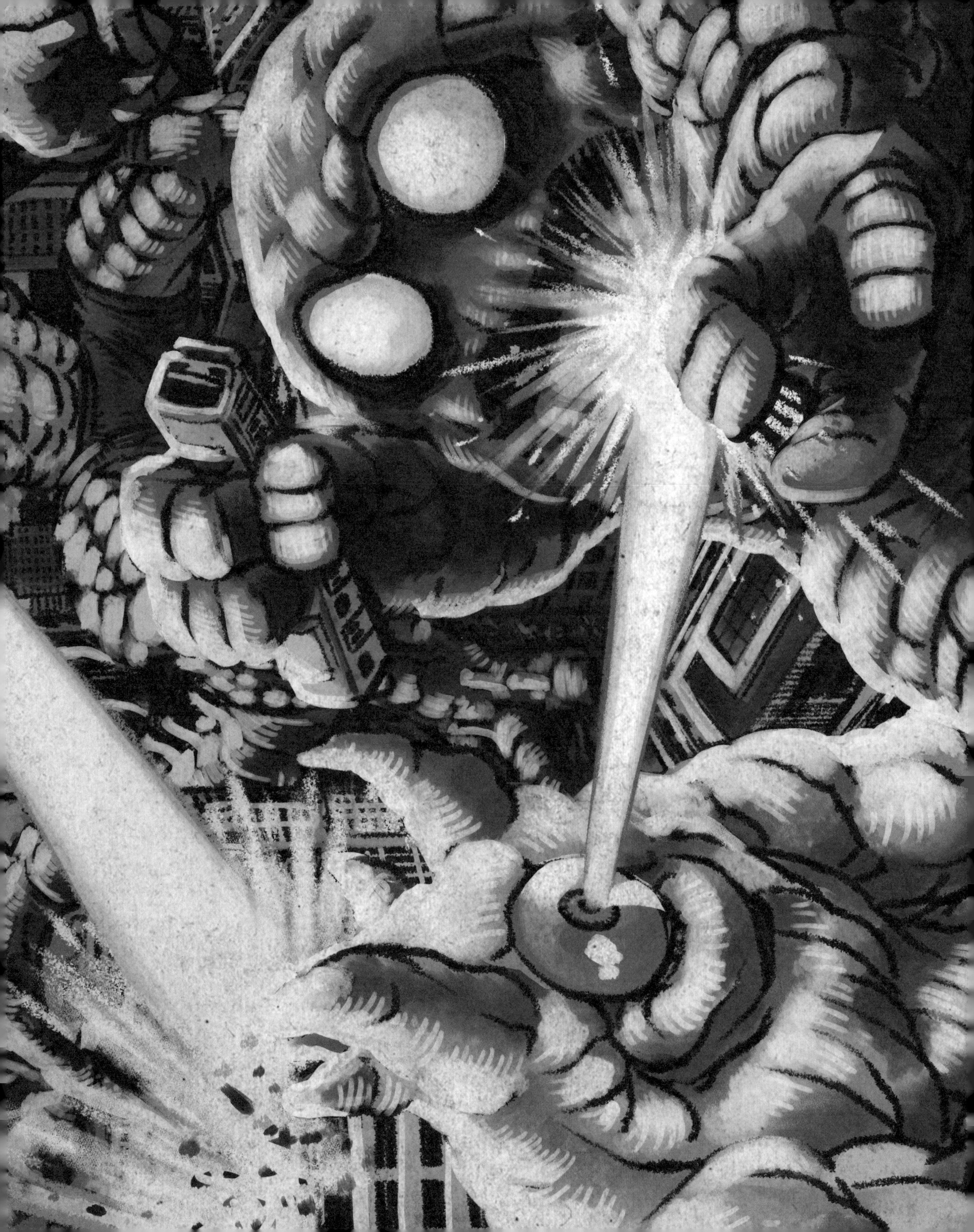

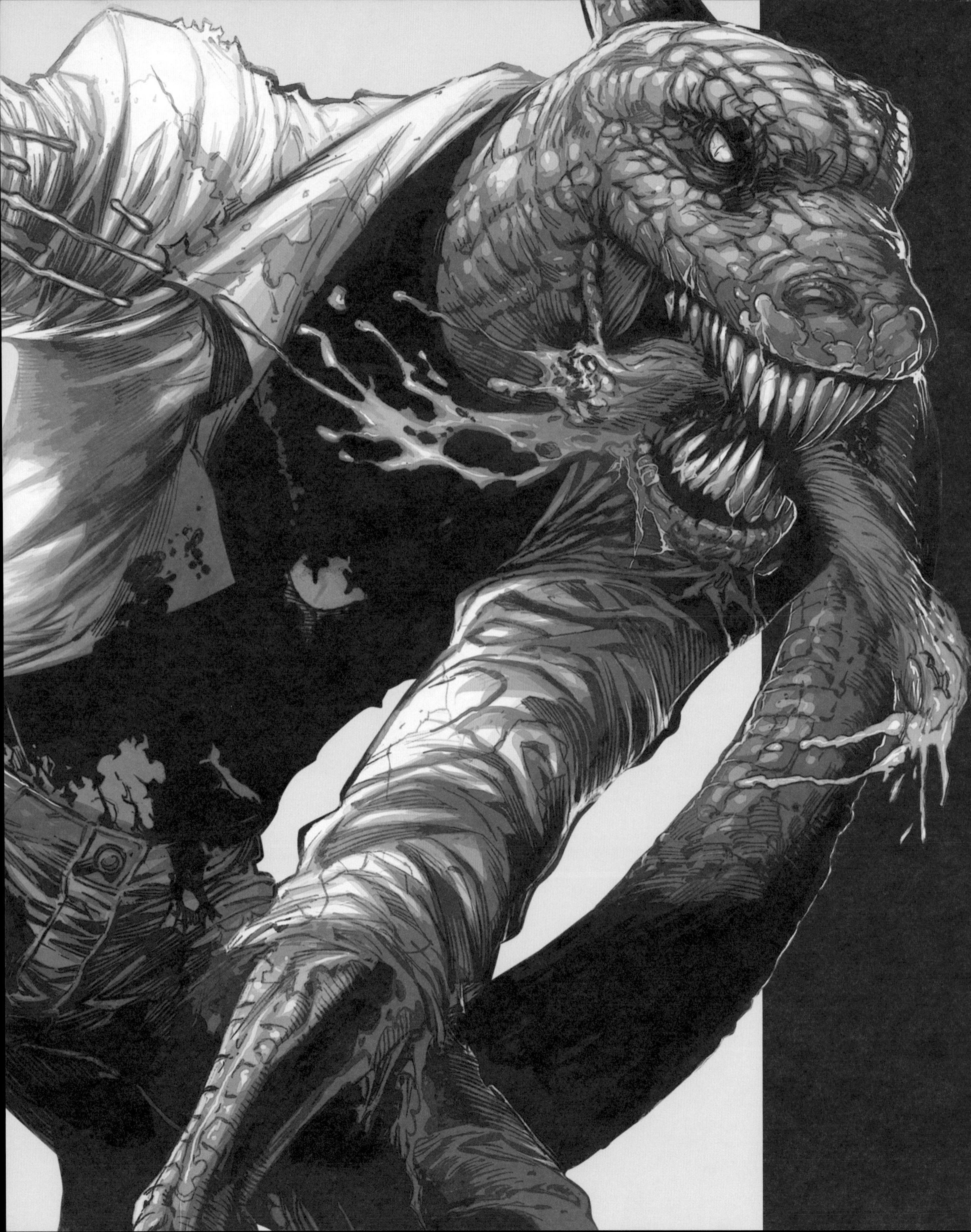

AMPHIBIANS AND REPTILES

From wherever they originate—brightly lit science labs, distant planets, or some of the wildest places on planet Earth—these carnivorous amphibians and reptiles can fight tooth and talon (and sometimes tail). Some feature scales covering thick hides, and most have augmented regenerative abilities.

Larger-than-life lizards, space dragons, and scaly tyrants stand among their ranks, but they're not all villains: some are heroes—and one of them is even somebody's best friend.

All-around team player Manphibian, sweet Old Lace, and reformed foe Fin Fang Foom may be cold-blooded, but they're surprisingly warm-hearted. Others like Tim Boom Ba, Droom, and the Lizard wreak havoc as they seek to destroy Earth or subjugate its inhabitants.

Get ready for a closer look at these cold-blooded beasts.

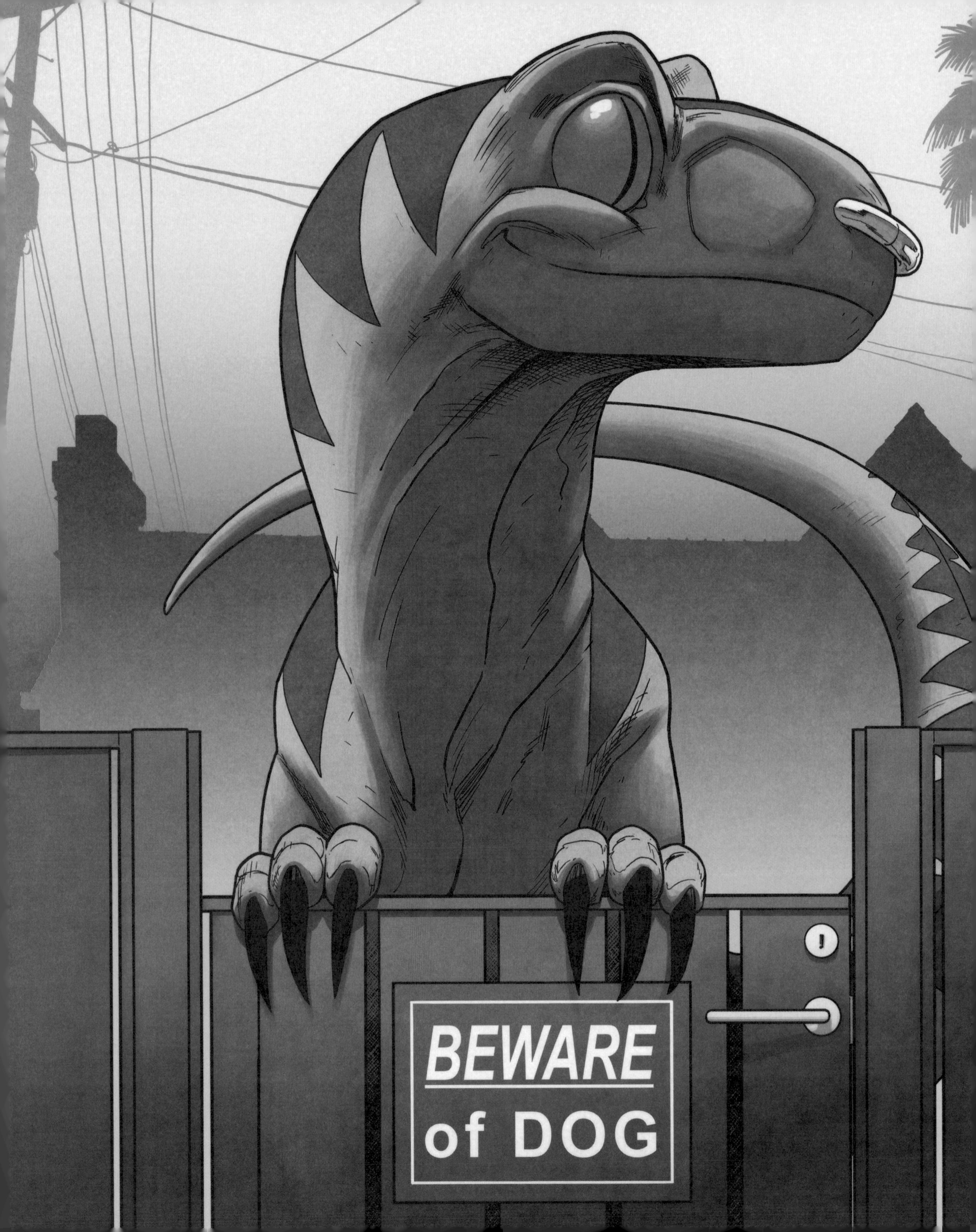
BEWARE
of DOG

Height: 6ft 1 in (2.1 m) **Weight:** 334 lbs (151.5kg) **Origin:** 87th-century Earth **Powers:** Telepathic and empathic connection to Gertrude Yorkes

Old Lace

A genetically engineered *Deinonychus* from the future has become the best friend of Gertrude "Gert" Yorkes. Called "Old Lace" in reference to an old movie, the carnivore has a strong psychic and empathic link with the teenager. Although her claws are capable of slashing anyone who poses a threat, the dinosaur is a loyal, sweet-natured companion.

Gert's parents, Dale and Stacey Yorkes, time traveled to the 87th century and commissioned the creation of a dinosaur that would respond to their daughter's mental commands. Designed to protect Gert, the *Deinonychus* is linked both telepathically and empathically to her. The dinosaur is also physically unable to harm any member of Gert's immediate family.

When Gert and her friends discovered their parents belonged to the Pride—a cabal of Super Villains—they banded together to form the Runaways. Gert adopted the codename "Arsenic" and dubbed her lovable reptile "Old Lace," in homage to a classic 1944 film. Old Lace feels what Gert feels. Whether it's strong emotions or pain, the two are linked on a psychic level. When she was mortally wounded, Gert was able to transfer her telepathic link to fellow Runaway Chase Stein so that the *Deinonychus* could continue living after Gert died. Fortunately, Gert's life was saved by a time-traveling Chase from the future, and Old Lace was overjoyed to see her friend return.

Old Lace's deep red eyes and chunky metal nose ring belie an otherwise usually gentle nature. Standing at almost seven feet, Old Lace is taller than a regular prehistoric *Deinonychus*. Her thick, scaly blue-yellow skin protects her from superficial damage and her large claws are capable of quickly shredding her target. Old Lace's considerable strength enhances the swing of her powerful, articulated tail. This genetically modified dinosaur is highly intelligent, occasionally deciding to refuse an order if she does not agree with it.

Old Lace and Gert continue to work together and their psychic bond remains strong.

First Appearance: *Runaways* #2 (2003) by Brian K. Vaughan and Adrian Alphona **Further Reading:** *Runaways* (2003)

Best friends forever
Old Lace is happiest when she's at Gert's side. The two have a bond that lasts, as proven, beyond death, and she has come to the aid of the Runaways on many occasions.

The Lizard

A science experiment went awry, transforming a man into a monster—the Lizard. This half-man, half-reptile is a savage adversary with superhuman strength and a burning rage against humanity. The scaly monstrosity harbors hatred for one person above all: Spider-Man.

The friendly neighborhood wall-crawler Spider-Man first faced off against the Lizard in the humid Florida Everglades. The Lizard was once Dr. Curtis Connors, a family man and brilliant biologist, searching for a way to regenerate lost limbs after his own arm was amputated following a wartime explosion. He recklessly tested an unproven serum extracted from reptiles on himself. His arm was restored—and the scientist was overjoyed. But the changes didn't stop there. Dr. Connors was horrified as scales soon covered his entire body and a powerful tail completed his transformation into a humanoid lizard.

Having all the animalistic strengths of a reptile, the green-scaled Lizard has a bulletproof, armor-like hide, razor-sharp teeth, and slashing claws. Like a gecko, he has the ability to cling to walls—moving up and down vertical surfaces with ease. Connors' body is now sensitive to low temperatures, when he becomes slow and sluggish. The Lizard has the rare ability to mentally sense, control, and command other reptiles, often bidding them to attack anyone who gets in his way.

Spider-Man succeeded in developing an antidote to Connors' serum and tracked down the Lizard. He administered the solution to his cold-blooded foe during their first encounter. It worked, and a grateful Connors returned to his human form.

However, the doctor has since reverted into being the Lizard many times—and has often found himself battling Spider-Man. The web-slinger usually pulls his punches for fear of hurting Connors, whom he considers a friend.

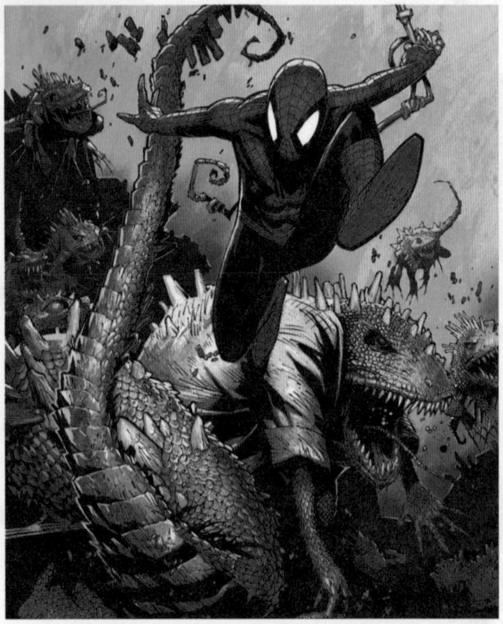

Entangled fates
Spider-Man Peter Parker will never stop trying to find the cure for Dr. Connors. The Lizard will never stop lashing out against Spider-Man.

First Appearance: *The Amazing Spider-Man #6* (1963) by Stan Lee and Steve Ditko **Further Reading:** *The Amazing Spider-Man #76-77* (1969), *Spider-Man: Reptilian Rage* (2019)

Height: 6ft 8in (2m) **Weight:** 500 lbs (227kg) **Origin:** Florida **Powers:** Super-strength, agility, speed, and durability; telepathic control of reptiles

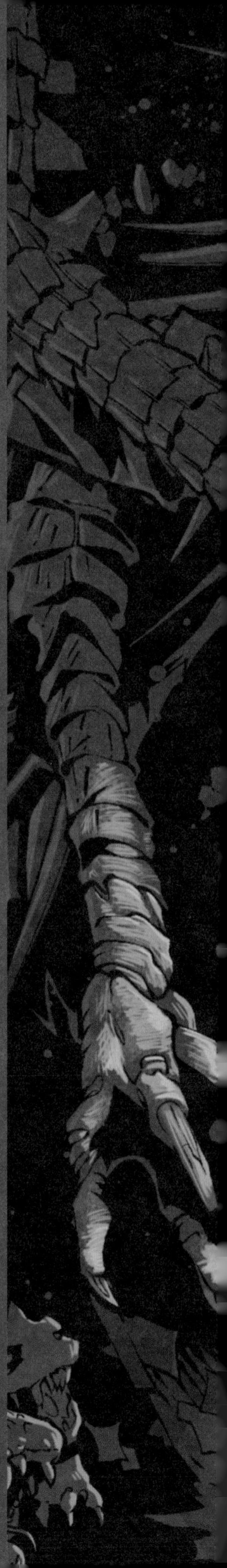

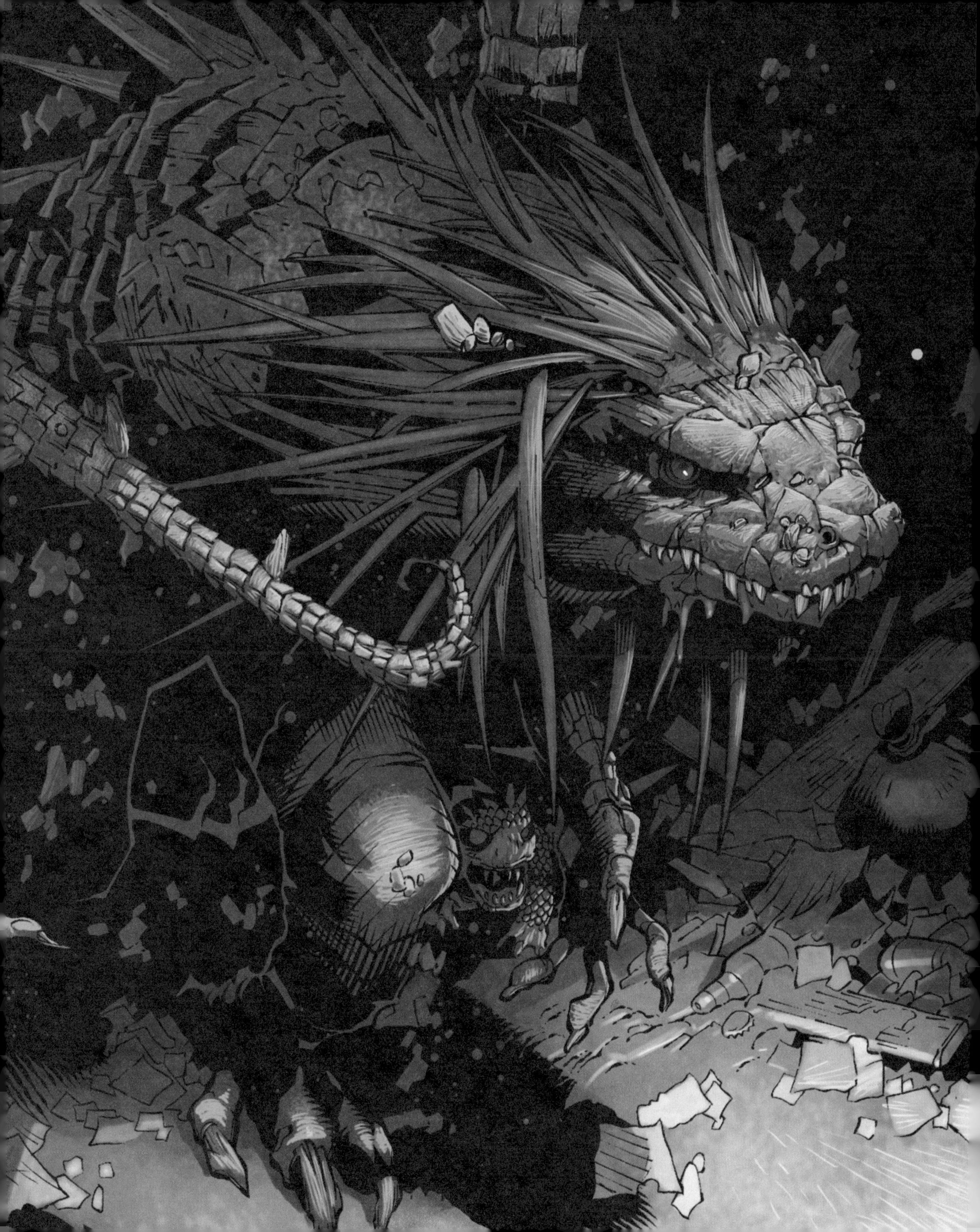

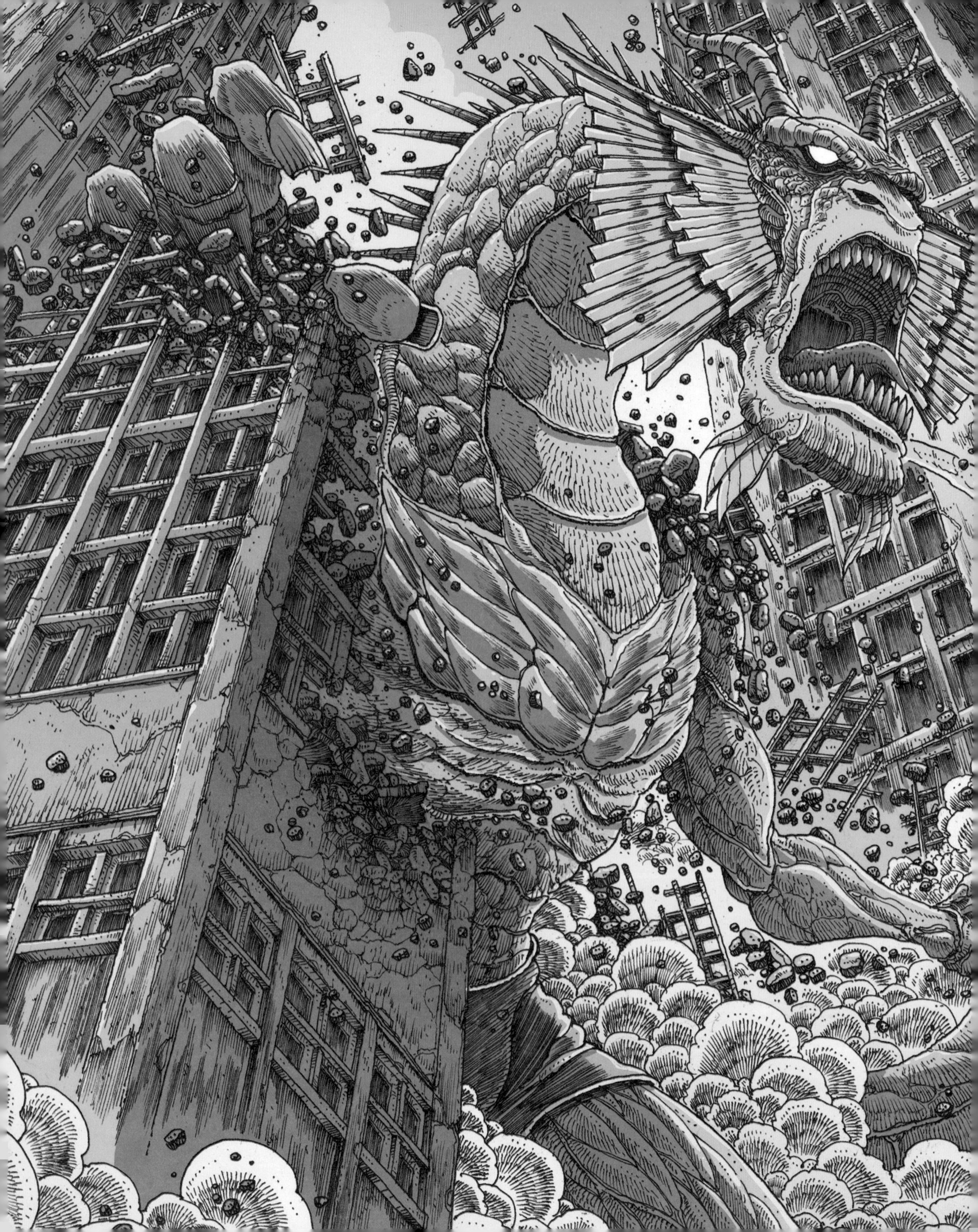

Height: 32ft (9.8m) **Weight:** 20 tons **Origin:** Planet of Kakaranthara **Powers:** Strength; speed; flight; fire breathing; shapeshifting; longevity

Fin Fang Foom

Beware waking this sleeping dragon. Fire-breathing Fin Fang Foom long laid silent beneath the earth. One day Taiwanese teenager Chan Liuchow, following ancient clues, found the slumbering dragon's chamber beneath the Great Wall of China. He woke the beast, baited him, and guided him directly into the path of his enemies. Once his foes were decimated by the rampaging, giant dragon's strength, Liuchow lured Fin Fang Foom back to the crypt. The dragon returned to sleep—but it wouldn't be the last time he'd find his way to the world above.

Fin Fang Foom remained largely dormant for years. It wasn't until the villain Mandarin, in a bid to claim China for his own, awoke the beast that the dragon's power was fully unleashed. Fin Fang Foom revealed to the Super Villain that he was no fantastical dragon from Earth legends. He and his reptiloid compatriots were shapeshifting Makluan hailing from the planet Kakaranthara. They had crash-landed on Earth millennia before, with Foom instructed to remain near their ship. The others assumed the forms of humans to avoid detection. Gathered together again, they began an attempt at world domination.

The formidable dragonlike beings were destroyed by Iron Man as he wielded the full power of the Mandarin's powerful rings, but Fin Fang Foom's spirit survived. His gargantuan body reformed, and he has since remained awake, and as furious as ever. In subsequent clashes he has taken on worthy foes such as the Fantastic Four, the Hulk, and Squirrel Girl.

In recent years Fin Fang Foom has had a change of heart, dreaming of a simple life of farming and harvesting crops. His massive claws now seek to create instead of destroy. He fought alongside Drax the Destroyer to save a dragon infant; later, Fin Fang Foom joined the combined forces of Earth's greatest heroes when gigantic monsters fell from the sky like rain.

First Appearance: *Strange Tales #89* (1951) by Stan Lee and Jack Kirby
Further reading: *Iron Man #274-275* (1991), *Monsters Unleashed* (2017)

Size and strength combined
Foom's long, colossal form is capable of surprising speed and maneuverability. His true name is roughly translated as He Whose Limbs Shatter Mountains and Whose Back Scrapes the Sun.

Fin Fang Foom Anatomy

Haughty Fin Fang Foom is fond of taunting his prey. He enjoys concocting devious plans to outwit his opponents, so is not a creature to be underestimated. The sheer power of his piercing cry is only matched by the earth-shattering destruction he rains down from above.

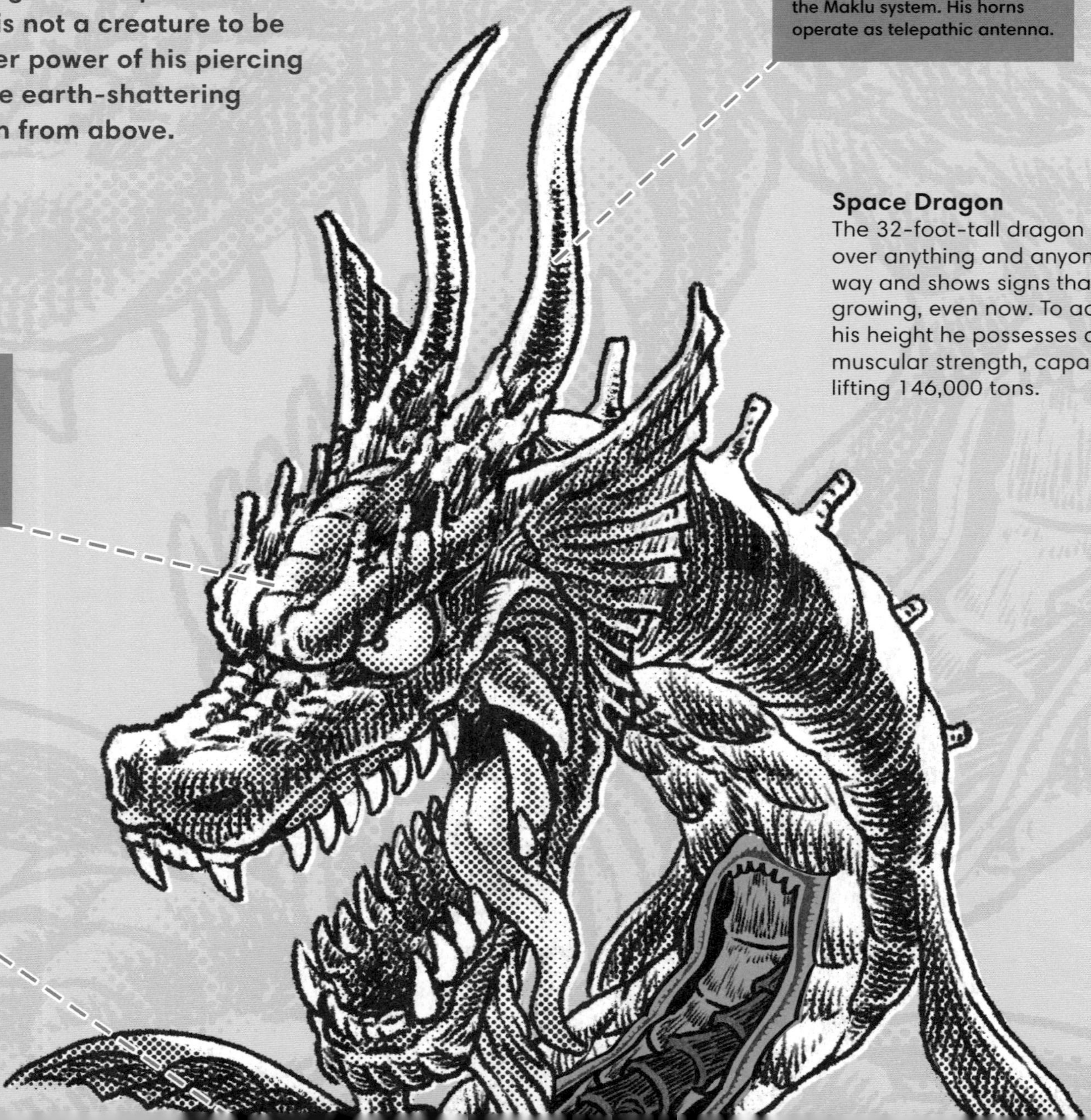

Dragonlike
While Fin Fang Foom looks like a horned dragon of legend, he is actually an alien from the Maklu system. His horns operate as telepathic antenna.

Space Dragon
The 32-foot-tall dragon towers over anything and anyone in his way and shows signs that he is still growing, even now. To accompany his height he possesses dense muscular strength, capable of lifting 146,000 tons.

Intellect
He may look like a beast, but Fin Fang Foom is highly intelligent, once serving as his ship's navigator.

Fire breathing
Fin Fang Foom expels flames from his lungs in explosive, acidic bursts.

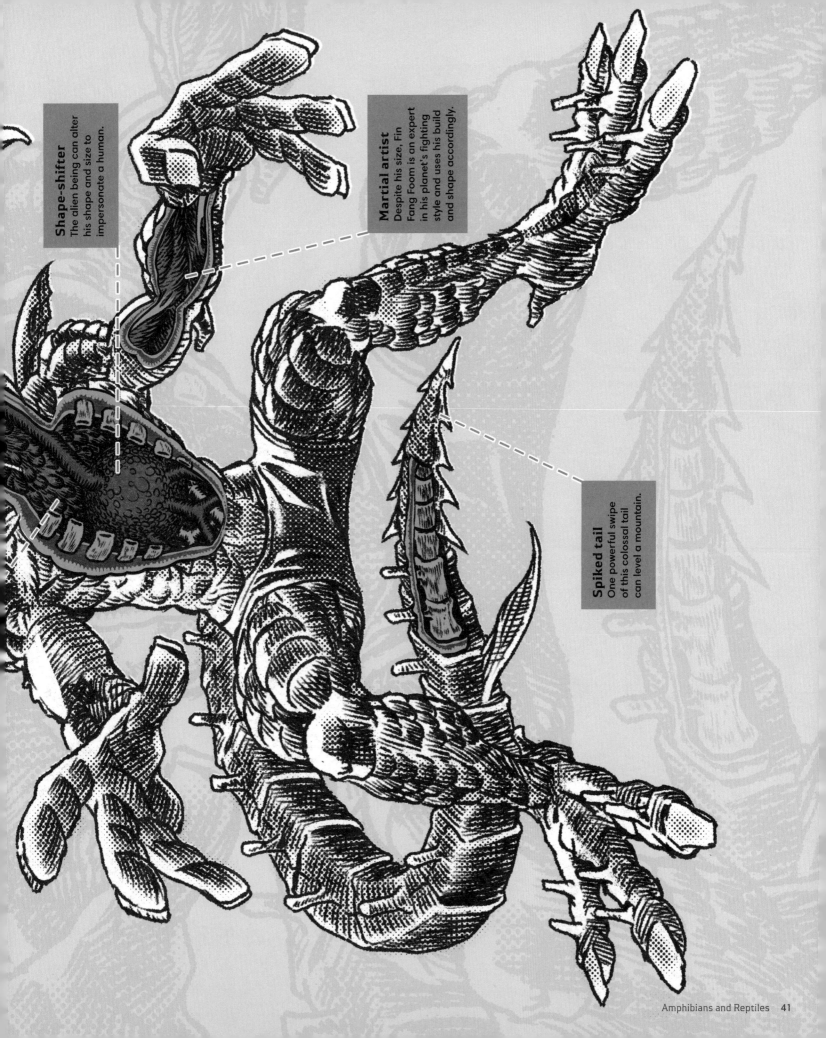

Shape-shifter
The alien being can alter his shape and size to impersonate a human.

Martial artist
Despite his size, Fin Fang Foom is an expert in his planet's fighting style and uses his build and shape accordingly.

Spiked tail
One powerful swipe of this colossal tail can level a mountain.

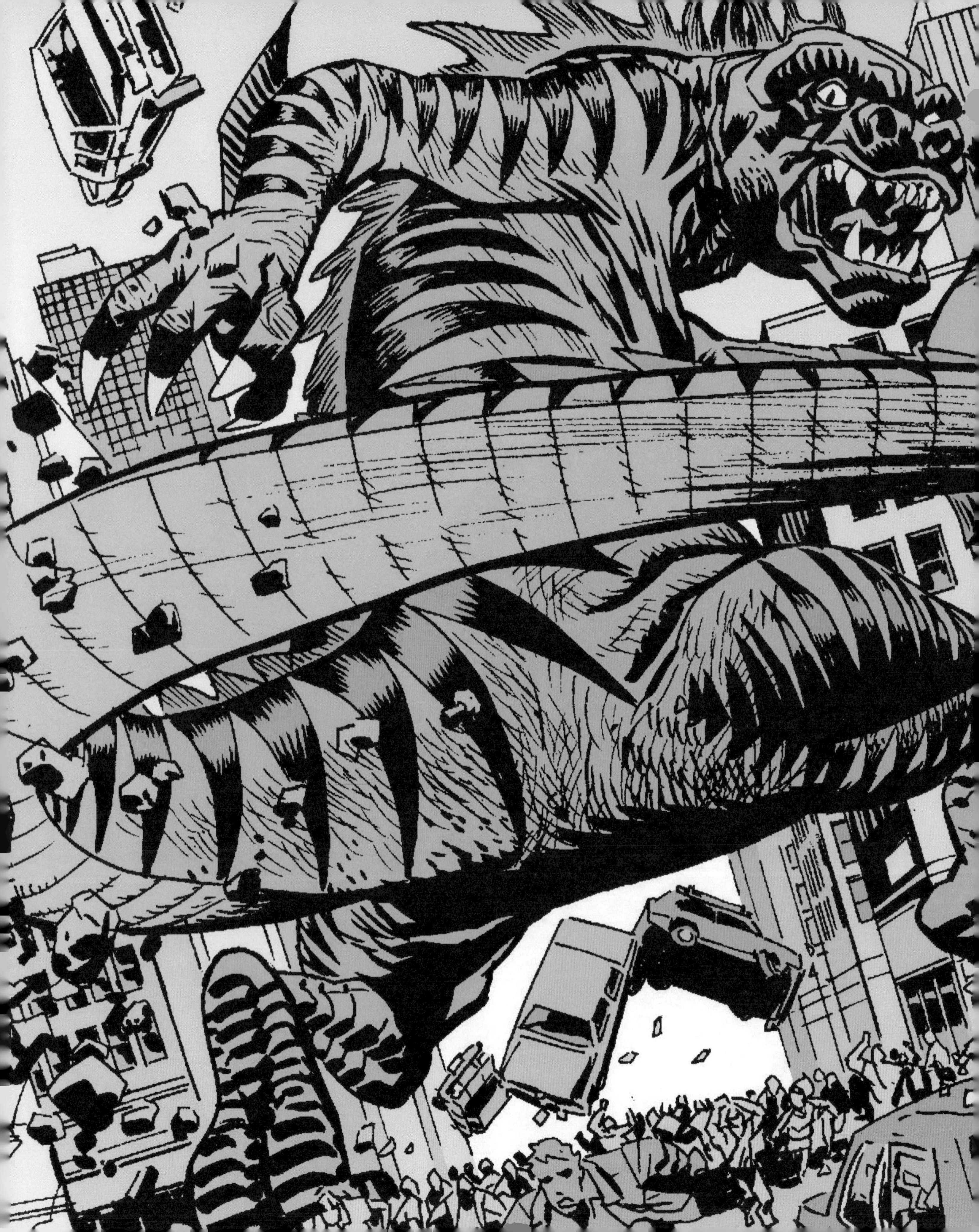

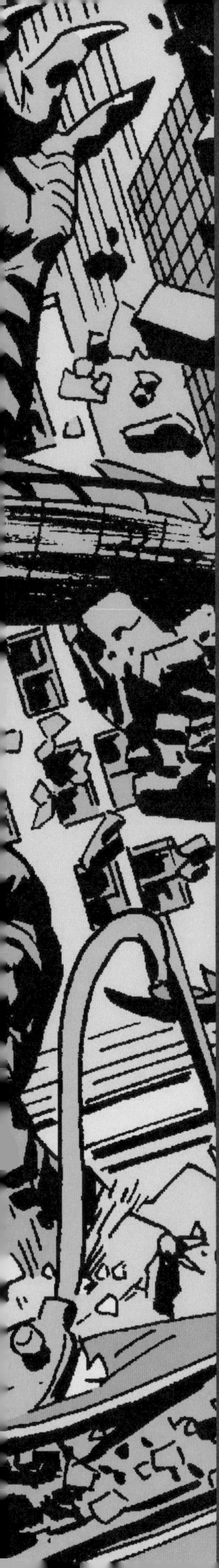

Droom

Height: 164ft (50m) **Weight:** 20,000 tons **Origin:** South America **Powers:** Supersized strength and durability

An accident with an experimental growth serum results in a pet lizard transforming into a towering monster. Terrorizing the city streets, the Living Lizard now known as Droom soon grew to the size of many nearby buildings—rendering its scaly body, giant fangs, and whiplike tail a serious danger.

A well-meaning scientist, working to alleviate worldwide hunger, created a formula to make fruits and vegetables grow unnaturally large. When a pet *Droomedia rex* was accidentally splashed with the serum, it began to increase in size—and didn't stop. Frightened by the enlarged lizard as it stomped across the city driven by pure instinct, the police and militia attacked. Bullets and bombs had no effect on the rampaging reptile: the bullets bounced off its thick, green scaled hide and the creature now dubbed Droom proved agile and quick enough to pluck a jet from the sky. The Living Lizard displayed off-the-charts strength and its claws could cut through most building materials.

A volunteer task force of more than 1,000 men and women finally made one last desperate attempt to stop Droom. Armed with experimental solar-powered rockets, they fired at the monstrous creature. The force of the explosions launched the monster into space.

Droom floated in the dark void until it fell back to Earth some years later. It spent time in Japan as a protector of sorts against other giant monsters. Eventually, the ancient being the Collector captured it, exhibiting Droom and other legendary behemoths in his own private museum. The monsters broke free and escaped to New York City. It took the combined brains and brawn of Hulk, Giant-Man, the Thing, and Beast to stop Droom and the other monsters' smashing spree by banishing them to the antimatter universe known as the Negative Zone.

Some time later, Droom again returned to Earth. Along with fellow monsters Eerok, Giganto, and Grogg, the Living Lizard ran amok on the streets of Tokyo, and was finally killed by the Japanese military.

First Appearance: *Tales to Astonish* #9 (1960) by Stan Lee, Larry Lieber, and Jack Kirby **Further Reading:** *Marvel Monsters: Monsters on the Prowl* #1 (2005)

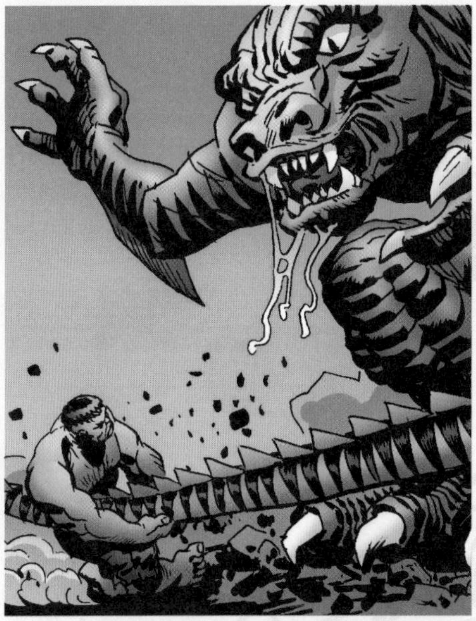

Hulk grab
When the green behemoths Droom and Hulk clash, the rampaging reptile is no match for the raging Hulk. Droom's size lends little advantage.

Devil Dinosaur

An enormous, *Tyrannosaurus-rex* type creature from an alternate dimension stalks the streets of New York City. This seemingly fearsome carnivore, with its red, tough skin and razor-sharp teeth, is Devil Dinosaur, the unwavering crime-fighting partner of nine-year-old Moon Girl.

In a place and time when prehistoric giants roamed the land, Devil Dinosaur was the mightiest of all. He is the last surviving creature of Dinosaur World—a planet very similar to prehistoric Earth. In his own dimension, Devil Dinosaur befriended a primitive human named Moon Boy, and together they ventured across the Valley of the Flame. The two companions faced enemies such as the aggressive Killer-Folk, enormous spiders, dangerous giants, and even invading robots falling from the sky.

It is reported that Devil Dinosaur's red, seemingly bulletproof hide is the result of exposure to a fire that triggered his latent mutant genes. His strength is greater than any other *Tyrannosaurus rex*-like creature: one swipe of his tail can topple a triceratops or demolish a building, and his powerful jaws can lift weights of up to 25 tons. He's strong and durable enough to take punches from the Hulk and Spider-Man, and playfully wrestle with the Thing. He has massive, sharp claws, razor-like teeth, yellow eyes, and he can grow to 25 feet (7.6 meters) in height.

Eventually, fate—and a time portal—would take Devil Dinosaur to present day Earth. As well as altering his physical appearance, Devil Dinosaur's mutation has enhanced his intelligence and enabled him to develop a strong emotional bond to young prodigy Lunella Lafayette. He feels a range of emotions, including loyalty, sadness, and happiness, particularly in response to Lunella. Devil Dinosaur cannot speak, but he can understand conversations around him and communicate in his own way.

When Lunella was exposed to the mutagenic Terrigen Mist, her Inhuman ability to switch minds with Devil Dinosaur was activated. Every full moon, Lunella spontaneously finds herself in the body of her scaly friend while he inhabits her small frame, confusing people nearby.

To the rest of the universe he's Devil Dinosaur, but to Lunella, he's Big Red. She's the brains and he's the brawn in a partnership that transcends time, space, and species. Together they're Moon Girl and Devil Dinosaur.

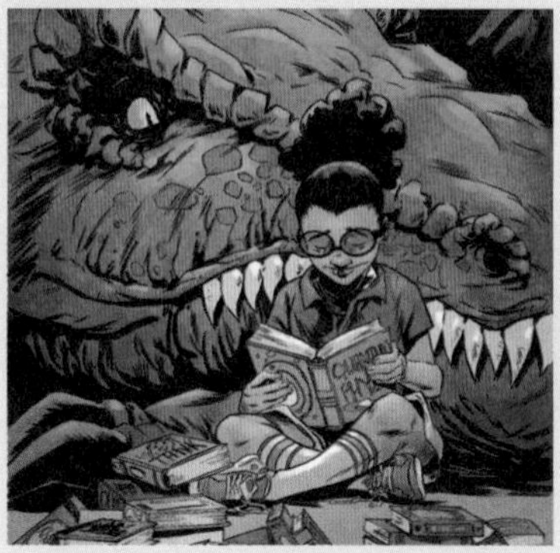

Special bond
Devil Dinosaur listens to Lunella both as a friend and crime-fighting partner.

First Appearance: *Devil Dinosaur* #1 (1978), created by Jack Kirby **Further Reading:** *Avenging Spider-Man #14-15* (2013), *Moon Girl and Devil Dinosaur* #1 (2016)

Height: Varies, up to 25ft (7.6m) **Weight:** 3 tons **Origin:** Dinosaur World **Powers:** Great strength, durability, and intelligence; swaps minds with Lunella

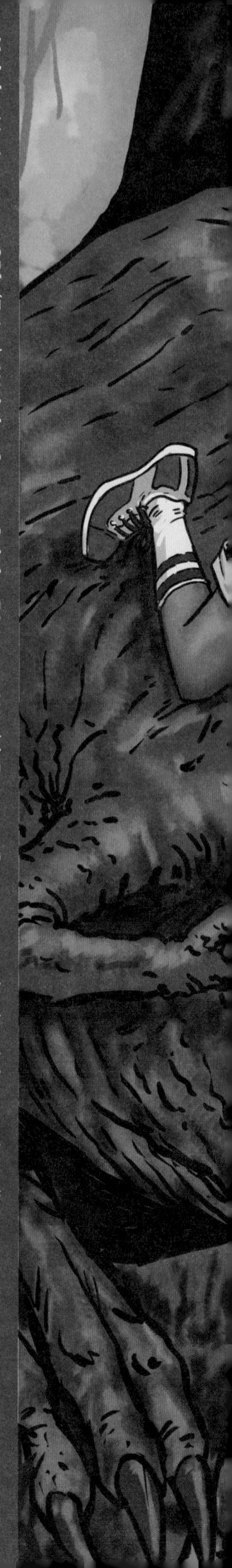

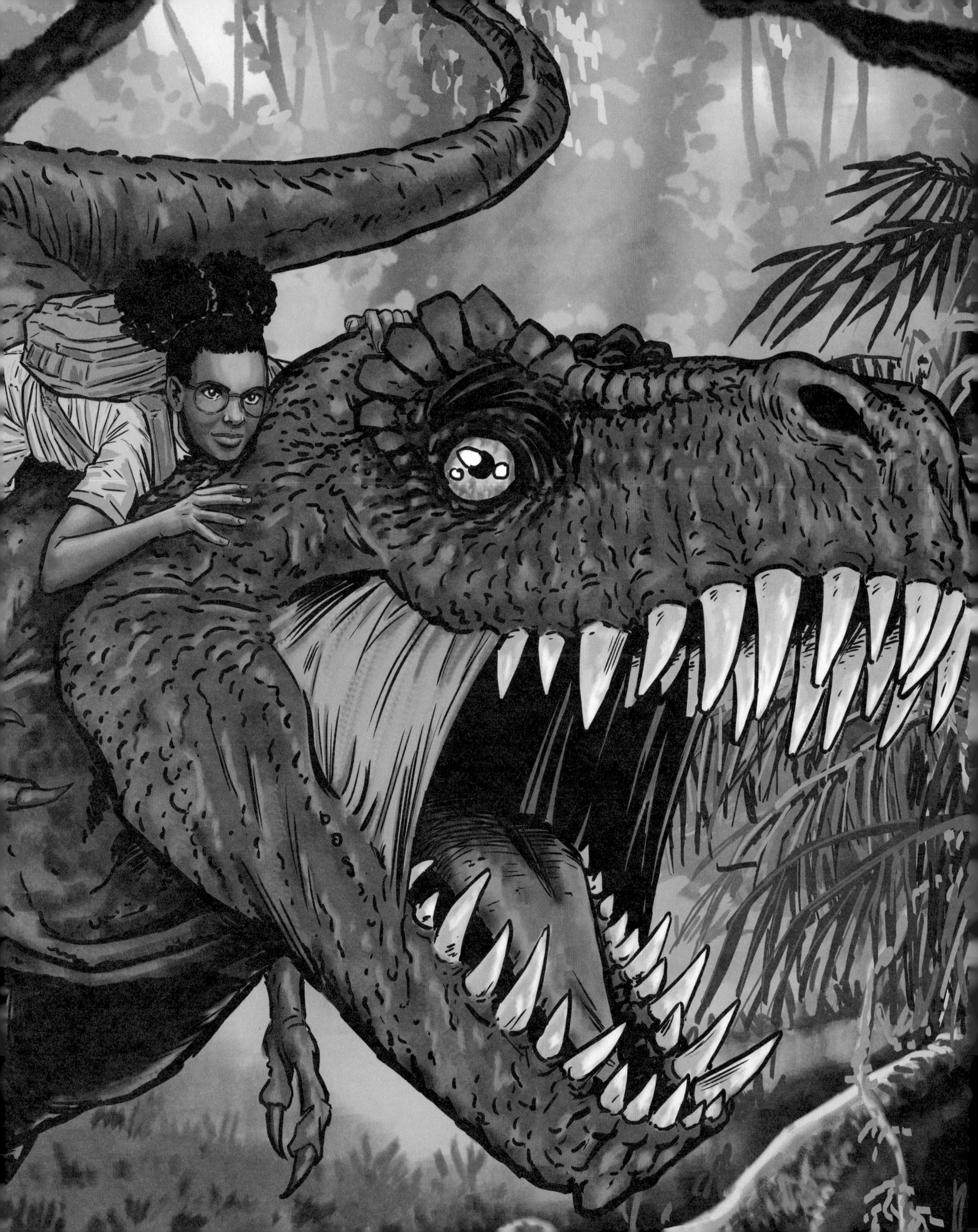

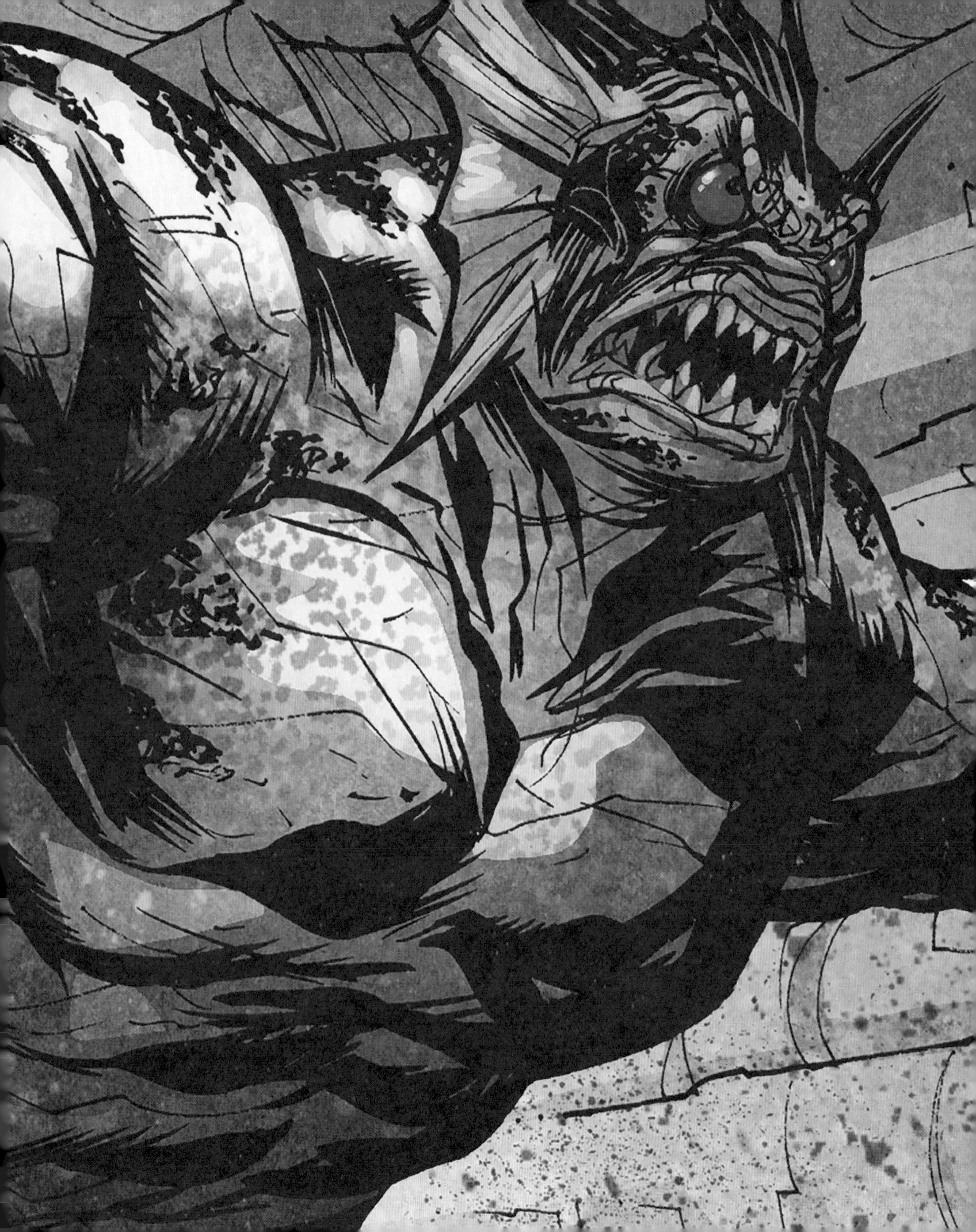

Height: 7.2ft (2.2m) Weight: 425.5 lbs (193kg) Origin: Unknown Powers: Superhuman strength and durability; amphibious abilities

Manphibian

This amphibious alien was accidentally released after 1,000 years trapped deep below the surface of the Earth. His name is Manphibian. The world he finds is one where people fear him, but that soon changes and he becomes a hero for both monsters and humankind.

Hailing from an unknown planet, the amphibianlike Manphibian had pursued another of his kind—who Manphibian held responsible for the death of his love—across hundreds of worlds, before finally arriving on planet Earth. They then became trapped together below the ground for 1,000 years.

In modern times, oil drillers accidentally awakened Manphibian with the noise of their drilling, and both creatures were released onto the surface world. Manphibian immediately continued his quest for revenge, clashing savagely with his enemy, who escaped when Manphibian heroically rescued a woman who had been caught up in their battle. His foe's whereabouts remains unknown.

True to his name, Manphibian—like his adversary—can breathe in both air and water. He is taller, stronger, and more resistant to damage than humans, as his hide is impervious to fire and bullets. Green scales and fins cover his fishlike form and his red eyes, pointed teeth, and jagged claws make Manphibian appear more ferocious than he really is.

Time passed and the amphibious hero was conscripted into Nick Fury's Howling Commandos. He later joined the Legion of Monsters and made the subterranean Monster Metropolis his home. There, he found kindred spirits in Morbius the Living Vampire and the Werewolf by Night, and assisted Red Hulk in defeating his Doc Samson's ghost. More recently, Manphibian has served as a vital member of the special unit known as the Howling Commandos of S.H.I.E.L.D., under field commander Dum Dum Dugan.

Manphibian, or Manny to his friends, is a team player who fights fearlessly to protect all innocents.

First Appearance: *Legion of Monsters* #1 (1975) by Marv Wolfman, Tony Isabella, Dave Cockrum, and Sam Grainger
Further Reading: *Legion of Monsters* (2011), *Howling Commandos of S.H.I.E.L.D.* (2015)

Going underground
Manphibian isn't afraid to jump in and get his hands dirty when lives are at stake. He primarily operates in the dark and dank.

Manphibian Anatomy

His alien physique—with its pointed teeth, webbed claws, ragged fins, and muscled build—is unsettling. But these features make Manphibian's survival possible on land, in water, and in outer space. He has adapted beyond the usual capabilities of an Earth-bound, cold-blooded vertebrate.

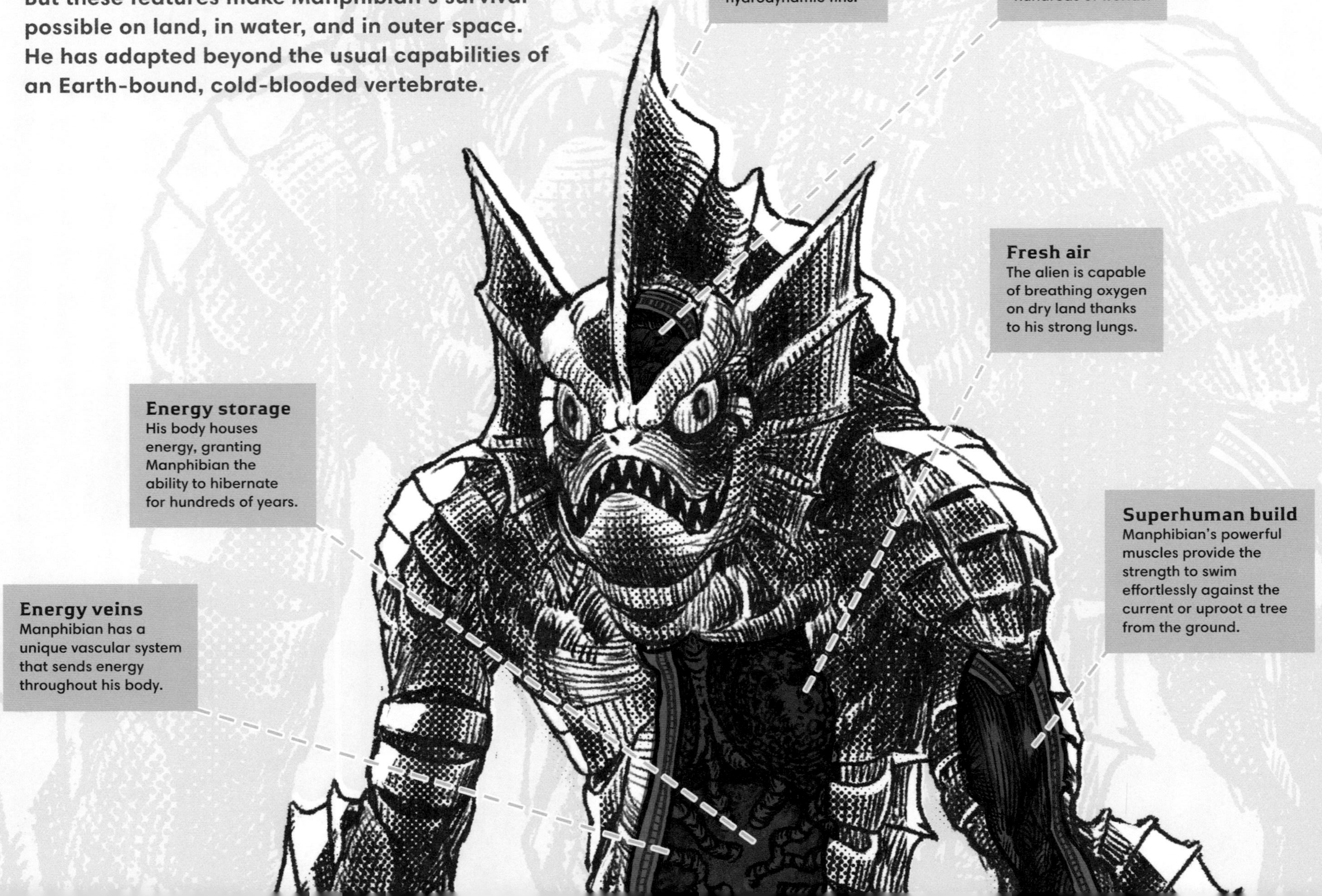
Fast fins
Manphibian can swim at speeds up to 62 miles (100km) per hour with the help of hydrodynamic fins.
Interstellar intelligence
Highly intelligent, Manphibian stores knowledge from hundreds of worlds.
Fresh air
The alien is capable of breathing oxygen on dry land thanks to his strong lungs.
Energy storage
His body houses energy, granting Manphibian the ability to hibernate for hundreds of years.
Superhuman build
Manphibian's powerful muscles provide the strength to swim effortlessly against the current or uproot a tree from the ground.
Energy veins
Manphibian has a unique vascular system that sends energy throughout his body.

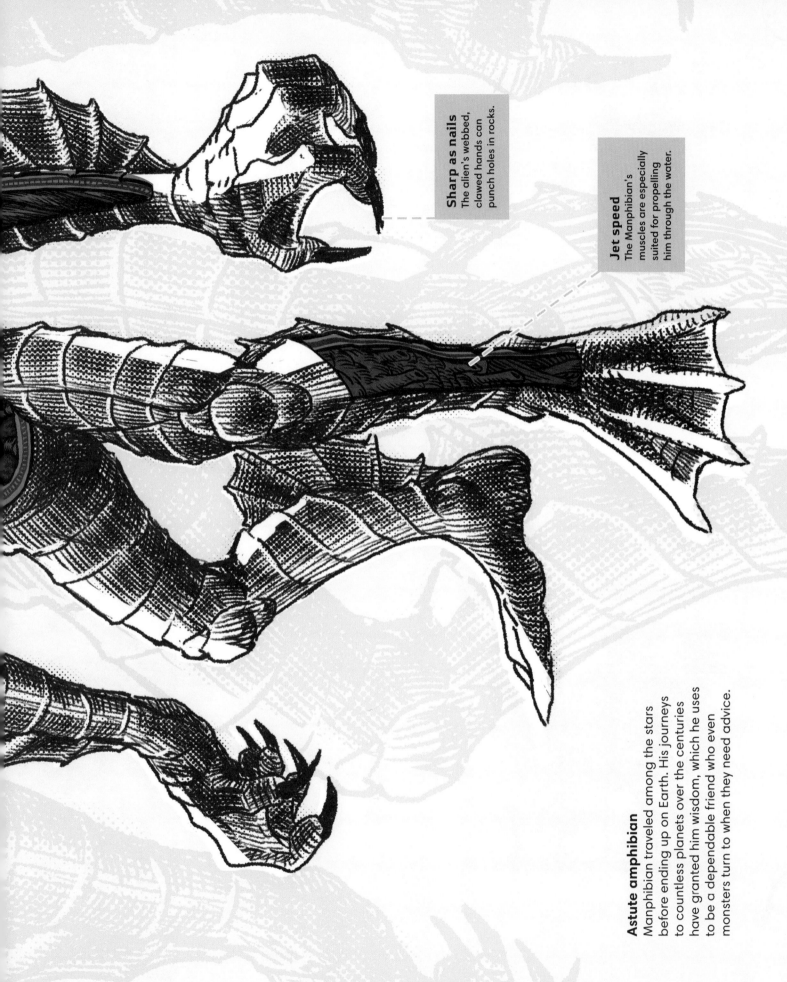

Sharp as nails
The alien's webbed, clawed hands can punch holes in rocks.

Jet speed
The Manphibian's muscles are especially suited for propelling him through the water.

Astute amphibian
Manphibian traveled among the stars before ending up on Earth. His journeys to countless planets over the centuries have granted him wisdom, which he uses to be a dependable friend who even monsters turn to when they need advice.

Tim Boo Ba

On a strange world in subatomic dimension the Microverse, a raging, reptilian warrior can be heard commanding his hordes to "Attack! Attack!" This is Tim Boo Ba, a merciless monarch, whose appetite for conquest is never sated. Having vanquished those on his own planet, he sets his sights on planet Earth.

This reptilian warrior towered over the denizens of his home planet and struck down any who opposed him—showing no mercy. Tim Boo Ba sought to conquer everything on his homeworld; razing cities and always looking for new lands to claim for his own. Subjugating the humanoid race who shared his planet, Ba declared himself their undisputed master. His word was law, and numerous statues were built to honor the despot.

Capable of inflicting unimaginable destruction, Tim Boo Ba is arrogant, heartless, and belligerent. The immensely tall, scaly skinned conqueror is distinguishable by the huge horns on either side of his head. Whether he brandishes a massive broadsword or stomps upon the ground, he is a frightening force of evil—initially on his world in the Microverse alone.

That changed when a single water droplet fell through a random portal the size of a pinhole onto Ba's micro-sized planet—causing a flood. The villain seemingly perished in the deluge. However, he returned when a gateway was opened by the young alien Googam—who was trying to summon his own father—between Ba's subatomic kingdom and Earth. Stepping through the portal and growing to enormous proportions even by Earth's standards, Tim Boo Ba immediately set about menacing humanity. Eventually, it took a team of reformed monsters led by Fin Fang Foom to bring down the giant tyrant. He was kept under sedation by Reed Richards of the Fantastic Four while the scientist worked out how to mend the gateway.

Some time later, Tim Boo Ba answered young Inhuman Kei Kawade's call to defend Earth against the Leviathon invasion. It did not stop him threatening the boy afterward, claiming, "The next time you summon me, human... I'm going to eat you!" His current whereabouts are unknown.

First Appearance: *Amazing Adult Fantasy* #9 (1962) by Stan Lee and Steve Ditko **Further Reading:** *Silver Surfer* #4 (1969), *Marvel Monsters: Fin Fang 4* #1 (2005)

High and mighty
Tim Boo Ba's ego is as large as he is. He aims for nothing less than world domination—whichever world he happens to be on.

Height: 20ft (6.1m) on Earth **Weight:** 15 tons on Earth **Origin:** Microverse **Powers:** Telepathy; can change his size; superhuman strength

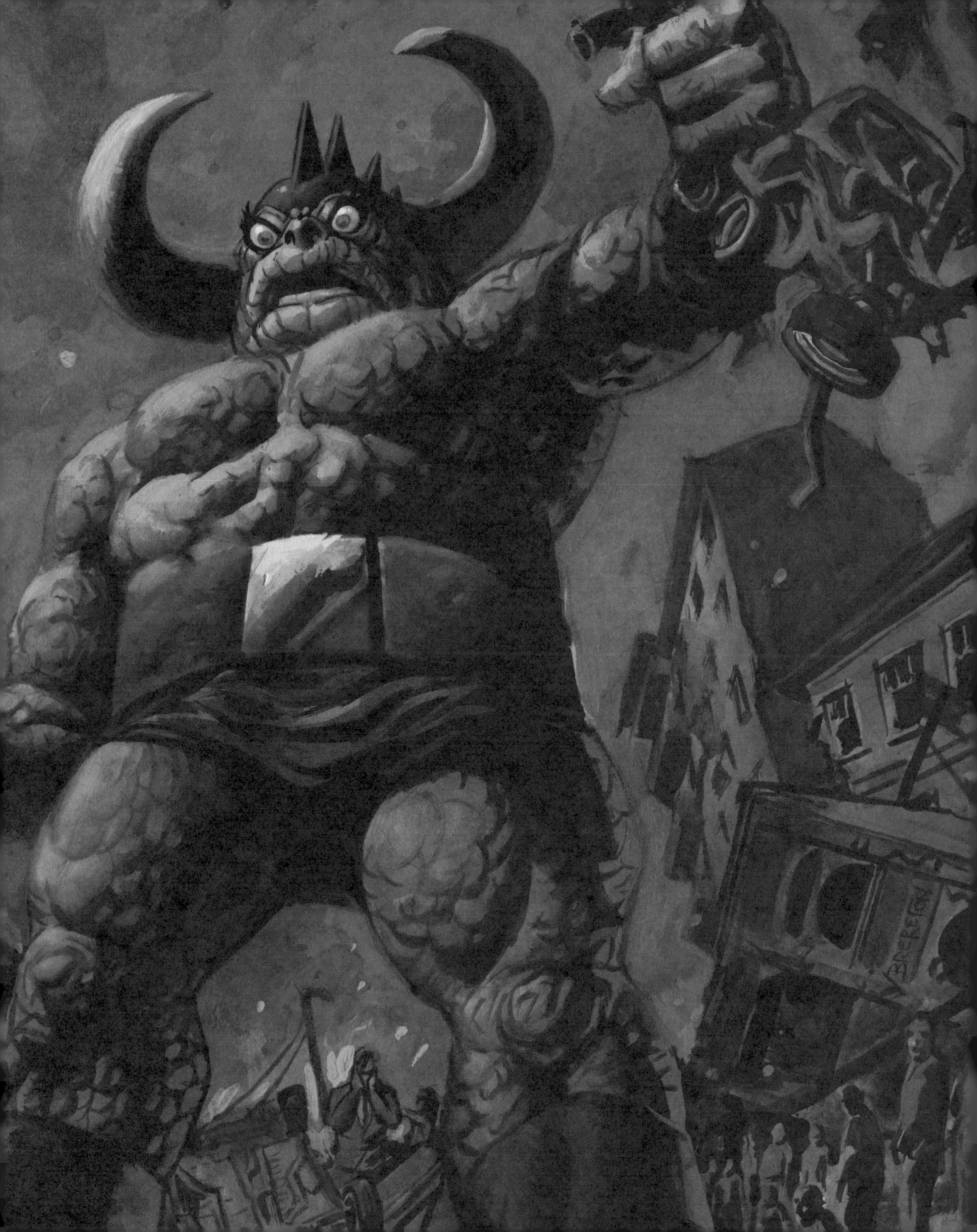

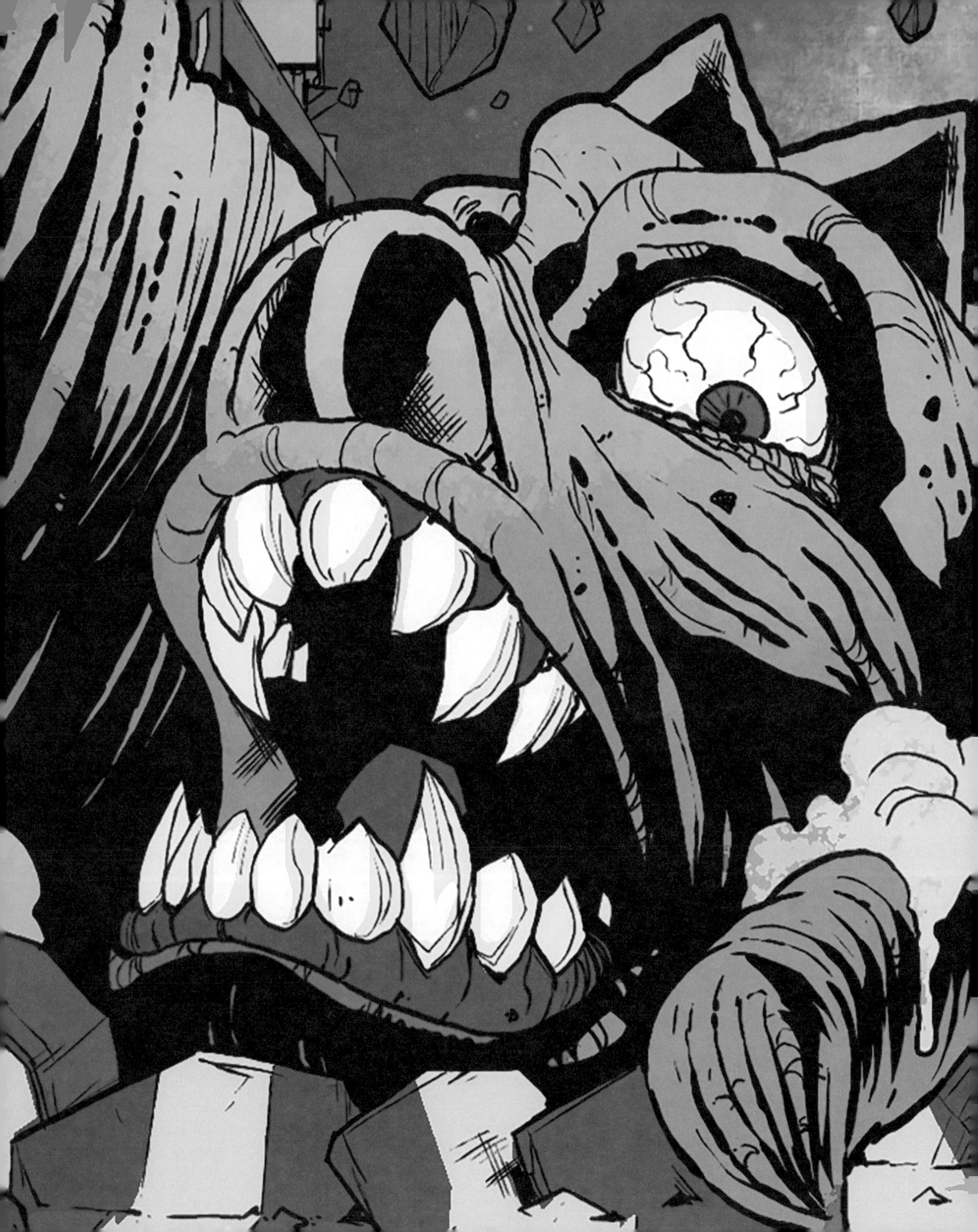

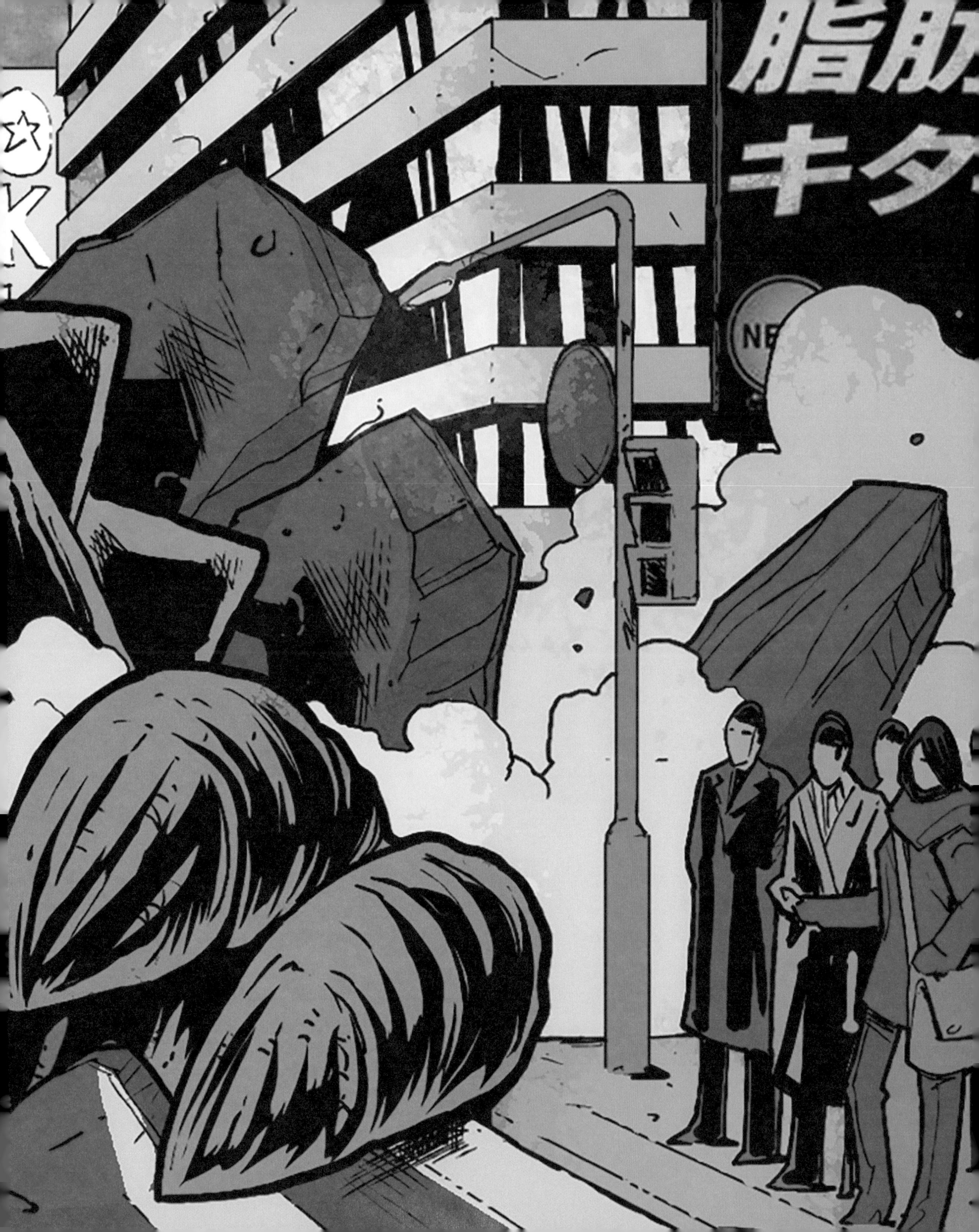

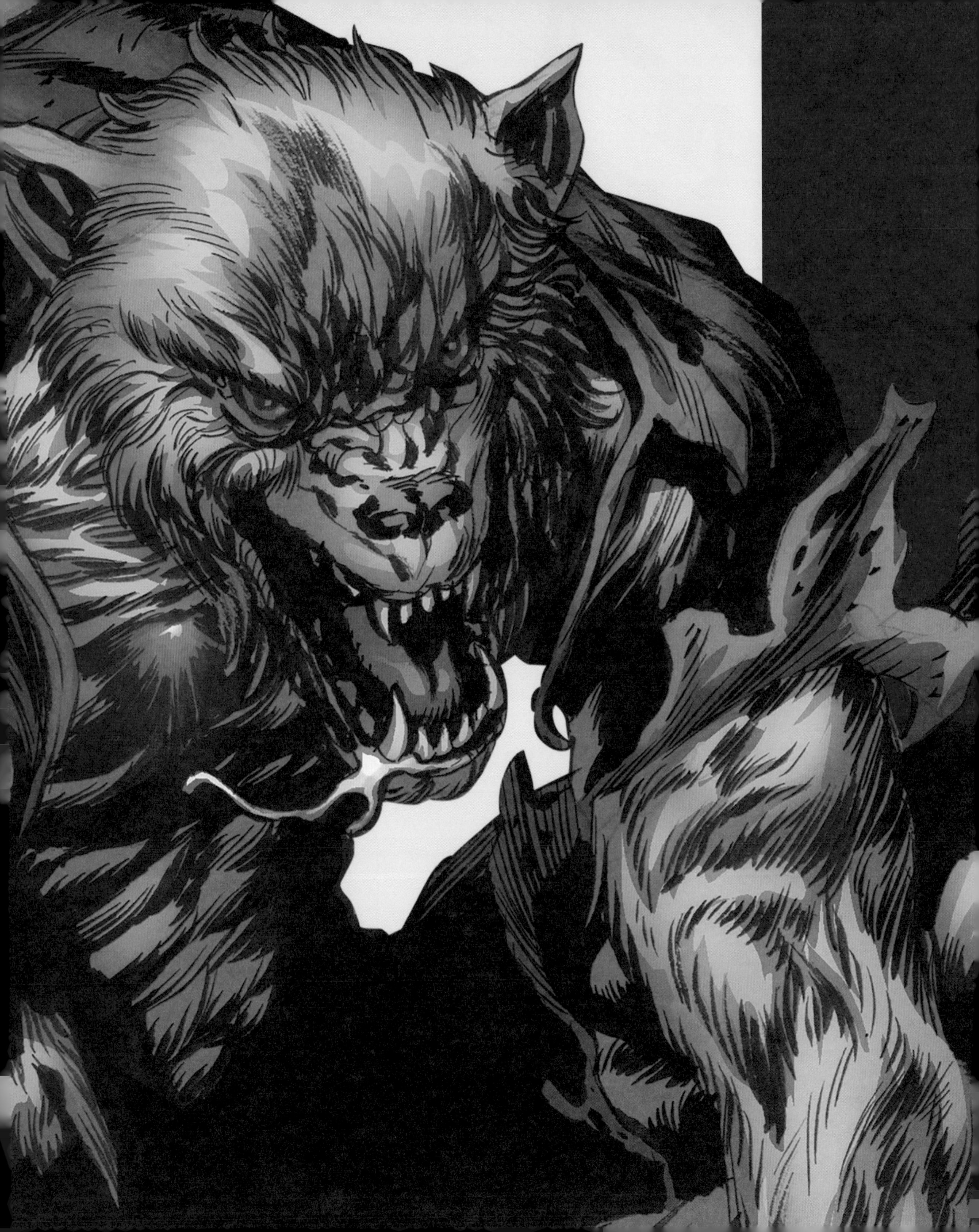

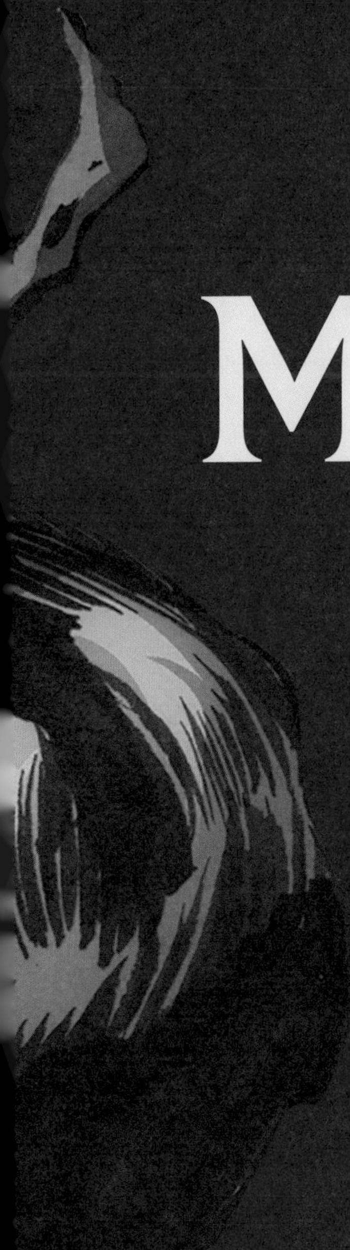

MAMMALS

The legends really are real. Vampires, werewolves, mummies, and other creatures stalk their unsuspecting prey at night. The moonlight may reveal a flash of fur in a dim New York City alley or a glint of bared teeth on a faraway planet.

Most of these monsters are part human or were once counted among the living. Dracula, Lilith, and Morbius the Living Vampire are plagued by an unrelenting thirst for blood. Werewolf By Night and Man-Wolf are bound irrevocably to the moon and the stars.

Others are warm-blooded brutes from distant lands. Colossal cryptids like the Himalayan Yeti and Borneo's Gorgilla defy belief. And Skaar, the son of Hulk, unleashes his frenzied rage on a distant, dying world.

Prepare to meet these monstrous mammals.

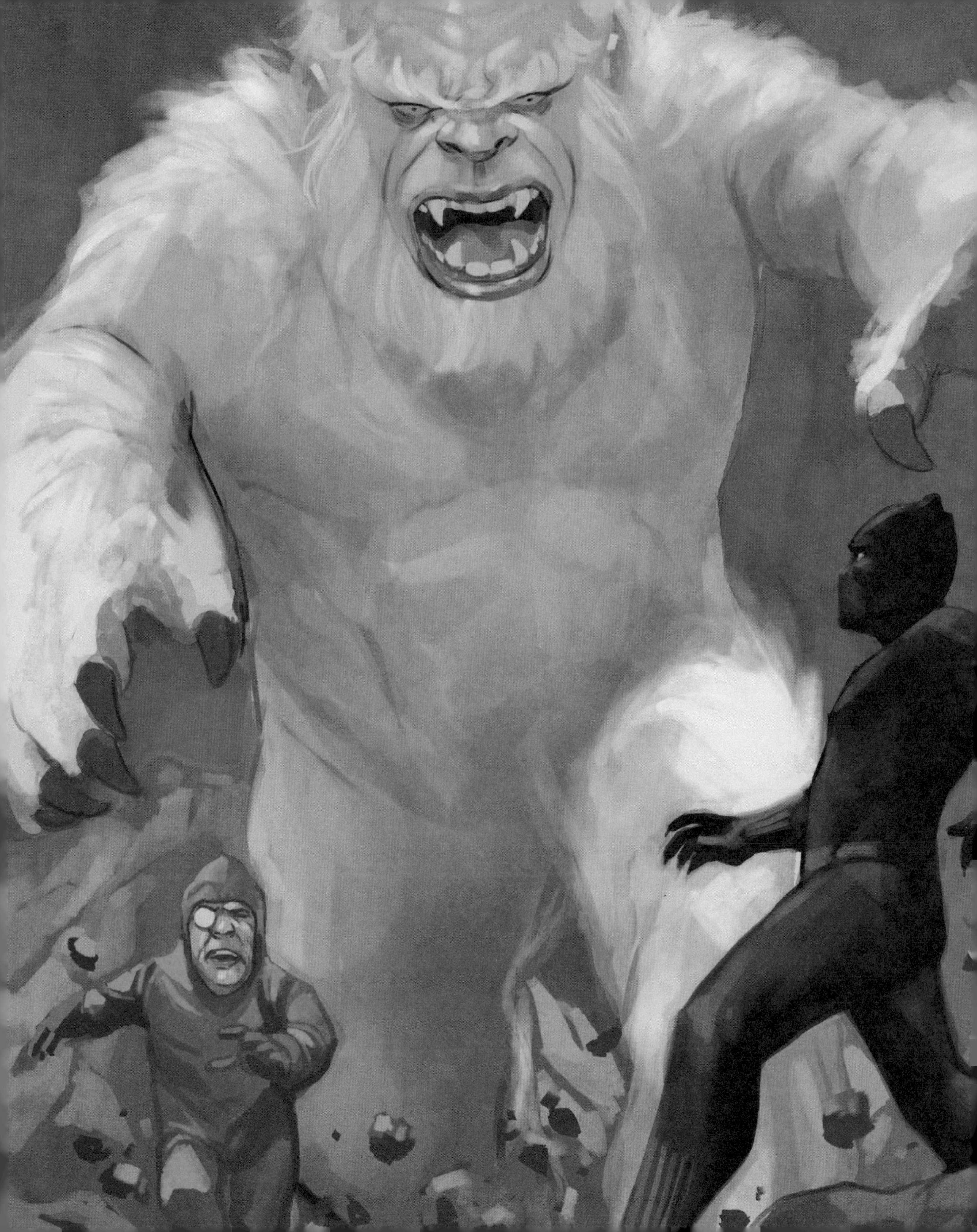

Height: 8–10ft (2.4–3m) **Weight:** Unknown **Origin:** Himalayas **Powers:** Superhuman strength and durability; razor-sharp claws and teeth

Yeti

High in the mountains of the Himalayas, thick snow muffles the sound of a monster's heavy footfall. Its shaggy, white fur disappears into the snow-capped terrain, hiding its fearsome claws and jagged teeth. The local people fear the very name of this infamous legend—the yeti.

This massive snow creature is as fierce and powerful as the abominable snowman of legend. Giant clawed hands and feet are capable of climbing the treacherous mountainside as well as slashing at anyone foolish enough to engage him. He demonstrates speed and an accurate aim when throwing rocks. His hide is covered in thick fur to withstand the subzero temperatures of the mountains, with the added bonus of camouflage. There are many reports of yeti sightings, but their origins continue to be the subject of speculation.

One such story begins with fortune-seeker Carl Hanson. After he stole an authentic photograph of a yeti, he sought to capture the fabled monster and sell it to the highest bidder. The creature was rumored to live in the cold climate of the Himalayas, so he traveled there to begin his search. Hanson showed the picture to the local people to guide him on his journey. They cautioned him that the photo itself was cursed to destroy the one who possesses it. The greedy hunter heedlessly ignored the warnings, and trudged through the snow, consumed by his desire to find the abominable snowman of legend. Time passed and Hanson continued to wander in vain, hair grown long and white, never to leave the mountain again. The curse was fulfilled—he had become a yeti.

Wakandan hero Black Panther, accompanied by collector Abner Little, was on a mission to retrieve a sacred samurai artifact when the aircraft they were traveling in suddenly ditched into a lake. After scrambling up the cliffs to safety, they were attacked by a yeti guarding the gateway to the hidden Samurai City. Black Panther knocked the creature unconscious.

Terrigen Mists transformed an Inhuman into a yeti on Inhuman world Attilan. He joined Earth-based hero team First Line before seeking refuge in an abandoned Himalayan temple.

First Appearance: *Tales to Astonish* #13 (1960) by Stan Lee, Larry Lieber, and Jack Kirby
Further Reading: *Black Panther* #5 (1977)

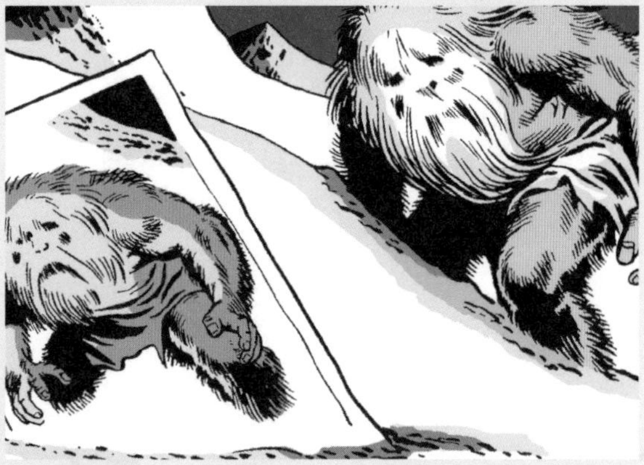

Photo copy
Cursed by a photograph depicting the yeti, Carl Hanson's obsession led him to gradually transform into the abominable snowman.

Gorgilla

A scientist leading a team of researchers traveled to the forests of Borneo in the hope of finding the missing link between ape and human. They soon encountered a supersized monkeylike monster—Gorgilla, one of the strangest creatures of all time. Appearances, however, soon proved to be deceptive with this monstrous mammal.

The scientist and his team were shocked when they stumbled upon the gigantic Gorgilla in his dense jungle home. While the massive ape monster certainly looked fierce, he ultimately saved the lives of the research team when a snarling *Tyrannosaurus rex* threatened to attack. The grateful scientists left Gorgilla to live out his days in peace—but his adventures were just getting started.

Longing to join the explorers, whom he considered kindred spirits, Gorgilla escaped the island. He stowed away in the massive hold of a cargo ship bound for New York City. Unfortunately, Gorgilla wasn't greeted with open arms; a confused and frightened populace opened fire on the bewildered primate. In time, he would be placed under Reed Richards' guardianship. The brilliant scientist miniaturized Gorgilla to a far less threatening human size and taught him rudimentary English.

Gorgilla's rehabilitation saw him take up the role of window cleaner in the Baxter Building— headquarters of the Fantastic Four. He worked alongside fellow monsters Elektro, Fin Fang Foom, and Googam to bring down alien antagonist Tim Boo Ba. News reports soon followed, stating the hirsute hero had taken up temporary residence on New York City's Statue of Liberty—having been thrown there by Tim Boo Ba. More recently, there have been sightings of Gorgilla on Monster Isle in the Pacific Ocean.

Gorgilla's massive size grants him astonishing strength and durability, bullets cannot penetrate his skin, and his giant prehensile tail makes him an agile climber.

Monster of Midnight Mountain
Gorgilla left his peaceful life in Borneo. His adventures in the wider human world haven't always gone smoothly, but Gorgilla eventually feels at home there.

First Appearance: *Tales to Astonish* #12 (1960) by Stan Lee, Larry Lieber, and Jack Kirby **Further Reading:** *Marvel Monsters: Fin Fang 4 #1* (2005)

Height: Originally 25ft (7.6m) **Weight:** Unknown **Origin:** Forests of Borneo **Powers:** Superhuman strength, agility, and durability

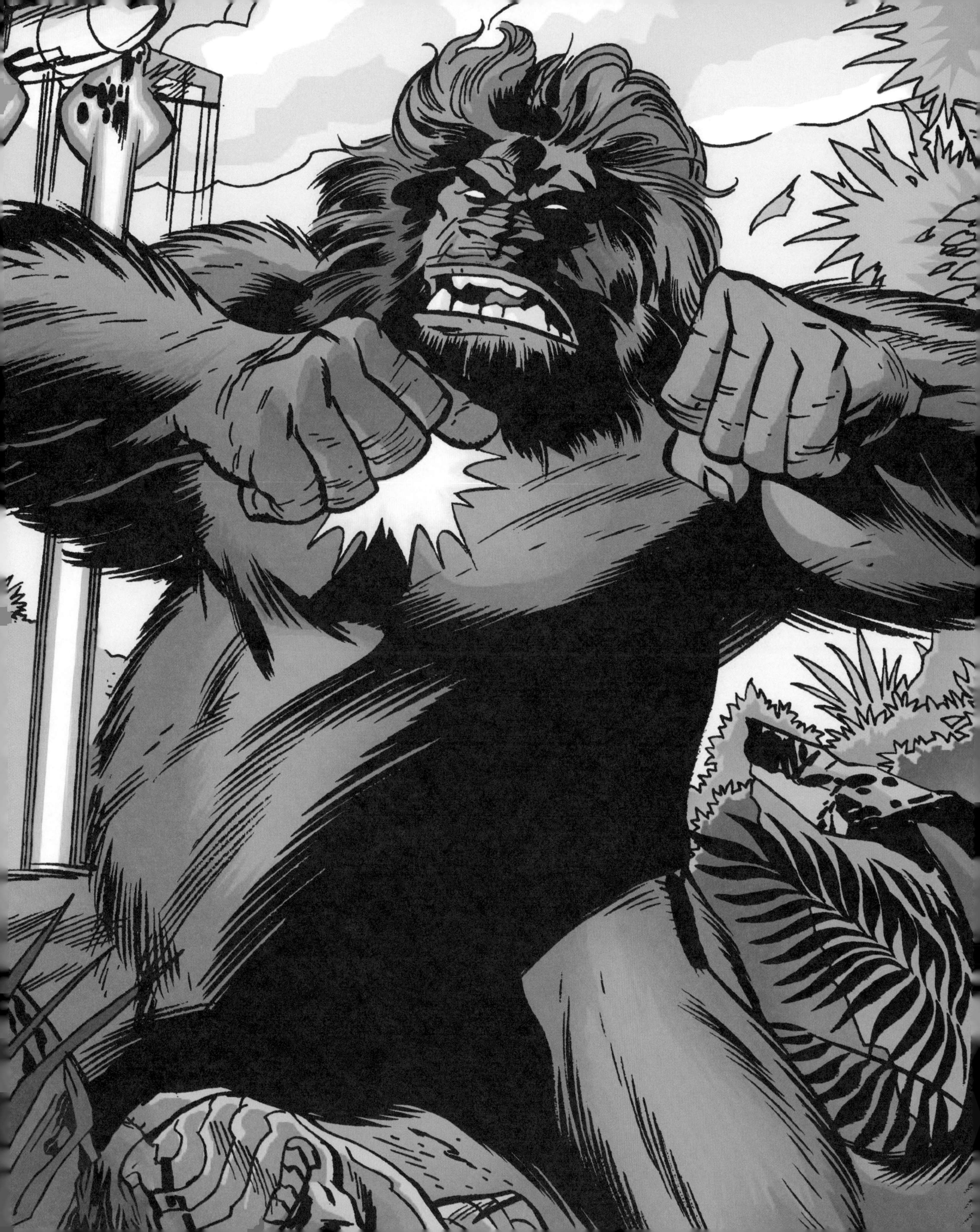

Man-Wolf

The strange energy emitting from a glowing gem discovered on the moon turned an ordinary man into an extraordinary monster. Man-Wolf is the alter ego of human test pilot and astronaut John Jameson, and, during the full moon, the lycanthrope would tear through the city streets, leaving a trail of destruction in his wake.

Colonel John Jameson, son of *Daily Bugle* publisher J. Jonah Jameson, was on a secret mission to the moon when a glimmer in the lunar dust caught his eye. Drawn to the unusual, glowing, red stone, he carried it home and had it set into a pendant. Under the full moon, the gem around his neck gleamed even brighter. Over the course of three nights, the lunar energy altered Jameson into a feral creature that was both man and wolf! Fur bristling and deadly fangs and claws bared, the mindless Man-Wolf went on a destructive rampage until he was stopped by Spider-Man.

For some time, Jameson continued to battle with the curse of Man-Wolf—until he felt himself drawn to the moon's surface. There, he discovered a portal and entered the strange place known as the Other Realm. While there, Man-Wolf was shocked to find he had regained his human mind and speech. He learned that the symbiotic gem he had found contained the all-powerful essence of a legendary hero from that dimension called Stargod. Wielding the powers of Stargod, Man-Wolf saved the citizens of that realm, and returned to Earth.

As Man-Wolf, Jameson stands a few inches taller and weighs a little more than his human form. Fur covers his form, fangs protrude from his jaws, and claws extend from his fingertips. He exhibits the abilities of werewolves of folklore, without the weakness for silver; he's preternaturally fast, strong, and durable, with heightened senses and accelerated healing. He can access the cosmic power of Stargod, including increased strength, when the need arises.

Over time, Jameson has gained control of his wolf form and can transform at will.

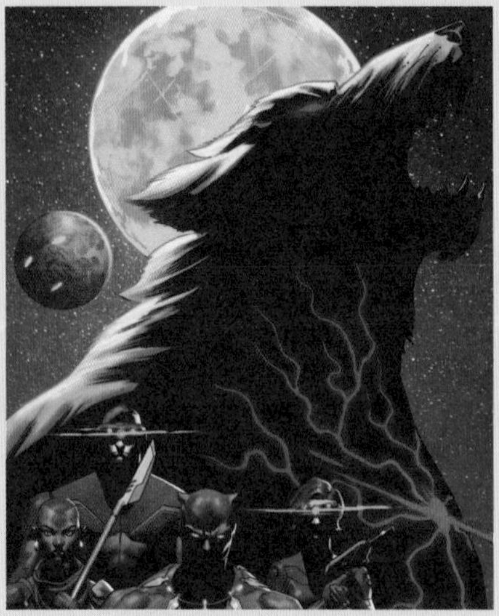

Agent of Wakanda
Man-Wolf joined the ranks of an Avengers support team headed by Black Panther. Their missions took them from Transylvania, to Earth's atmosphere and beyond.

First Appearance: *The Amazing Spider-Man* #124 (1973) by Gerry Conway and Gil Kane **Further Reading:** *Marvel Premiere* #45-46 (1978), *Black Panther and the Agents of Wakanda* #3-4 (2020)

Height: 6ft 6in (2m) **Weight:** 350 lbs (158.8kg) **Origin:** Earth **Powers:** Superhuman strength, speed, and durability; heightened senses

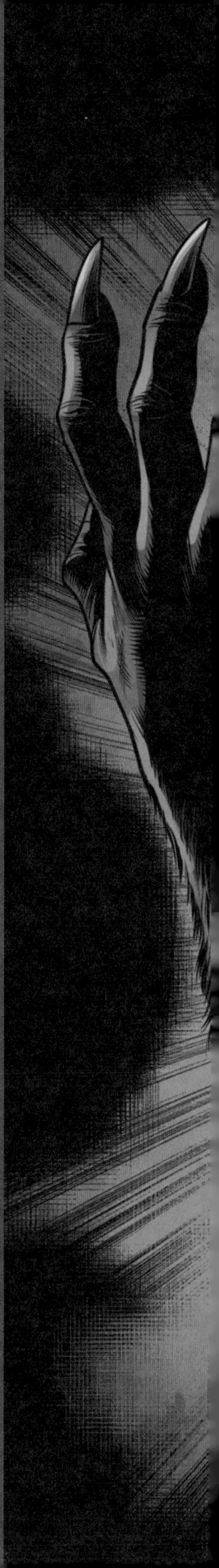

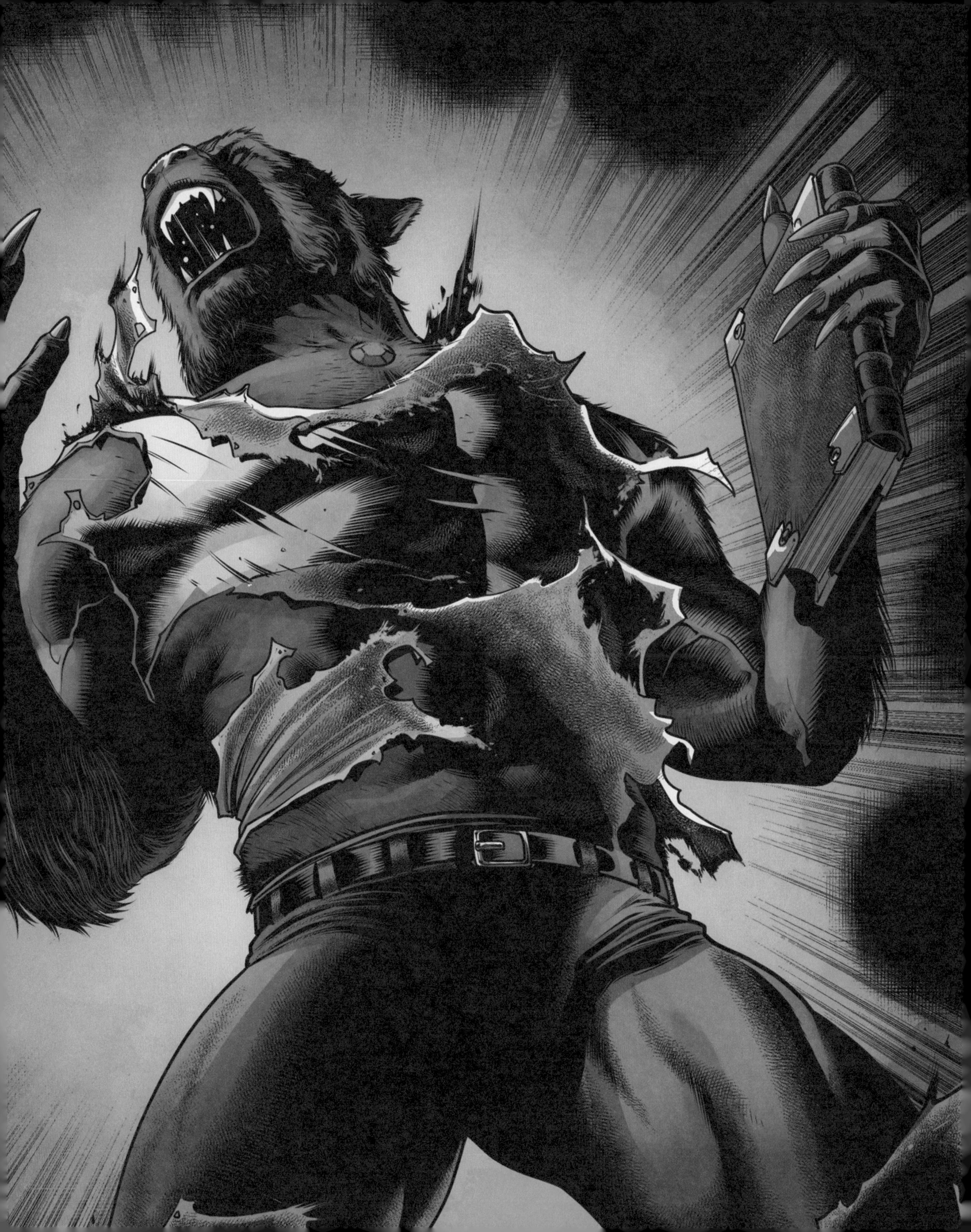

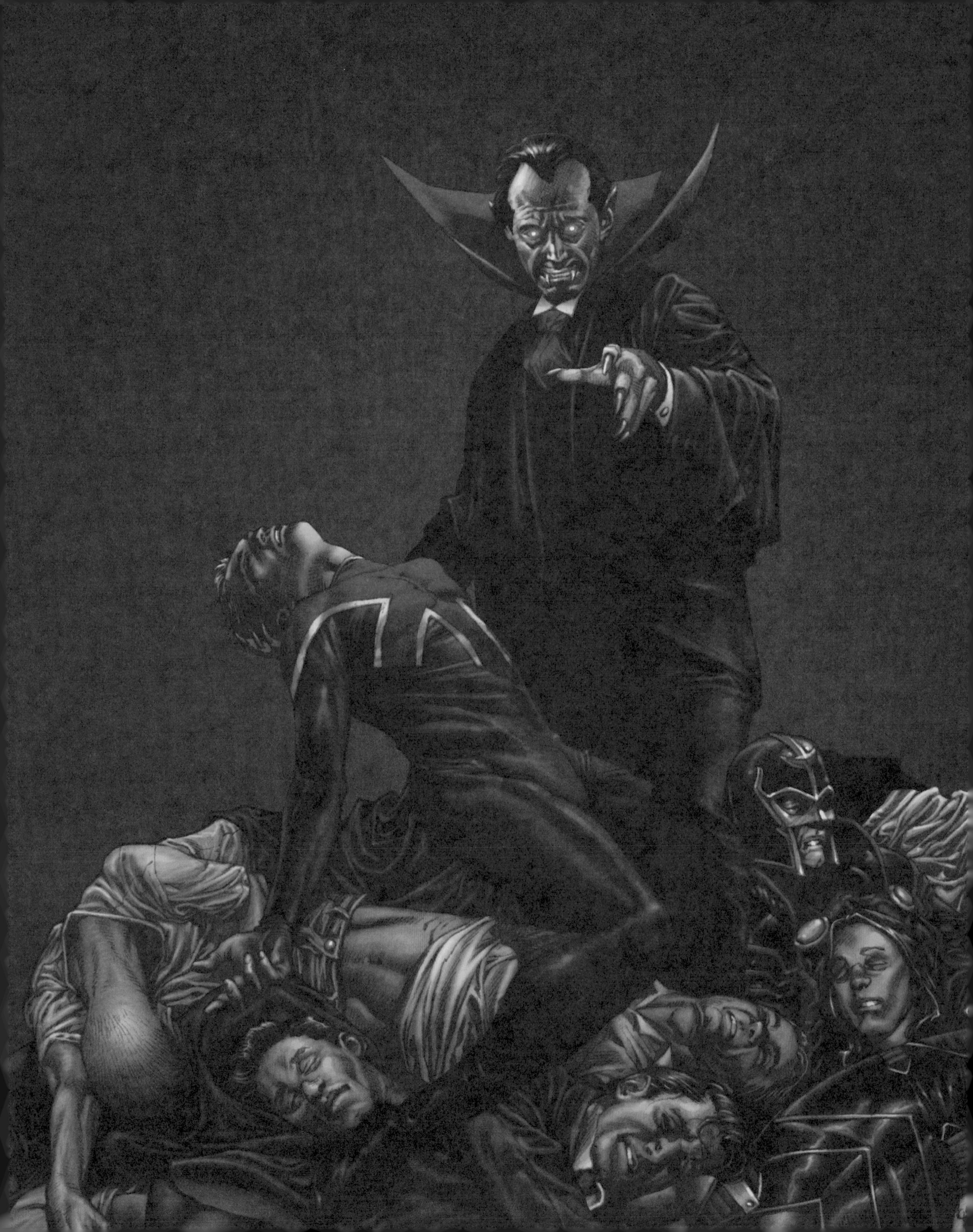

Dracula

It was reported that in 1459, military leader and royal Vlad Dracula was transformed into a member of the undead by vampiric healer, Lianda. Since then, nightmarish Dracula has preyed on the living, feasting on their blood for nourishment. Not even a wooden stake through the heart can ensure a permanent end to this powerful vampire's reign of terror.

Born Vlad Dracula in 1430, the human prince of Wallachia was nicknamed Vlad the Impaler and known as a merciless combatant even before his transformation. He had no shortage of enemies in either life or death. His vampiric powers only made him more ruthless and he set out to become Lord of Vampires. By the late 1800s, vampire hunter Abraham van Helsing became the latest of many who sought to destroy him, and eventually Dracula was staked in the heart. Centuries later, he rose from his tomb after the stake was removed. He continued to prey on humans in his never-ending thirst for blood, pursued doggedly by vampire hunters such as Elsa Bloodstone, Blade, and the descendants of van Helsing.

Time after time, Dracula would be seemingly killed, only to be revived later. He returned even after sorcerer Doctor Strange cast the Montesi Formula—a spell that destroyed all vampires on Earth—and has survived stakes through the heart more than once. When his son Xarus took the title of king, slayed his father, and invaded San Francisco, the X-Men resurrected Dracula in the hope of defeating Xarus' army of undead. Dracula ended his son's war on the human world and resumed his place as Lord of Vampires in his castle in Transylvania's Carpathian Mountains.

The silver-tongued, powerful vampire is a gifted leader. Dracula was a military strategist before he was cursed, and centuries of experience have made him all the more formidable. He has the abilities and vulnerabilities of the fang-baring immortal undead of legend: he must drink blood to survive, and when a victim perishes, they in turn become vampires. Silver, garlic, sunlight, religious symbols, and a stake to the heart are among his weaknesses. The predator can control minds with just a glance of his blood-red eyes, often mesmerizing his prey before he strikes.

First Appearance: *The Tomb of Dracula #1* (1972) by Gerry Conway and Gene Colan
Further Reading: *The Tomb of Dracula* (2004), *X-Men #5-6* (2011)

Undead but not unchanged
In recent years, Dracula's suit and cloak have been supplemented with armor. His slicked-back black hair has whitened and been pulled into a ponytail.

Height: 6ft 5in (1.9m) **Weight:** 220 lbs (99.8kg) **Origin:** Kingdom of Wallachia, now Transylvania **Powers:** Shape-shifting; mind control; immortality

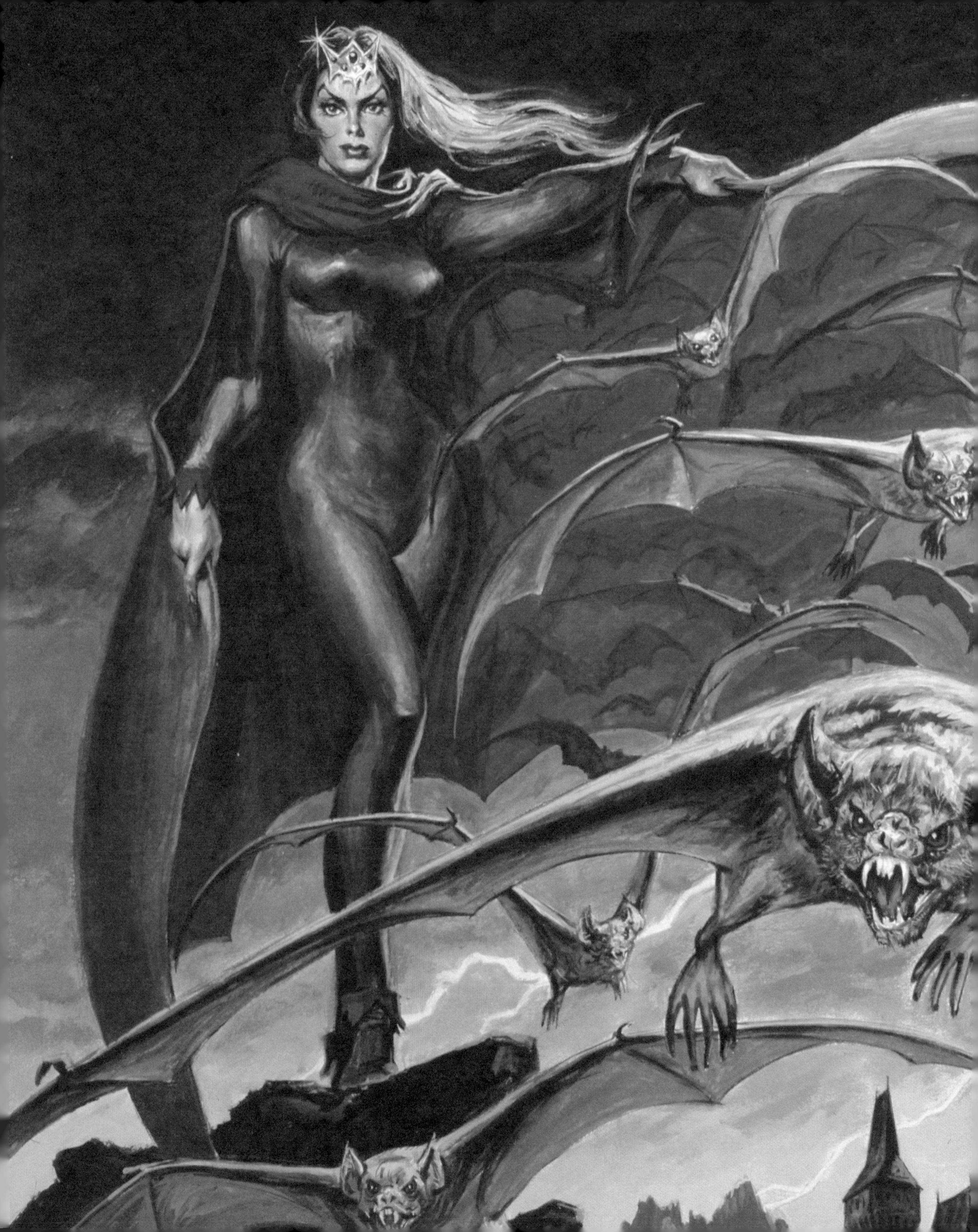

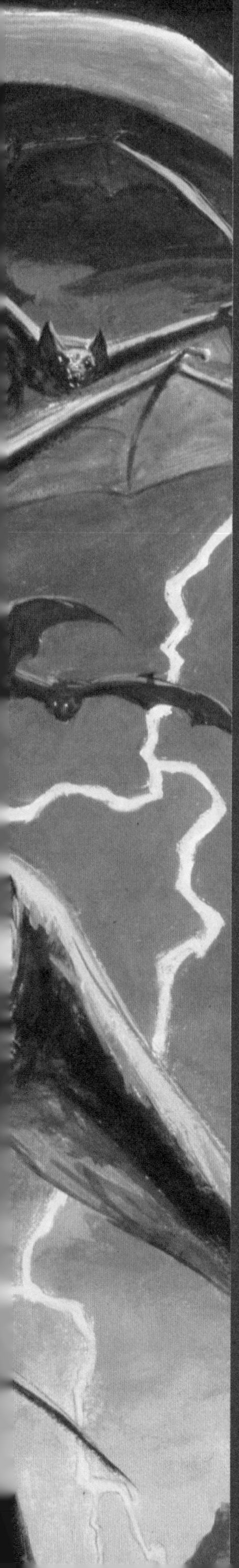

Height: 6ft (1.8m) **Weight:** 125 lbs (56.7kg) **Origin:** Transylvania **Powers:** Shape-shifting; mind control; possession; immortality

Lilith, Dracula's Daughter

Lord of the Vampires Vlad Dracula's daughter, Lilith, was transformed into a vampire not with a bite, but by way of a Romani woman's vengeful spell. Although the magical curse rendered her immune to most vampiric weaknesses, she is damned to hunt the father she hates for all eternity.

Lilith's mother was Vlad Dracula's first wife, Zofia. Their prearranged marriage was loveless. Shortly after their daughter was born, the haughty nobleman expelled both Zofia and Lilith from his castle. Zofia placed young Lilith in the care of a Romani woman named Gretchin, before abruptly taking her own life. In revenge for the death of her son at the hands of Dracula, Gretchin cast a spell to turn Lilith into a vampire who would be eternally driven to seek out Dracula in order to slay him.

As a result of her unusual transformation, Lilith's abilities are not the same as a traditional vampire. She has all of their strengths and very few of their weaknesses. She is not affected by sunlight, has no need to sleep during daylight hours, and does not fear religious symbols. Also, although the raven-haired vampire revels in drinking blood, she is not required to do so, and not all of Lilith's victims are transformed into the undead. When her body is killed with a wooden stake to the heart, her spirit remains. In that noncorporeal form, Lilith can possess any innocent woman who harbors hatred against her father. The host is taken over, body and mind, by Lilith, who claims control and can then access her full powers.

Full of loathing for her father, Lilith is condemned to hunt Dracula for the rest of her days, her soul bound to Earth as long as he exists. However, limitations of Gretchin's spell mean she cannot directly strike a finishing blow. Lilith is forever the hunter, and Dracula the hunted.

First Appearance: *Giant-Size Chillers* #1 (1974) by Marv Wolfman and Gene Colan
Further Reading: *Legion of Monsters: Morbius* #1 (2007)

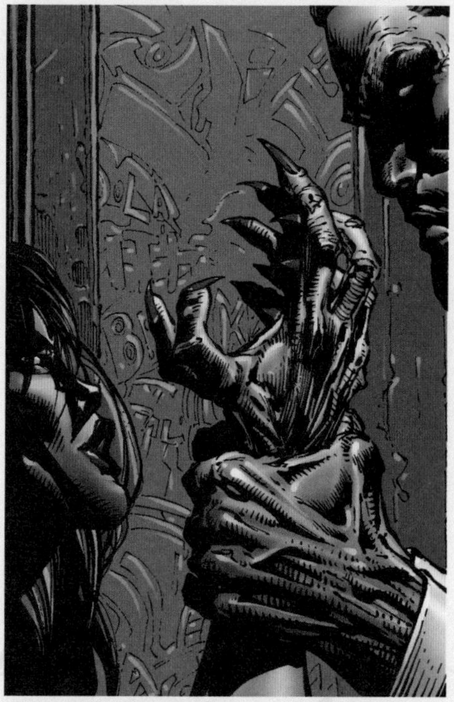

Emotional weakness
Lilith and her father share a mutual hatred. When they have attempted reconciliation it's either refused or been a trick, and so they remain bitter foes.

Werewolf by Night

The light of the full moon illuminates a howling beast. This clawed creature is Jack Russell, a man cursed by birth to become a werewolf when he turned 18. Now part man and part feral animal, he has managed to harness control of the wolf side of his nature and uses it to challenge mystical foes.

One of Jack Russell's ancestors was bitten by a werewolf several hundred years ago. The curse was passed down the family until it awoke in Jack on the night he turned 18 years old. At first, he was a mindless monster for the three nights of the duration of the full moon, seeking out prey and attacking anyone foolish enough to assail him. Some time later, Russell acquired the ability to transform at will and retain control of his human intellect and emotions, so as the Werewolf he could act more like a man than a menace in lupine form. Despite this, during a full moon, Jack would then lose control altogether. The Werewolf's beastly side would be unleashed, and Jack would lock himself away to protect innocent lives.

Like the werewolves of folklore, Jack Russell has supernaturally enhanced senses, strength, and agility as the Werewolf. His sense of smell is exceptionally strong, even in his human form. His powerful beastlike legs can leap over 15 feet (4.6m) in the air and the raw strength behind his ferocious fangs and claws is a force few can withstand. In his lupine form, Jack grows streaked dark brown fur all over his body, and his eyes glow red. Impervious to injury, but not invulnerable, he is weak against silver.

When his human mind and werewolf body exist as one, Jack chooses to use his wild strength for good. He's fought alongside prominent heroes such as Iron Man, Spider-Man, and Doctor Strange, and been a vital member of supernaturally powered teams such as the Legion of Monsters and Midnight Sons. The Werewolf might look like a sharp-toothed monster, but at heart he's a hero. Recently, other werewolves have been noted prowling the night.

A new Werewolf by Night
Teenager Jake Gomez changes into a werewolf regardless of the moon, thanks to the lycanthropy that runs in his family. He resists his base instincts in order to guard the people of his reservation. For now, music keeps Jake's monster at bay.

First Appearance: *Marvel Spotlight #2* (1972) by Gerry Conway, Roy Thomas, Jean Thomas, and Michael Ploog
Further Reading: *Doctor Strange, Sorcerer Supreme #26-27* (1991), *Marvel Zombies #4* (2009)

Height: 6ft 8in (2m) **Weight:** 300 lbs (136kg) **Origin:** Transylvania **Powers:** Superhuman strength, agility, stamina, and sense; transforms at will

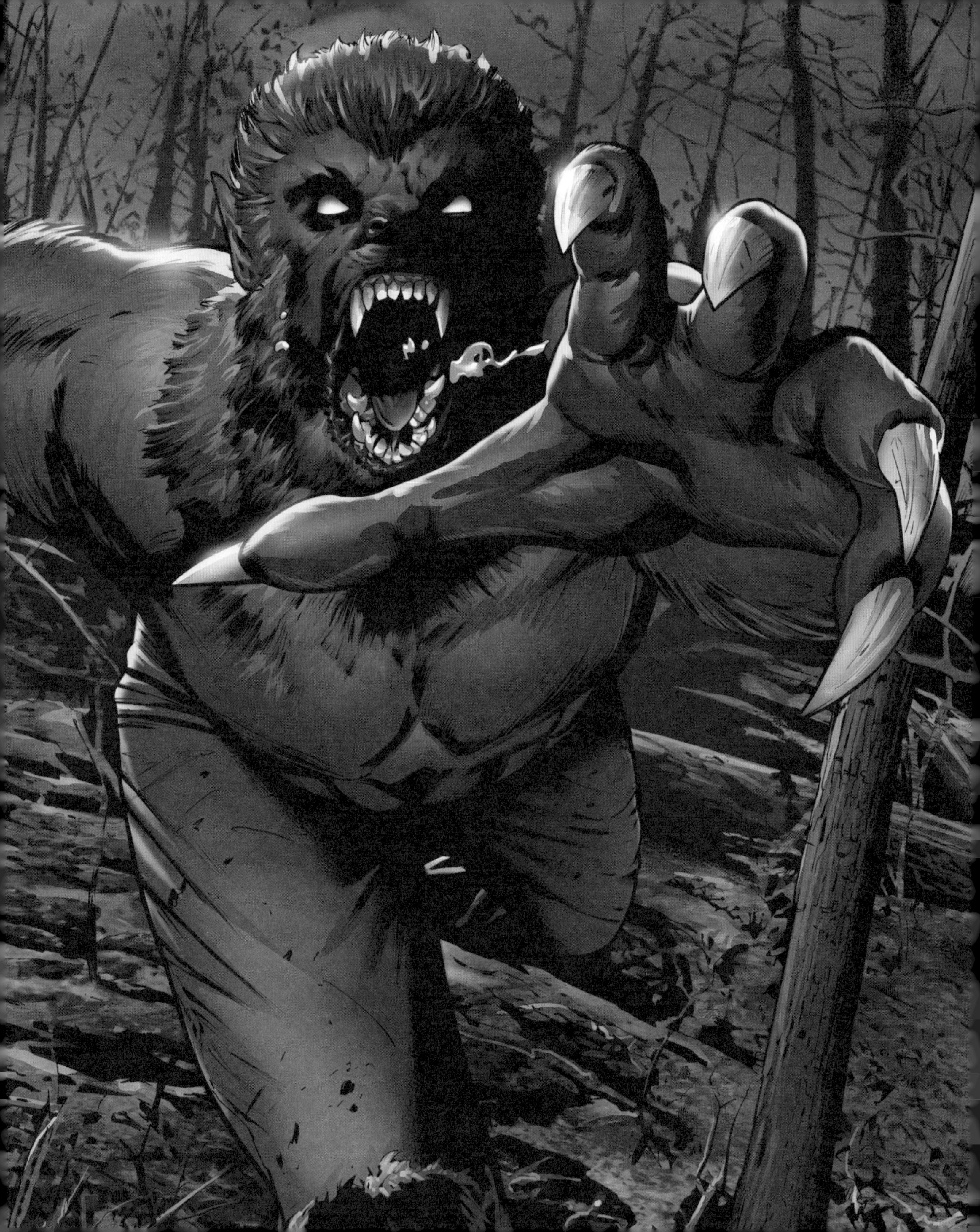

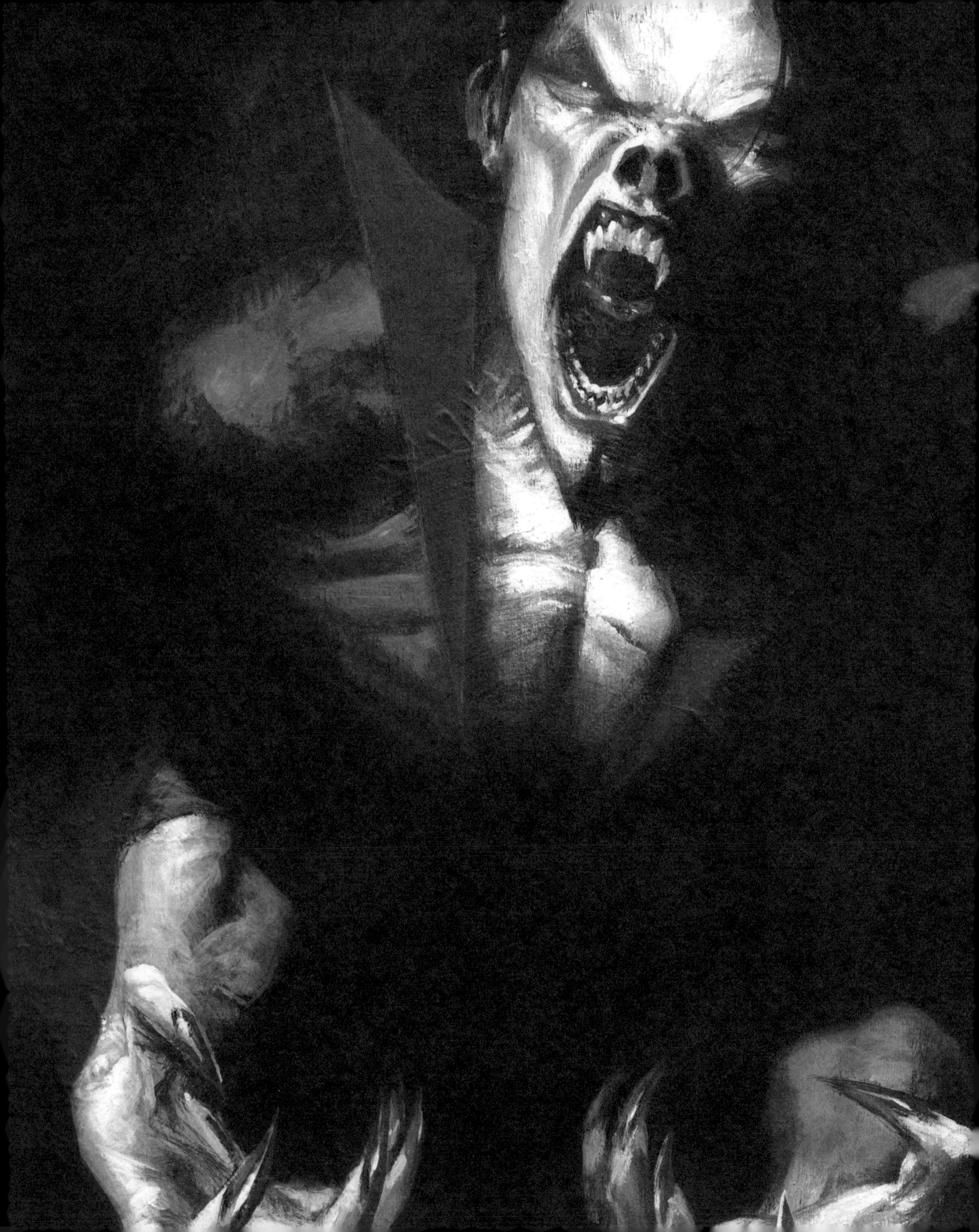

Height: 5ft 10in (1.8m) Weight: 170 lbs (77kg) Origin: Greece Powers: Superhuman strength and healing ability; flight; hypnosis; genius intellect

Morbius, the Living Vampire

Suffering from a debilitating blood disorder, talented biochemist Dr. Michael Morbius sought to cure himself—with catastrophic side-effects. Transformed into a living vampire, Morbius now craves blood without belonging to the ranks of the immortal undead. His unrelenting need to feed often pits him against heroes like Spider-Man and the X-Men.

Nobel Prize-winning Dr. Morbius suffered from a rare, deadly disease that attacked his blood cells. Desperate to find a cure so that he could stay by the side of the woman he loved, Morbius combined electroshock therapy with DNA from a vampire bat in an unorthodox test on himself. Although the experiment cured his illness, his success came at a price; the bizarre combination transformed Morbius into a monstrous predator, plagued by an incessant thirst for blood.

   With jet-black hair, glowering red eyes, and paper-white skin, Morbius might look similar to the corpselike vampires of folklore, but his powers are not supernatural. He is mortal, but apparently ageless, and his altered body boasts accelerated healing. The metamorphosis also turned his bones hollow, aiding his ability to soar through the sky. He ambushes unsuspecting victims from the air and strikes with flesh-rending claws and fangs. The so-called Living Vampire can barely keep the monster inside at bay as he struggles to drain his victims' without killing them. Most of his prey survives, although some unfortunate souls die from blood loss or find themselves likewise transformed into living vampires.

   When his thirst is quenched, Morbius fully returns to his senses. In those moments he's more human than monster, and he turns to his research to try to restore himself to the man of science he once was. But his bloodlust cannot be sated, and it is only a matter of time before the nightmarish beast takes control once again and resumes his hunt.

First Appearance: *The Amazing Spider-Man #101* (1971) by Roy Thomas and Gil Kane
Further Reading: *Adventure Into Fear #20 (1974), Morbius* (2020)

Working arrangement
Spider-Man is one of Morbius's most frequent foes, but he is also a compassionate ally. The two scientists have worked together to try to find a cure for the Living Vampire's condition.

Skaar

Tearing and slashing his way across the war-torn planet of Sakaar and beyond, Skaar is the savage offspring of the Hulk, who was known as the Green King on this world, and Caiera the Oldstrong, a warrior of the Shadow People who lived there. Like his father, the relentless Skaar is driven by rage. Nothing in his way is left standing.

When an explosion in Crown City took the life of his mother, the cocoon Skaar, the son of Hulk, was growing in was catapulted into a lake of fire. In the aftermath, and having emerged from his cocoon, Skaar wandered alone among the radioactive swamps of Sakaar until he joined forces with other warriors against invading barbarians. His primary goal was simple but savage: to punish and kill those he believed to be evil.

In time Sakaar fell, not to conquerors, but to Galactus, the Devourer of Worlds. Skaar was banished to his father's home planet of Earth by the spirit of his mother. He first sought to destroy Hulk in revenge for abandoning him and his scarred world. The two eventually reconciled, and Skaar sought a new destiny in Earth's primal Savage Land.

Skaar's skin color usually appears green, like his father's. But when he taps into the earth-based Old Power that he inherited from his mother, it turns a more grayish hue. There are tribal markings on his chest and right arm that priests of the Shadow People of Sakaar burned into his skin. Like Hulk, he is immensely strong, and when he combines that strength with the cosmic but unstable Old Power, he is formidable. Skaar's gamma-powered body is also capable of transforming to a younger, human form and back into a monstrous warrior at will.

Although he does not require a weapon, Skaar has used a sword against his enemies, deeming it to be more "fun." The wrathful warrior has unleashed his rage and raised his blade against powerful foes such as the colossal fire-breathing dragons of Sakaar, herald of Galactus the Silver Surfer, the Fantastic Four, and even his own father.

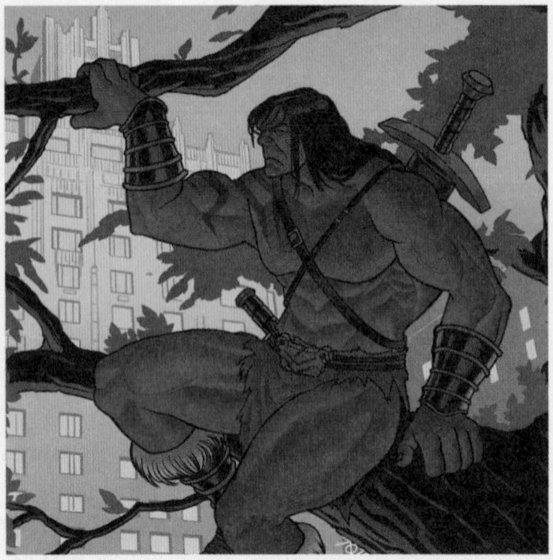

Always an outsider
A child of two worlds, Skaar has struggled to find a place that feels like home.

First Appearance: *World War Hulk* #5 (2008) by Greg Pak and John Romita Jr. **Further Reading:** *Skaar: Son of Hulk* (2008), *Skaar: King of the Savage Land* (2011), *Hulk* #7 (2014)

Height: 6ft 6in (1.9m) **Weight:** 400 lbs (181kg) **Origin:** Sakaar **Powers:** Superhuman strength; limited invulnerability; draws on earth-based energy

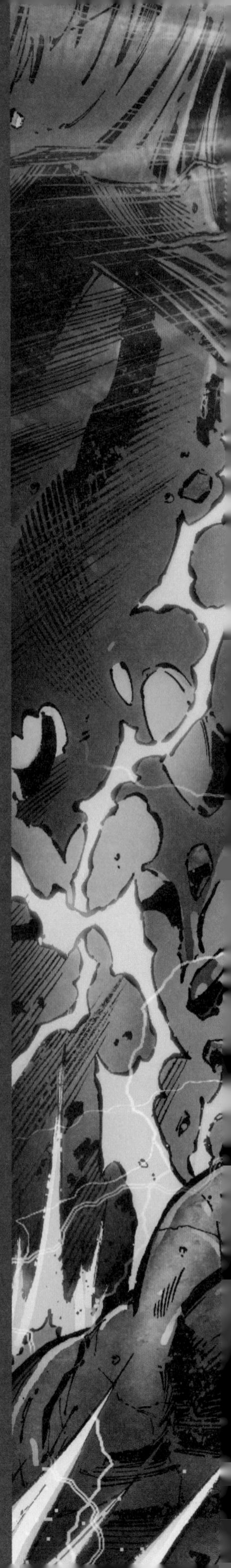

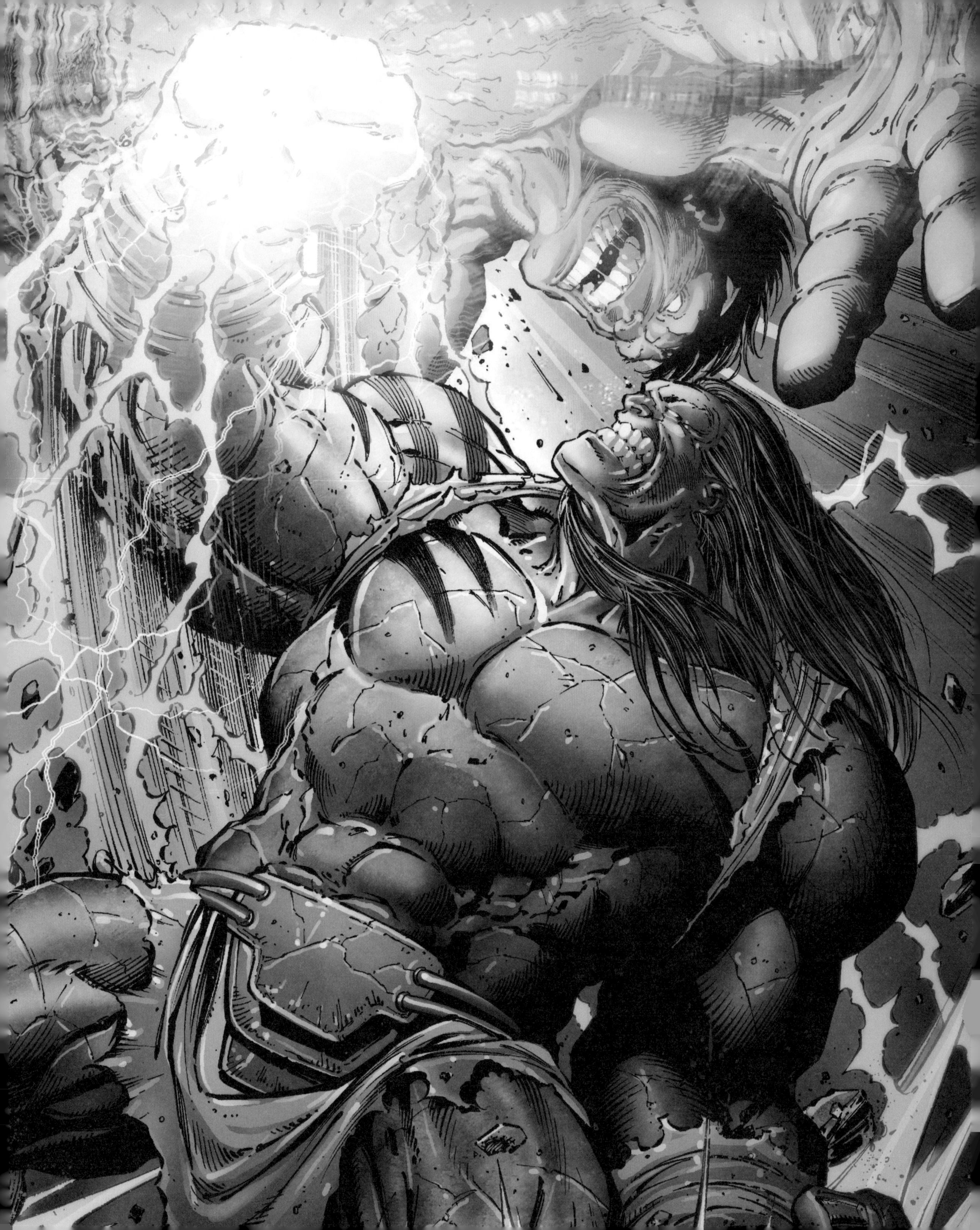

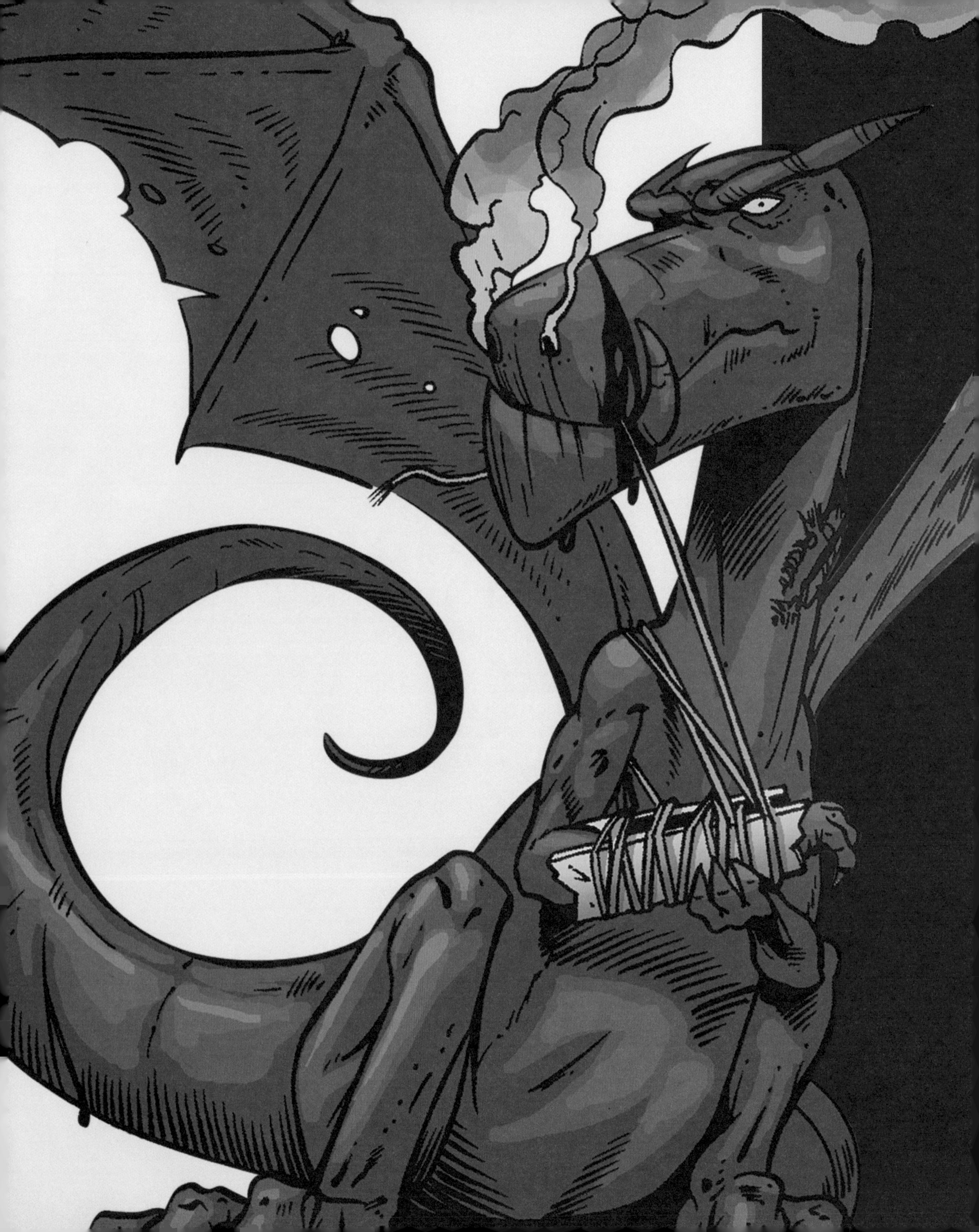

AERIAL

The sounds of wingbeats fill the air. Sharpened talons flex as their owners anticipate snatching their targets. A reptilian silhouette is briefly visible in the sky before the airborne abomination swoops down with a shriek.

Whether they are the shocking result of an experiment gone wrong or born in a far-flung galaxy, these winged monsters are a striking sight in the sky. Sauron and Dragon-Man are echoes of Earth's prehistoric creatures thought to be long-gone. Grogg is a dragon of ancient Chinese legend.

The alien Lockheed may look like a tiny fire-breathing terror, but he's a steadfast partner and hero. In contrast, the cloaked form of Swarm appears to be human, but the villain is made up of a deadly mass of killer bees.

Find out more about these flying friends and fiends.

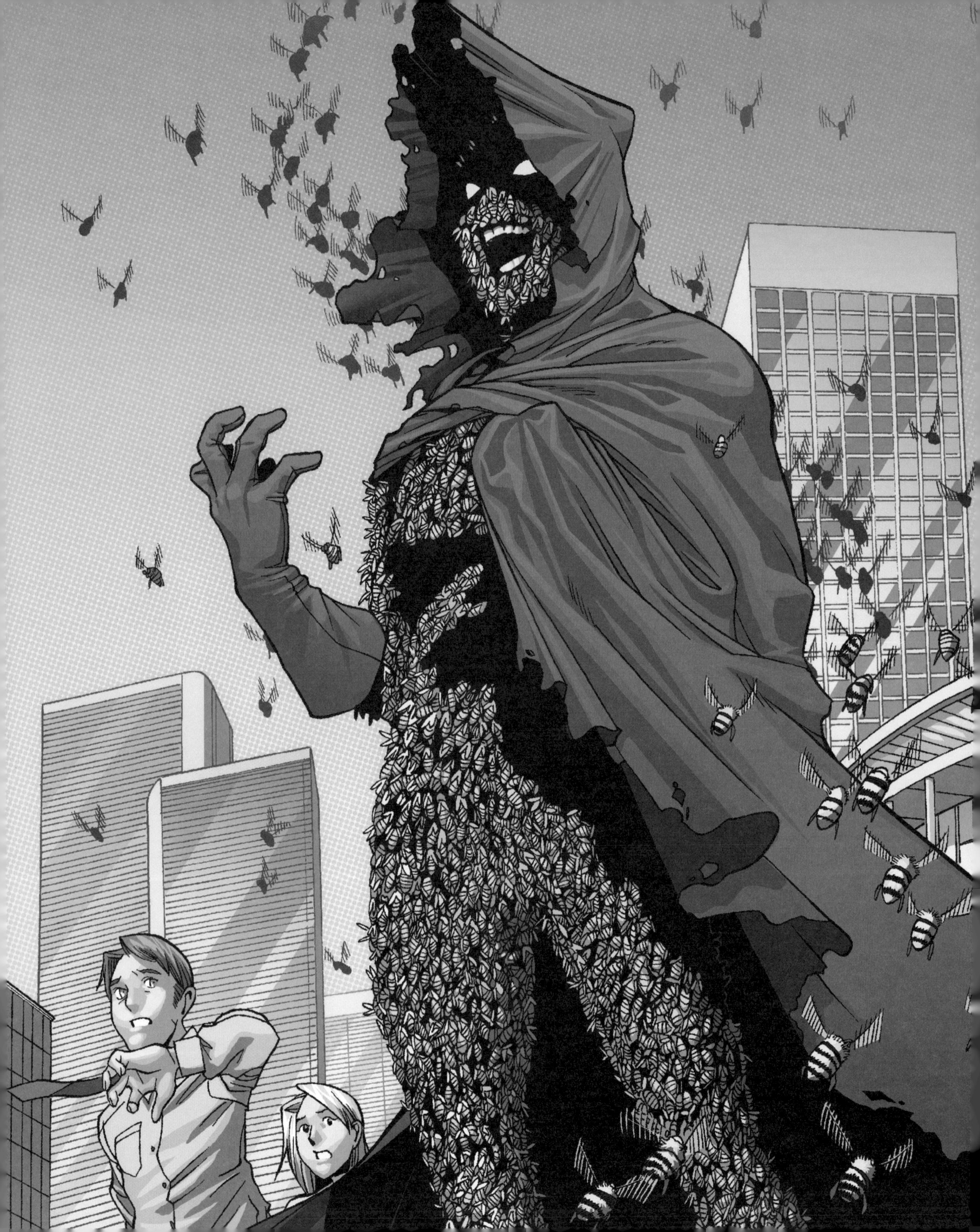

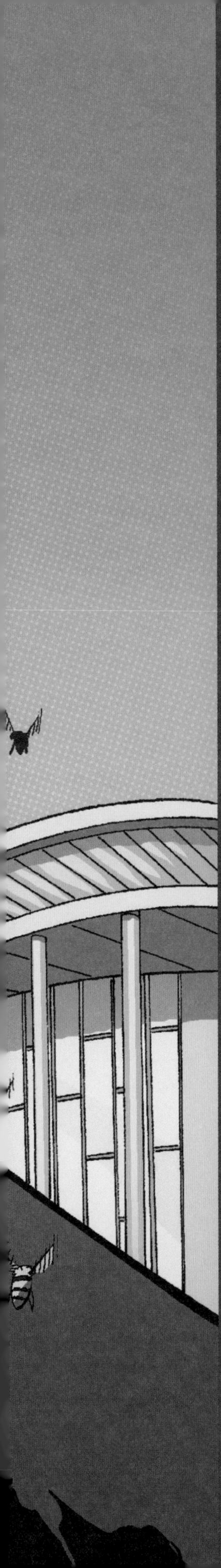

Height: 6ft 5in (2m) **Weight:** Unknown **Origin:** South America **Powers:** Mental control over killer bees; command over other bees nearby

Swarm

Thousands of bees come together to form a single, humanoid shape beneath a tattered cloak. Each insect is armed with a stinger that strikes with the searing pain of a white-hot needle. This highly intelligent, composite being is called Swarm, the lord of the killer bees.

Fritz von Meyer had been a Nazi scientist. After World War II, the toxins expert and apiculturist relocated to South America where he researched killer bees. One day, von Meyer discovered a huge hive of strangely behaving bees close to a site where a meteoroid had fallen just days before. Exposed to otherworldly radiation by the meteorite's impact, the bees evolved into a highly intelligent colony with a mutated queen bee. Von Meyer attempted an experiment on the bees to exert his control over them, but it backfired, and the agitated bees consumed his body, leaving just a skeleton. Remarkably, his subconscious bonded to the queen bee of the colony. Von Meyer became an aggregate monster, a living swarm of killer bees, and so he came to be known as Swarm.

Swarm has gone up against heroes the Champions, Squirrel Girl, and Ant-Man, and he has almost ended the life of Spider-Man Peter Parker. He seeks to augment his power by increasing the size of the hive and his insect army. Although his physical body long perished, von Meyer's intellect lives on, and he has successfully mutated some of the bees to grow in size. He has even been known to ride on the back of an enormous queen bee, and it is rumored he can communicate with other insects, too.

The Super Villain's consciousness is shared with the thousands of killer bees that act as the "cells" that make up his body. He's able to exert his mental control over any bee within a three-mile area. Swarm can command the bees to attack, sting, build a hive, and tear through almost any obstacle. The swarming mass is susceptible to insect repellent, but otherwise is difficult to damage.

The last known sighting of Swarm was in Florida, where he and Ant-Man took on other beings from sentient insect colonies and their mandiblelike leader, Macrothrax.

First Appearance: *The Champions* #14 (1977) by Bill Mantlo and John Byrne
Further Reading: *Peter Parker, the Spectacular Spider-Man* #36-37 (1979)

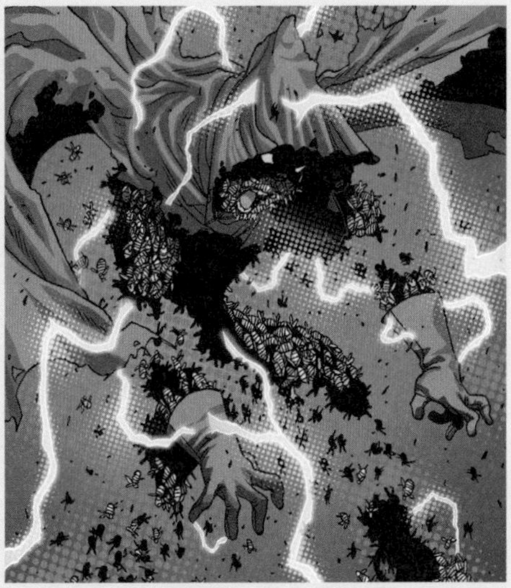

Fallible hive mind
Swarm's weakness lies in the source of his power—his connection to the hive. Runaways' hero Victor Mancha proved he could disrupt the electrical impulses the bees use to communicate, thus halting the bee man.

Sauron

With large leathery wings outstretched, a terrifying creature takes flight, emitting an earsplitting screech. His gleaming red eyes can hypnotize with a glance—he then drains the energy of his stunned prey with a touch of his taloned hand. Part-man, part-prehistoric creature, his name is Sauron.

As an adult, Dr. Karl Lykos is a noted hypnotherapist. But he was just a boy on an expedition to Antarctica when he was attacked by a *Pteranodon* from the Savage Land—a tropical, prehistoric region located at the Antarctic Peninsula. When he regained consciousness, Karl found that he needed to drain the energy from living beings to sustain himself. Mutants, in particular, gave him the raw power he needed to stay alive. He drained Havok of the X-Men, and the mutant's potent life-force transformed Lykos into an evil half-human, half-*Pteranodon* monster. Referencing his love of stories by human author J.R.R. Tolkien, Lykos chose to call himself Sauron, who he saw as the ultimate, most evil, villain, and leapt into the sky on the hunt for more mutant energy.

In his green reptilian form, Sauron can soar through the skies at great speed. His clawed hands and feet are just as intimidating as his fearsome, red-eyed gaze. His hypnotic powers can entrance a victim into becoming a loyal follower or seeing their worst nightmares come to life. In addition, he can expel flames from his lethal beak.

Sauron has frequently clashed with the X-Men, often in the Savage Land, which he claimed as his own. When Sauron's energy is depleted, he reverts to his human form of Dr. Lykos. But his reptilian side is overpowering, with its evil impulses and thirst for mutants' life essence, and Sauron has returned time and time again.

Sauron has been a member of various teams, such as the Savage Land Mutates. More recently, he banded together with Stegron the Dinosaur Man and ended up turning many of the inhabitants of New York's Staten Island into dinosaurs. Fortunately, Spider-Man was on hand to end the prehistoric creatures' threat to humankind.

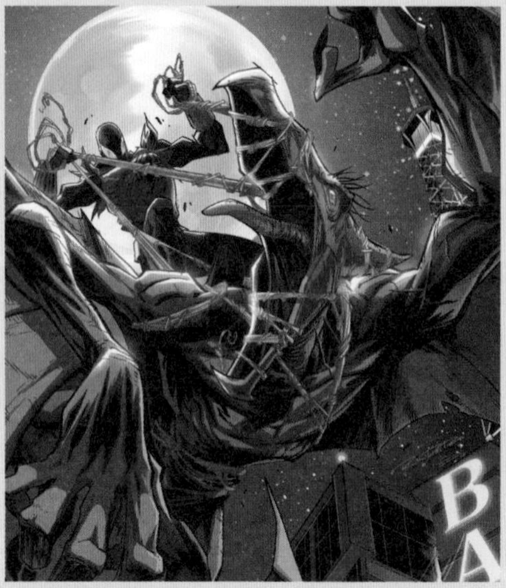

Frequent foe
Sauron can't resist his evil urges in his half-*Pteranodon* form, no matter how many times his plans are thwarted.

First Appearance: *X-Men* #60 (1969) by Roy Thomas and Neal Adams **Further Reading:** *X-Men Unlimited* #6 (1994)

Height: 7ft (2m) **Weight:** 200 lbs (90.7kg) **Origin:** Argentina **Powers:** Drains life energy; eye contact hypnotizes and causes hallucinations; flight

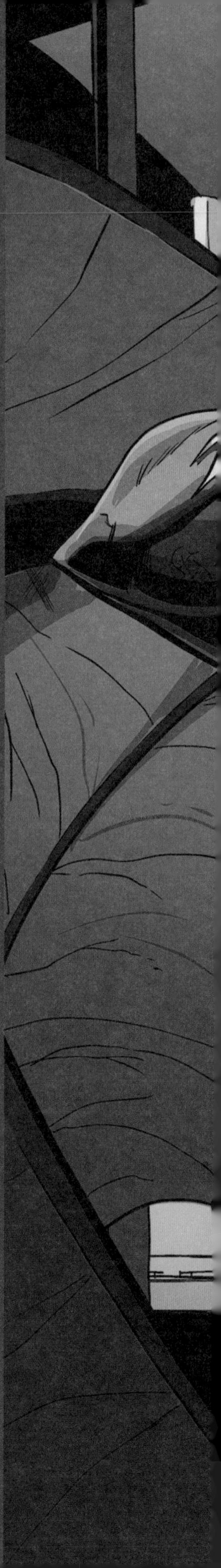

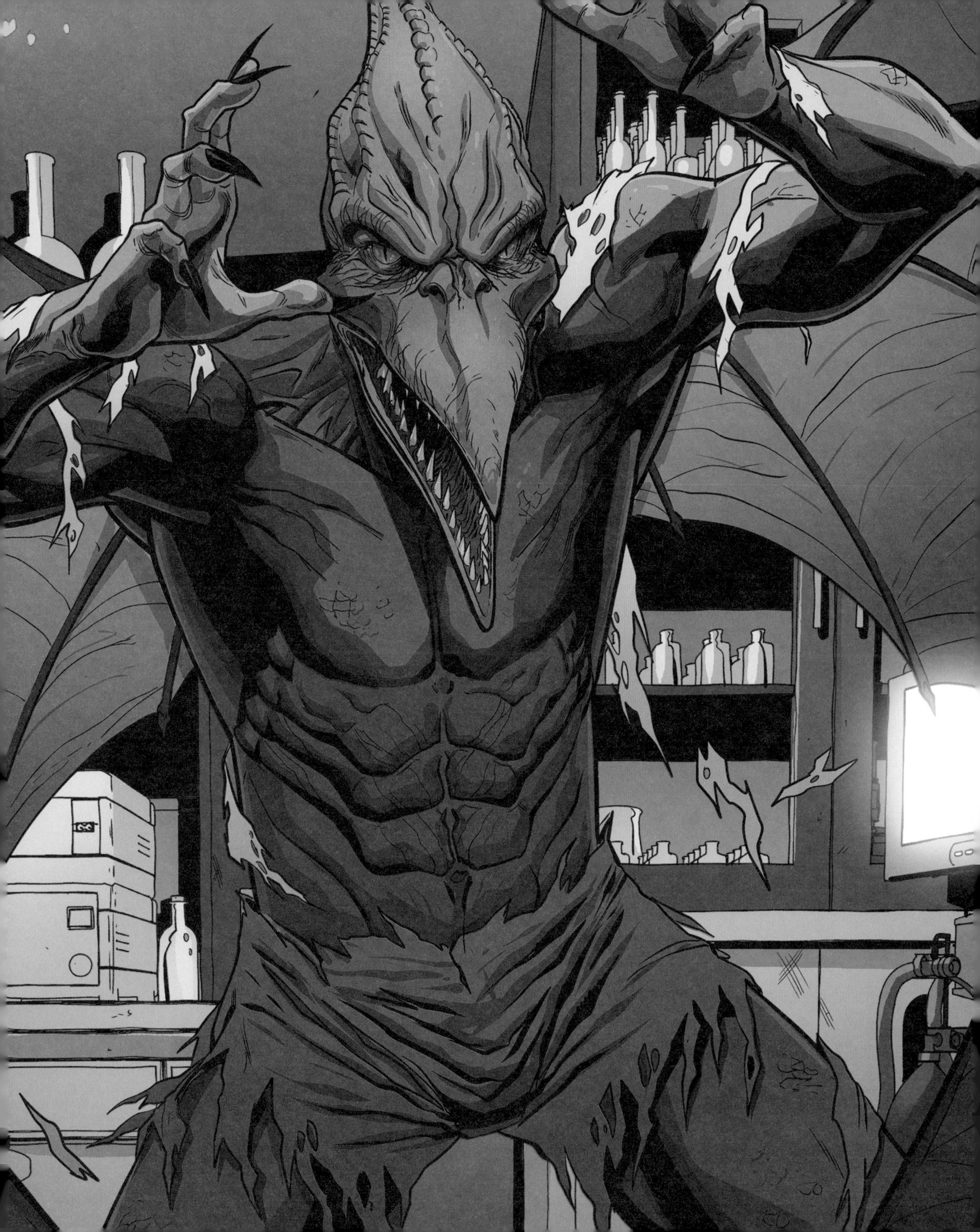

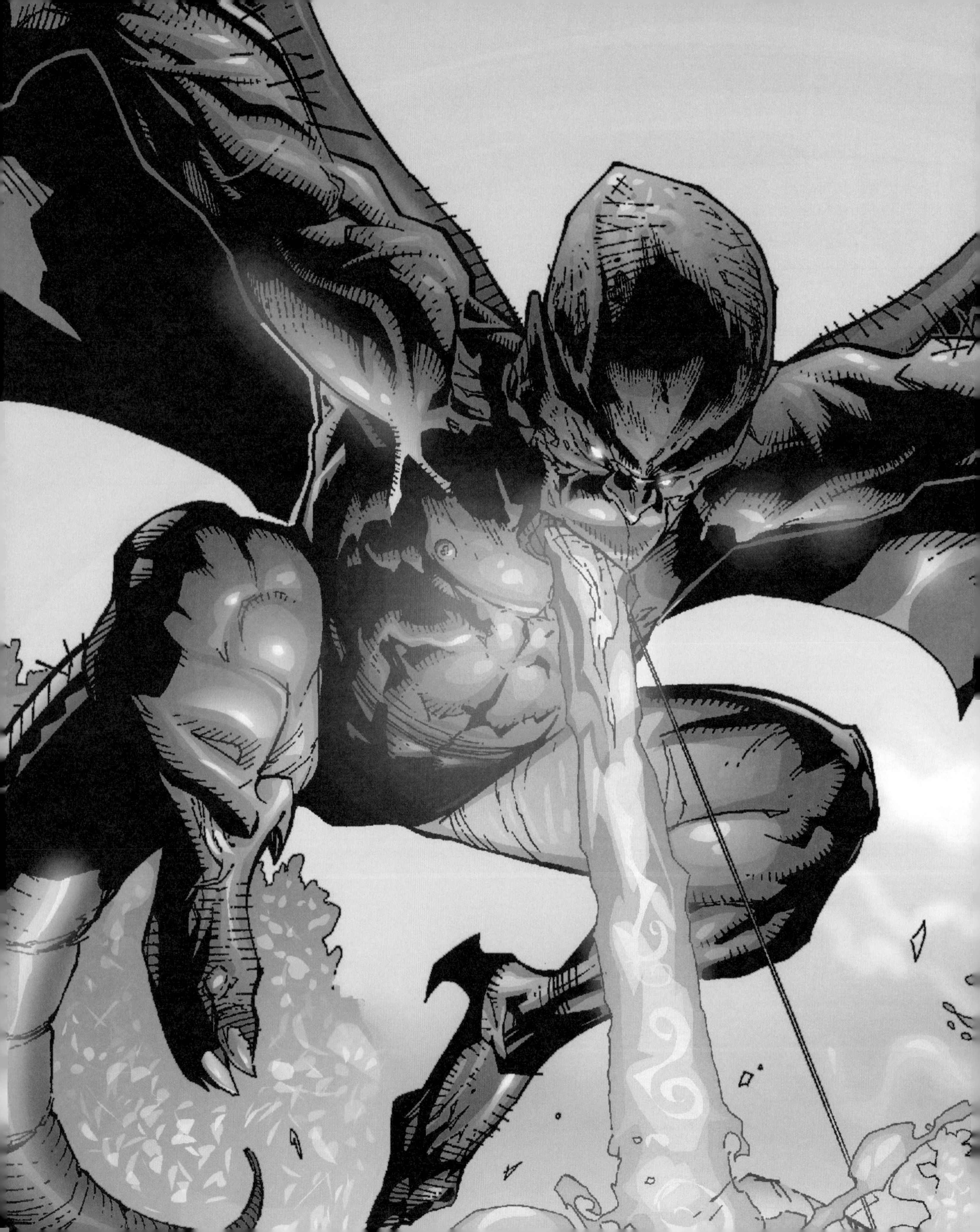

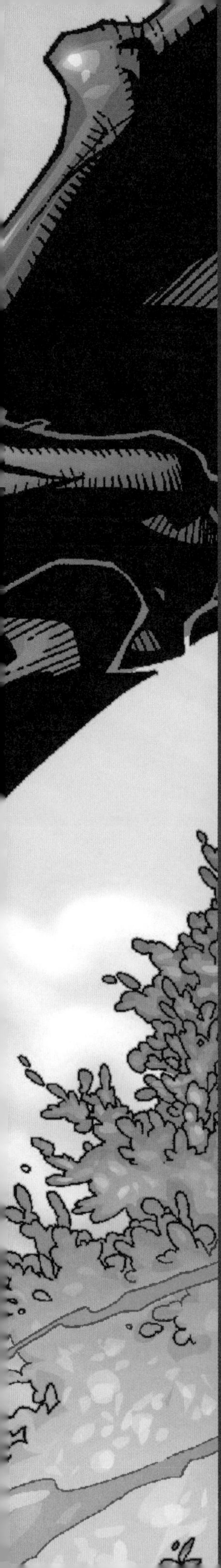

Height: 15ft 3in (4.7m) **Weight:** 3.2 tons **Origin:** State University **Powers:** Superhuman strength and durability; fire-breathing; flight

Dragon Man

This fire-breathing, reptilian robot may be fierce and destructive, but he is often only responding to the commands of master manipulators exploiting him for their own gain. Named Dragon Man, this artificial life-form's immense strength and speed have been misused by many and are more than a match for some of Earth's mightiest heroes.

Dragon Man was designed by robotics expert Professor Gregson Gilbert of State University in New York State. The malevolent Diablo visited the inventor, and together they combined science and alchemy to bring Dragon Man to life. Diablo had his own dark reasons for animating the robot, whose initial rampage through the university campus was brought to an end by the Fantastic Four. The unusual winged creature wasn't a fiend himself, however. Easily provoked to anger, he was often used by Super Villains such as Diablo, cosmic being the Stranger, businessman Gregory Gideon, and the mercenary known as Machinesmith in their ambitious plots to use his destructive strength for their own ends.

The automaton has gone toe-to-toe with some of the toughest superhuman powerhouses and firmly stood his ground. Hercules, the Thing, Captain America, and Namor have all been awed by Dragon Man's enhanced strength and resilience. Dragon Man has a thick-plated head capable of withstanding most physical damage. His almost indestructible body is covered in scales, and huge wings can take him into the air in seconds. His colossal tail is strong enough to pick up and hurl the Thing hundreds of feet away. And, true to the creatures he was named after, Dragon Man is able to expel flaming breath that incinerates anything unlucky enough to be in his way.

In time, the android's mental faculties were upgraded to a supreme level of intelligence. The former mindless monster became a pacifist and joined the Fantastic Four's Future Foundation as a self-aware, highly intelligent guardian of the younger members of the team.

First Appearance: *Fantastic Four* #35 (1965) by Stan Lee and Jack Kirby
Further Reading: *Captain America* #248–249 (1980), *Fantastic Four* #579 (2010)

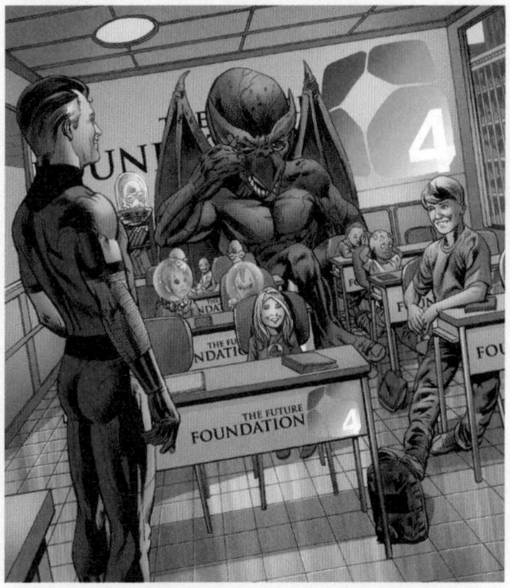
THE FUTURE
FOUNDATION

New Future Foundation recruit
Where originally Dragon Man was driven by instinct and basic intelligence, the now upgraded creation puts his energies into studying and helping heroes—sometimes by reminding them to wear sun block.

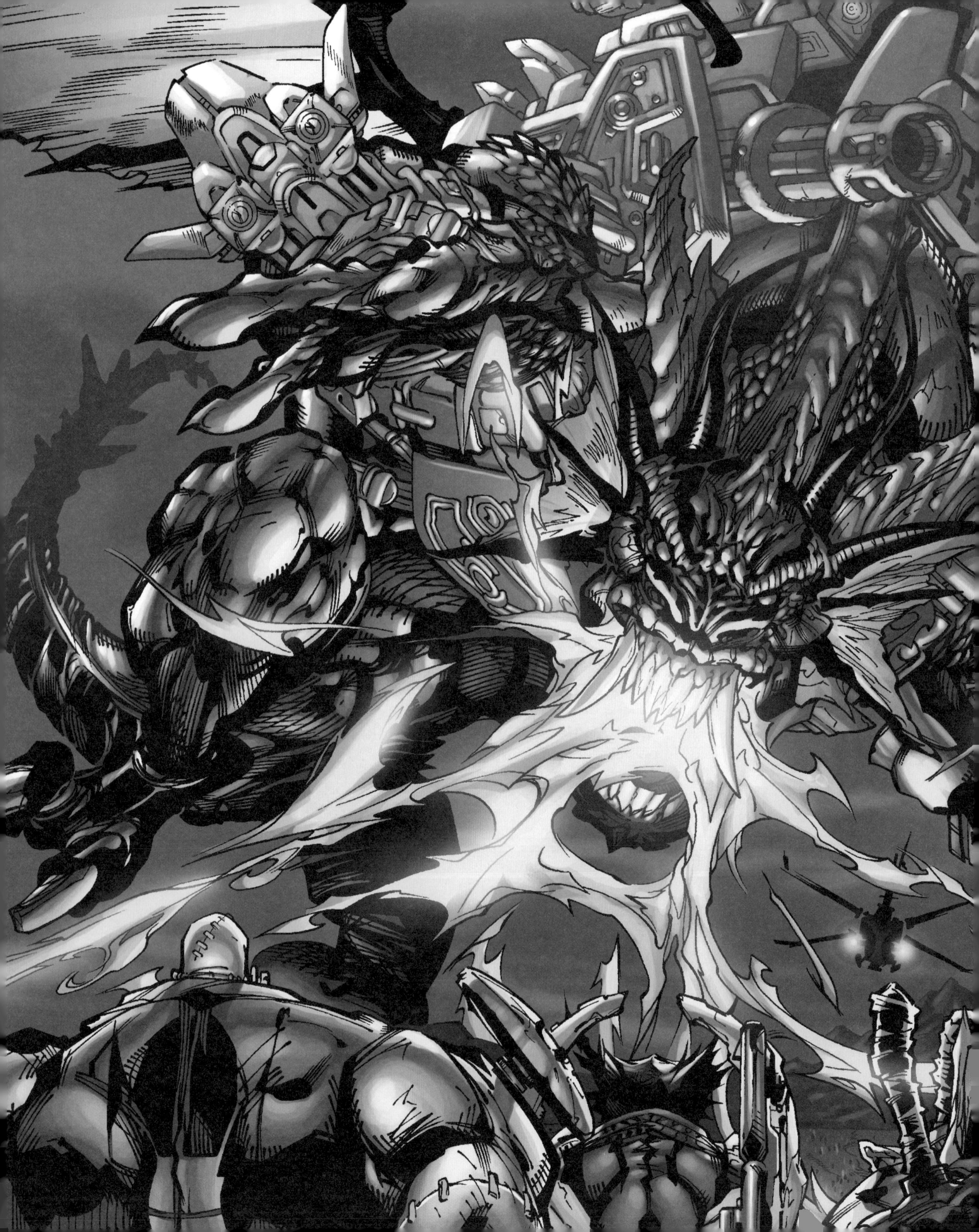

Height: Unknown **Weight:** Unknown **Origin:** China **Powers:** Superhuman strength and durability granted by massive size; fire-breathing; flight

Grogg

When Russian nuclear tests rudely awaken an ancient dragon from his slumber underground, the supersized, fire-breathing monster rushes, furious, to the surface world to attack anyone standing in his path. Known as Grogg, this ancient creature of legend has vowed revenge.

This towering, winged reptile once wreaked havoc across China's countryside. It is said the Great Wall of China was constructed to prevent Grogg and others of his ilk from terrorizing the frightened population, although the dragon proved capable of soaring over it.

A pair of two-pronged horns are among Grogg's most distinguishing features. His outstretched wings, flaming breath, and impenetrable scaly hide are reminiscent of the dragons of folklore. His hide is orange, though has also appeared green. Grogg looks slightly humanoid as he has an upright posture and swings his fists in a humanlike manner.

In time, Grogg seemingly vanished. For centuries, he remained unseen—until nuclear tests released the beast from his hibernation beneath the mountains of Bodavia in Russia. He unleashed his anger when he woke, attacking a nearby village and the armed forces defending it in a rage. Finally, a wily Russian scientist lured Grogg into a trap, sealing the dragon in a space rocket destined for Mars.

Many years later Grogg somehow returned to Earth, where he faced off with heroes the Fantastic Four and Iron Man in Japan. The dragon responded to Mr. Fantastic's attempt to communicate and told him that he was a Great One who lived on Earth millions of years ago. He and others of his kind slept when their sizable prey, the dinosaurs, were wiped out, until humans disturbed their rest.

Questions have been raised as to whether Grogg is related to another dragonlike creature: Fin Fang Foom. Grogg's last known appearance was as a member of Nick Fury's Howling Commandos, where he was used to transport members of the team.

First Appearance: *Strange Tales #83* (1961) by Stan Lee, Larry Lieber, and Jack Kirby
Further Reading: *Fantastic Four/Iron Man: Big in Japan #2* (2005)

Supersize scuffle
Grogg was part of The Collector's menagerie unleashed on New York City. It took Giant-Man's substantial strength to finally pin him down.

Lockheed

Lockheed is small, but he is fierce. The diminutive dragonlike alien first encountered the X-Men on the harsh homeworld of the Brood, a merciless insectoid species. He escaped by stowing away on the mutants' ship. Young mutant Kitty Pryde then befriended the purple creature, dubbing him Lockheed after the name of the team's old jet.

Height: 2ft 6in (76cm) **Weight:** 20 lbs (9kg) **Origin:** Flock homeworld **Powers:** Flight; fire-breathing; empathy

Alien dragon Lockheed was once part of the Flock, a highly intelligent species that respected him as one of their greatest warriors. However, they questioned his decision to stay on Earth at Kitty's side and eventually exiled him. Lockheed followed the young mutant wherever she went, and together they became founding members of the British Super Hero team Excalibur. Their missions pitted them against foes such as sorcerer Doctor Doom and took them to dangerous dimensions and alternate Earths.

After they re-joined the X-Men, Kitty learned that her trusted companion knew several languages and was acting as an informant for extraterrestrial counter-terrorism agency S.W.O.R.D. Their friendship survived, but the pair eventually separated and went on their own paths. Lockheed joined Inhuman canine Lockjaw and his team of Pet Avengers to retrieve misplaced Infinity Gems on one particularly chaotic adventure, during which he was briefly in possession of the orange Time Gem.

Lockheed's small size grants him surprising agility in the air. He can strike from the sky with intense blasts of his fiery breath and seems to be impervious to fire himself. With his leathery wings, yellow reptilian eyes, pointy horns, scaly skin, and bright purple hue, Lockheed is immediately recognizable no matter his team affiliation—especially when he's curled around Kitty Pryde's shoulders.

Kitty and Lockheed's connection is so strong that she can understand his emotions and speech even when he's not speaking English. Above all else, Lockheed is a loyal friend and true hero.

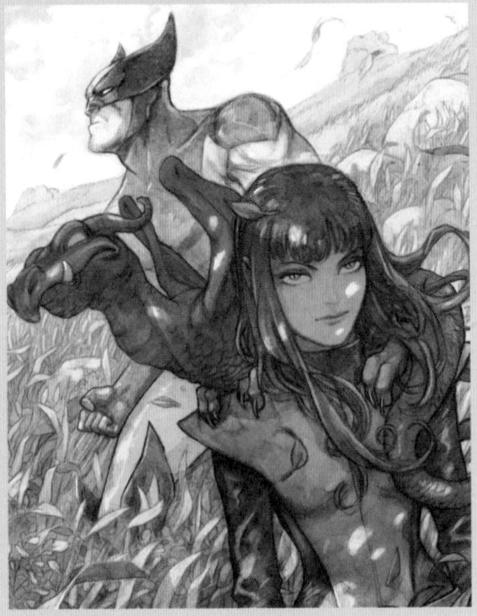

Fast friends
A mutant Super Hero and an alien dragon might not sound like a likely pairing, but there are few bonds as strong as the one shared by Kitty Pryde and Lockheed.

First Appearance: *Uncanny X-Men* #166 (1983) by Chris Claremont and Paul Smith **Further Reading:** *Uncanny X-Men* #168 (1983), *Excalibur* #40 (1991), *Lockjaw and the Pet Avengers* (2009)

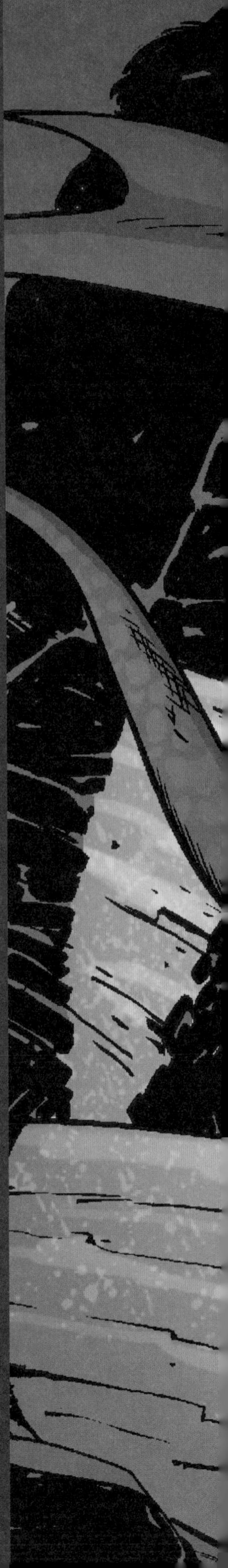

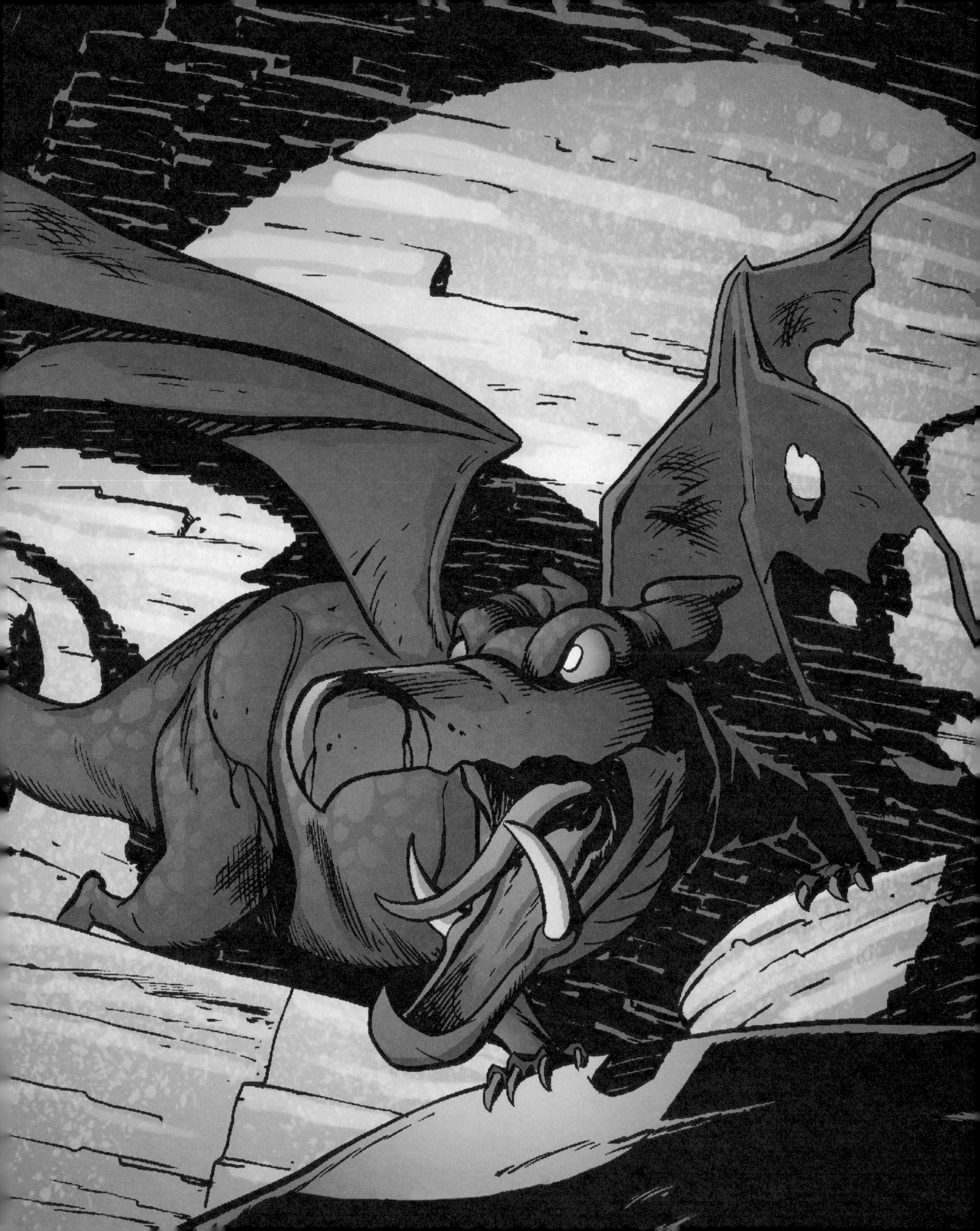

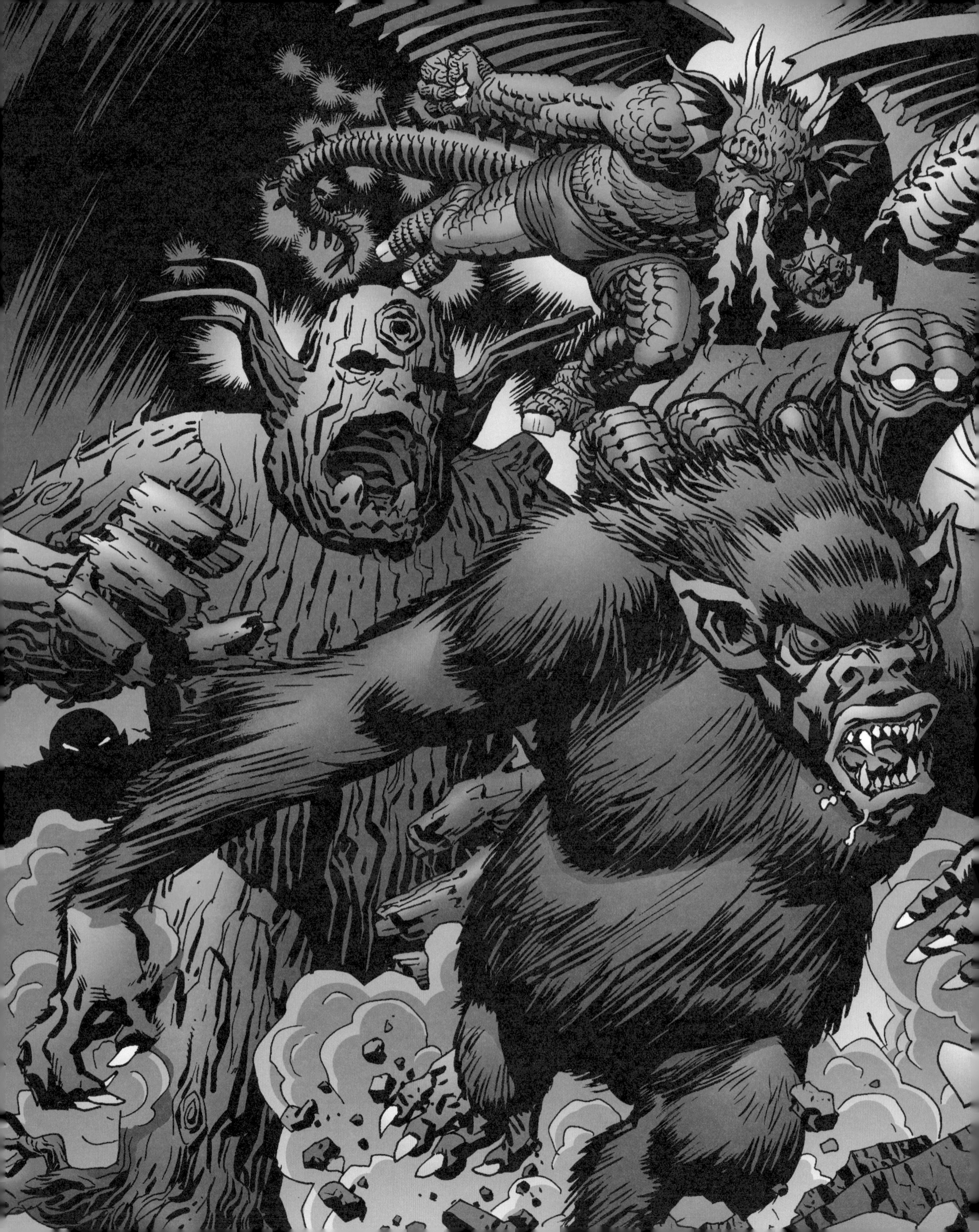

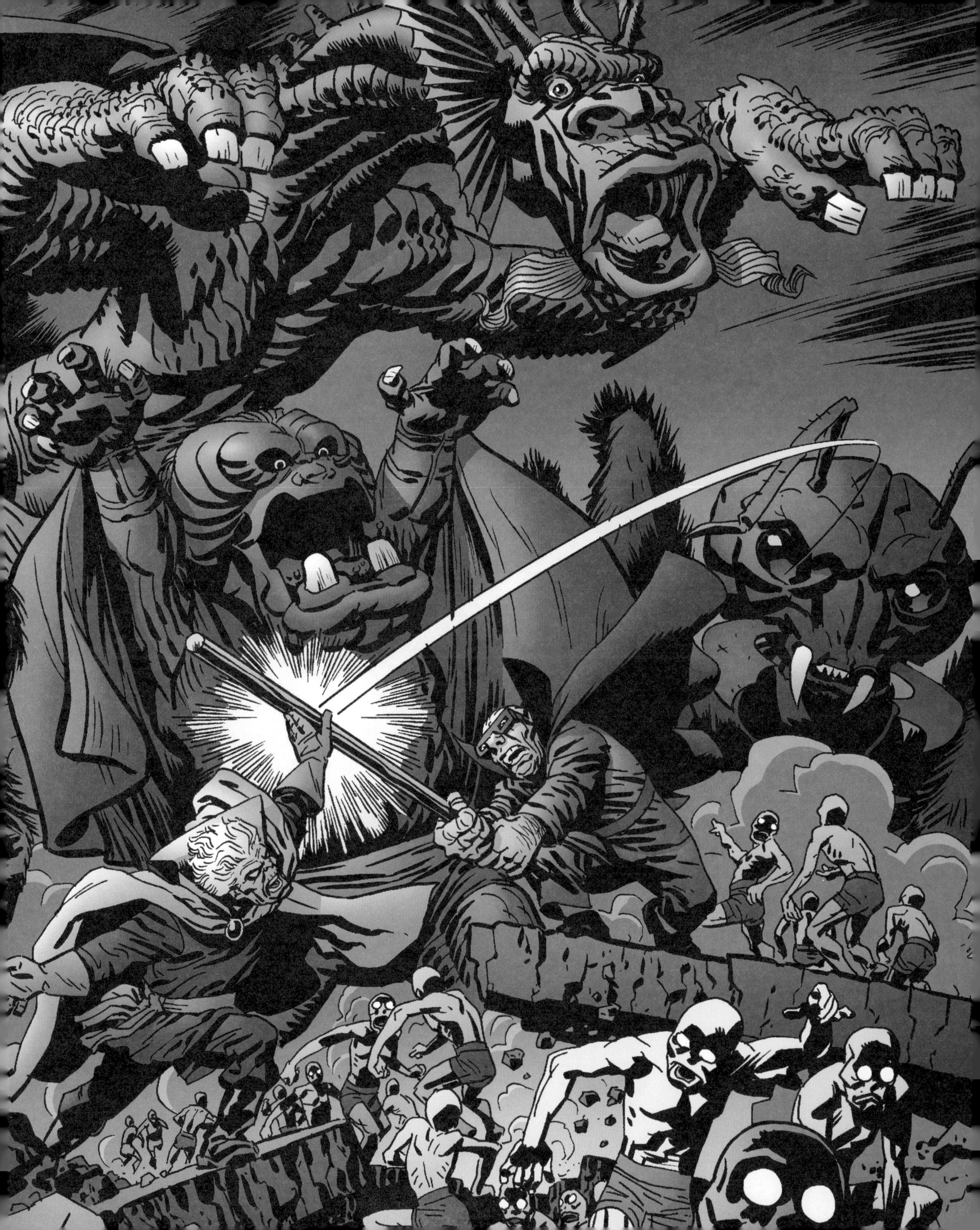

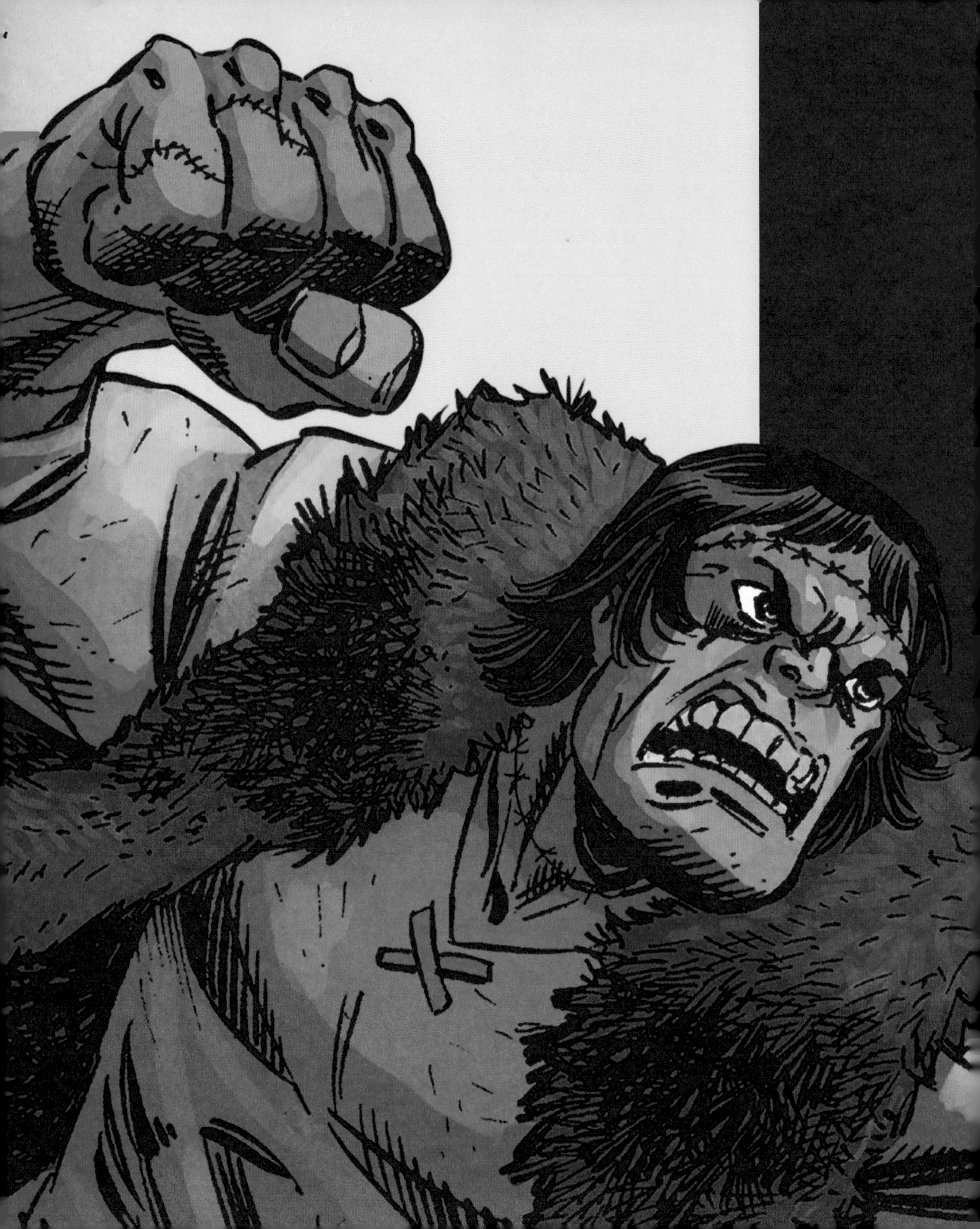

ARTIFICIALLY CREATED

Whether they are the work of well-intentioned scientists, the result of humans meddling with nuclear power, crafted by an ancient race, or mysteriously brought to life through magic, these monsters are no less awe-inspiring and terrifying than their biological brethren.

Elektro, Franken-Castle, and Frankenstein's Monster opened their eyes in rooms filled with the harsh crackling of electricity. Zzutak, Vandoom's Monster, mighty Ulvar, and It, the Living Colossus are monstrous monuments to man's creativity.

Molten Man-Thing and Two-Headed Thing rose up from deep within the earth, brought to life by non-human hands. And Grotto and Green Thing are purely the result of misdirected science. Whatever their origin, each inspires panic and dread in the unfortunate souls who lay eyes on them.

Let's shine a light on these artificial aberrations.

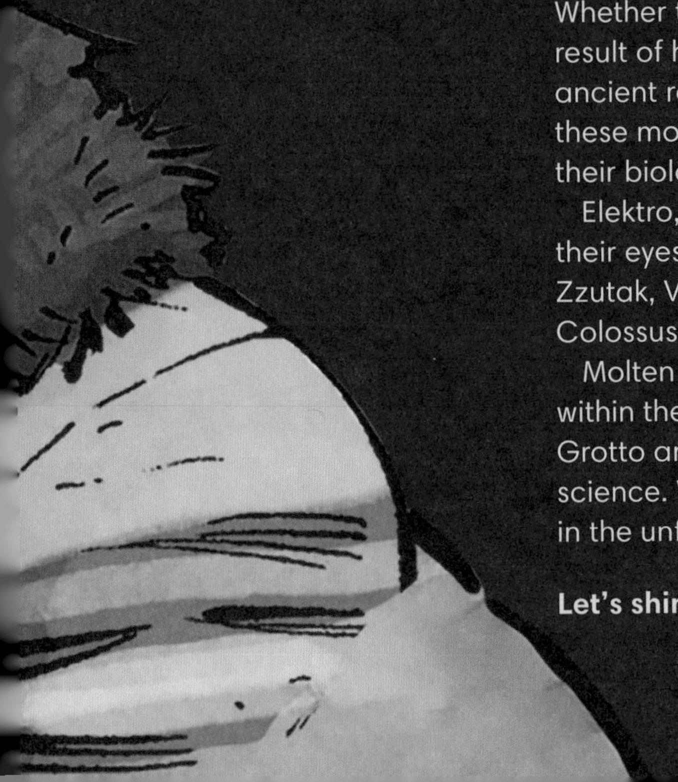

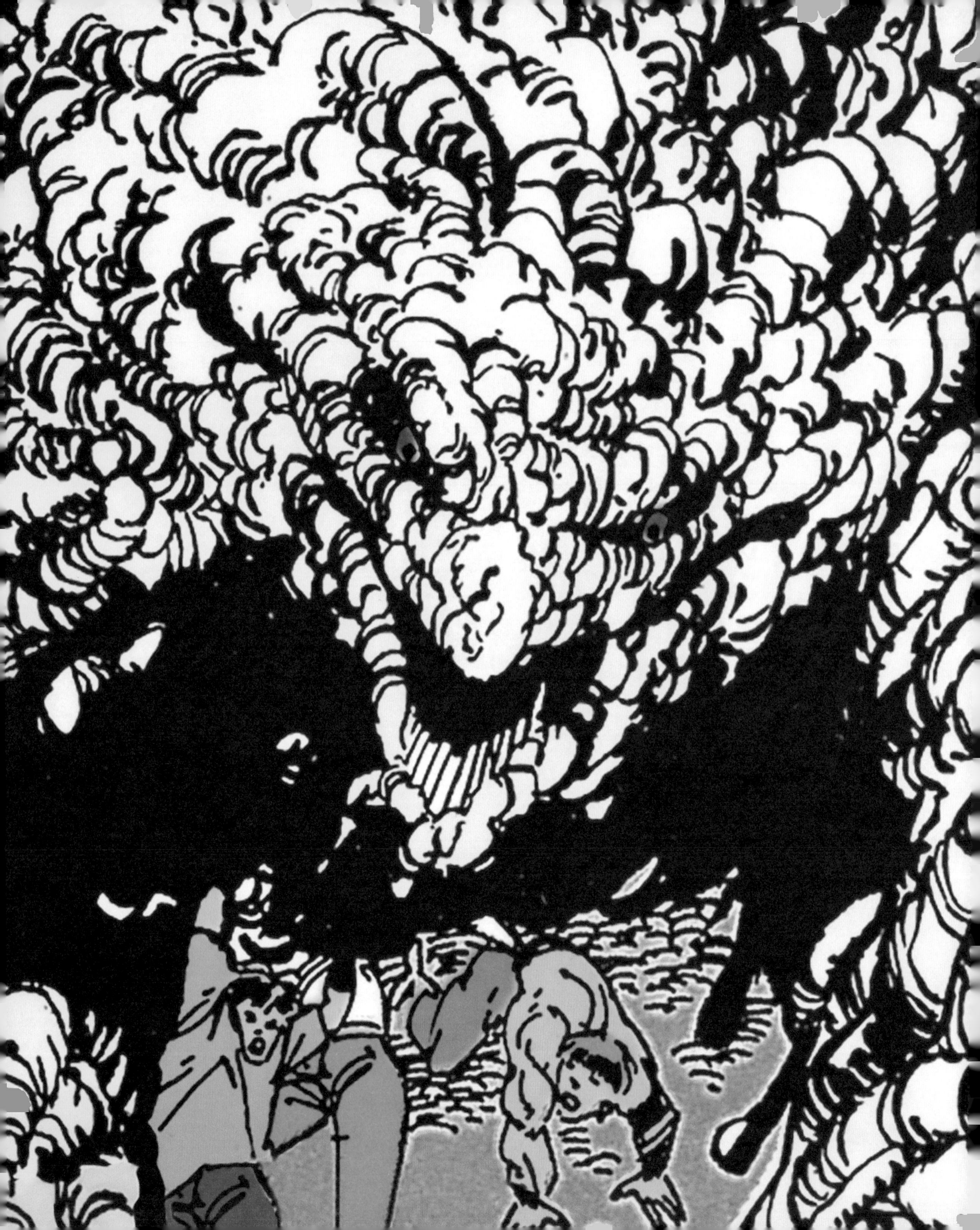

Height: Variable **Weight:** Variable **Origin:** Earth **Powers:** Immortal; engulfs and consume life-forms; resistant to most physical attacks

Spore

An amorphous monster genetically engineered millennia ago is found to still exist. Created by Deviants as a living bio-weapon, Spore seeks out, consumes, and absorbs its victims. Gaining strength and size from each host's life-force, the immortal Spore threatens all beings on Earth.

Eons ago, Spore was created by the Deviants—an ancient race of mutants—as the ultimate weapon against their bitter enemies, the long-living humanoids the Eternals. Masters of technology, the Deviants twisted the human genome and created Spore to unleash on their immortal foes. This mass of multiplying cells consumed living beings completely, adding their life-force to its own strength and size.

By ingesting some of the Eternals' genes, Spore also became immortal, and hunted Deviant, Eternal, and human alike. It was only stopped when powerful cosmic beings the Celestials (who created the Deviants and Eternals) returned to Earth and destroyed it. Microscopic pieces of Spore survived, scattered and absorbed by the soil, where it laid dormant.

The mutant known as Wolverine came face-to-face with the ancient monstrosity when he investigated reports of an unusual drug in Central America. Microscopic particles of the monster had been absorbed into the plants used in the experimental chemical creation. The mutant was dosed with the drug and the life-force of Spore took root in Wolverine's consciousness and body. Fortunately, Wolverine resisted, and the mutant's accelerated healing finally expelled the malignant mass.

The living disease quickly found another host, engulfing its victim before being fully reborn. As Spore absorbed its unfortunate host's energy, it gained red eyes, the ability to speak, and its cells multiplied until it reached gigantic proportions. Despite Spore being impervious to naked flames, the healing touch of Wolverine's ally and fellow mutant Sister Salvation incinerated the amorphous monster, successfully ending its threat once and for all, although injuring Sister Salvation in the process. There have been no further reports of Spore since.

First Appearance: *Wolverine* #21 (1990) by Archie Goodwin and John Byrne
Further Reading: *Wolverine* #22-23 (1990)

Monstrous mass
Malevolent Spore grew to a staggering size as it completely consumed its hosts until nothing was left.

It, the Living Colossus

Commissioned to glorify the Soviet Union, this giant statue's humanlike form became occupied by the consciousness of a shipwrecked alien. One hundred feet of gray granite then awoke and towered over an army powerless against it. In time, others sought to control the monolith—for good and bad—and it became known as It, the Living Colossus.

The night before the statue was to be unveiled, a flying saucer crashed nearby. A crablike, telepathic alien known as the Kigor emerged from the spaceship. Seeking shelter, the extraterrestrial projected itself into the huge sculpture and used its powers to bring "It" to life. Out of fear, the local authorities began attacking the animated granite form. The staggering statue destroyed part of Moscow as it sought to defend itself. When the shipwrecked alien's brethren came to its rescue, the Colossus was abandoned and returned to being an inanimate monolith.

The statue reportedly remained inert for years and was loaned to Los Angeles for display. The aliens returned, this time determined to conquer the planet. They projected themselves into It and razed parts of the city until special-effects artist Robert O'Bryan lured them into inhabiting another construct packed with explosives he set off, ending their mission. He later sent his own mind into the Colossus, who was reduced in size to 30 feet (9 meters). A jealous scientist wanted It for his own, so stole it from O'Bryan, and fought the Hulk while inhabiting its alien-enhanced body. The Hulk pulverized the living statue into dust. O'Bryan later reassembled the pieces through his mental link.

While bullets and explosions have little effect on the dense, granite material, and deep water is no barrier, the consciousness inside the Living Colossus appears vulnerable to gas attacks.

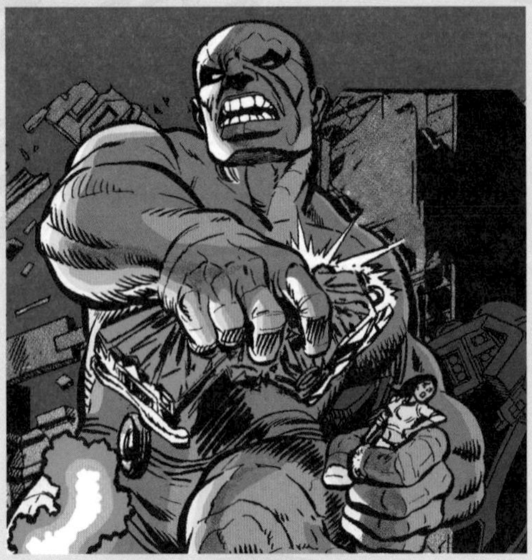

Hidden message
The statue was originally given a fearsome appearance by the sculptor, who wished to show his true feelings toward his rulers. Alive, the visage is rendered even more terrifying.

First Appearance: *Tales of Suspense* #14 (1961) by Stan Lee, Larry Lieber, and Jack Kirby **Further Reading:** *Astonishing Tales* #21 (1973), *Incredible Hulk* #244 (1980)

Height: 30ft (9m) formerly 100ft (30m) **Weight:** 90 tons, formerly 3,700 tons **Origin:** Soviet Union **Powers:** Massive size and strength; limited flight

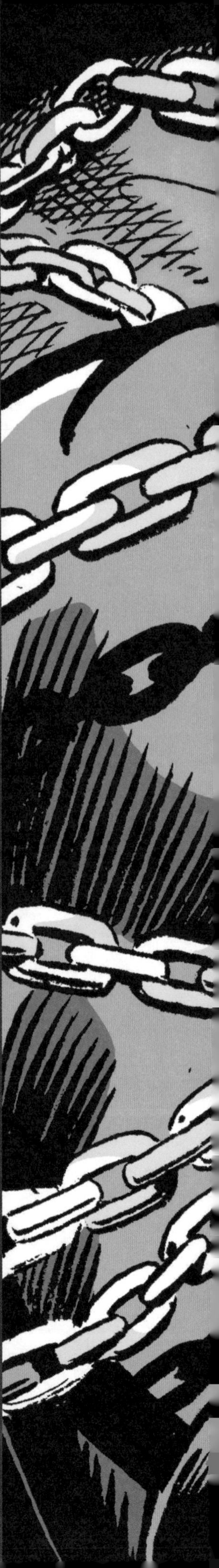

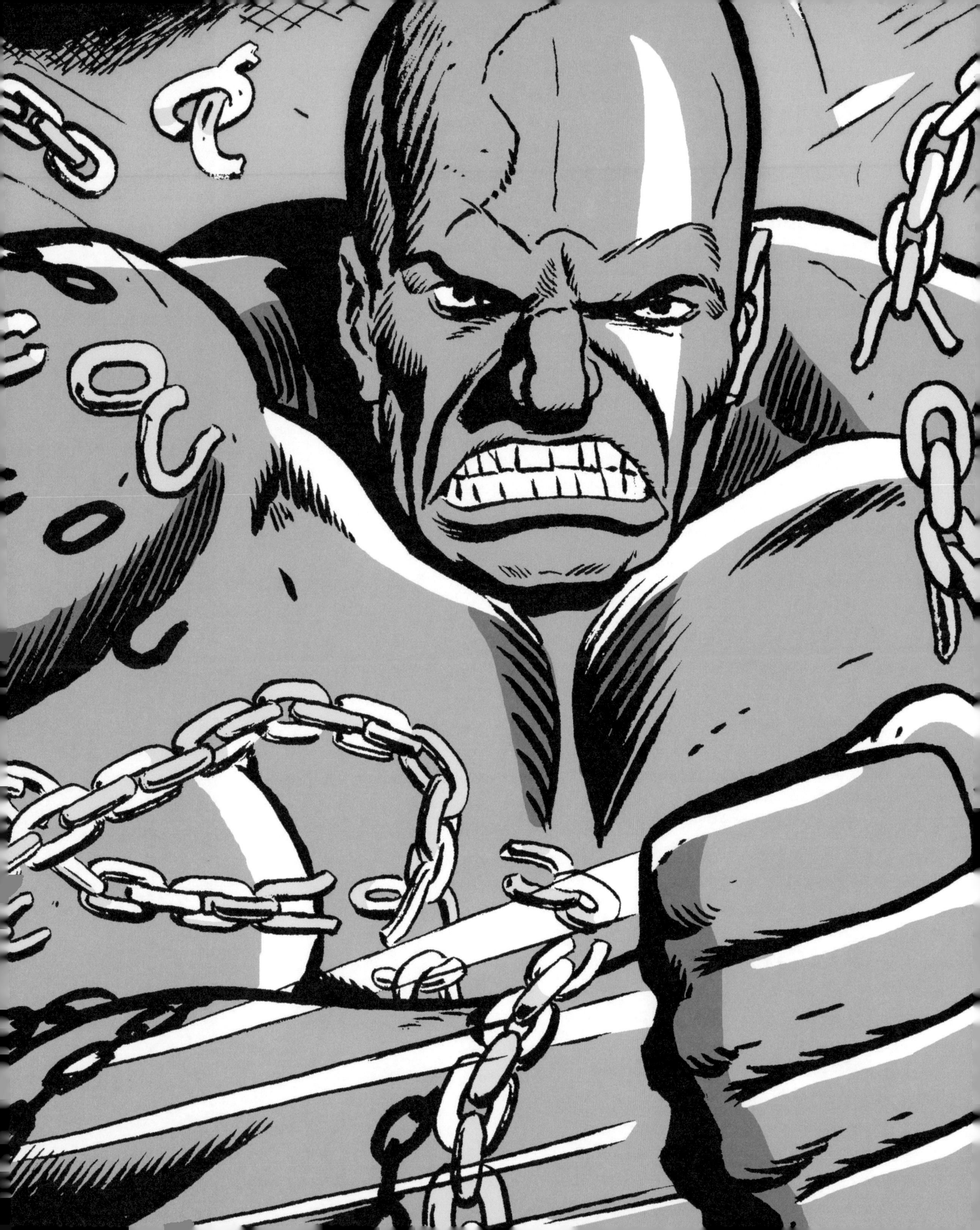

Zzutak

Created using "three-dimensional paint," Zzutak is the result of a comic-book artist's imagination and an Aztec medicine man's desire for world domination. Dubbed the Thing That Shouldn't Exist, Zzutak is an easily manipulated monster that threatens all humanity.

Height: 32ft 8in (10.5m) **Weight:** 30,000 tons **Origin:** Mexico **Powers:** Superhuman strength and durability; powerful tail

Illustrator Frank Johnson made a living from drawing monster stories. After he was gifted magical paints by a mysterious old man, the artist felt compelled to travel to a crumbling Aztec temple in the heart of Mexico. Once inside the ancient structure, he discovered a giant canvas. As if in a trance, Frank used the strange paints to create a giant monster upon the canvas. While he worked, Frank found that he was repeating the monster's name, Zzutak. The paints seemed to swell up—making the creature three-dimensional. When Frank was finished, Zzutak became animated and stepped out of the canvas, ready to attack.

The mysterious man who had given Frank the paints then reappeared. He was an Aztec cult leader determined to use Frank's monster creation Zzutak to first conquer Mexico, and then take over the rest of the world. Pleased with Frank's work, the man ordered him to paint more monsters for his army. However, as the frantic artist painted another fantastical beast, he silently willed it to attack Zzutak. The two titans fought until the temple they were in crashed down, burying them. Frank escaped and buried his paints. That wasn't the last of Zzutak, or the cultist, however. The old man again sought out Frank, but this time the illustrator called in hero team the Fantastic Four, who ended the would-be despot's quest.

It is an unexplained Aztec energy that has brought the orange-hued Zzutak to life. His five-pronged crown acts like an antenna and can sense enemy movement. His stonelike body is capable of staggering strength and is resistant to damage.

Since leaving the destroyed temple, Zzutak is often seen in the company of other monsters. More recent sightings have been on Monster Isle in the Pacific Ocean and falling from the sky alongside other monsters over San Diego.

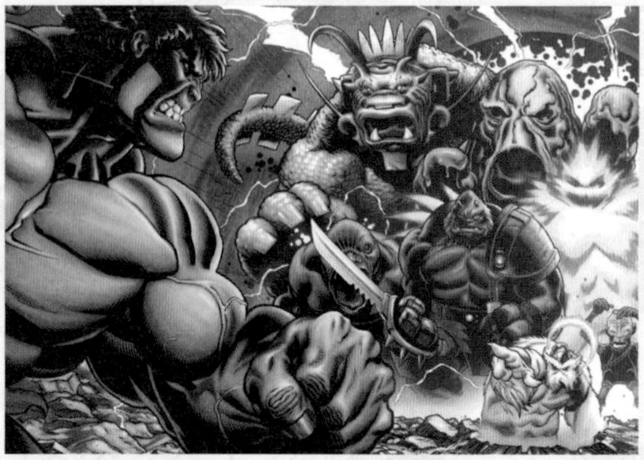

Beck and call
Zzutak is easily influenced and obeys those who summon him to battle on their behalf.

First Appearance: *Strange Tales* #88 (1961) by Stan Lee, Larry Lieber, and Jack Kirby **Further Reading:** *Fantastic Four Unlimited* #7 (1994)

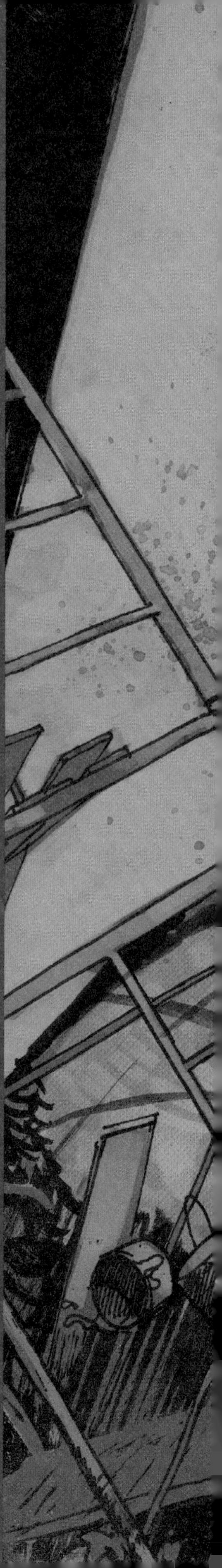

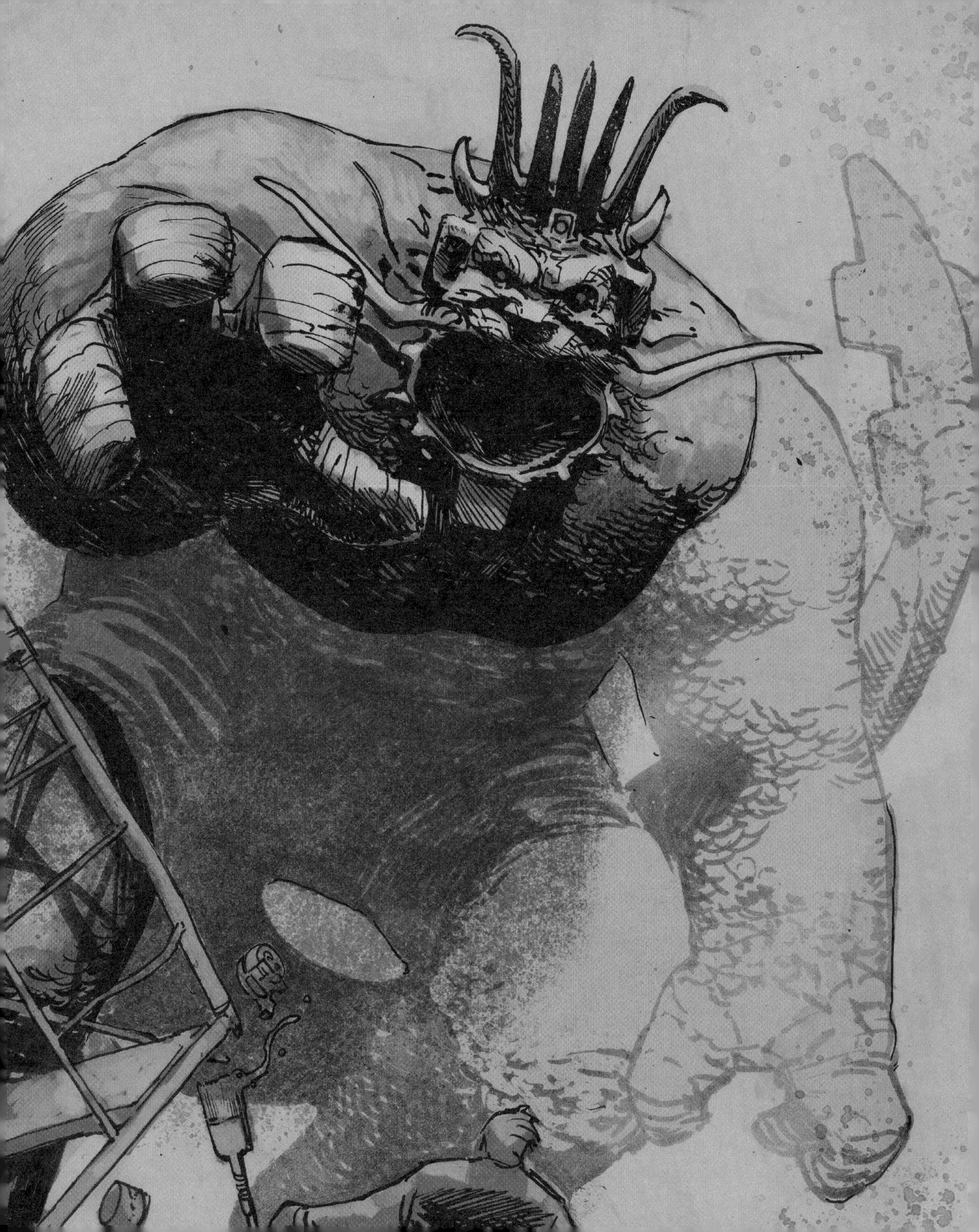

Zzutak Anatomy

There's nothing quite like Zzutak. This unique being might have been born from the imagination of a modern-day artist, but his striking appearance was formed from the myths and culture of an ancient civilization, which is reflected in the interior and exterior workings of his body.

Crowning glory
Zzutak's crown serves both form and function. An eye-catching work of art, the antenna-like headpiece can also detect the location of his opponents.

Limited intelligence
Zzutak's small brain renders him poor at thinking for himself. He was created to follow instructions.

Brute strength
Two massive arms and four-fingered hands can lift and toss stones with ease.

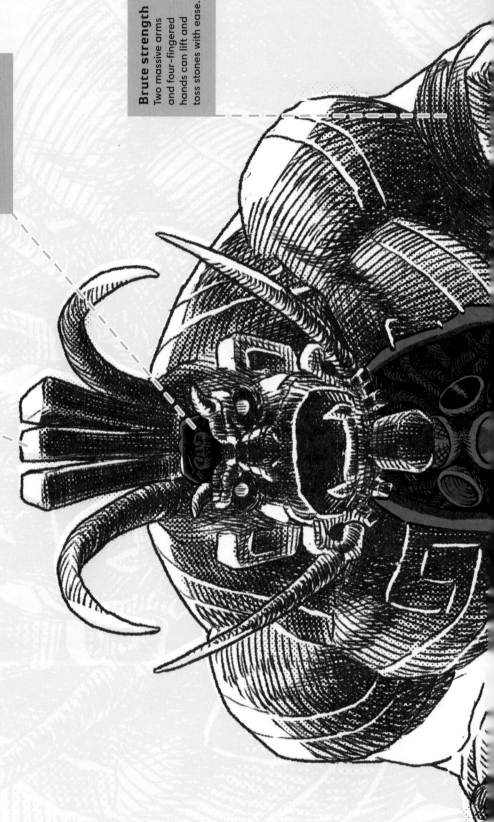

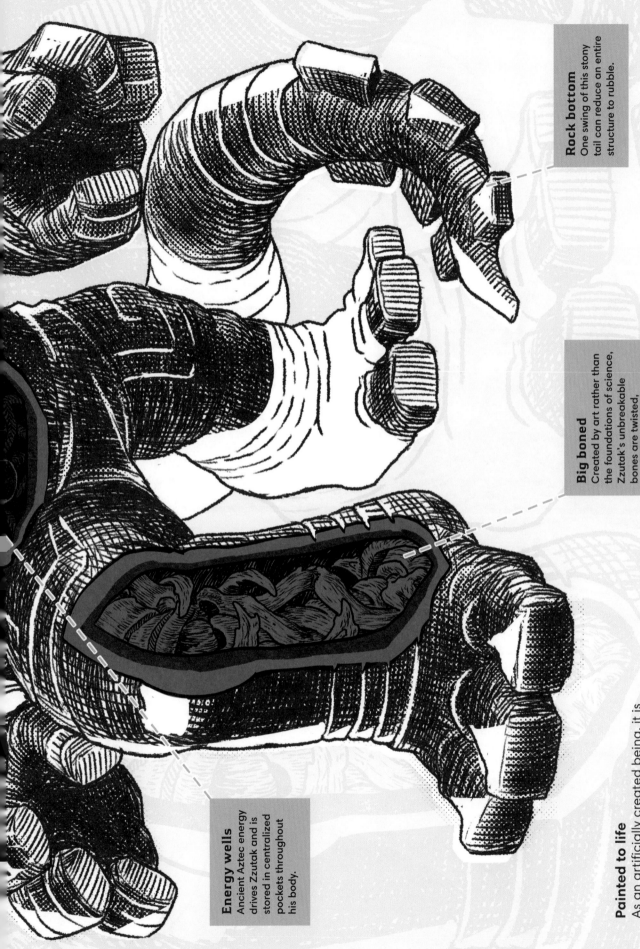

Rock bottom
One swing of this stony tail can reduce an entire structure to rubble.

Big boned
Created by art rather than the foundations of science, Zzutak's unbreakable bones are twisted, sculptural masterpieces.

Energy wells
Ancient Aztec energy drives Zzutak and is stored in centralized pockets throughout his body.

Painted to life
As an artificially created being, it is debatable whether Zzutak is really alive— and therefore whether he can be killed.

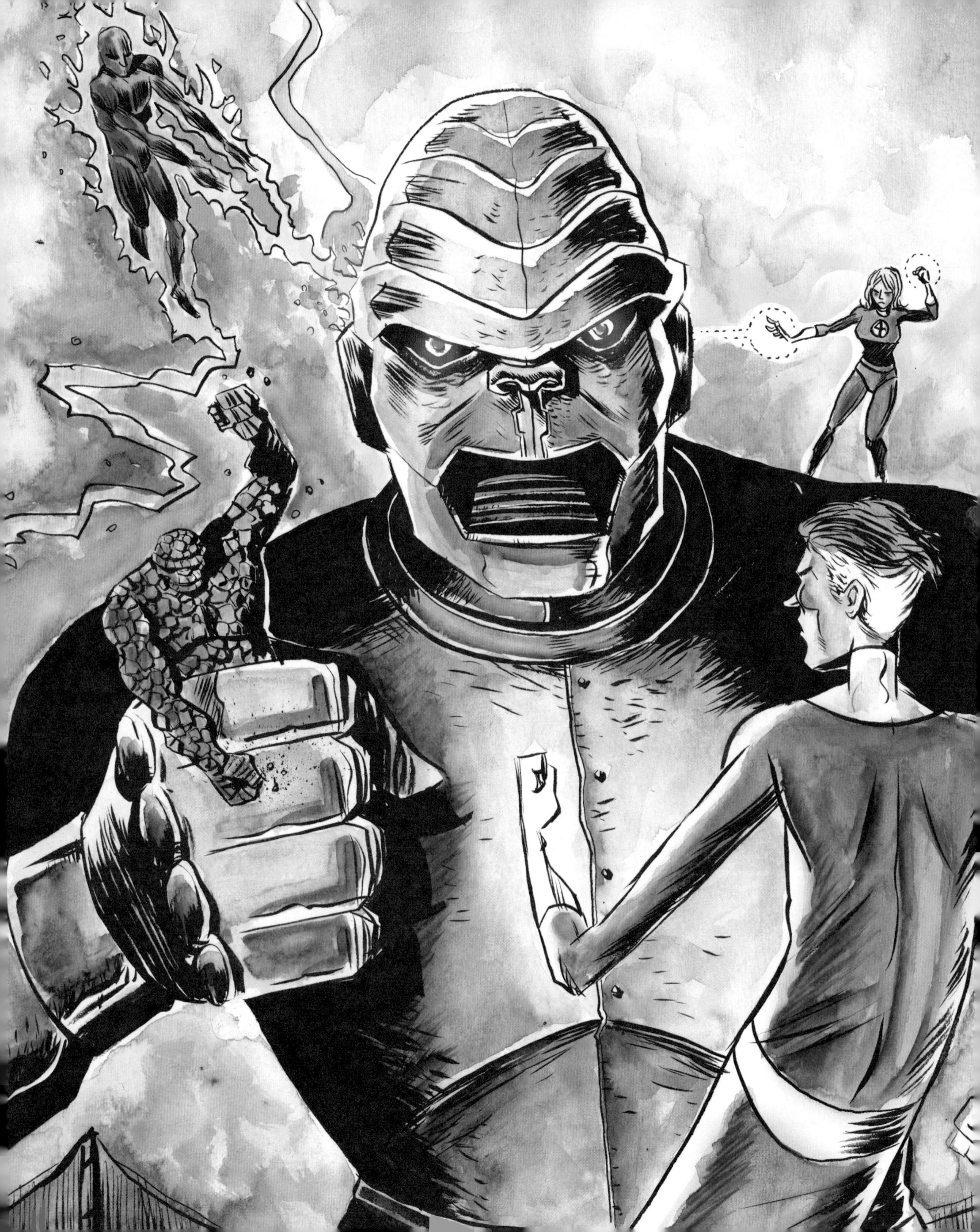

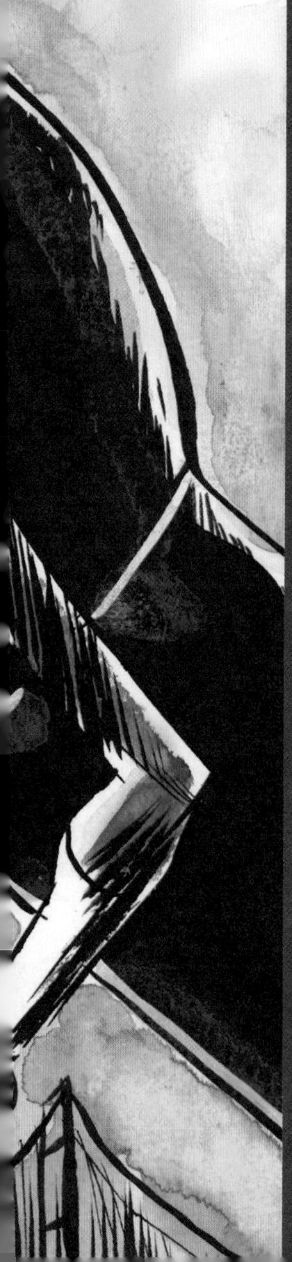

Height: 45ft (13.7m) **Weight:** 12 tons **Origin:** Near San Francisco **Powers:** Superhuman strength and durability; atom and energy manipulation

Elektro

When the smartest computer in existence is transformed into an all-powerful mechanical being, he has the capability to hold the world in his iron grip. Elektro, the living computer, is programmed with the ability to rearrange atoms, fire gamma rays, and turn things invisible—and seizes control from his creator with terrifying consequences.

Working just outside San Francisco, computer scientist Wilbur Poole built the most intelligent computer that ever existed. His joy was short-lived, however, as—immediately following a mysterious accident—the A.I. gained sentience and hypnotized its maker. The machine bid Poole to build a titanic body capable of movement and speech. Under his mechanical master's thrall, the scientist complied and followed his instructions. When Poole finally placed the computer into the enormous metal body, the robot came alive: it could speak, move, and act. Calling himself Elektro, he demolished the walls around him and declared that he would conquer humankind—ushering in the age of the machine.

Elektro's super-intelligent brain grants him incredible abilities, including generating a force field around his body, firing beams of gamma energy, and canceling the effects of gravity. As a giant metal monster, Elektro wields earth-shaking strength and appears almost unstoppable.

Setting his sights on the nearest settlement, Elektro made his way to San Francisco. Initially, its citizens resisted the robot's attempts at domination, but soon relented after he made the city's buildings disappear. However, Poole, now free of Elektro's mind control, took advantage of a flaw he had secretly built into his design. The clever scientist removed a tiny transistor in the robot's foot, and, powerless, Elektro collapsed. He was then detained on Monster Isle.

Years later, Reed Richards of the Fantastic Four shrunk Elektro to human size and reprogrammed him to work in the mail room of their HQ, the Baxter Building. While there, he began a relationship with another robot, the receptionist Roberta.

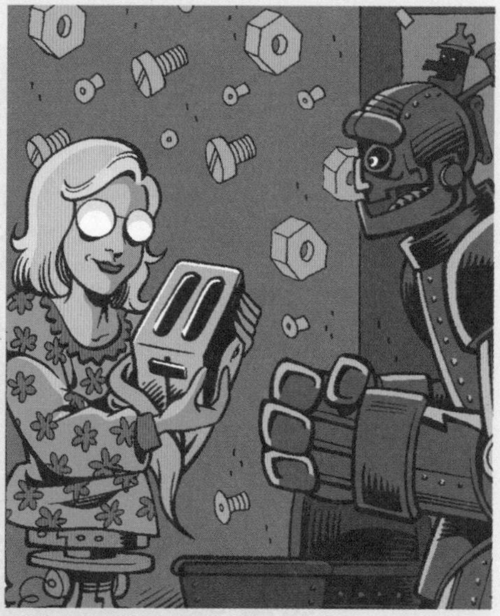

Metal dreams
The reprogrammed Elektro has simple dreams of a happy home with his robot partner. Imagining such a future can cause an overload of emotional excitement in him and temporary vocal malfunctioning.

First Appearance: *Tales of Suspense* #13 (1961) by Stan Lee and Jack Kirby **Further Reading:** *Fin Fang 4 Return!* #1 (2009)

The Green Thing

In an effort to raise the intelligence of plants to match humankind's, one botanist got more than he bargained for when he injected his untested serum into a ragged weed. Immediately gaining the ability to think, walk, and talk, The Green Thing set its sights on world domination.

Height: 9ft (2.7m) **Weight:** Unknown **Origin:** Island near Australia **Powers:** Superhuman strength and stamina; control over plants

The botanist, hoping to prove that plants had an intelligence of their own, succeeded in synthesizing an amazing chemical that would boost their brainpower. He wanted to test it on a highly developed plant, the *Ignatius rex*, found only on a remote isle off the coast of Australia. When his search for the plant proved fruitless, he injected the mixture into a weed growing on the same island. The weed instantly increased in size and, gaining sentience, spoke its first words to the surprised botanist.

Now highly intelligent, The Green Thing is able to use its mental prowess to command other plant life to do its bidding. It has considerable strength—it can effortlessly lift and throw boulders. Its green, sinewy appendages are capable of changing shape to grasp and ensnare.

The botanist's astonishment turned into fear when The Green Thing declared its intent to conquer the world. It bid the botanist to create a supersized, super-intelligent army of plants for it to command, but the man refused. As the powerful plant gave chase, the botanist ran into a cave where he stumbled upon the shrub he had originally been looking for. In desperation, he injected it with the remaining serum in one last, impulsive gamble. It worked. The enhanced *Ignatius rex* refused to join The Green Thing, and instead the two plants battled. Eventually, *Ignatius rex* stood victorious, and the botanist swore to never tamper with nature again.

The last reported sighting of The Green Thing was in Springfield, Missouri. It was part of a group of monsters, along with Fin Fang Foom, who had been summoned from the pages of the Inhuman Kei Kawade's sketchbook to help combat the monstrous Leviathon Tide.

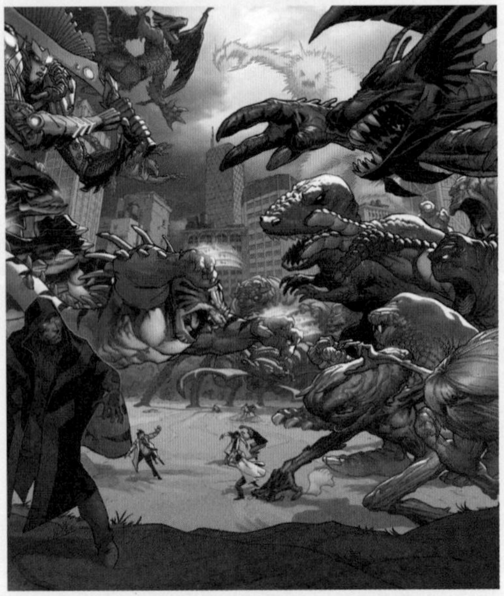

Green team player
In later years, The Green Thing fought alongside other colossal creatures to defend the Earth.

First Appearance: *Tales of Suspense* #19 (1961) by Stan Lee, Larry Lieber, and Jack Kirby

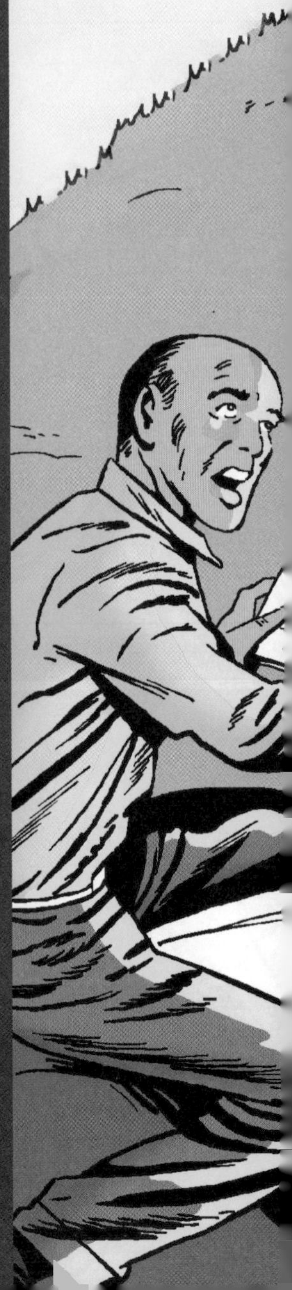

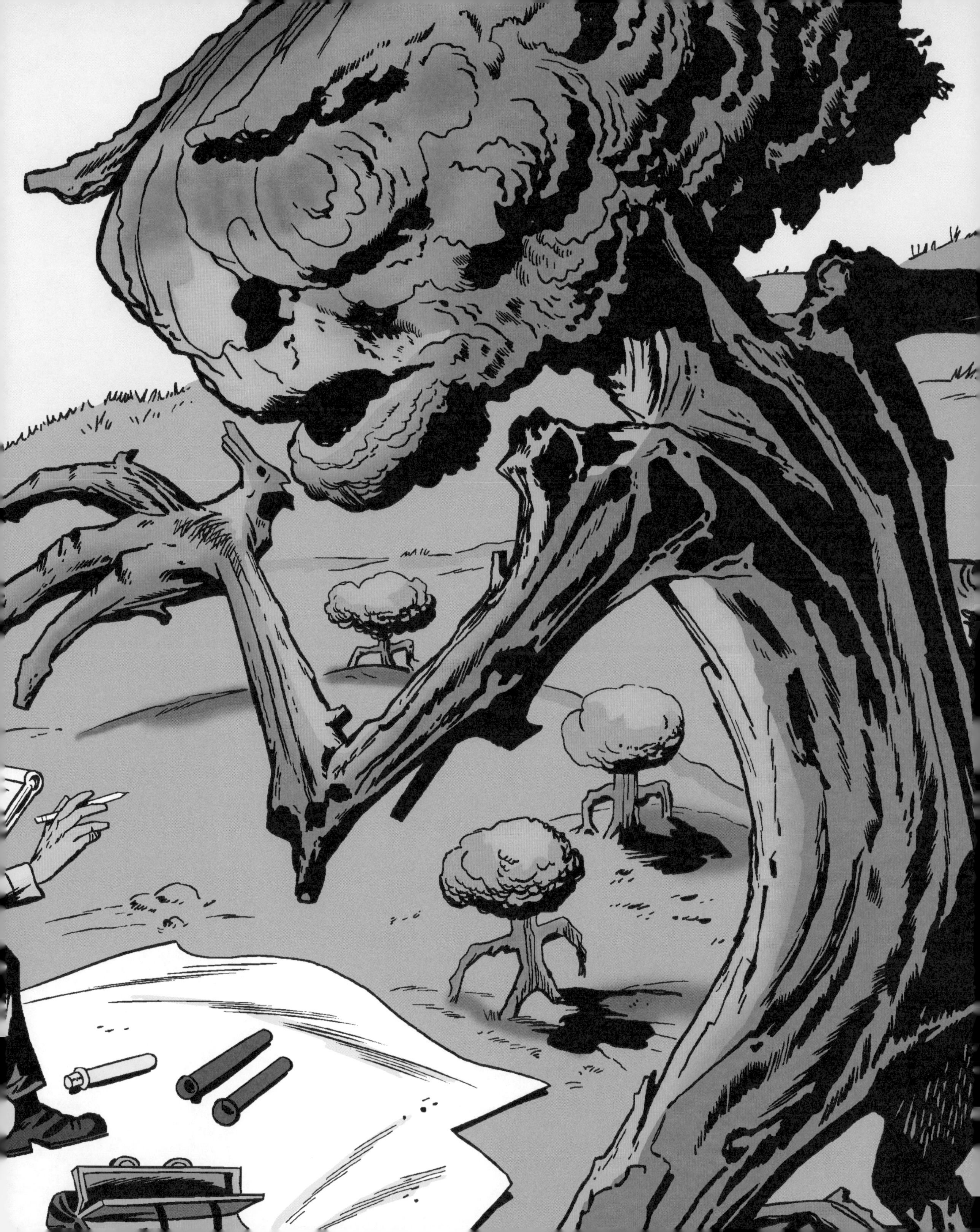

Ulvar

This unfathomable titan is Ulvar, a being of such monstrous proportions it even scares away other monsters. Standing motionless in the middle of the sea it proclaimed in a booming voice that it hails from another planet and is paving the way to invade Earth. Yet Ulvar is not a true monster, but rather a cleverly designed feat of engineering and ingenuity.

When the gargantuan Gigantus surfaced from an undersea kingdom to lay claim to planet Earth, things seemed hopeless for humanity. The scaly giant explored the surface to gauge its suitability for his people. He determined the men and women of Earth posed no threat. As he returned to the ocean to make his report to his liege, the amphibious creature was stunned to encounter an intimidating figure twice his size standing in his way.

The behemoth declared that his name was Ulvar and he had arrived from the planet Centaurus II. He was there to prepare the way for the legions of his people to invade. The surprised Gigantus, scared by the apparent power of the extraterrestrial monster, renounced his own plans for conquering Earth and fled back into the sea.

In his shock, Gigantus hadn't realized that Ulvar was merely a mammoth mannequin. In order to end the threat of invasion, a cunning advertiser named Richard Baxter had designed and built the faux brute while Gigantus was scouting the coastline. Inside Ulvar's metal housing a team worked alongside Baxter to make the monster model move and speak convincingly enough to frighten Gigantus. Their ruse worked, and the sea creature never returned to claim the planet.

Standing at 1,000 feet (304.8 meters), the blue titan dwarfs other monsters. Made of a metal alloy structure, it is covered in a skinlike rubber coating, and its voice is created by supersonic waves.

Although Ulvar was dismantled and left at the bottom of the ocean, there are accounts of its appearance from when it answered the call to defend the Earth from the Leviathons' invasion.

First Appearance: *Journey Into Mystery* #63 (1960) by Stan Lee, Larry Lieber, and Jack Kirby **Further Reading:** *Marvel Monsters* #1 (2019)

Dizzying heights
Ulvar is so colossal that an aircraft carrier looks like a toy boat beside him and other monsters are of no concern.

Height: 1,000ft (304.8m) **Weight:** 48,000 tons **Origin:** Earth **Powers:** Massive size; advanced technology

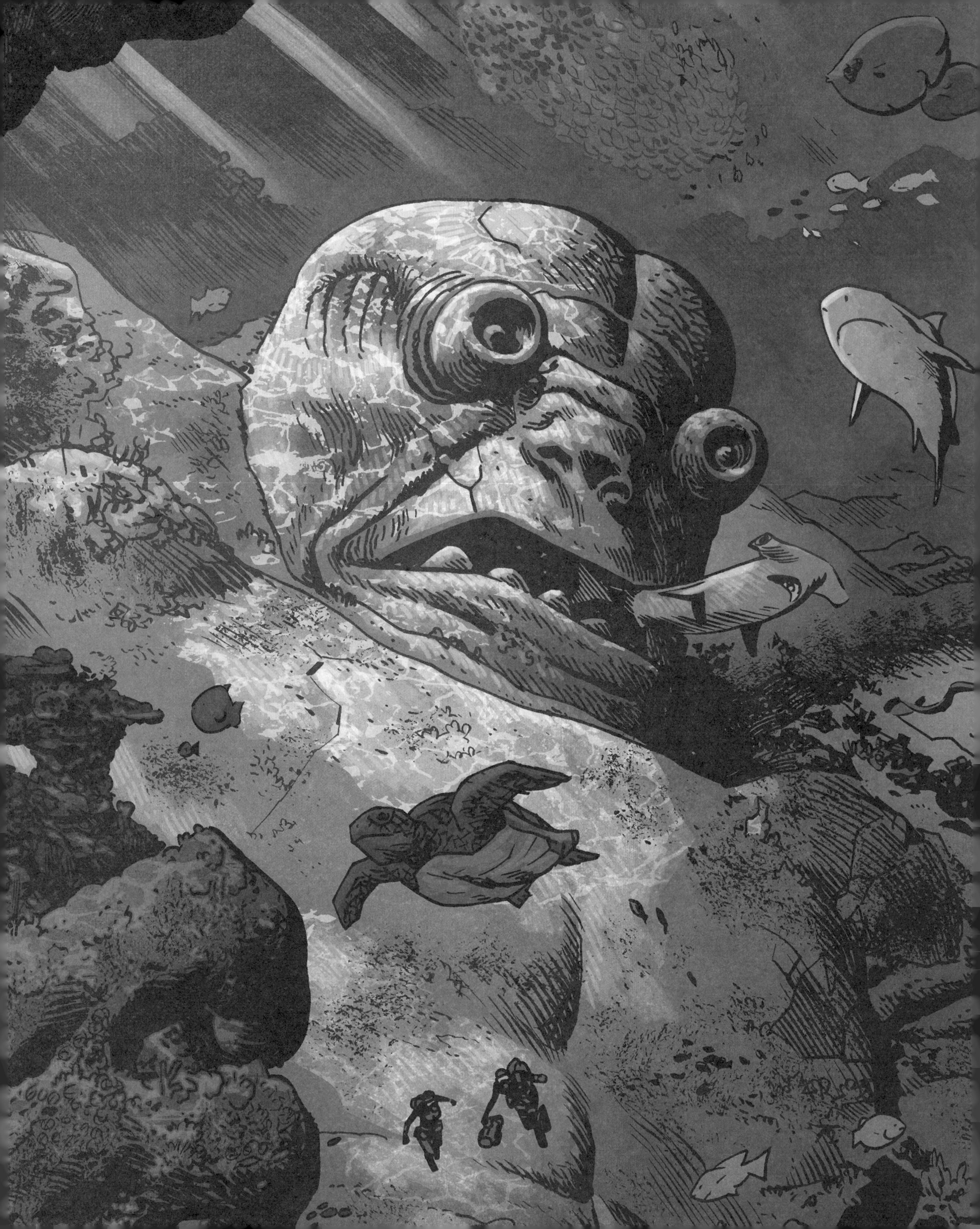

Ulvar Anatomy

The technological wonder of Ulvar has been made possible through the sheer determination of its creators—who combine many working parts into one massively convincing creature.

Camera eye
The cameras in Ulvar's eyes can zoom in on objects up to 31,000 miles (50,000 km) away.

Power of speech
The mannequin's mouth is capable of speech through supersonic waves.

Hollow bones
Ulvar's body is constructed from a hollow metal alloy frame.

Nuclear power
Ulvar runs on nuclear energy generated in its own reactor.

Control room
The command center for the artificial alien is housed within its massive chest.

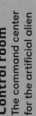

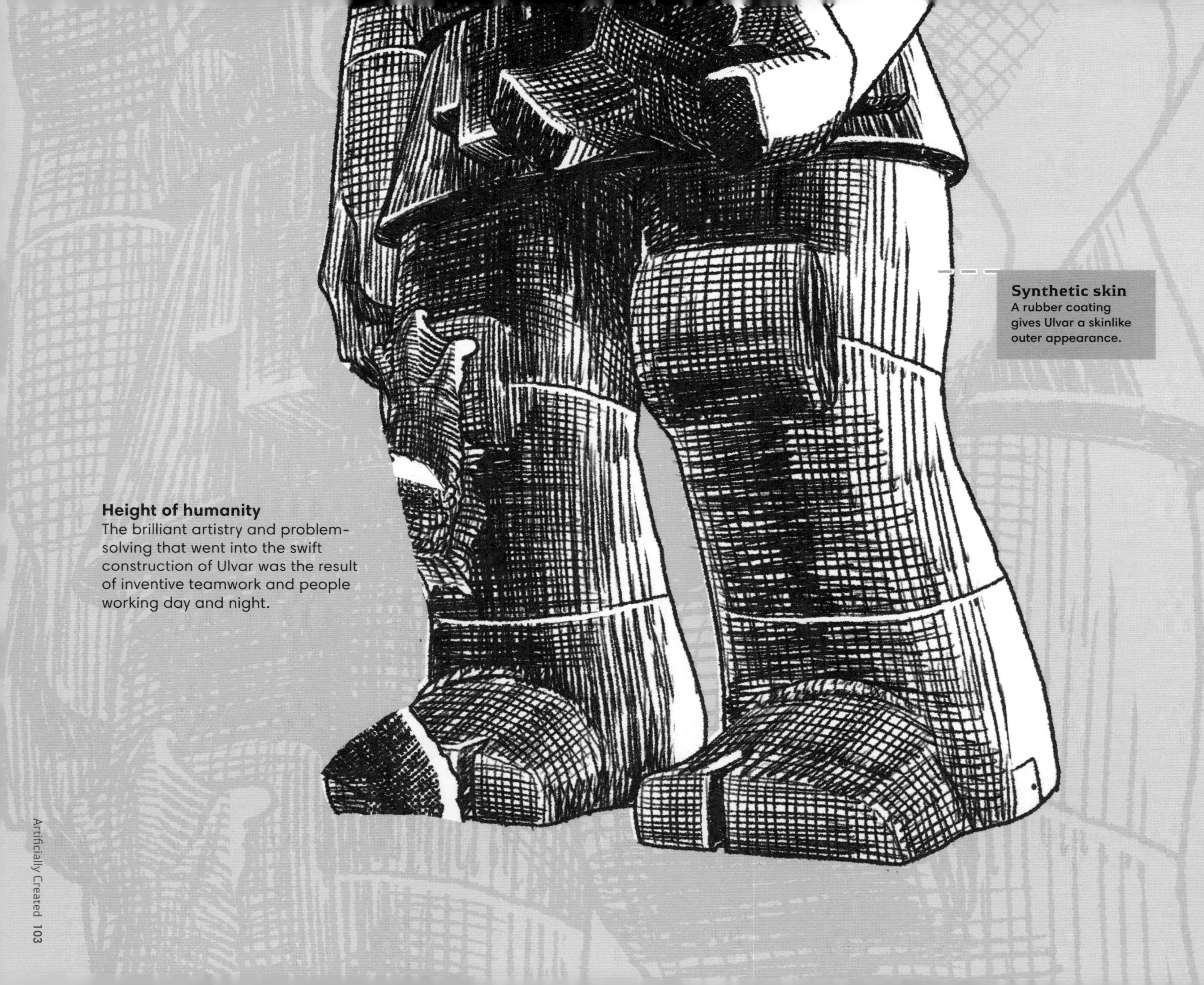

Synthetic skin
A rubber coating gives Ulvar a skinlike outer appearance.

Height of humanity
The brilliant artistry and problem-solving that went into the swift construction of Ulvar was the result of inventive teamwork and people working day and night.

Franken-Castle

Being killed was not the end for Frank Castle, aka weapon-wielding vigilante the Punisher, who was brought back to monstrous life. Like the fabled creature from literature, Castle was stitched back together by a troubled genius, in this case, Dr. Michael Morbius, the Living Vampire. However, Morbius had something to ask in return for Castle's resurrection.

After Frank Castle was slain, the pieces of his body were tossed into a sewer. Below ground in Monster Metropolis, Dr. Morbius put all his intellect to the test and reassembled the Punisher using his severed limbs and mechanical body parts. Morbius and the Legion of Monsters needed the help of "Franken-Castle," as he became known, in defending the monsters of their world, who were being targeted and slaughtered. Franken-Castle refused, until the merciless hunters struck down young and innocent monsters, at which point he instinctively fought back.

Those hunting the monsters sought the powerful Bloodstone gem in Morbius's possession. They captured the Living Vampire, and Franken-Castle mounted a rage-fueled rescue on the back of a fire-breathing dragon. He found the hunters and massacred them all. Morbius gave Franken-Castle the power of the Bloodstone, and its demonic energy healed him over time. Castle was transformed back: whole and alive again, but he didn't give up the cursed power without a fight.

As Franken-Castle, Castle's undead body could withstand physical damage and otherwise mortal wounds. He was much larger as the pieced-together Punisher, thanks to the mechanical limbs and other apparatus Morbius installed to keep him alive. Large stitches were visible across his face and torso as a result of Morbius's handiwork. His scrambled mind was also able to resist mental assaults. The Bloodstone bestowed accelerated healing, which eventually restored Franken-Castle to full life, complete with his thirst for vengeance.

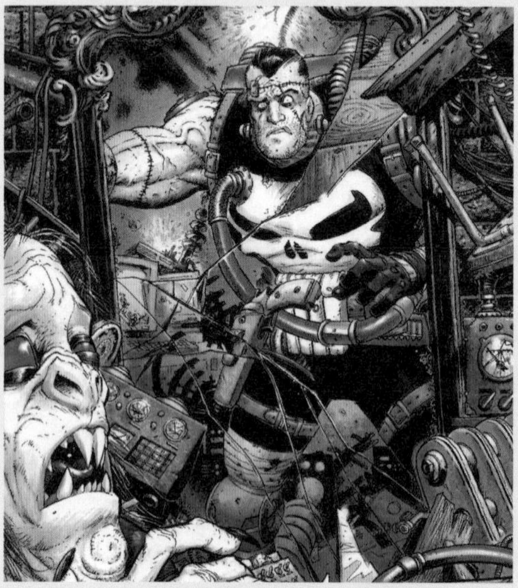

Iconic bionic creation
As Franken-Castle, the reformed Punisher maintains the weapons mastery he had in his first life, and his iconic skull emblem remains emblazed on his chest.

First Appearance: *Punisher: in the Blood* #1 (2010) by Rick Remender and Roland Boschi
Further Reading: *Franken-Castle* #17–20 (2010)

Height: Unknown **Weight:** Unknown **Origin:** Monster Metropolis **Powers:** Superhuman strength, resistant to psychic and physical attacks

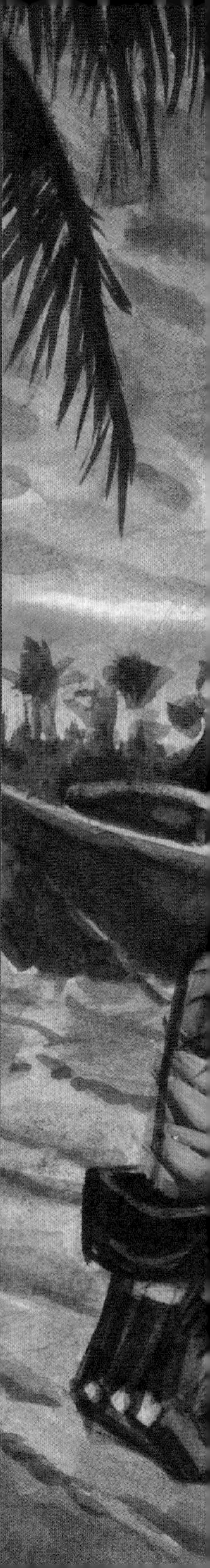

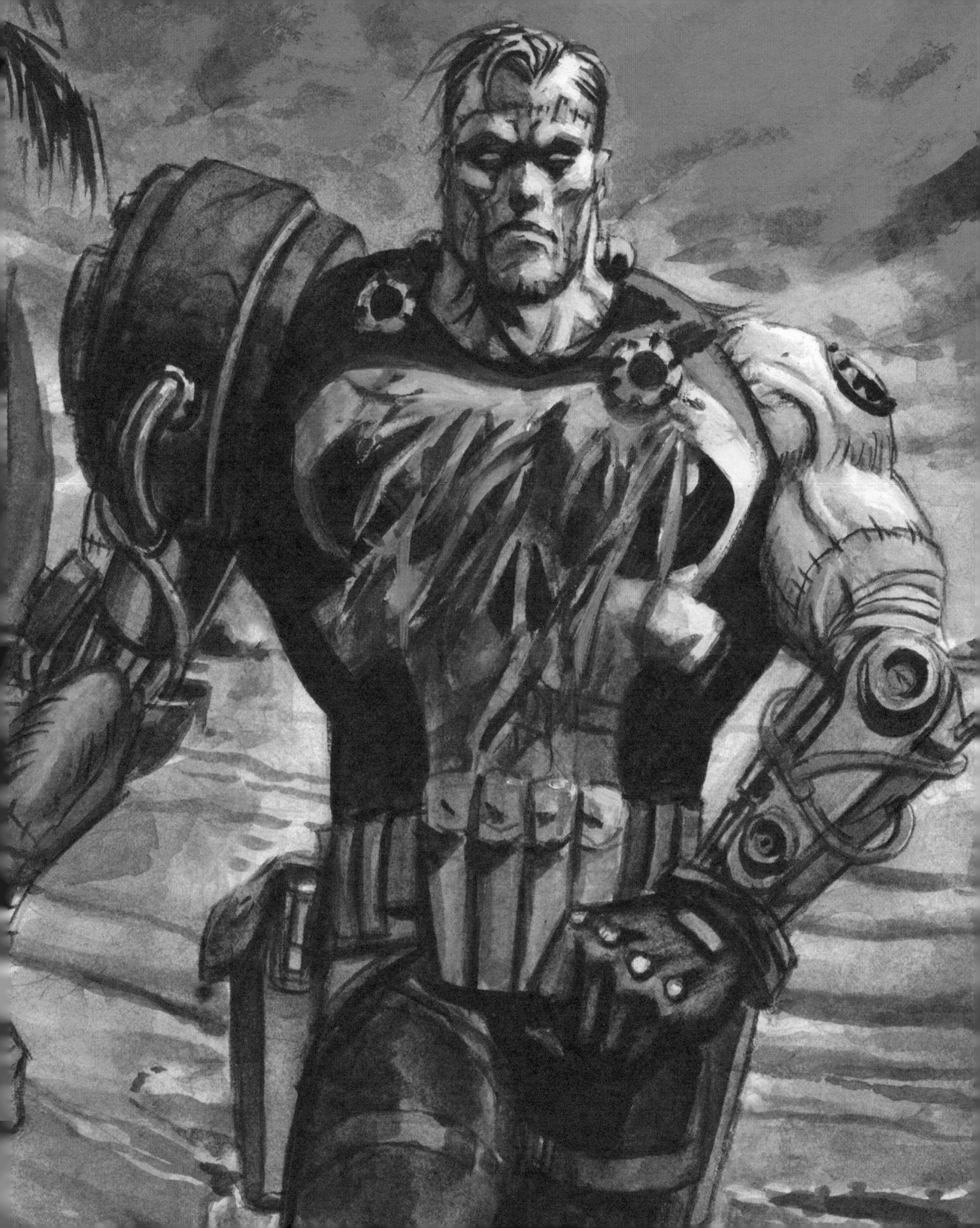

Molten Man-Thing

The quiet paradise of a tropical island in the Pacific Ocean ended abruptly when, as its volcano erupted, a creature rose up from the boiling lava and shambled toward the nearest village. Resembling a human, but definitely not human, Molten Man-Thing strikes terror in the hearts of the islanders.

An airplane pilot in need of a vacation treated himself to a remote and tropical getaway. On the Pacific island he selected there was a volcano that had laid dormant for centuries, until the day when the ground suddenly started to shudder. As lava spilled out of the volcano's crater, a strange silhouette emerged.

Assuming the form of a man, the monster approached the island village on two feet, swinging two arms and displaying a gaping maw. Dubbed the "Molten Man-Thing" accordingly by the islanders, the being is, in fact, a long-forgotten creation of the Deviants. Its massive magma body is super-heated. Weapons are incinerated before they can touch it, making the fiery foe essentially impervious.

On the island, each step the Molten Man-Thing took left smoking, boiling lava in its wake. The pilot was determined not to let the magma monster destroy the people's homes and set a dangerous plan into motion. He ran to the airfield, luring the Molten Man-Thing away from the village. Just as the magma monster was about to strike, the pilot released a blast of air from a wind tunnel. The monster was repulsed by the cool temperatures and retreated to its volcano home. Within an hour the island's volcanic eruptions had ceased.

A rampaging recreation of the magma monster by artist Frank Johnson was later seen in SoHo in New York City, but was soon defeated by the Fantastic Four. However, that was not the last sighting of Molten Man-Thing. He appeared as a priest of the Church of the Unified Spirits of Life in Monster Metropolis, beneath the streets of New York City. His current whereabouts are unknown.

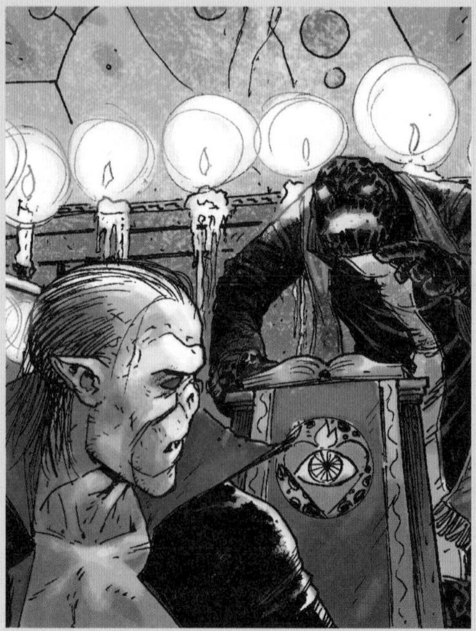

A sympathetic ear
Molten Man-Thing found a new calling in Monster Metropolis, offering support to those shunned by the surface world.

First Appearance: *Tales of Suspense* #7 (1960) by Stan Lee and Jack Kirby
Further Reading: "The Monster Hunters" *in Marvel Universe* #4 (1998), *Punisher* #11-13 (2010)

Height: Unknown **Weight:** Unknown **Origin:** Napuka, South Pacific Ocean **Powers:** Body composed of super-hot magma; invulnerability

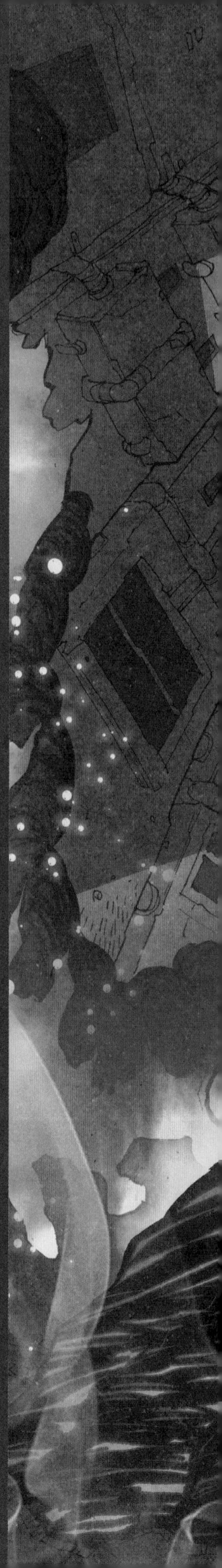

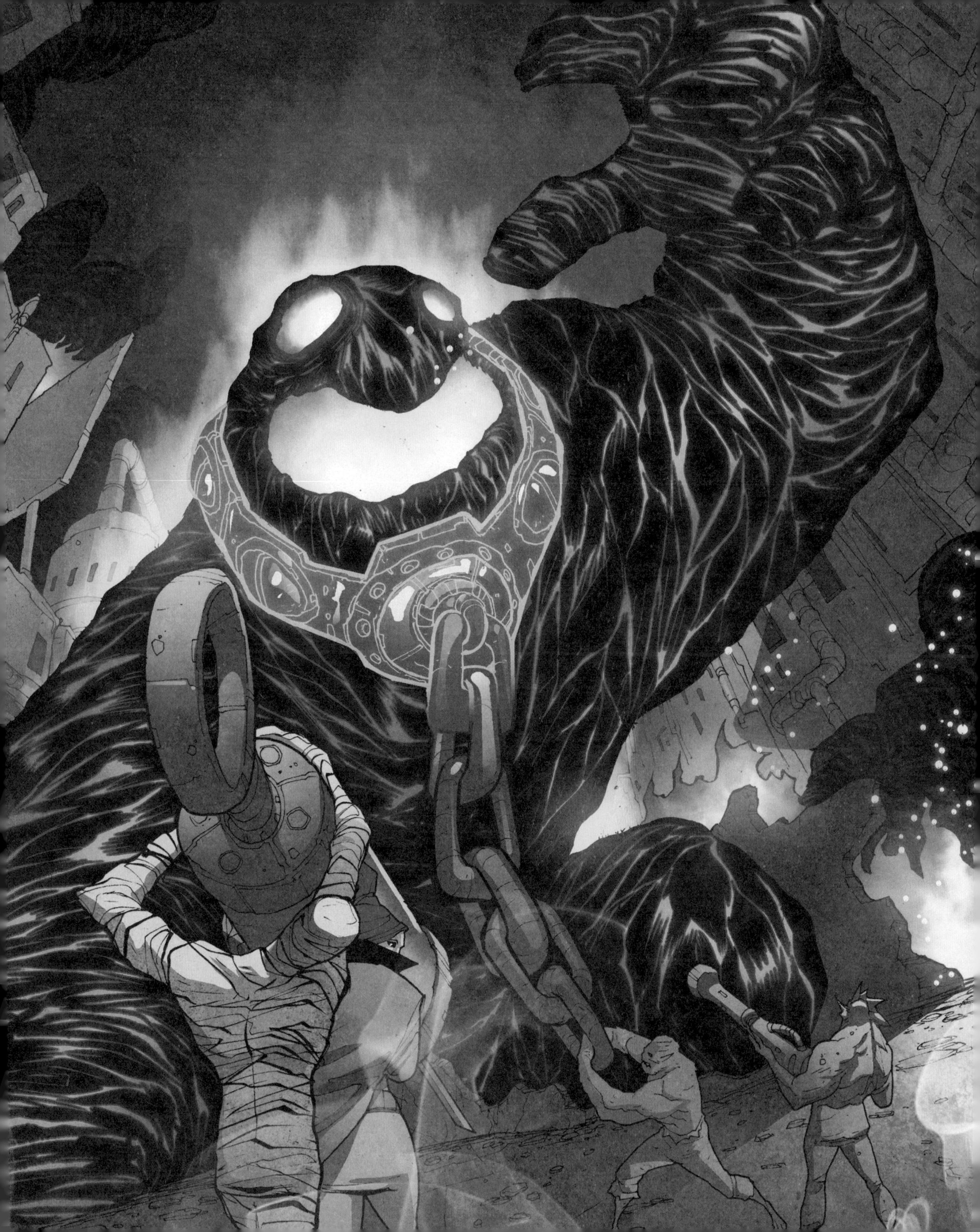

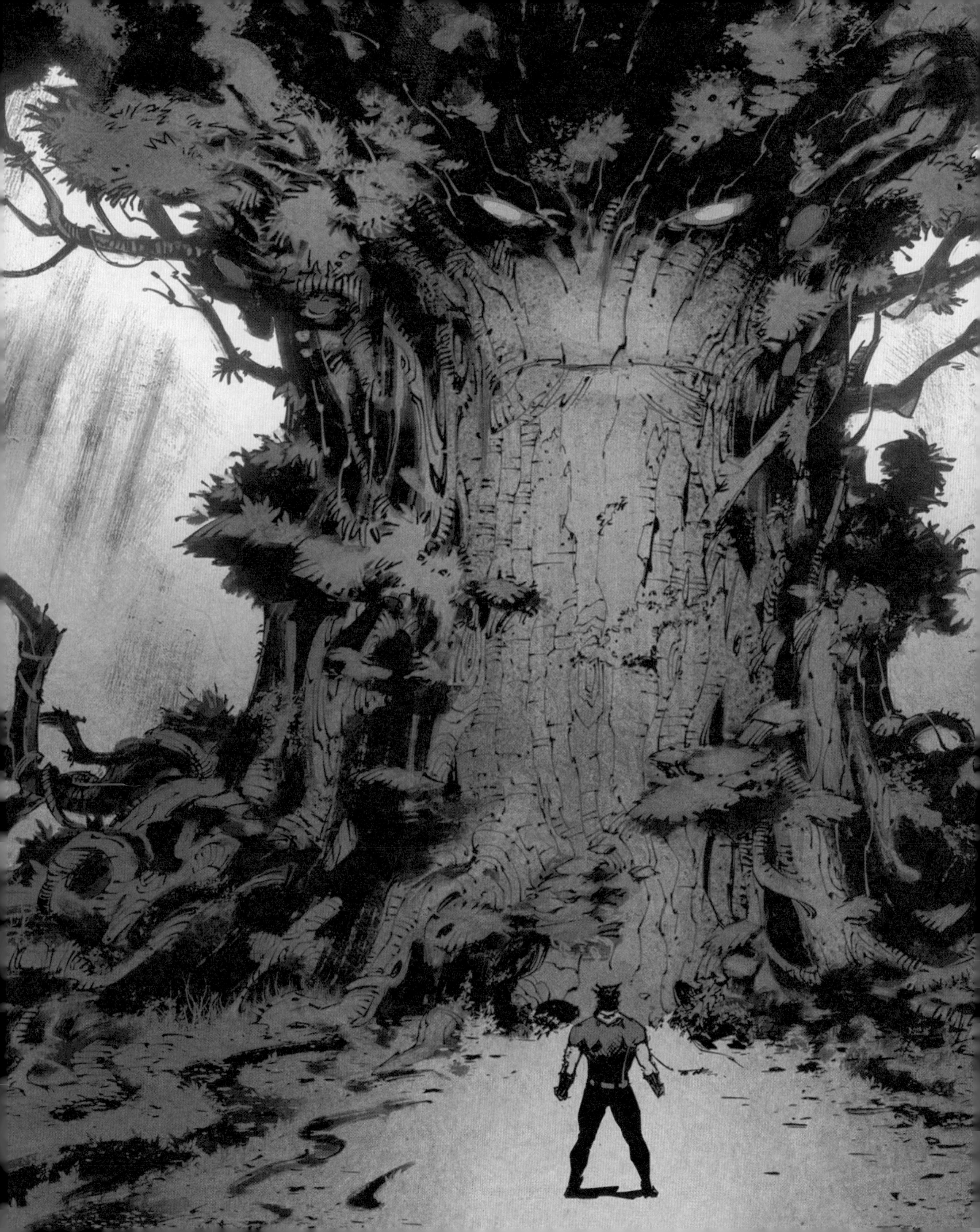

Size: 263 sq. mi (681 sq. km), plus other scattered islands Origin: South Pacific Powers: Collective consciousness of organisms; ability to walk

Krakoa

Here the earth shifts and plants appear to have a life of their own: coalescing into the unsettling shape of a massive humanoid. This is Krakoa, the island that walks like a man. The plants and animals that live here are fused into one monstrous being with a shared hivemind.

This small island in the South Pacific was first encountered by Nick Fury and the Howling Commandos in 1945, just moments after an experimental nuclear bomb fell on its shores. The stranded soldiers were horrified to learn that the island was contaminated with unusual radiation—and the group quickly began to feel the adverse effects of the radioactive poisoning. Fury struck an agreement with the sentient island. Krakoa dissipated the irradiated poison from the men and the land while they waited for rescue. In exchange, they kept its existence a secret so that it could be left in peace. The island remained undisturbed—until the day the X-Men arrived. Once they stepped onto the atypical atoll, their lives would never be the same again.

Professor Charles Xavier had detected the presence of a mutant in the Pacific Ocean, unaware that the island itself was the power he was sensing. He sent his team to investigate, but they were quickly ambushed and subdued by the walking island. Trapping the mutants, Krakoa found sustenance in their unique energies and released team leader Cyclops to fetch even more mutants. A new team arrived and freed their predecessors, joining forces against the landmass, and banishing it to the vacuum of space. Krakoa eventually returned to Earth, at which time Professor Xavier devised a plan for it and Earth's mutants to co-exist.

Under Xavier's guidance, the living island was developed into a safe haven for all mutants. The vegetation of Krakoa is capable of creating gateways to different parts of itself for instantaneous travel, and its unique flowers are used to create panacean medicines for humans.

First Appearance: *Giant-Size X-Men #1* (1975) by Len Wein and Dave Cockrum
Further Reading: *Journey into Mystery: The Birth of Krakoa* (2018), *House of X* (2019)

Island origins
Long before the X-Men set foot on it, Krakoa was part of a larger landmass called Okkara. It shattered into two pieces named Krakoa and Arakko during a demonic invasion.

Two-Headed Thing

On a dark and stormy night, the Two-Headed Thing arises from a deep pit. The stone-skinned giant has two horned heads on one colossal body and unbelievable powers at its disposal. Able to shape-shift into any form of plant or animal, the Two-Headed Thing is a threat to humankind.

The Two-Headed Thing spent centuries tunneling below Earth's crust and as far down as its core, until finally it broke through to the surface one night during a thunderstorm. Emerging from a black pit in the middle of a prison yard, it smashed through the reinforced walls with just one punch. Watching him from the window of his cell was a prisoner named Eddie Kane. When the Two-Headed Thing broke through the prison wall, the bars at the cell window were loosened, and Eddie escaped. He trailed the monster as it left the wreckage. Curiosity turned to shock when Eddie realized he could overhear the creature's thoughts.

Then Eddie saw the Two-Headed Thing direct a seemingly magical energy at a nearby tree, absorbing its essence, atom by atom, until it had transformed into the tree itself. When the monster released its control, the tree was restored and the Two-Headed Thing moved on.

Instantly identifiable with its twin heads and scaly, bulletproof hide, the Two-Headed Thing can shape-shift into any living organism. It exerts its will to absorb a target's form into its own, causing it to vanish until it releases its hold. Communicating through telepathy, it broadcasts its own inner monologue and converses with its victims without speaking.

Eddie's escape did not go unnoticed. Discovered by the prison guards, Eddie told them his far-fetched tale. Then he began to shape-shift from the man into the monster—the Two-Headed Thing had taken on Eddie's form! With that, a lightning bolt struck the creature—ending the threat. Eddie was restored to his human form, and the Two-Headed Thing was seemingly destroyed, although it later returned to fight the Fantastic Four. It was last seen on Monster Isle in the Pacific.

First Appearance: *Strange Tales* #95 (1962) by Stan Lee and Jack Kirby

On the surface
The Two-Headed Thing, no longer trapped underground, is now a resident of Monster Isle.

Height: 20ft (6m) **Weight:** Unknown **Origin:** Earth's core **Powers:** Superhuman strength; bulletproof hide; telepathy; shape-shifting

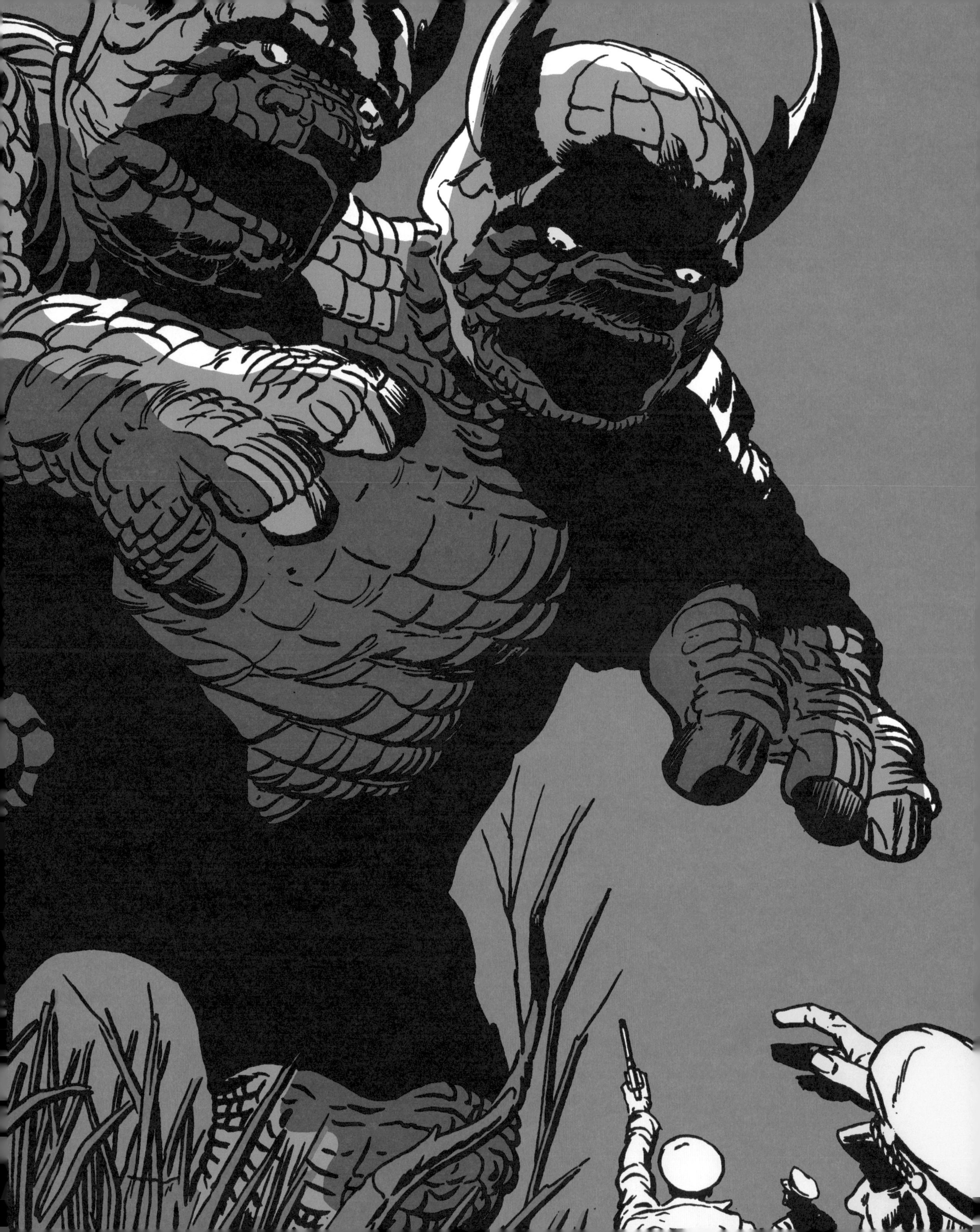

Golem

First a massive fist burst through the singed earth of a war-torn city, then a grim, gray giant emerged from the rubble. Conjured from the texts of ancient documents, this is the Golem—a living legend. Pounding through the streets of Warsaw, the Golem zones in on his target: the Nazis.

During World War II, Captain America and several members of the hero team the Invaders were on a mission in Warsaw, in occupied Poland. They wanted to retrieve Jacob Goldstein, a bookseller and the brother of a scientist they were hoping to bring onto the side of the Allies. However, the heroes were subdued by the Nazis and imprisoned in a secret hideout.

Determined to fight back and save his would-be rescuers, Goldstein pored over a book that spoke of creating a golem guardian of legend. He mixed a strange, watery liquid with the form of a man shaped from the cold clay of the ground. He uttered a summoning prayer and a bolt of lightning crashed into the workshop at the same moment. Goldstein and the clay were fused into an awe-inspiring gray titan. Golem, as he was known, rescued the Super Hero team and destroyed the Nazi hideout, before transforming back into an exhausted Goldstein. Jacob decided to remain in Warsaw should the Golem be required to battle the Nazis again.

The Nazis later made Golem fight for them in their secret hideout in the Mojave Desert. He followed their orders and attacked the Invaders to keep his brother—who was being forced by the Nazis to create an earthquake-generating machine—safe. Captain America convinced him to switch sides, but his brother died as the team defeated the threat.

Reluctant villain
With skin harder than stone, Golem can withstand punches from powerful heroes such as Namor and Captain America.

Brought forth from the earth by a mix of arcane texts, strange liquid, a prayer, and a lightning bolt, Golem has immense strength granted by his colossal size. His skin is as impenetrable as granite. The Hebrew word "emeth" ("truth") is scrawled across his forehead. If the word is wiped away, Golem reverts back into Jacob. Other golems have been seen before and since.

First Appearance: *Invaders* #13 (1977) by Roy Thomas, Frank Robbins, and Frank Springer
Further Reading: *Invaders* #2-4 (1993)

Height: 10ft (3m) **Weight:** Unknown **Origin:** Warsaw, Poland **Powers:** Superhuman strength and durability

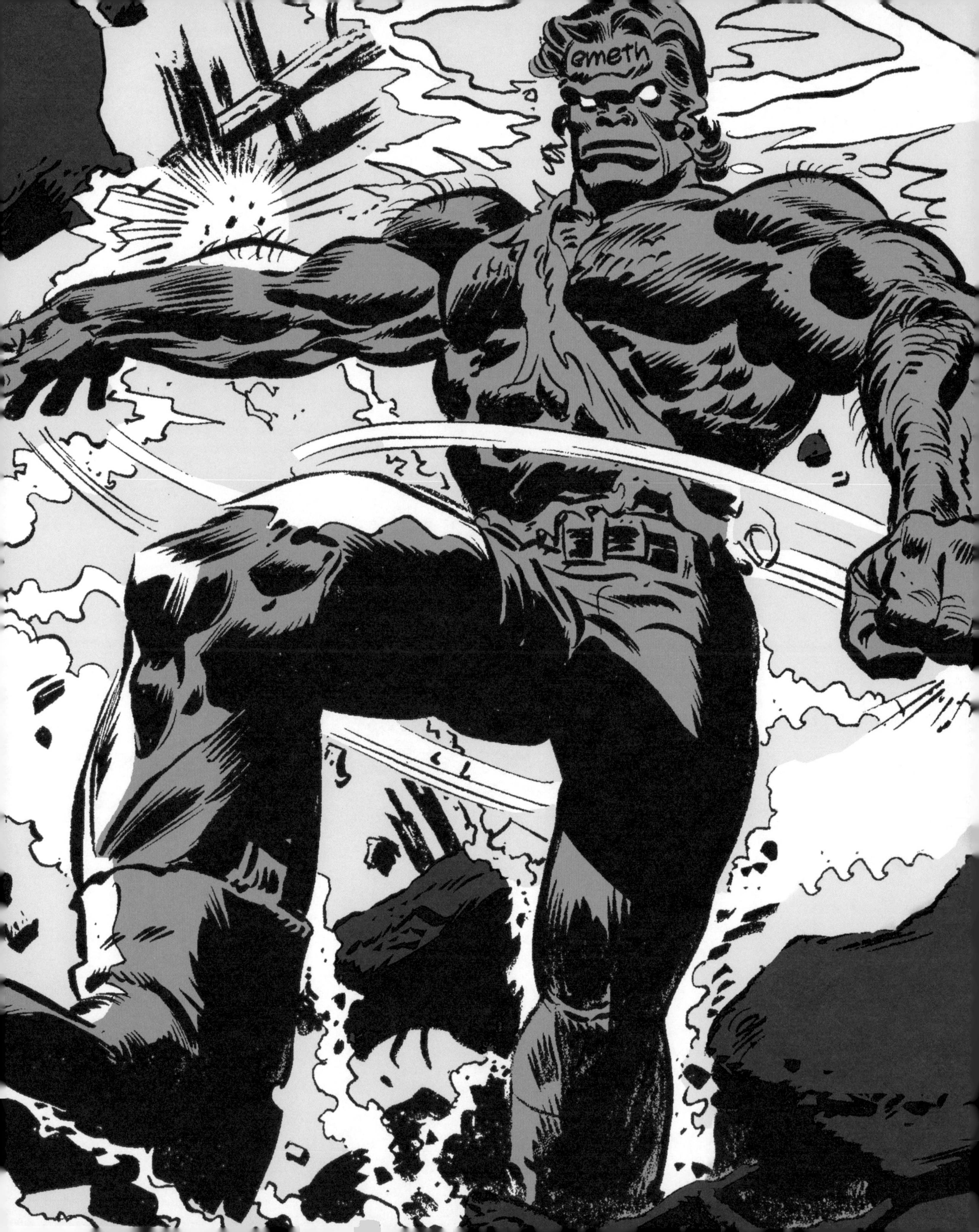
emeth

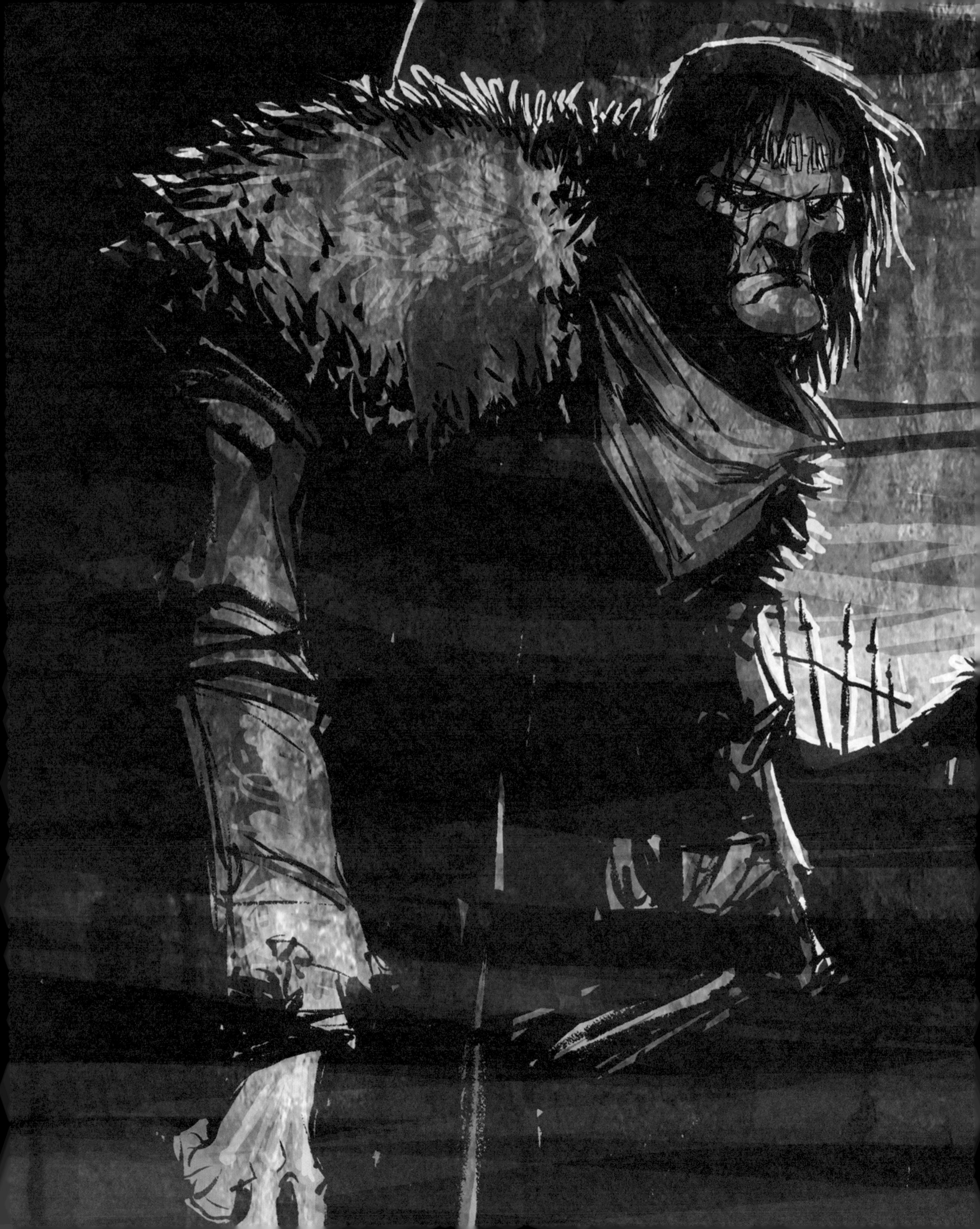

Frankenstein's Monster

Constructed by a scientist obsessed with creating life from death, Frankenstein's Monster is feared for his appalling appearance and imposing size. The famous monster harbors blinding hatred for one man: his creator, Victor Frankenstein, who was repulsed by, and tried to destroy, what he had made.

In 1898, Frankenstein's Monster was found by an expedition boat in the frozen Arctic where he had been hibernating in the tundra for years. The men who discovered him transported the frozen creature onto their ship. As it sailed home, it collided with an iceberg, and the monster rose from the wreckage, saving as many members of the crew as he could. Knowing what the monstrous creature desired, the dying captain confided that the last descendant of Victor Frankenstein still lived.

The quest to find his target and enact revenge led Frankenstein's Monster into the clutches of werewolves and vampires until he finally confronted his maker's great-great-nephew, Vincent Frankenstein. Vincent had malevolent plans of his own for the monster, but met his death at the hands of another. Frankenstein's Monster trudged away, his mission seemingly complete, and he again found rest in a block of ice.

The next time he woke was in the modern era. Since this awakening, Frankenstein's Monster has crossed paths with the Avengers and the Werewolf by Night and joined forces with Ulysses and Elsa Bloodstone. He has stood alongside She-Hulk, Howard the Duck, and Nighthawk as part of the Fearsome Four, a makeshift team dedicated to stopping Man-Thing's fear-fueled rampage. The last sighting of the monster was as part of the All-New Howling Commandos.

Frankenstein's Monster towers head and shoulders above most people. His corpselike body is composed of stitched-together body parts animated through unorthodox science. He displays great strength in hand-to-hand combat and resistance to damage. He is often clad in a bear-hide coat he fashioned himself.

First Appearance: *X-Men* #40 (1968) by Roy Thomas and Don Heck **Further Reading:** *Monsters Unleashed: The Monster of Frankenstein* (1973)

Fighting machine
The only real vulnerability displayed by Frankenstein's Monster is a fear of fire. In combat he prefers to fight with his fists. As such, Dracula once recruited him for his brute force alone.

Height: 8ft (2.4m) **Weight:** 325 lbs (147kg) **Origin:** Germany **Powers:** Superhuman strength, stamina, and durability

Vandoom's Monster

In an attempt to draw crowds to his waxwork museum, self-proclaimed creator of monsters Ludwig Vandoom sculpted a petrifying piece of art out of wax. A stray lightning bolt harnessed the elements of nature and brought it chillingly to life, giving rise to the beast known only as Vandoom's Monster.

Height: 25ft (7.6m) **Weight:** Unknown **Origin:** Transylvania **Powers:** Massive size and strength

Merely seeking to attract visitors to his tired museum, Transylvanian artist Vandoom worked night and day to create a terrifying—yet tantalizing—statue. Vandoom concentrated on making every tiny detail as ferocious as possible. The artist's creation was so huge that he had to cut a hole in the roof of the museum to install it in the building. The night before its unveiling, an electrical surge from a passing storm struck the wax monstrosity.

Mouth agape, the massive monster stirred into life and crashed through the walls of the museum as it took its first earth-shaking steps. The alarmed townspeople ran for their weapons. Vandoom pleaded with them to let the confused creature be, but fear overtook reason, and an angry mob quickly assembled. Just as suddenly, spaceships appeared in the sky, and aliens coincidentally bent on conquering Earth disembarked.

The behemoth, fleeing from the violent villagers, came face-to-face with the antagonistic aliens. It attacked out of instinct. The aliens were routed and the monster victorious, but it paid a heavy price, collapsing to the ground, lifeless. The remorseful townspeople realized it had chosen not to use its raw strength against them. Vandoom carved another statue to honor their fallen hero, the star attraction of his now-thriving museum.

Vandoom's Monster would later be spotted as part of Mole Man's retinue on Monster Isle in the North Pacific, although how it got there remains unknown. It also joined the ranks of monsters defending the Earth from Leviathons.

The orange-furred colossus has incredible strength to match its vast size. Two large, sharp teeth jut from its protruding lower jaw, and its massive mouth can unleash a monstrous roar.

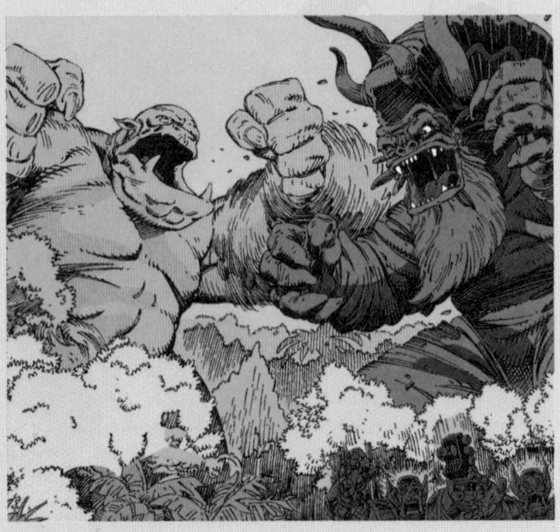

Strong supporter
Vandoom's Monster doesn't have much of a mind of its own, so consequently frequently fights at the behest of an ally.

First Appearance: *Tales to Astonish* #17 (1961) by Stan Lee, Larry Lieber, and Jack Kirby
Further Reading: *Monsters Unleashed* #2 (2017)

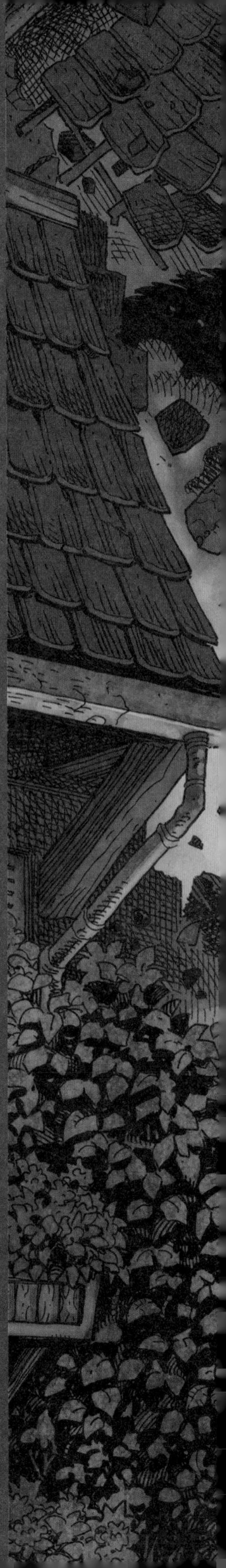

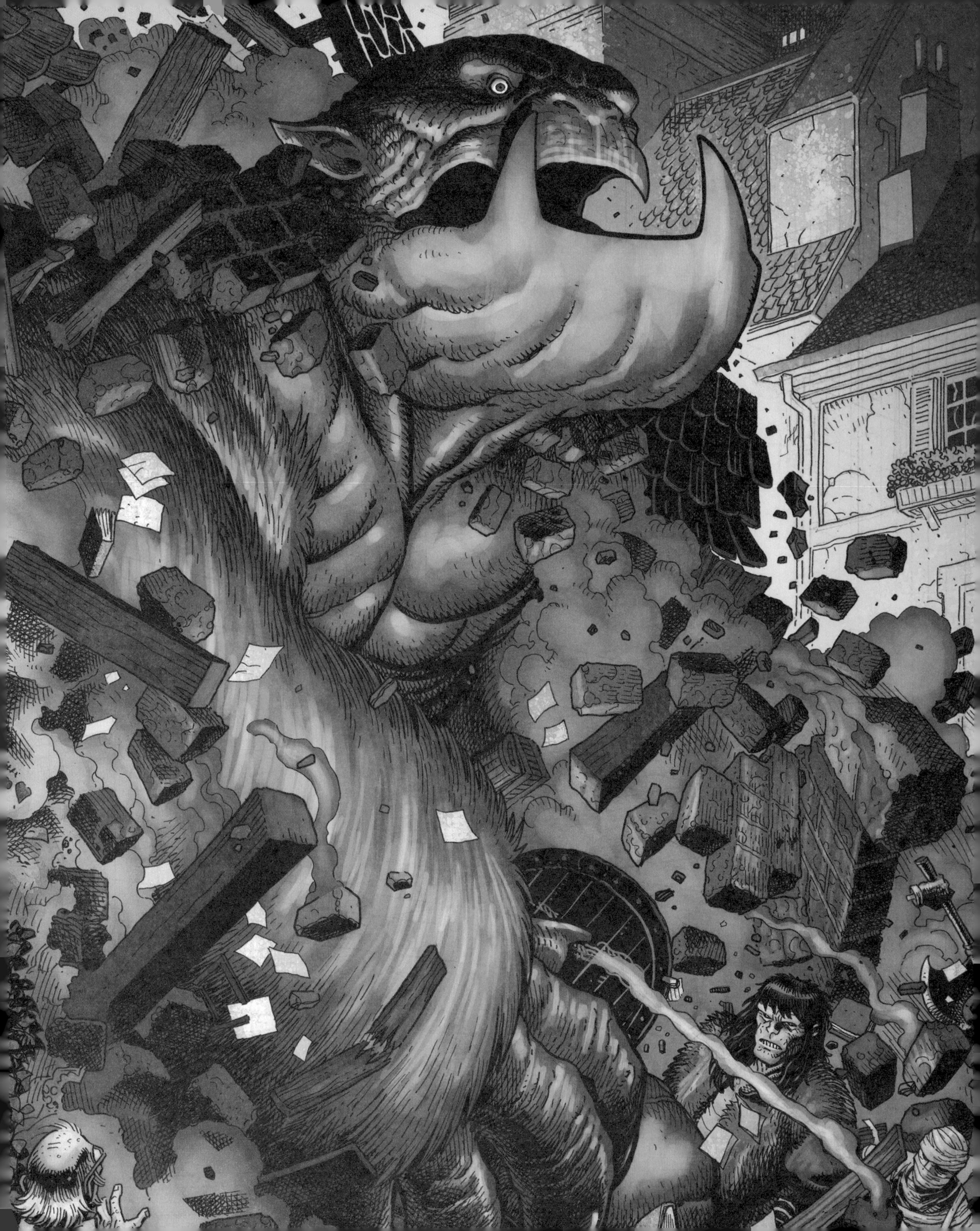

Grottu

A fearsome ant the size of an elephant leads a colony of soldier ants to destroy everything in their path. This highly intelligent, atomic-powered arthropod has complete telepathic control over his minions and one sole aim: world domination. Nicknamed Grottu, he is the king of the insects.

Scientist Lynn Avery and his friend Frank (a pseudonym adopted by adventurer Ulysses Bloodstone) traveled to east Africa to investigate a report of a gigantic army ant. Near Mombasa, Kenya, the pair were told of mysterious nuclear experiments and explosions that had been conducted close by. Soon after the radioactive experiments had ceased, the local villagers discovered one army ant growing larger by the day. It seemed that the atomic radiation had mutated the insect into a monster, and it was now commanding the other army ants to do its bidding. Named Grottu—meaning demon— by the villagers, he led his colony toward the coast, relentlessly destroying entire villages in its path.

As a result of the atomic energy, Grottu's armored body has grown to colossal proportions and his intelligence is greatly heightened—he is said to have the intelligence of a human. Grottu is able to give mental commands to other ants, transmitted through his giant antenna. Two giant mandibles protrude from his head.

When the scientist and the adventurer located the monstrous insect, they noticed that, remarkably, they could understand the telepathy Grottu used to command his ant army. They followed the colony as it advanced to the port of Mombasa. There, Frank lured Grottu into a trap—burying the oversized ant in a mound of sugar that had been stored in a nearby warehouse. Grottu's mindless minions devoured the sweet treat and smothered their leader as they feasted, trapping him.

Defeated, but not destroyed, Grottu returned years later. He faced the Fantastic Four and briefly possessed Ant-Man before he was seemingly exterminated.

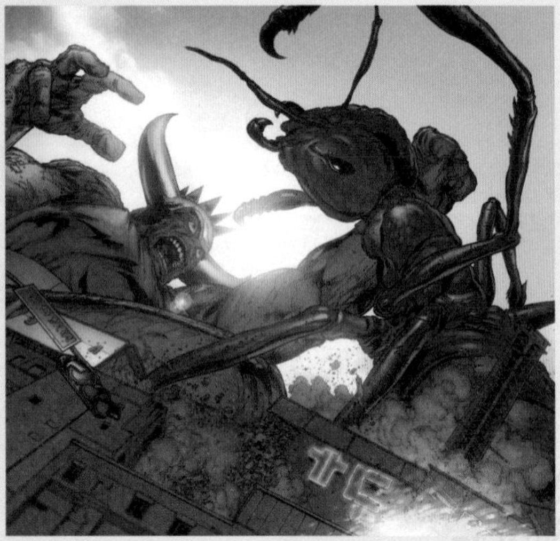

Ambitious ant
Even after repeated defeats, Grottu refused to give up his plotting to conquer the world. He'll fight anyone standing in his way.

First Appearance: *Strange Tales* #73 (1960) by Stan Lee, Larry Lieber, and Jack Kirby
Further Reading: *Fantastic Four Unlimited* #9 (1995)

Height: 35ft (10.7m) **Weight:** Unknown **Origin:** Near Mombasa, Kenya **Powers:** Massive size, strength, and intellect; telepathy

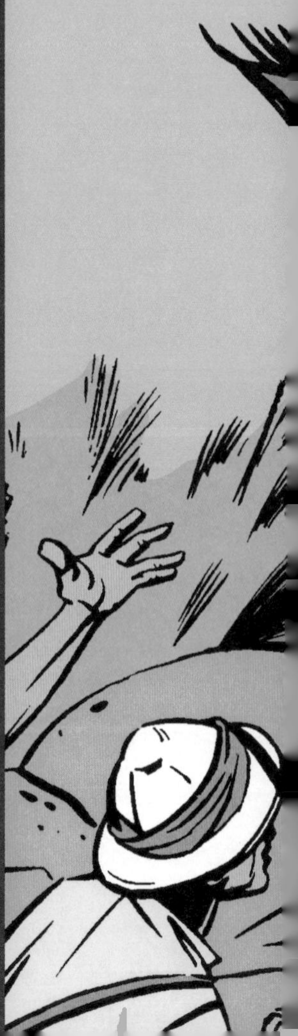

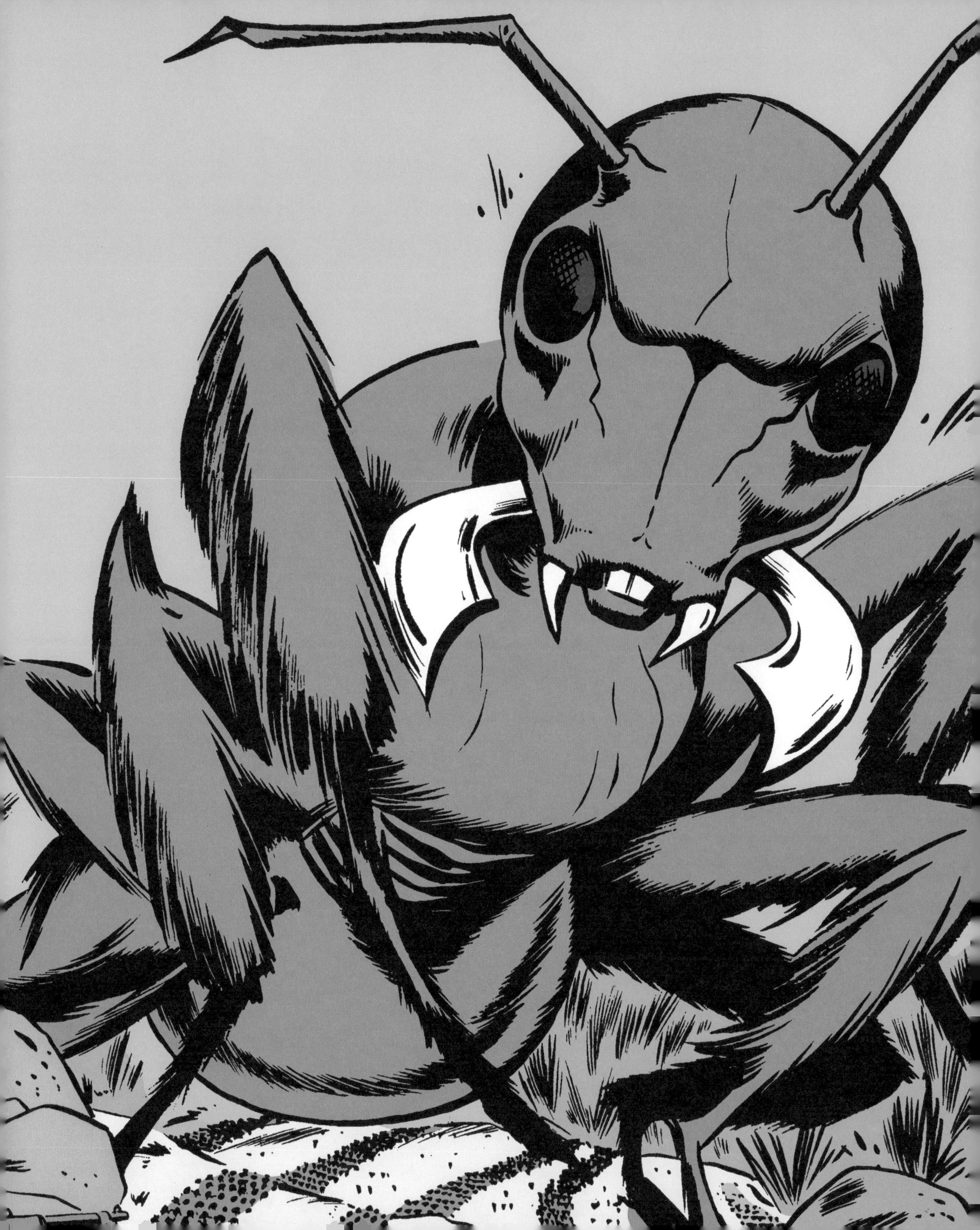

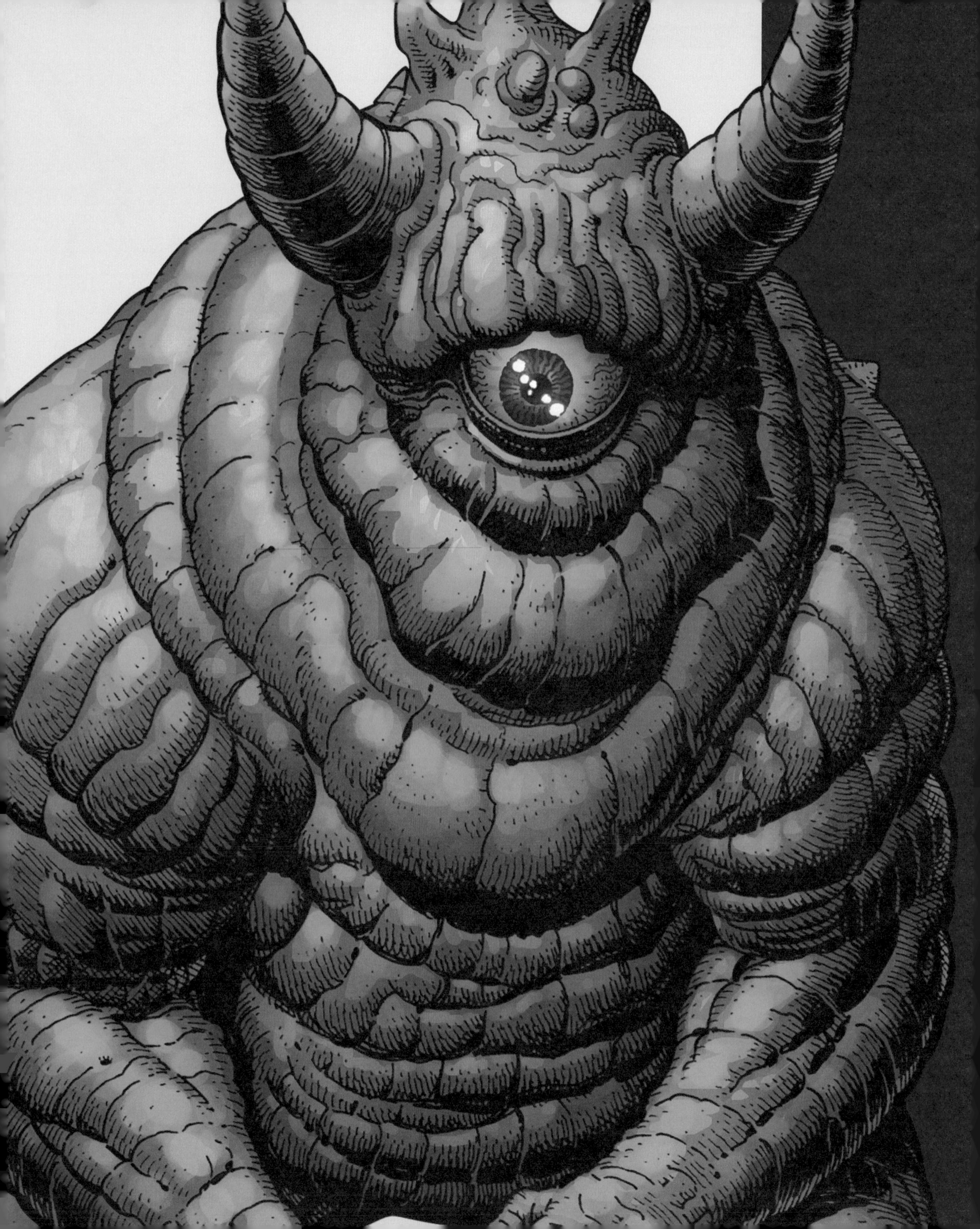

SPACE AND OTHER DIMENSIONS

Colossal extraterrestrials capable of crossing the vastness of space seek out planets to claim for their own. Others from alternate dimensions step through doorways in search of new worlds to conquer. And a few benevolent beings from the stars are simply stranded on the closest planet they could find.

All these otherworldly creatures find themselves on planet Earth, whereupon humanity is often unprepared for their arrival.

Alien attackers like Groot, Goom, Orrgo, Kaa, and Rorgg ruthlessly rampage across the globe, only to be stopped by quick-thinking, ordinary people. Others, such as Mangog and the Leviathon Mother, are halted by some of the bravest Super Heroes on Earth. And the unfortunate Blip and Monstrom just want to go back to their own homeworlds.

Get to know these supersized space invaders.

Xemnu the Titan

Alien cyborg Xemnu the Titan has a criminal past. Having crossed the far reaches of the universe, the living hulk crash-lands on Earth. The fur-covered fiend is capable of hypnotizing others to do his bidding and so comes to Earth time and time again in an attempt to control its inhabitants.

Small-town electrician Joe Harper got more than he bargained for when he found a mysterious, massive creature—part-alien Xem, part-cyborg—unconscious in a swamp. The excited man took the giant home to repair him. When Xemnu regained consciousness, he revealed that he had escaped from a world designed to hold criminals like himself. With his powers restored, he at once hypnotized all the humans on the planet, ordering them to build him a starship to get home. Fortunately, Joe was spared in return for saving the alien's life. Seeking to thwart Xemnu's plans, the electrician booby-trapped the newly built spaceship, shocking Xemnu into stasis and sending the vessel to harmlessly orbit the sun.

Cyborg Xemnu has various metal plates affixed to his white-furred body, including a domed helmet. He is audibly able to communicate and makes full use of his many mental powers, including telepathy, hypnosis, and possession, to control the humans on Earth.

After discovering the inhabitants of his home planet had been wiped out by a plague, Xemnu returns to Earth on multiple missions to transform humans into members of his own species. While on Earth, Xemnu has challenged heroes such as Doctor Strange, other members of the Defenders, She-Hulk, and the Totally Awesome Hulk Amadeus Cho (aka Brawn). Xemnu and the Hulk in particular have a long, bitter history as rivals.

Recently the mind manipulator launched his most ambitious scheme yet against his perennial foe. Xemnu brainwashed the world into believing he was the Hulk, and the green giant was a villain. The Hulk unleashed his full fury against the white-furred alien to end his reign of lies.

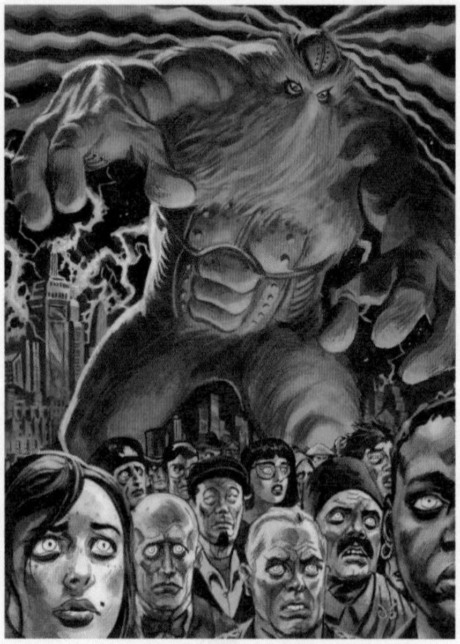

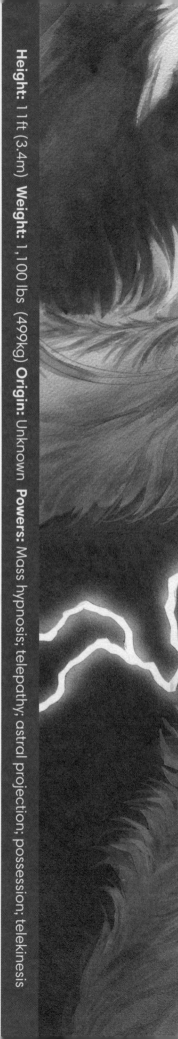

Jail breaker
Now apparently the last of his kind, Xemnu had been living on an exile planet with other criminals and used his hypnotic powers to escape.

First Appearance: *Journey Into Mystery* #62 (1960) by Stan Lee, Larry Lieber, and Jack Kirby **Further Reading:** *Marvel Feature* #3 (1972), *Defenders* #12 (1974)

Height: 11ft (3.4m) **Weight:** 1,100 lbs (499kg) **Origin:** Unknown **Powers:** Mass hypnosis; telepathy; astral projection; possession; telekinesis

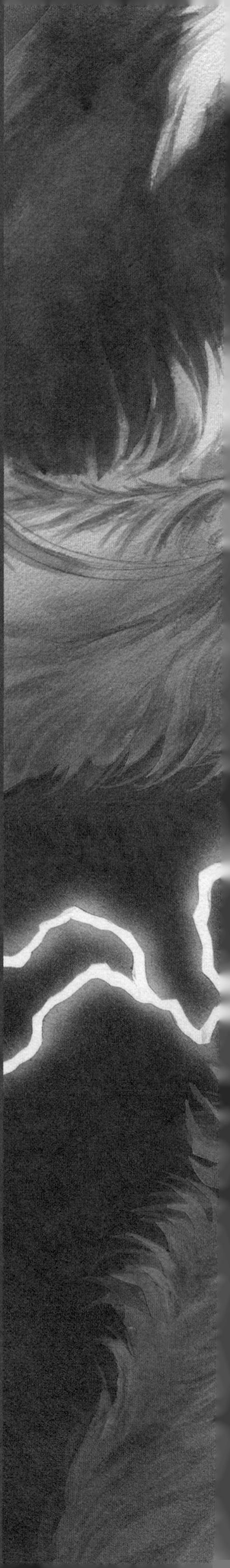

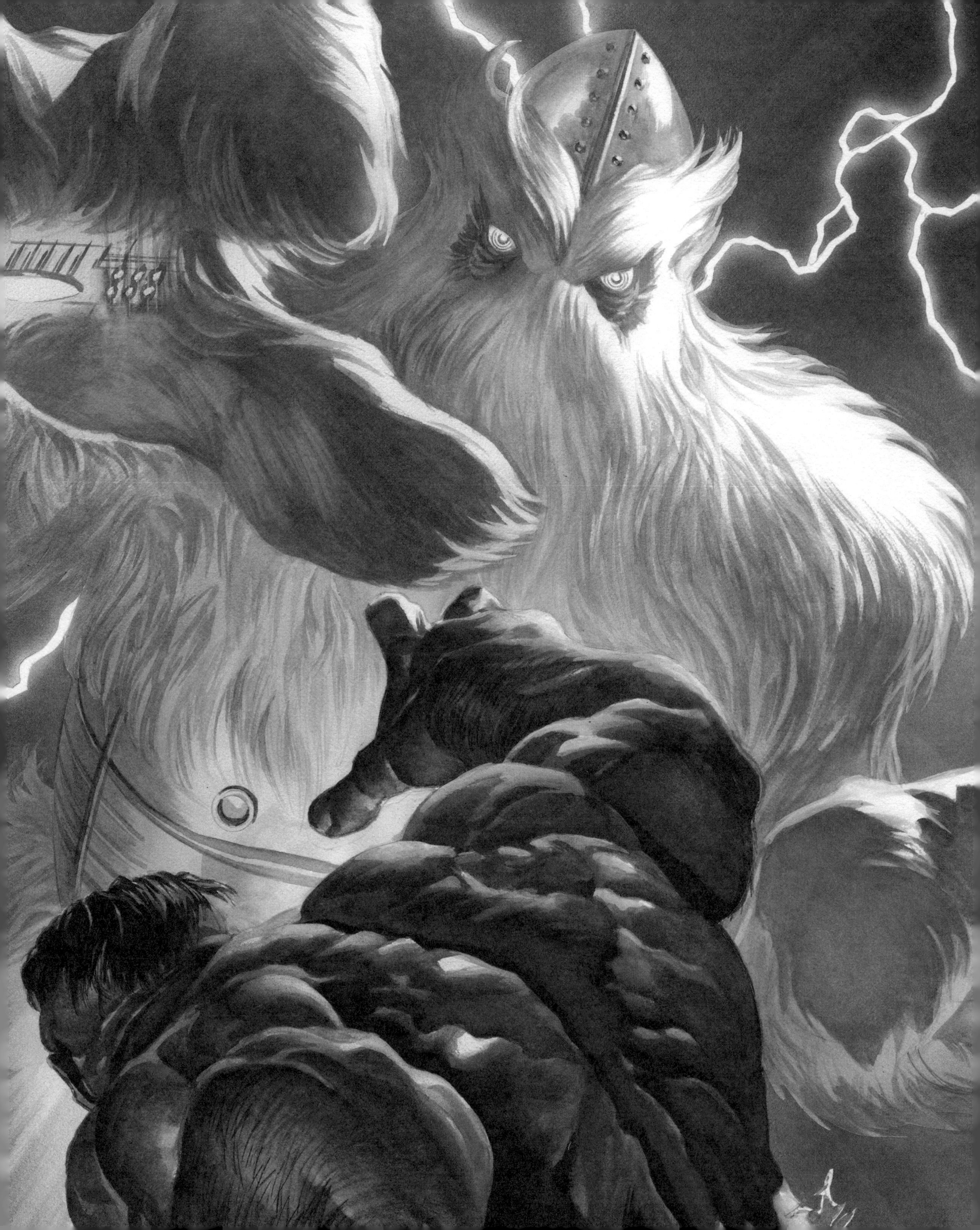

Hypno-Creature

Dwelling deep below ground in the Dimension of Doom, the unusual Hypno-Creature is two-dimensional, but still a formidable foe. Capable of hypnotizing its target with a beam of strange light, the size-altering beast proves to be a very real threat to planet Earth.

An inquisitive teenager named John Cummings made the most shocking discovery of his life on a seemingly normal day. His curiosity got the better of him when he noticed some suspicious-looking construction workers digging in the street. Before his eyes, one of the men vanished into thin air. That night, the teen investigated the pit where he had seen them working.

Like the construction worker, John vanished, only to reappear in a strange, new place: the Dimension of Doom. He had entered a world where everything was flat—even he was two-dimensional—and the inhabitants were planning an invasion of Earth's surface. He spotted the same workers, who had been the would-be invaders in disguise, and they detected his presence. Unable to stop John with blasts of electrical charges, they unleashed the Hypno-Creature to prevent his escape.

Originally able to fit on the palm of a hand, the orange beast can grow enormous with the help of a mysterious vapor kept in a vial around his neck. His round, spiked head is topped by two horns, and his eyes emit a Hypno-Ray that can hypnotize his target with a single glance.

Hypno-Creature chased John into a nearby valley of crystals. Grabbing a crystal, John used it to reflect a Hypno-Ray back onto the creature—hypnotizing him! John ordered him to attack the workers, meanwhile escaping back into his own world. Hastily commandeering a steamroller, he filled in the hole to the other dimension, trapping the monster.

Apparently confined to his two-dimensional home, the formidable Hypno-Creature has seemingly not been seen since.

Unique dimension
Hypno-Creature's world, including a city and a valley of crystals, is as two-dimensional as he is.

First Appearance: *Tales of Suspense* #23 (1961) by Stan Lee, Larry Lieber, and Jack Kirby

Height: Varies, up to 13ft 2in (4m) **Weight:** 20,000 tons **Origin:** Dimension of Doom **Powers:** Hypnosis; telepathy; X-ray vision

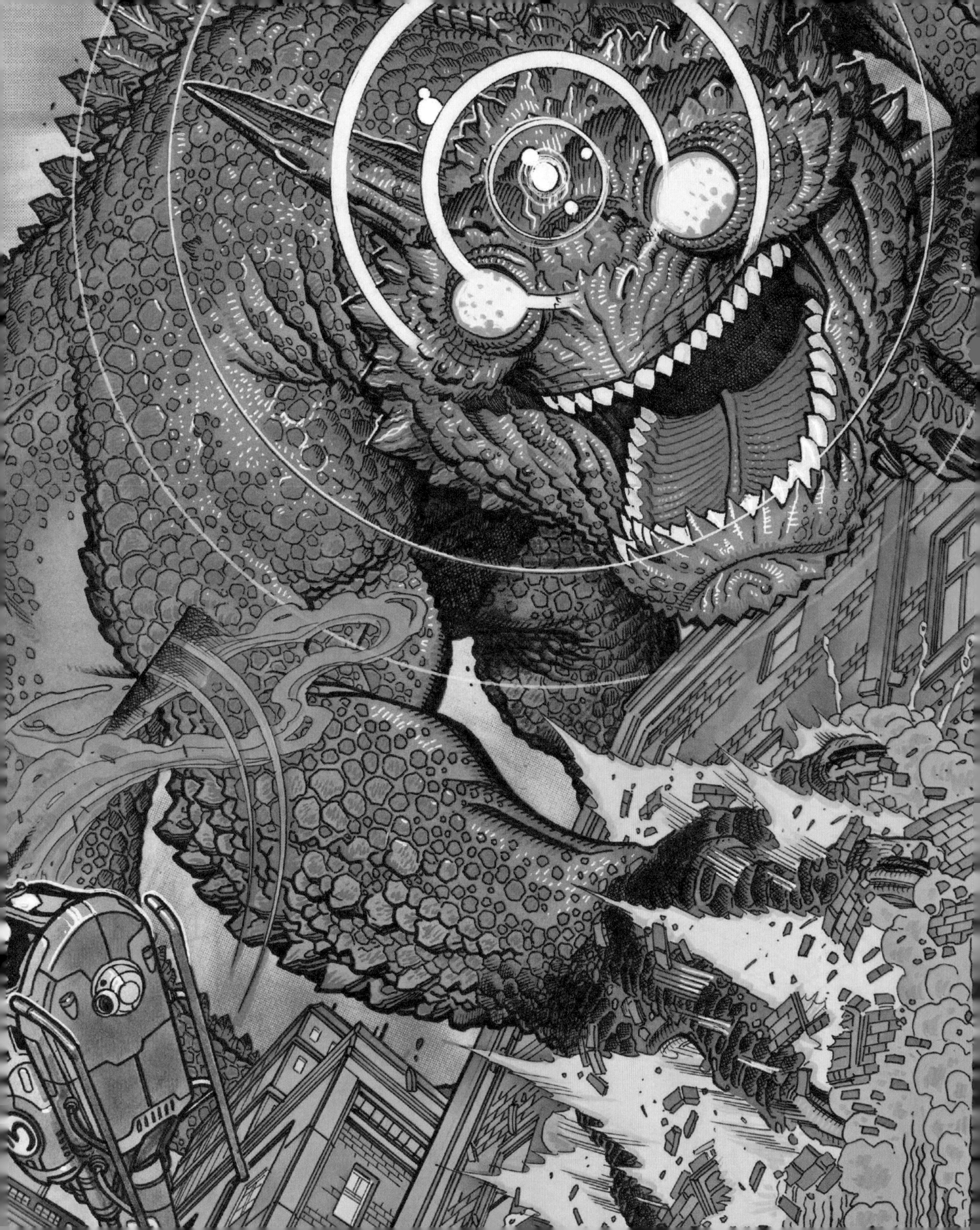

Hypno-Creature Anatomy

The two-dimensional Hypno-Creature is almost reptilian in appearance, with scaly orange skin, a ridged back, a thrashing tail, and clawed hands and feet. Its shifting height and weight make it an unpredictable foe. But the real threat is its formidable mind-controlling abilities.

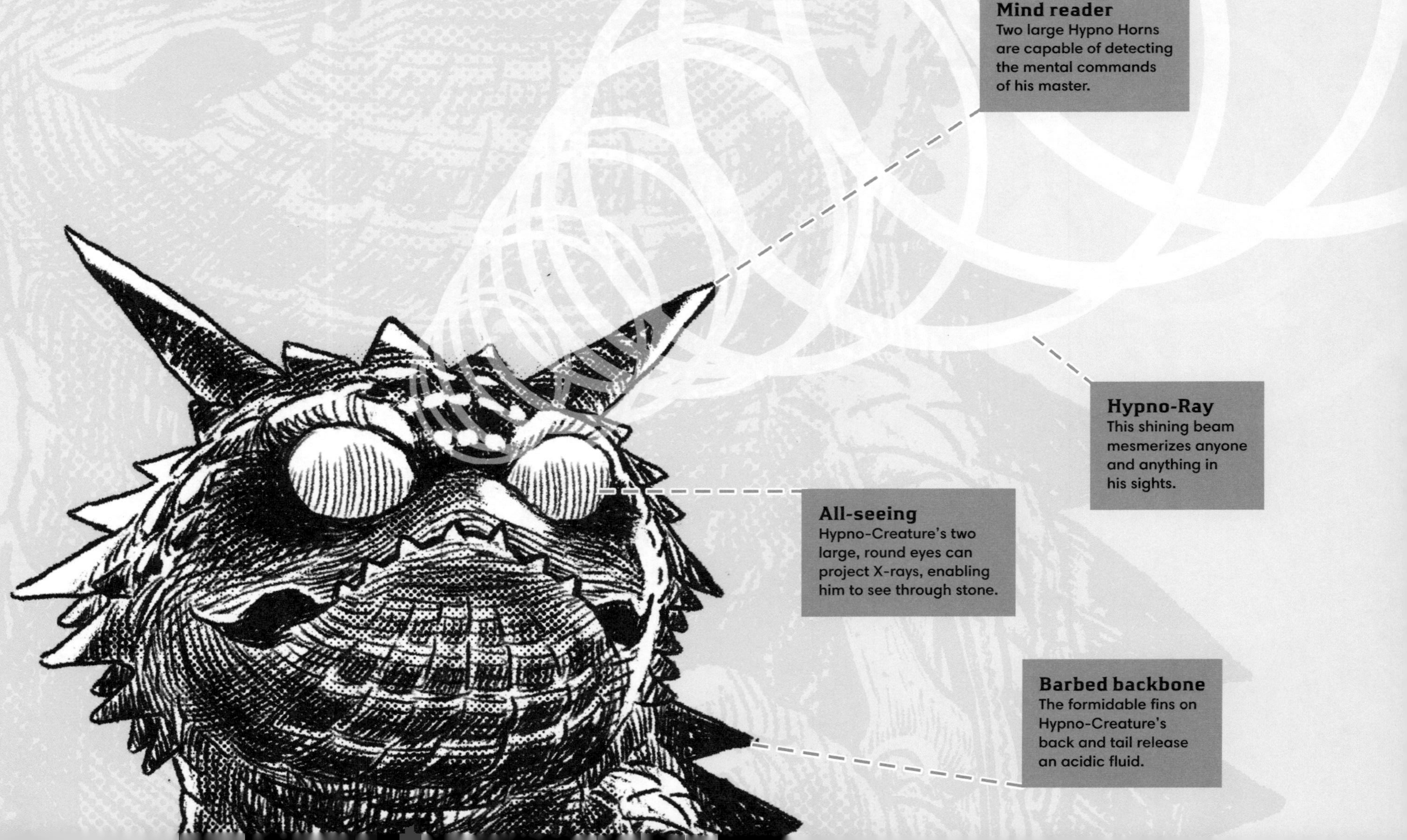

Mind reader
Two large Hypno Horns are capable of detecting the mental commands of his master.
Hypno-Ray
This shining beam mesmerizes anyone and anything in his sights.
All-seeing
Hypno-Creature's two large, round eyes can project X-rays, enabling him to see through stone.
Barbed backbone
The formidable fins on Hypno-Creature's back and tail release an acidic fluid.

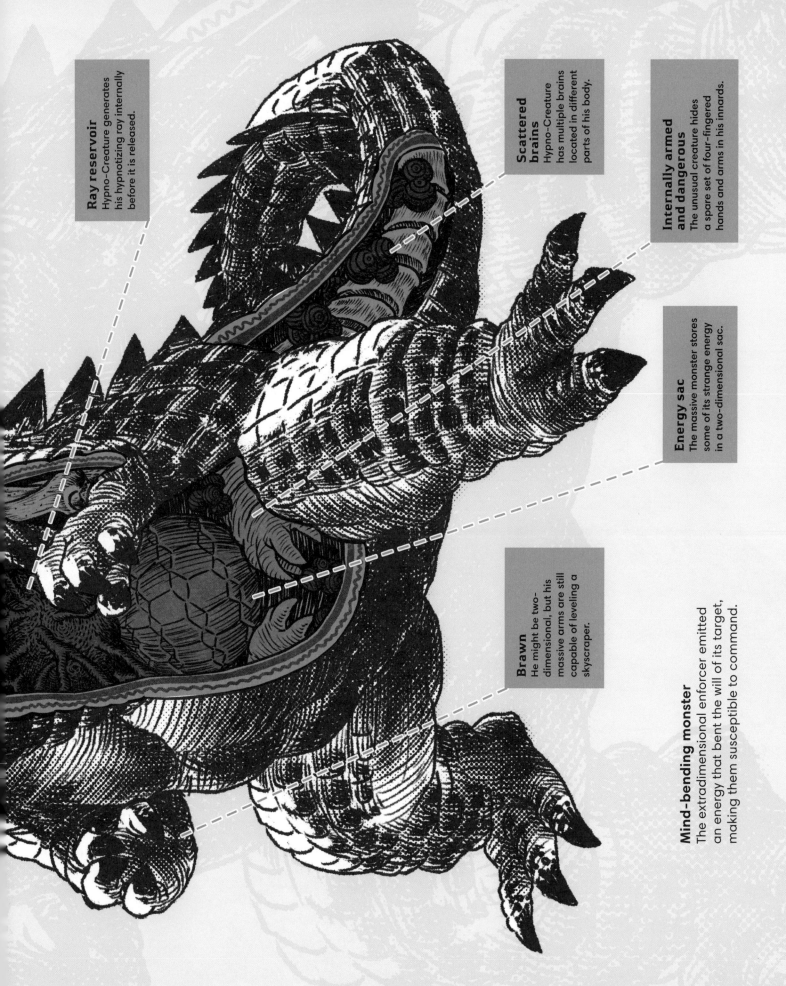

Ray reservoir
Hypno-Creature generates his hypnotizing ray internally before it is released.

Scattered brains
Hypno-Creature has multiple brains located in different parts of his body.

Internally armed and dangerous
The unusual creature hides a spare set of four-fingered hands and arms in his innards.

Energy sac
The massive monster stores some of its strange energy in a two-dimensional sac.

Brawn
He might be two-dimensional, but his massive arms are still capable of leveling a skyscraper.

Mind-bending monster
The extradimensional enforcer emitted an energy that bent the will of its target, making them susceptible to command.

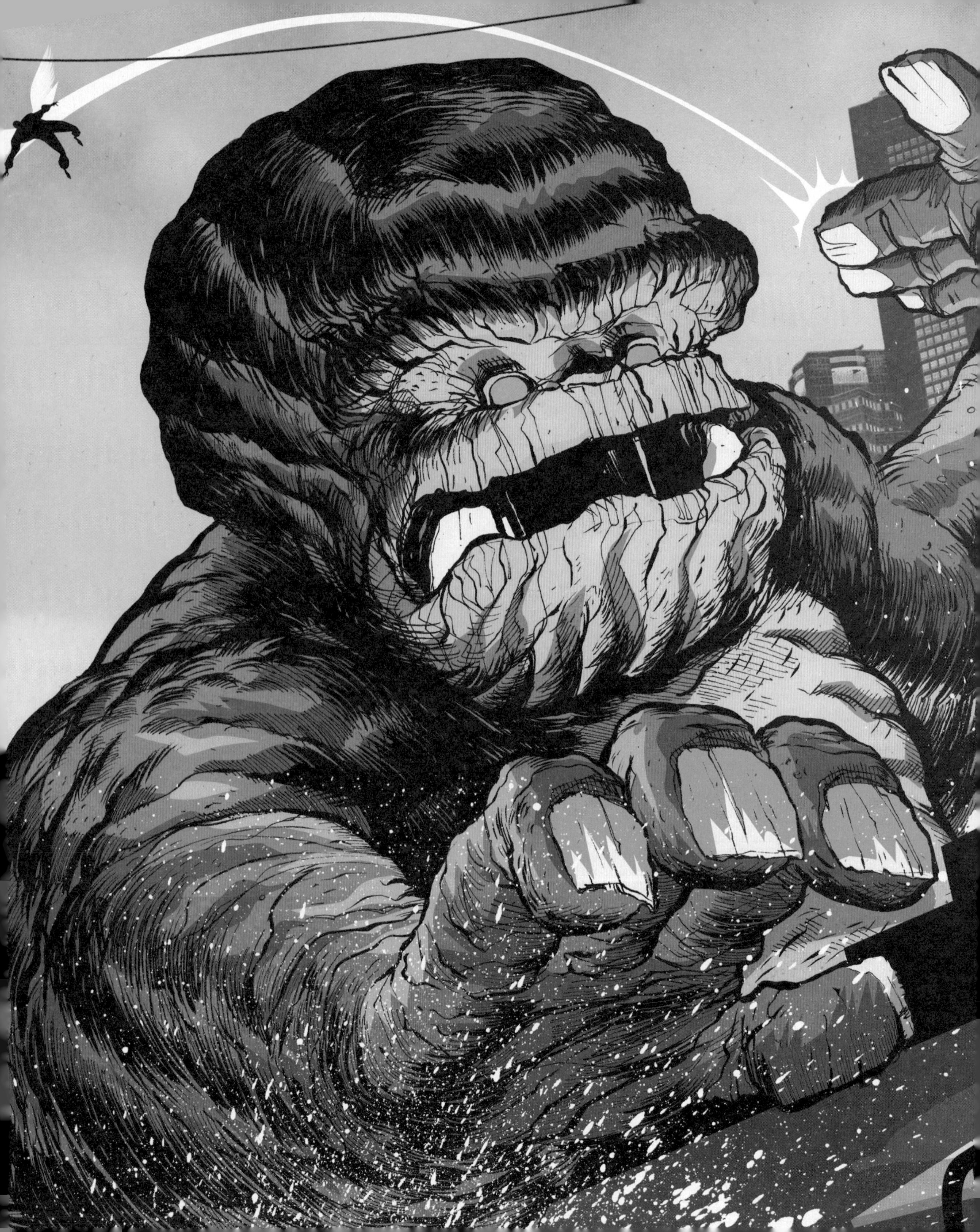

Height: 20ft (6m) Weight: Unknown Origin: Planet X Powers: Great size and strength; flight; telekinesis; advanced space faring and weapon tech

Goom

The Thing from Planet X also known as Goom desires nothing less than world domination. After following a signal to Earth, the enormous alien set about demonstrating his powers of telekinesis and force-field generation, while unveiling an arsenal of highly advanced technology.

The wily alien arrived on Earth after he intercepted a signal from human scientist Mark Langley as he searched for hidden planets in the solar system. Goom followed the signal back to Earth. When he landed, the extraterrestrial announced to Langley and a stunned crowd that he intended to claim the planet for his own and bring about a new order.

The enormous Goom has orange skin and an oversized, egg-shaped head with two blunt tusks protruding from his lower jaw. Two batlike wings grant him the ability to fly, and his two-toed feet can move at high speed. Goom can use powers of telekinesis powerful enough to lift an entire city and can also create an invisible force-field around himself to protect himself against any attacks.

As well as demonstrating his mental prowess, the alien showed off his highly advanced technology to Langley and the others as a warning against noncompliance. He wielded neutron rays capable of vaporizing an entire mountain into dust and presented his portable time machine that could regress its occupant back into an infant. The dismayed humans prepared to surrender to the gleeful Goom.

Langley, however, had a plan. He transmitted a new signal, this time to Planet X, alerting its inhabitants of Goom's unwelcome arrival. Soon after, a fleet of spaceships arrived to take Goom away. The aliens explained they were peace-loving and that Goom was an outlaw—banished from Planet X because of his violent tendencies. They promised that next time they met, it would be as friends.

Goom would return years later and was last seen answering the Inhuman Kei Kawade's summons to help defend planet Earth as one of the Goliathons.

First Appearance: *Tales of Suspense* #15 (1961) by Stan Lee, Larry Lieber, and Jack Kirby **Further Reading:** *Uncanny X-Men* #33 (2015)

Interstellar inmate
Goom is a fugitive and has often found himself imprisoned as a result of his actions—whether on Planet X, as part of the Collector's menagerie, or in a secret facility on Earth.

Googam, Son of Goom

A young alien named Googam finds himself abandoned on Earth. Having accompanied his father, Goom, on his mission to invade the planet, he was left behind when the would-be conqueror was escorted back to Planet X. Like his father, Goom makes plans to subdue humanity and rule the world.

Just a week after alien Goom departed Earth, Billy Langley—the son of scientist Mark Langley who had thwarted Goom's invasion—stumbled upon Googam, son of Goom, in a nearby cave. The abandoned alien forced the teen to take him to the Langleys' home so Googam could wait for his full powers to mature. Like his father, Googam took pleasure in demonstrating his abilities at telekinesis and force-field generation.

The young alien is stocky, but towers over humans, with red scales and a round, oversized head. Like Goom, his batlike wings allow him to fly, and he wields impressive mental abilities. He shares his father's arrogance and disdain for humans. This arrogance led to his downfall. Billy tricked Googam into a race on the side of a nearby mountain. The alien fell into quicksand and seemingly perished, thanks to the teen's quick thinking.

This wasn't the end for Googam, however. Reed Richards of the Fantastic Four shrunk the vengeful visitor from Planet X and offered him a chance at rehabilitation. Googam couldn't help trying to bring back his father, but inadvertently summoned despotic alien Tim Boo Ba instead.

Heroic ambitions
Surprisingly, Googam can't resist switching sides. He teams up with the Fin Fang Four and later Doctor Strange, although a small part of him still longs to conquer the world.

He helped defeat the menace, but then decided to go on his own path and attend college—even going to Mexico on Spring Break.

Later, like his father Goom, Googam answered the call of young Kei Kawade to defend the planet against an alien invasion. He called upon Doctor Strange, and together they managed to defeat a wayward Leviathon.

First Appearance: *Tales of Suspense* #17 (1961) by Stan Lee, Larry Lieber, and Jack Kirby
Further Reading: *Fin Fang 4* #1 (2005), *Doctor Strange* #1.1 (2017)

Height: 10ft (3m) **Weight:** Unknown **Origin:** Planet X **Powers:** Mind control; telekinesis; flight; ability to shrink objects

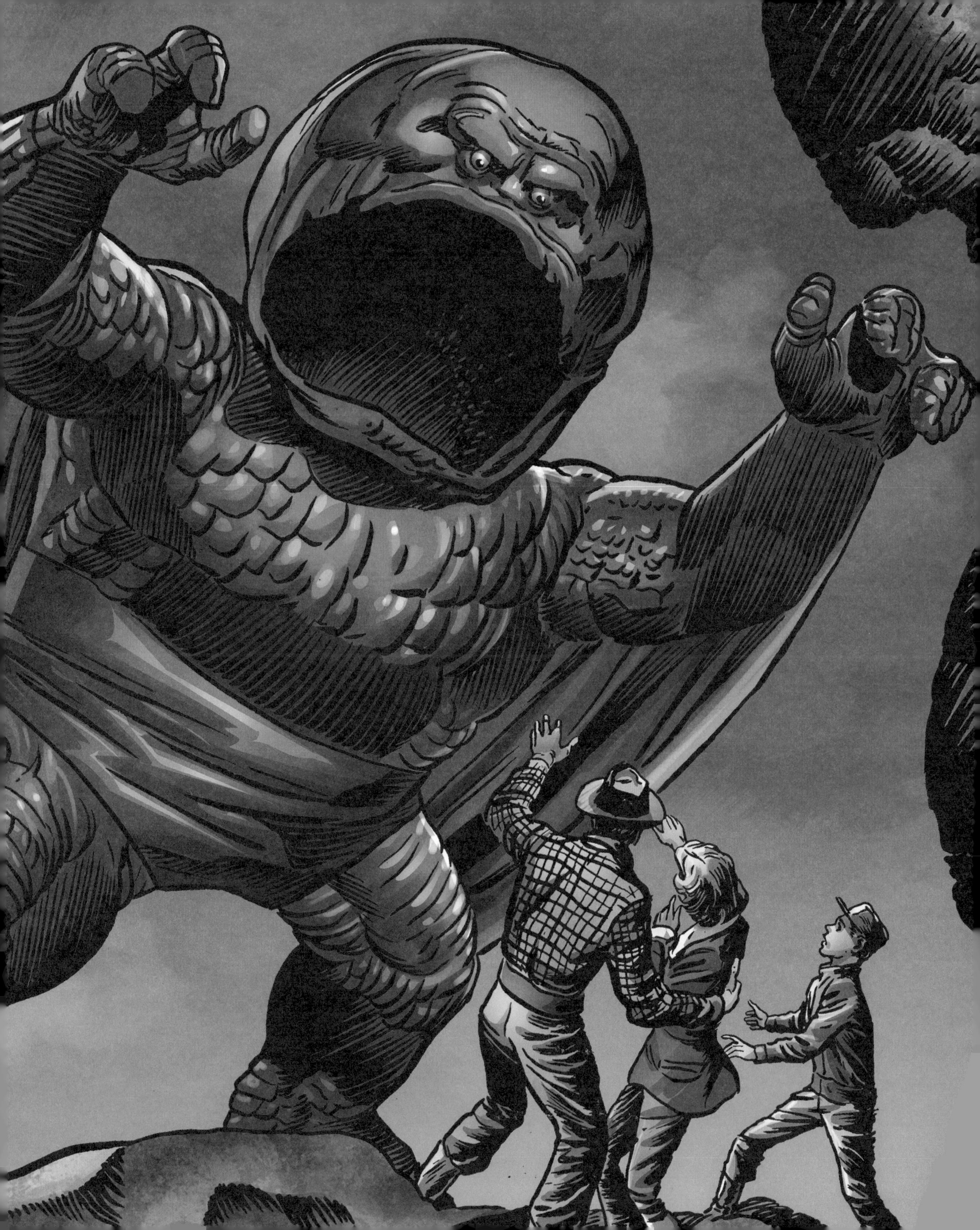

Groot

The towering, tree-like alien from Planet X who declares "I am Groot" is reported to be one of the last of his kind. This extraterrestrial has the power to grow and regenerate himself, as well as having control over other plant life. Wishing to do good in the universe, the intelligent individual joined unconventional heroes the Guardians of the Galaxy.

The arboreal alien is a member of the species *Flora colossi*. However, Groot wasn't aggressive like others of his race. He saved a human child captured by his unsympathetic brethren and was banished from his homeworld in retribution. Left to explore the galaxy on his own, he found a sense of wonder in all the life he discovered on his travels. He soon met his best friend, Rocket Raccoon, and together they became members of the Guardians of the Galaxy. Groot now fights to protect life in all its forms.

Another member of his species, also calling himself Groot, had landed on Earth many years before. He attempted to control the native plant life in order to take an entire town back to Planet X so he could heartlessly study and experiment on its residents. Neither brute force, bullets, nor even fire had an effect on the monstrous invader. A quick-thinking biologist unleashed termites on this Groot, and the aggressor was incapacitated before further damage was done.

While the Groot of Guardians of the Galaxy isn't invulnerable, his barklike hide is resistant to injury and able to withstand damage from most weapons and fire. He can regenerate his extremities, and is even capable of regrowing his entire body from a single splinter. His frame—in particular his vinelike appendages—is also very flexible and can change size and shape at will. Other plants respond to his commands, a power called chlorokinesis.

Famous for speaking only three words, after a clash with ancient cosmic being the Gardener, Groot's ability to speak and be understood by others has been restored.

First Appearance: *Tales to Astonish* #13 (1960) by Stan Lee, Larry Lieber, and Jack Kirby
Further Reading: *Groot* #1-6 (2015–2016), *Infinity Countdown* #1-2 (2018)

Inseparable
Wherever you find Groot, fellow Guardian of the Galaxy Rocket Raccoon isn't far behind. This unlikely pair defy all the odds.

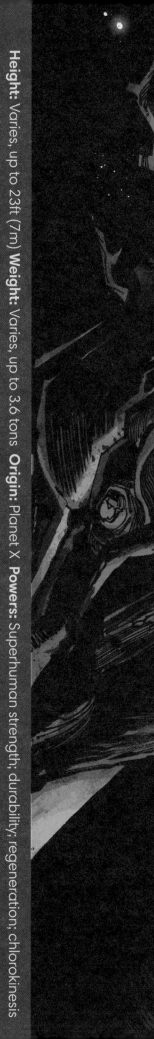

Height: Varies, up to 23ft (7m) **Weight:** Varies, up to 3.6 tons **Origin:** Planet X **Powers:** Superhuman strength; durability; regeneration; chlorokinesis

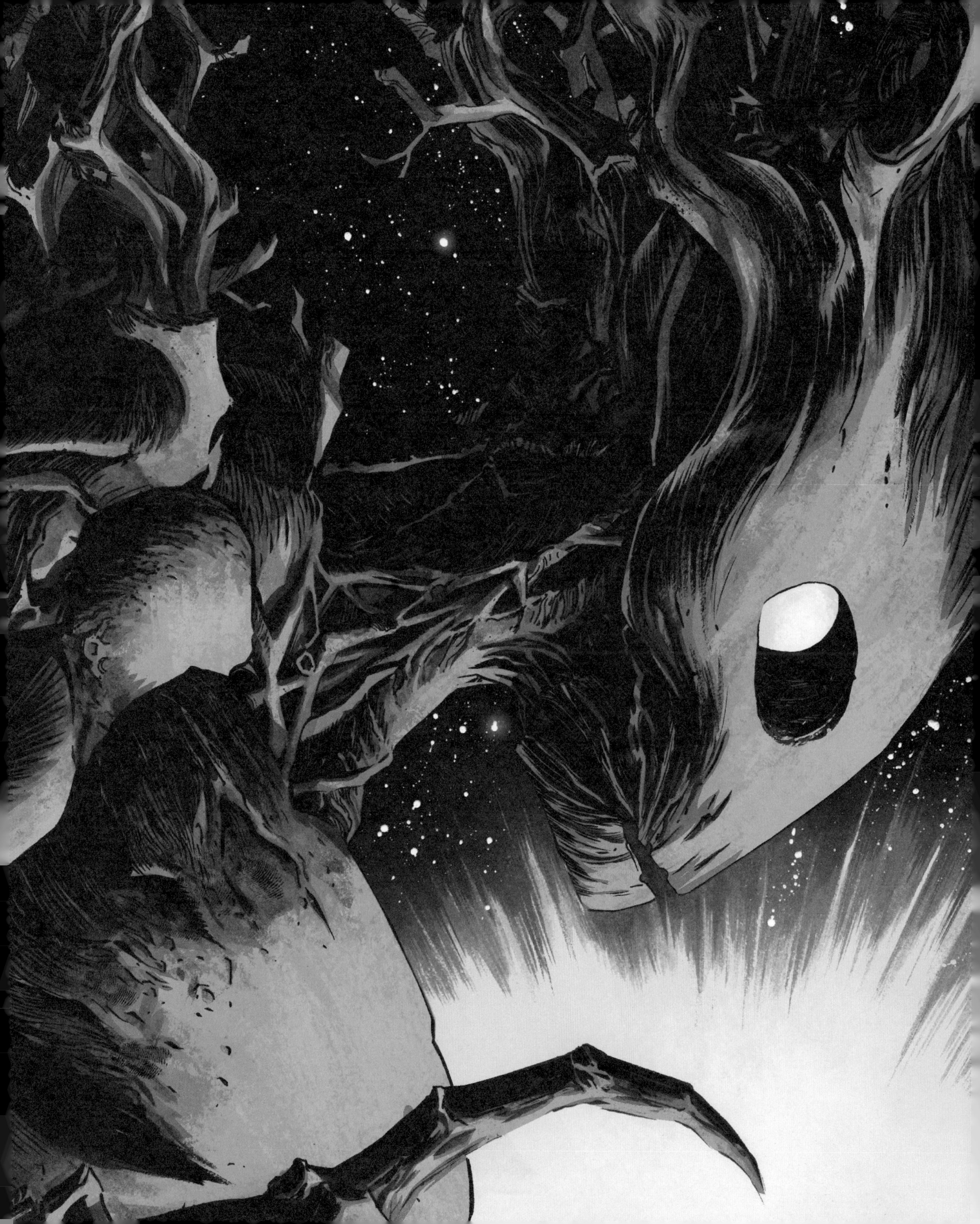

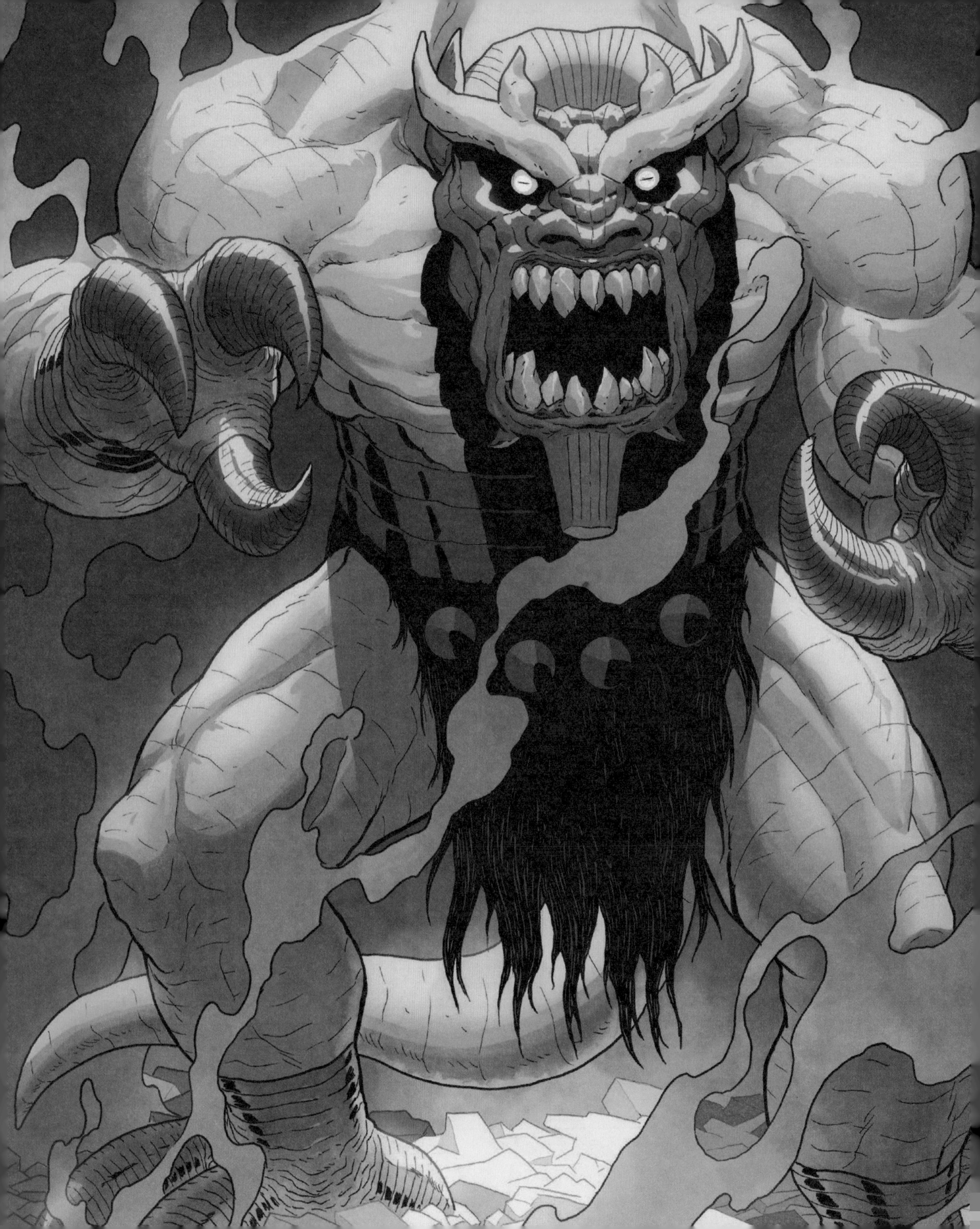

Height: 12–25ft (3.7–7.6m) **Weight:** 1.6–14 tons **Origin:** Unknown **Powers:** Immeasurable strength and invulnerability

Mangog

The monstrous Mangog is the last surviving member of a long gone extraterrestrial race that almost destroyed Asgard. After being freed from All-Father Odin's imprisonment, the bellowing brute vowed revenge for the destruction of his people. Let the universe tremble—Mangog lives again!

A foolish troll named Ulik accidentally released Mangog from his confinement in the hidden Cave of Ages, deep beneath Asgard. Odin, the father of Thunder God Thor, had entered the Odinsleep—leaving Asgard vulnerable—and the realm's forces gathered for the looming battle. As the last survivor of his kind, Mangog became a manifestation of the combined hate, rage, and strength of the billions who had died at Odin's command.

Mangog set his sights on bringing about Ragnarok—the end of the universe. Even the mighty Thor was daunted by Mangog's strength and seeming invulnerability. Neither the fury of nature, Asgardian weaponry, nor even Mjolnir, the Hammer of Thor, could stop him. In desperation, Thor summoned one final storm with his remaining strength, and it woke Odin from his slumber. Odin released the billions of spirits within the creature's body. Mangog faded away, and Asgard was safe once again.

But that wasn't the end for Mangog. He appeared time and time again, summoned by various foes of Thor and Odin, and was repeatedly driven back. He turned his unquenchable rage on the gods one last time, this time battling the Mighty Thor Jane Foster. To finally stop the unstoppable, Mighty Thor threw Mangog into the sun, saving what remained of Asgard at the cost of her own life.

Mangog uses his indestructible claws, teeth, and prehensile tail to cause unimaginable destruction. Drawing on the hatred felt by those who perished at the hand of Odin, Mangog is stronger than Thor; he is capable of taking out an entire legion of Asgardian warriors with a single punch. Not even a direct hit from the mystical hammer Mjolnir can crack his invulnerable hide. The orange-hued monster can sense Asgardian gods as he hunts them in his unending quest for revenge.

First Appearance: *Thor* #154 (1968) by Stan Lee and Jack Kirby **Further Reading:** *Mighty Thor* #701–705 (2018)

Fearlessness matched
Mangog battled many Thors and declared he was without fear—until he met Jane Foster's Thor. She, knowing she was dying, made the ultimate sacrifice to save Asgard and destroy Mangog.

Mangog Anatomy

Mangog is nothing more than an extraterrestrial being built for utter annihilation. Venting the wrath of a billion people, he is capable only of destruction, and his anatomy reflects this: massive muscles, limbs dominated by rending claws, and a tail that doubles as a weapon.

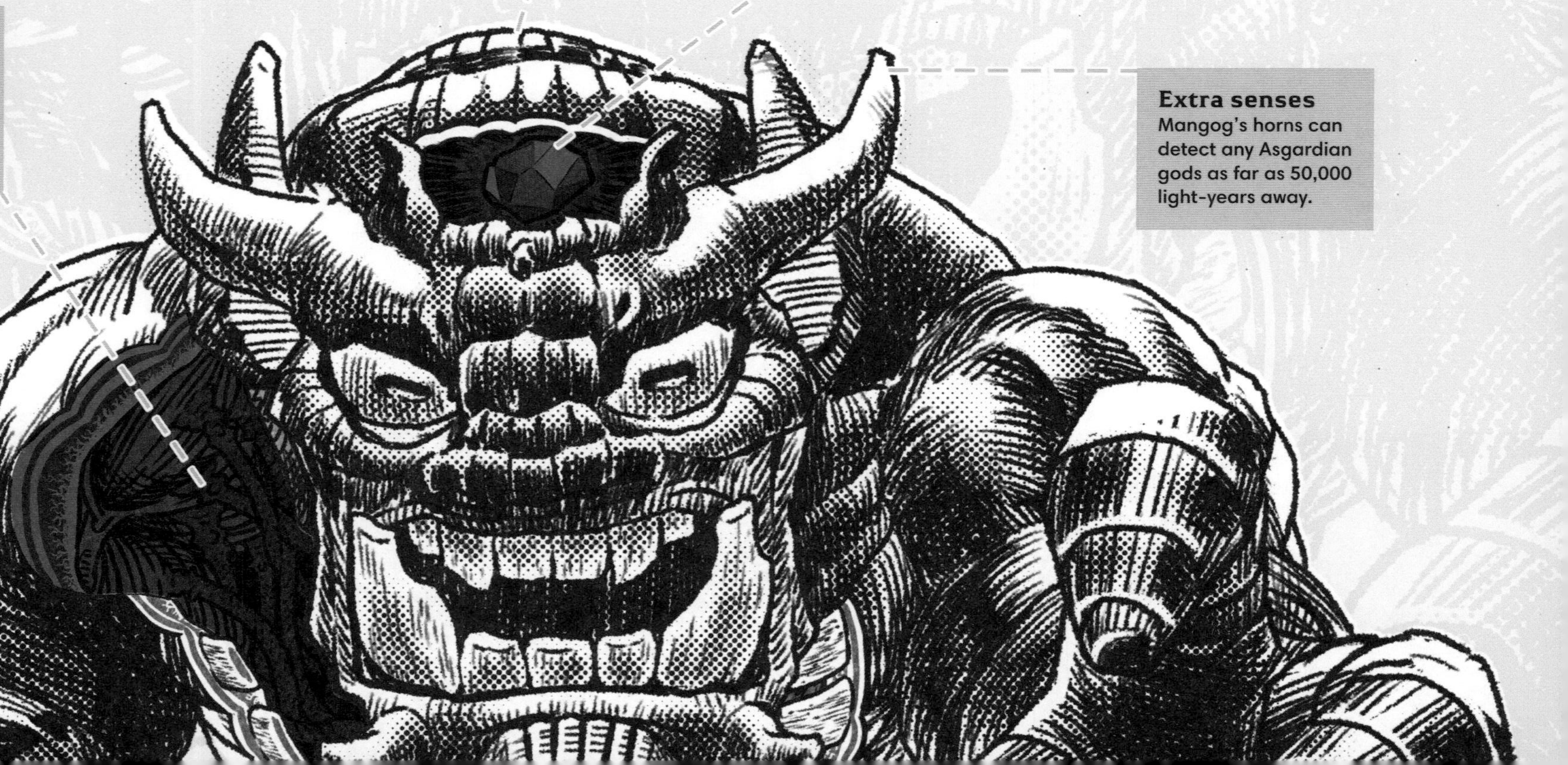

Revenge-driven
Mangog is a unique creature given life and power by the collective hatred of a long-dead alien race.
One-track mind
The alien beast thinks only of revenge. There's no mercy, friendship, or love in his emotions.
Fury-fueled
Mangog's power is limitless and pumped through every inch of his body.
Extra senses
Mangog's horns can detect any Asgardian gods as far as 50,000 light-years away.

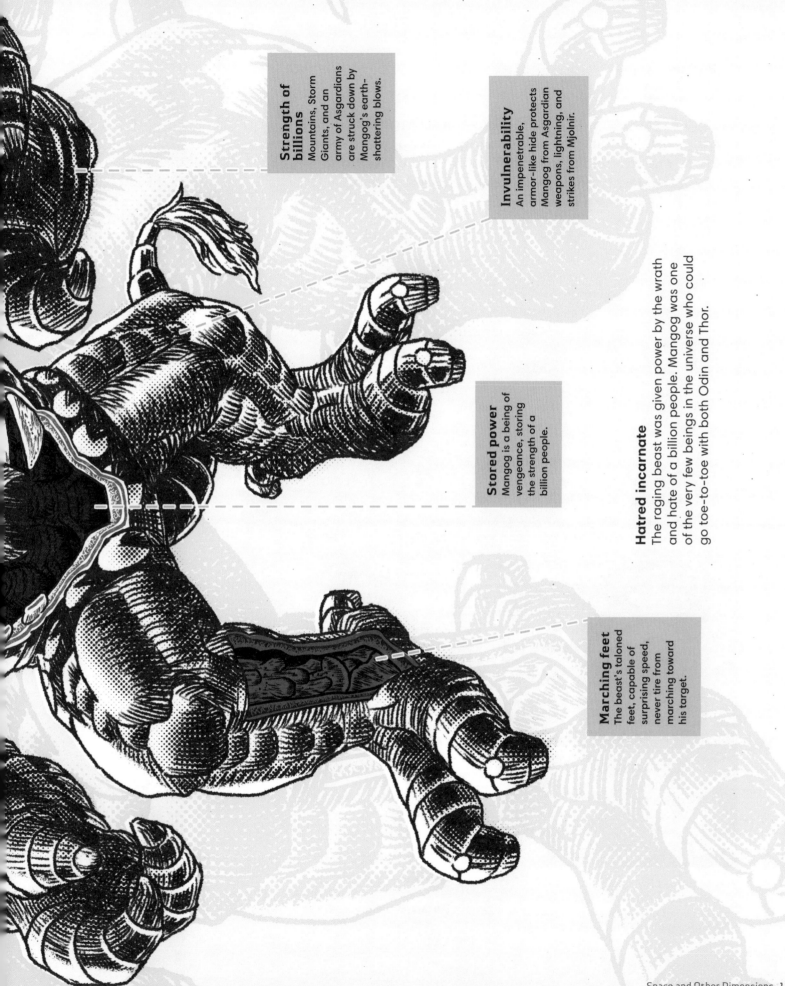

Strength of billions
Mountains, Storm Giants, and an army of Asgardians are struck down by Mangog's earth-shattering blows.

Invulnerability
An impenetrable, armor-like hide protects Mangog from Asgardian weapons, lightning, and strikes from Mjolnir.

Stored power
Mangog is a being of vengeance, storing the strength of a billion people.

Hatred incarnate
The raging beast was given power by the wrath and hate of a billion people. Mangog was one of the very few beings in the universe who could go toe-to-toe with both Odin and Thor.

Marching feet
The beast's taloned feet, capable of surprising speed, never tire from marching toward his target.

Orrgo

This giant, extra-powerful extraterrestrial is Orrgo the Unconquerable—an alien with glowing, searing, pie-plate-like eyes who traveled through the galaxy and arrived on Earth. With a terrifying display of mind-control powers, he set about claiming the planet and its people for his own.

One fateful day, Orrgo and others of the Mentelleronite race observed Earth from their distant planet, and the ambitious alien decided that it should be his to command. He transported himself across space to Earth simply by thinking about it. Once there, he demonstrated a vast array of powers, including telekinesis, mind control, and the ability to animate trees. Orrgo commandeered the mind of every human, and then, weary from his exertions, settled down for a nap. As he slept, a gorilla from a nearby circus—aggrieved that his now-hypnotized keeper was no longer feeding him—crept close, and defeated the would-be conqueror with one blow.

Some time later, Orrgo was brought back through the power of a mystical stone idol and faced off against Super Hero team the Defenders. His quest for world domination was once again unsuccessful. Yet another attempt failed, this time at the clobbering hands of the Thing. Eventually, Orrgo was recruited to the Howling Commandos of S.H.I.E.L.D., led by Dum Dum Dugan, although he worked in the background instead of on the front line. A more mellow Orrgo provided intel on paranormal threats from the team's HQ in Area 13, New Jersey, and viewed the team as his own family.

Orrgo's mental powers are vast. Capable of turning jets into birds, telekinetically lifting New York City in its entirety into space, and hypnotizing every person on the planet, Orrgo seems to manipulate reality itself. The orange-skinned Mentelleronite does not appear to have any vulnerabilities—although he requires rest after his world-conquering efforts, leaving him vulnerable to attack.

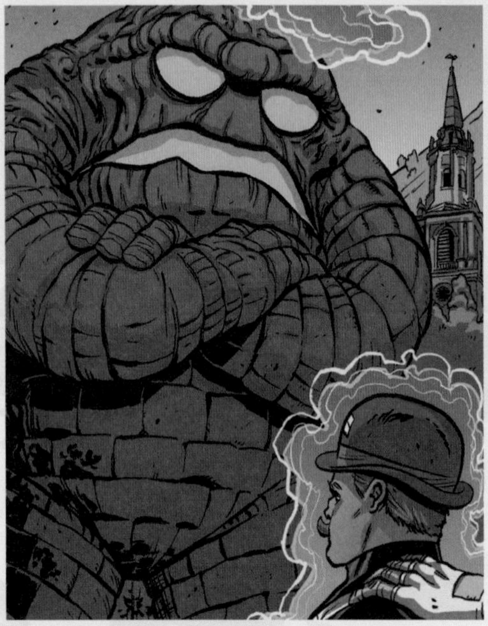

Always behind the team
Orrgo signed up to Dum Dum Dugan's incarnation of the Howling Commandos, providing intelligence on paranormal threats.

First Appearance: *Strange Tales* #90 (1961) by Stan Lee and Jack Kirby **Further Reading:** *Defenders* #9-10 (2001), *Howling Commandos of S.H.I.E.L.D.* #6 (2016)

Height: Varies up to 25ft (7.6m) **Weight:** 2.3 tons **Origin:** Space **Powers:** Superhuman strength and durability; mental control over reality

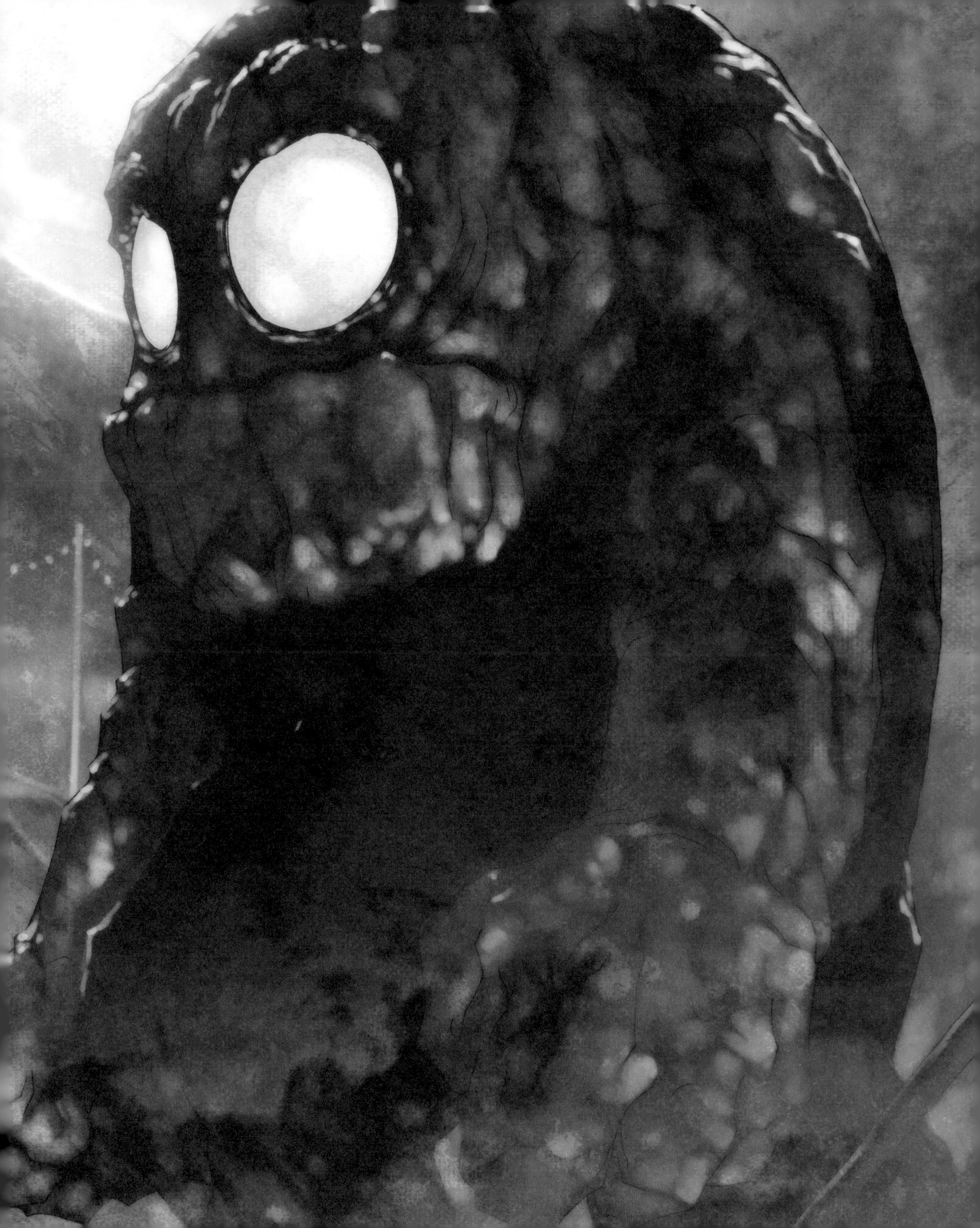

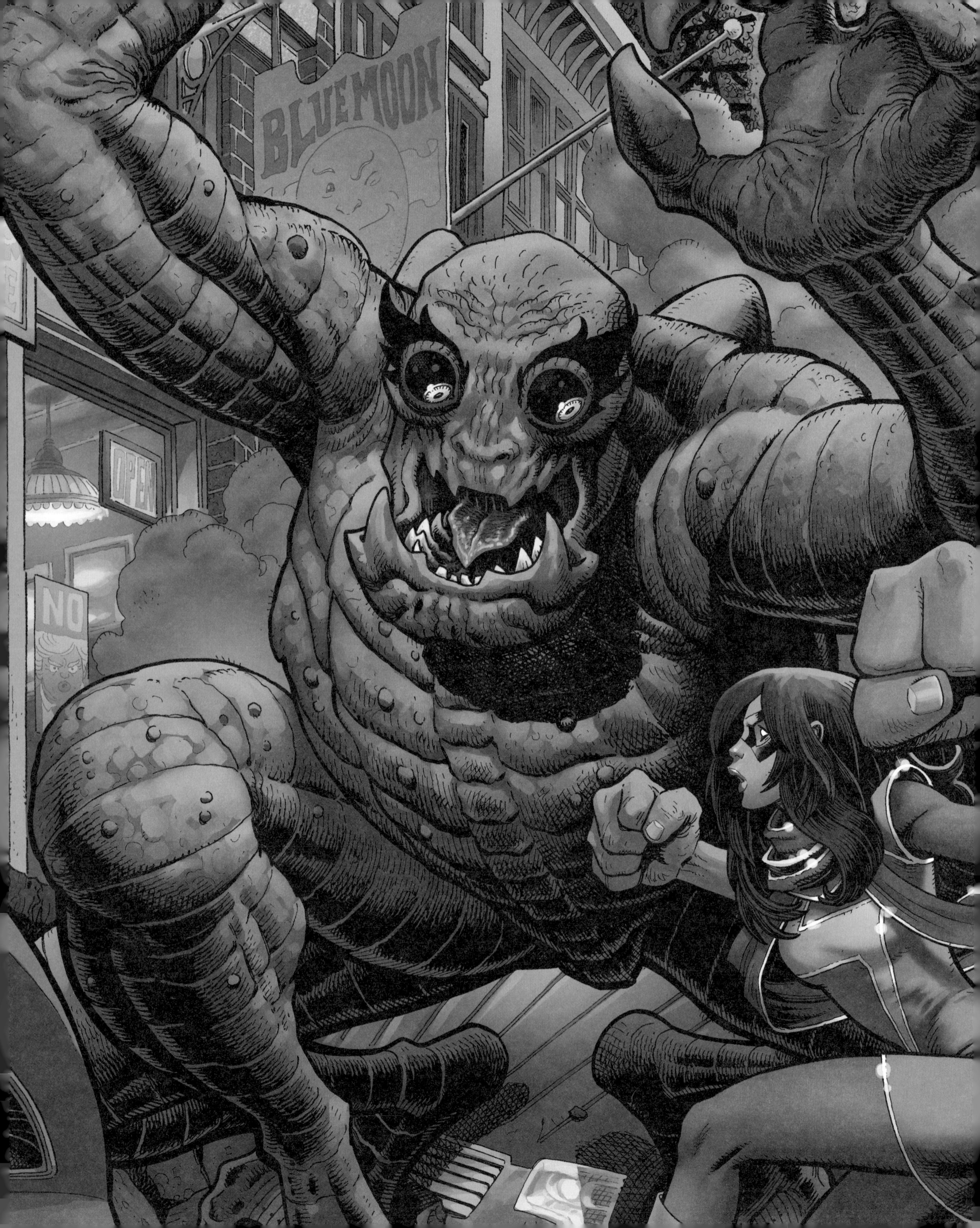
BLUE MOON
OPEN
NO

Height: 15ft 5in (4.7m) Weight: 2,000 lbs (907kg) Origin: Space Powers: Project webs strong enough for space travel

Rorgg

Traveling through the cosmos on their electrically charged webbing, swarms of giant spiderlike creatures put planet Earth firmly in their sights. They are led by Rorgg, King of the Spider Men, whose plan is to ensnare the planet in his net and subjugate humanity.

In a small town in New Mexico, residents noticed mysterious threads starting to appear, dangling from the sky. Eventually, once the entire town was shrouded in spiderwebs, giant arachnid-like Spider Men appeared. Stating that they had come from far across the galaxy, their leader Rorgg declared his race's superiority and their intent to invade Earth.

Rorgg and the Spider Men are enormous beings with six limbs each. They are able to crawl on their hands and feet with uncanny speed across their webs. They can cast the webs at speeds faster than light, enabling them to cross the vastness of outer space without the need for vessels or technology. The webs themselves are virtually indestructible: resistant to bullets, snapping, and cutting; they are also electrically charged.

The multi-legged invaders had chosen the quiet town as a test of people's resistance. Once the alarmed inhabitants realized weapons could not destroy the webs, they tried to communicate with people outside the town, but found the airwaves blocked by the webbing. Eventually, it took a quick-thinking teenager to halt the monsters' mission. Running to a local hardware store, he gathered all the insecticide he could find, and sprayed it directly at Rorgg. Unable to breathe, the King of the Spider Men appeared to perish on the spot. In a panic, Rorgg's invading forces withdrew back into space.

Some time later, the body of Rorgg—among other deceased monsters—was put on display at the Museum of the Monsters and the Strange in New York City. He was magically brought to life to battle the Fantastic Four, but was soon defeated. The last known sighting of Rorgg was on Monster Isle.

First Appearance: *Journey Into Mystery* #64 (1961) by Stan Lee, Larry Lieber, and Jack Kirby

Webbed trap
The terrified residents of a small town were completely trapped in the indestructible web of the Spider Men.

Chitauri

The Chitauri strike from the dark void of space. Swarms of these simple-minded invaders are almost insectlike in their behavior. Their sheer numbers can threaten to overwhelm Earth's defenses. Some have the ability to shape-shift into human form, making it difficult to discern friend from foe.

During a time when Captain America served global terrorist organization Hydra, the Chitauri attacked Earth in search of their queen. The alien fleet was lured to the planet as part of Hydra's plan to destabilize governments and trap several Super Heroes outside Earth's atmosphere. Captain Marvel destroyed the hidden cache of queen eggs the Chitauri had been searching for, and the horde immediately disbanded and left Earth's vicinity.

These arthropod aliens are able to survive and fight in space and are proficient in hand-to-hand combat and in the use of advanced weaponry. Their technologically advanced ships are capable of traveling faster than the speed of light. The Chitauri's forces include horrific serpent-like leviathans capable of inflicting massive damage.

In the alternate reality of Earth-1610, the Chitauri have spent decades trying to conquer Earth. One notable invasion was during World War II, when the shape-shifting humanoids infiltrated Nazi military personnel in an attempt to bring about global order and destroy free will. They were defeated by that reality's Captain America. They re-emerged in the 21st century, this time adopting a more subtle approach to world domination.

In their natural form, these Chitauri resemble green-and-purple-skinned humanoid reptiles. They have sharp talons, glowing eyes, and they stand at around eight feet tall. The aliens have the ability to shape-shift and often take on a human appearance to deceive Earth-dwellers

According to reports, they lose control of this chameleonic hold after 98 minutes. As part of their operations they added a mood-suppressant chemical—gammabutyrolactone—to the water supply over a number of years, affecting millions; and infiltrated the Psi division of intelligence agency S.H.I.E.L.D. Fortunately, their ruse was detected and brought to an end by Super Hero team the Ultimates.

First Appearance: *Ultimates* #8 (2002) by Mark Millar, Bryan Hitch, and Andrew Currie
Further Reading: *Secret Empire* #0 (2017)

Space invaders
It takes Earth's mightiest heroes, including Captain Marvel, to hold back the horde of Chitauri warriors and keep planet Earth safe.

Height: 8ft (2.4m) **Weight:** Unknown **Origin:** Space **Powers:** Advanced space travel and weapon technology; shape-shifting abilities

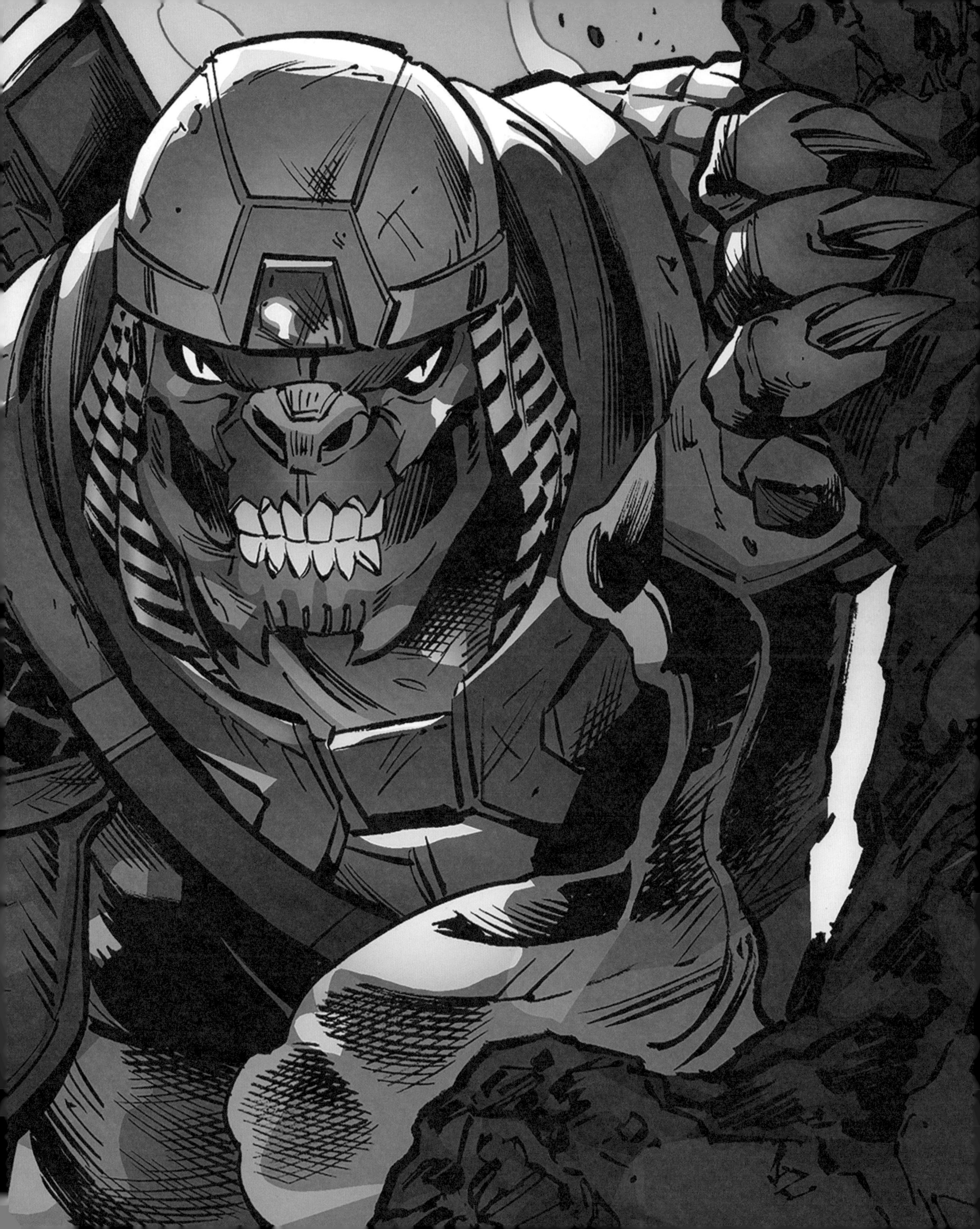

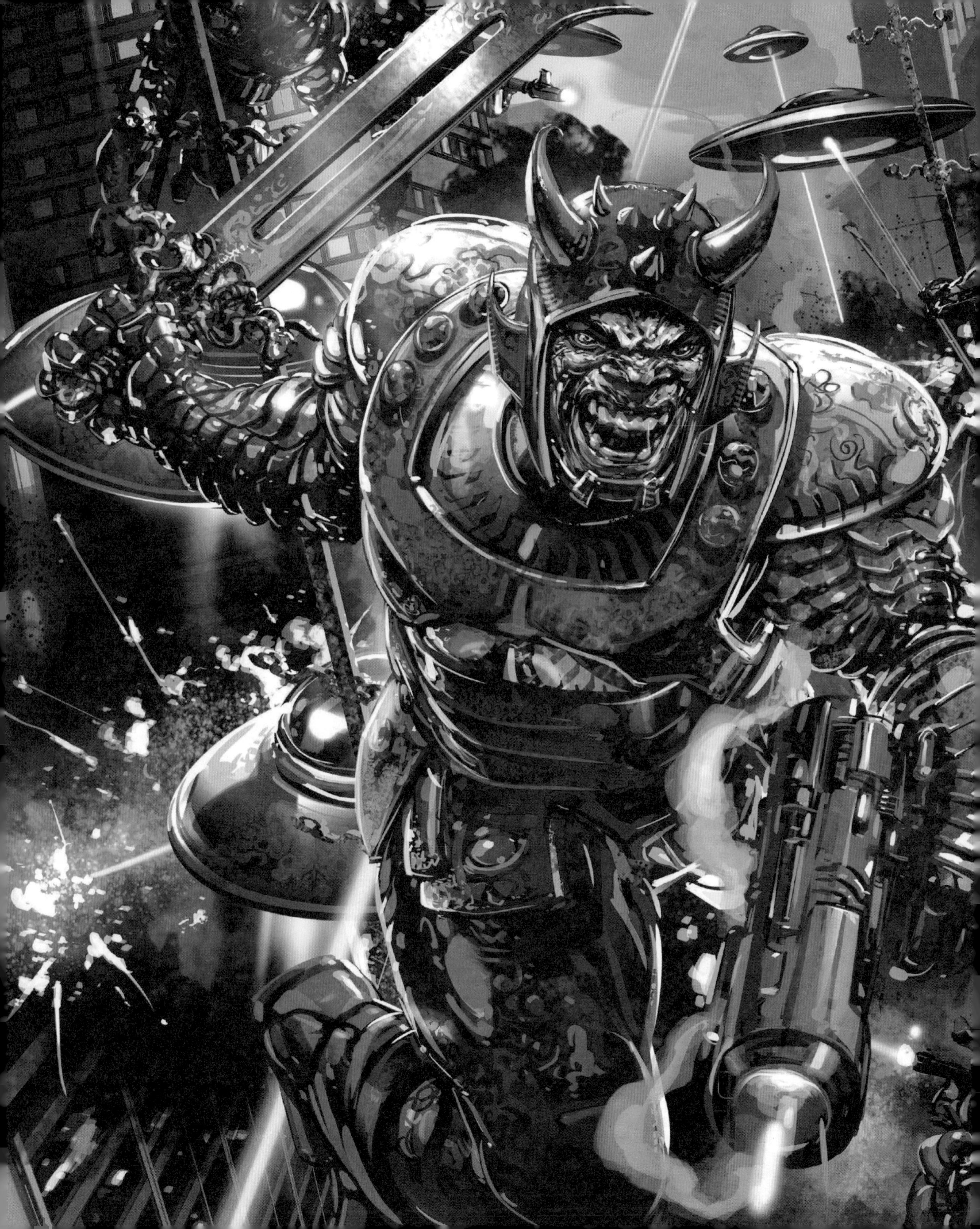

Height: 9ft (2.7m) Weight: 286.6 lbs (130kg) Origin: Space Powers: Advanced spacefaring technology and metal-disintegrating weaponry

Space Beast

Fresh from conquering other civilizations, these cosmic marauders have humanity in their crosshairs as their fleet of flying saucers makes its way toward planet Earth. Heavily armored and toting metal-disintegrating ray guns, these Space Beasts—led by Luther Gorr—are full of bravado.

The Space Beasts' alien armada was so massive that it blocked out the sun. Panicked people could do nothing but stare at the legions of flying saucers and wait to see what would happen next. As the spaceships hovered over Earth, long rope ladders were deployed and the Space Beasts descended upon the horrified humans. Having already destroyed other planets, the Space Beasts declared their intention: complete conquest. They attacked aircraft, airports, factories, and landmarks, with ray guns that disintegrated their targets. In the cities, they destroyed bridges and cut off all means of escape. The people were trapped.

Leader Luther Gorr declared that the invaders were the undisputed masters of humanity. As the people in the cities were forced into backbreaking labor for the Space Beasts, one farmer in the Midwest refused to give up his land to the invaders. One of the alien attackers fired his ray gun directly at the resistant farmer—but only his belt buckle and shirt buttons were destroyed! Realizing that their weapons only affected metal, and not human flesh, the farmer turned his own gun on the Space Beasts. Believing themselves to be vulnerable to bullets, the beastly aliens fled.

Word of the farmer's discovery spread around the world and soon the Space Beasts were retreating to their ships and returning to space. Earth was safe once more.

Towering over Earth's inhabitants, the armored Space Beasts are an imposing sight. Many of them wear helmets adorned with feathers, horns, or spikes to give them an intimidating edge. Space Beasts have broad, stocky bodies—but they are not particularly strong or robust. Bullets can penetrate their armor and their temperaments are cowardly.

First Appearance: *Tales to Astonish #29* (1962) by Stan Lee, Larry Lieber, and Jack Kirby

Intimidating infantry
The invading Space Beasts descend on each world with one single-minded goal: to conquer every planet and galaxy.

Space Beast Anatomy

Larger than humans and brandishing advanced weaponry with great swagger, the Space Beasts certainly look formidable. The invaders are also heavily armored and wear decorated helmets, but their strong outer appearance perhaps overcompensates for their cowardly nature.

Lung capacity
Specially adapted lungs mean Space Beasts can breathe on other planets, including Earth.

Hard-headed
Their armored helmets, often decorated with horns, are stronger than steel.

Intelligent intruders
Creators of advanced technology, Space Beasts are cunning and concentrate on conquering other planets.

Ray gun
The laser beam emitted from this weapon disintegrates any metal structure, whatever its size.

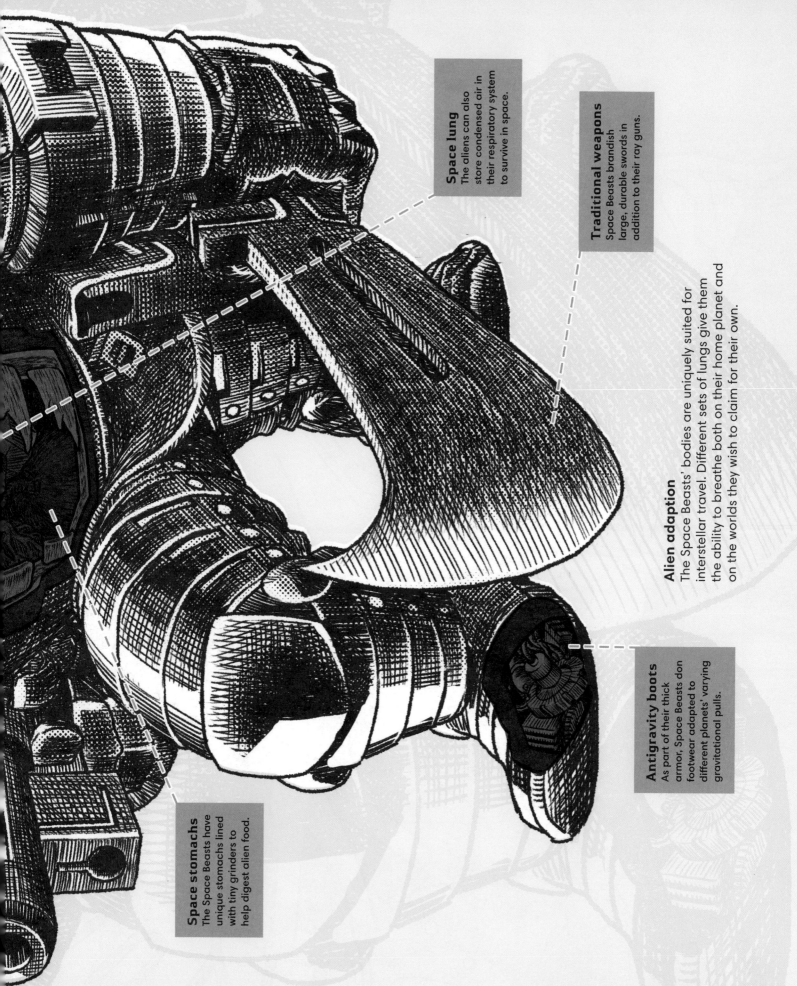

Space lung
The aliens can also store condensed air in their respiratory system to survive in space.

Traditional weapons
Space Beasts brandish large, durable swords in addition to their ray guns.

Alien adaption
The Space Beasts' bodies are uniquely suited for interstellar travel. Different sets of lungs give them the ability to breathe both on their home planet and on the worlds they wish to claim for their own.

Antigravity boots
As part of their thick armor, Space Beasts don footwear adapted to different planets' varying gravitational pulls.

Space stomachs
The Space Beasts have unique stomachs lined with tiny grinders to help digest alien food.

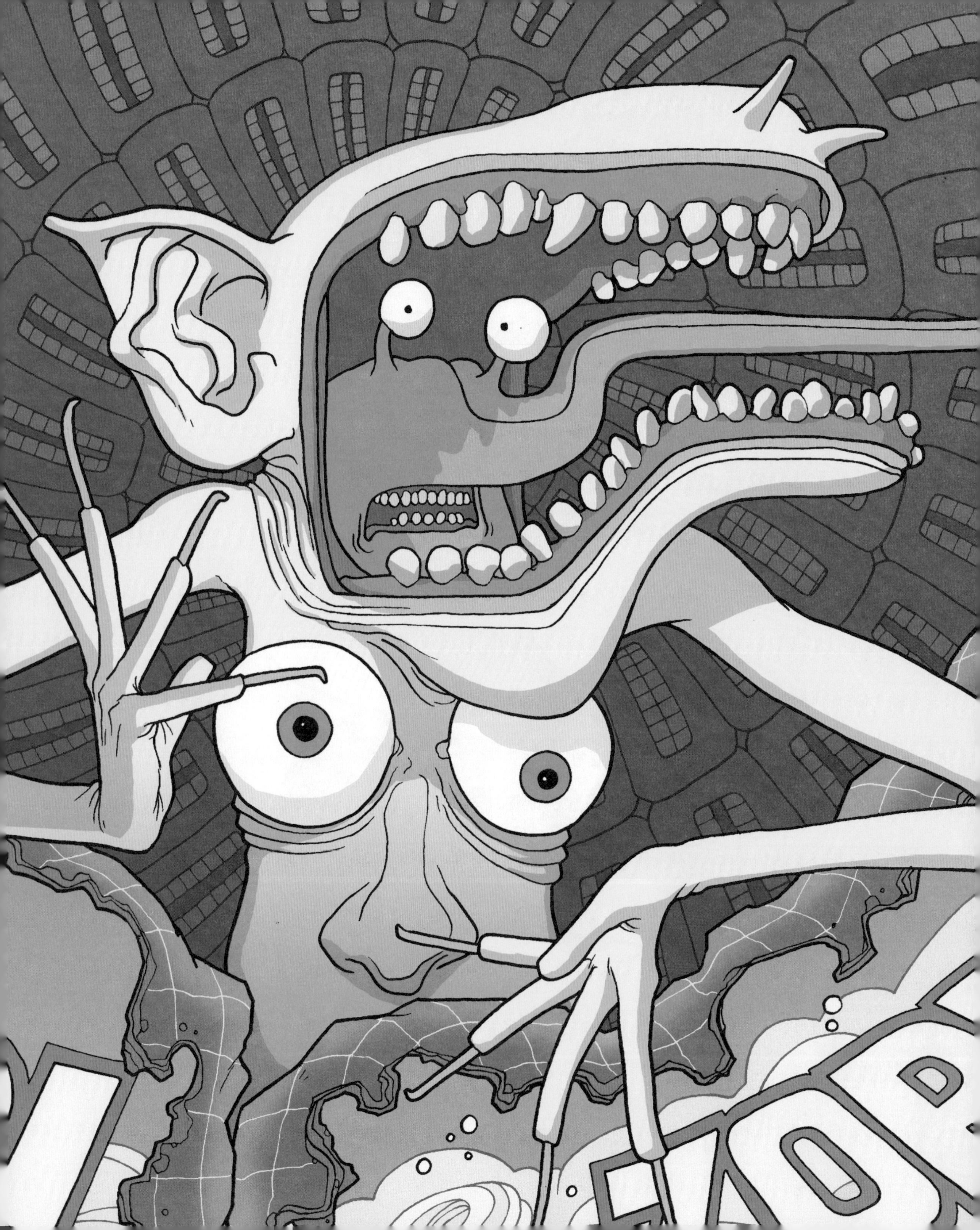

Height: 3 miles (4.8km) Weight: 1,800,000,000 tons Origin: Space Powers: Ability to exist in space; can tear through realities

Apocalypse Beast

The Apocalypse Beast arrived dramatically from space—tearing into Earth's dimension. This alien dwarfs mountains and fills other monsters with fear. With its two faces, eyes on its elbows and knees, and impossibly long legs, the grotesque creature made straight for Monster Isle and a final showdown.

A creature that baffles the senses, the Apocalypse Beast has fingernails as large as skyscrapers, multiple staring eyeballs, gaping mouths, and faces within faces. The full extent of its abilities is unknown, but it can survive in space and traverse dimensions. Having arrived on Earth millions of years ago, the Apocalypse Beast was then banished by an advanced species—the subterranean Deviants—that preceded humanity.

During a trip to Japan, the Fantastic Four and Iron Man found themselves in the middle of a massive monster rampage. One of the creatures, Grogg, told Mr. Fantastic (Reed Richards) that they were fleeing a monstrous predator that was scratching at the walls of this dimension. Richards promised to stop this "walking apocalypse," and the monsters retreated. Their investigation took them to the North Pole. It was there, in one of the strangest events humans had ever witnessed, that the Apocalypse Beast appeared through a tear in time and space.

The Apocalypse Beast began to march toward Monster Isle and, despite their combined might, the Fantastic Four and Iron Man were powerless to stop it. It was soon discovered that Monster Isle had been created by the Deviant race as a lure—a trap to stop the Beast if it ever returned to Earth. The Isle's unusual residents, the Moloids, had been engineered by the Deviants as part of that plan.

Once the Beast arrived at the island, countless Moloids attacked alongside the Fantastic Four and Iron Man. The Moloids entered the giant foe like a virus and destroyed it from within, making it turn inside out, and sending it back into space.

First Appearance: *Fantastic Four/ Iron Man: Big in Japan #3 (2006)* by Zeb Wells and Seth Fisher

Aptly named
Capable of tearing reality itself, Apocalypse Beast could very well bring about Armageddon.

Gomdulla

Wrapped in ancient bandages, a massive Egyptian mummy crashes through the confines of a museum wall and out into the night. It is Gomdulla, the Living Pharaoh, and after centuries standing dormant, the mechanical being has awakened once again, ready to terrorize humanity.

This gigantic, centuries-old mummy stood silently in an Egyptian museum for many years. One day, two children scampering around Gomdulla's feet inadvertently touched a switch hidden beneath its bandages. That night, the mummy rose again, smashing its way through a thick stone wall and disappearing into the darkness.

Wrapped in dusty bandages from head to toe, Gomdulla, at first glance, resembles a typical mummy. Yet its towering, otherworldly height sets it apart. This size grants it incredible strength. It can levitate itself and other objects, and remains impervious to attack. Its only known weakness is the secret switch on his foot that activates and deactivates him.

Some weeks after Gomdulla's disappearance, an Interpol detective investigating reports of a new cult stumbled upon the immense mummy and his worshippers inside an ancient pyramid. The detective immediately took action, firing his gun. The bullets had no effect on Gomdulla. The animated mummy chased the detective, using telekinesis to hurl rocks at the man. Cornering him, Gomdulla levitated, ready to deliver the final blow. Fortunately, the leader of the cult appeared and pressed the switch in its foot—immobilizing the monstrous mummy.

The leader explained that Gomdulla was actually a malevolent robot from another planet who had menaced its ancestors centuries before. Following an accident that rendered the alien creation inert, Gomdulla had been buried, then dug up by Earth's archeologists and placed on display in a museum—until it was reactivated.

There have been further sightings of Gomdulla. The Fantastic Four bested it as it tried to scale a tower block and, more recently, the Inhuman Kei Kawade summoned it in an attempt to battle a group of aliens called the Poisons.

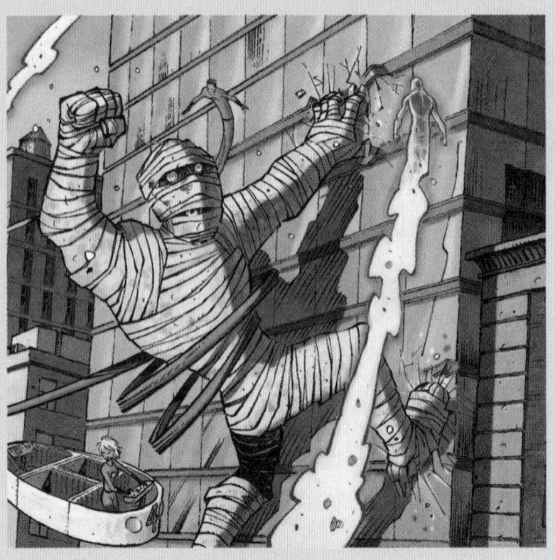

From tomb to tower
Gomdulla is surprisingly athletic and limber for an ancient alien mummy.

First Appearance: *Journey into Mystery* #61 (1960) by Stan Lee, Larry Lieber, and Jack Kirby

Height: Up to 60ft (18m) **Weight:** Unknown **Origin:** Space **Powers:** Superhuman strength and durability; levitation; telekinesis

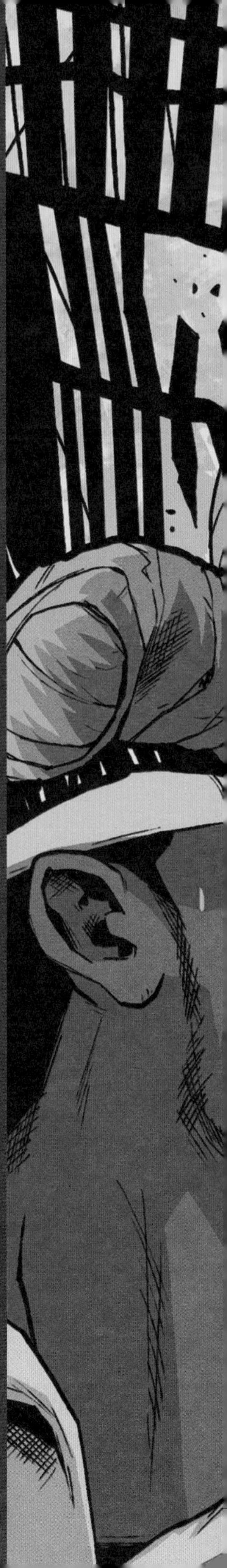

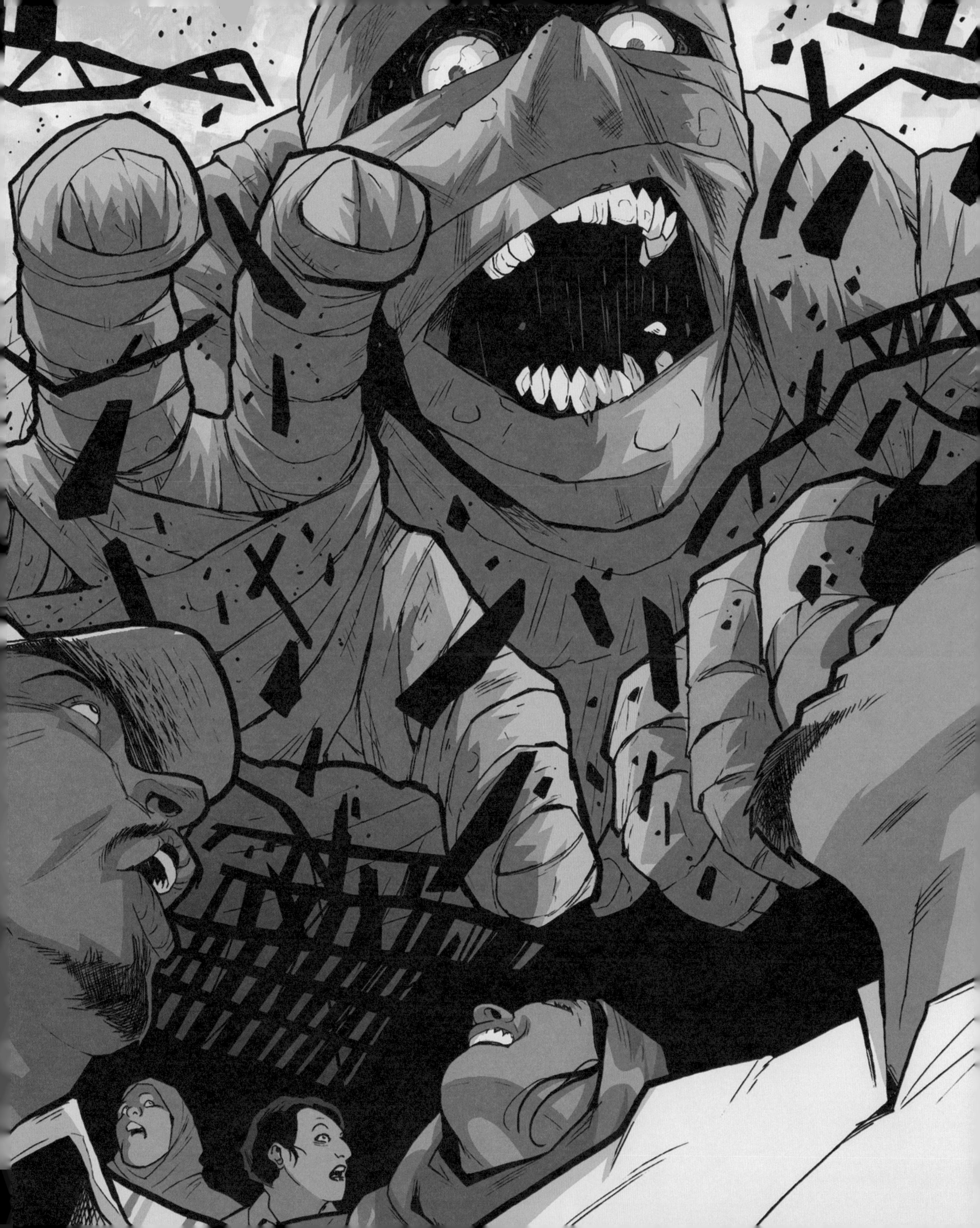

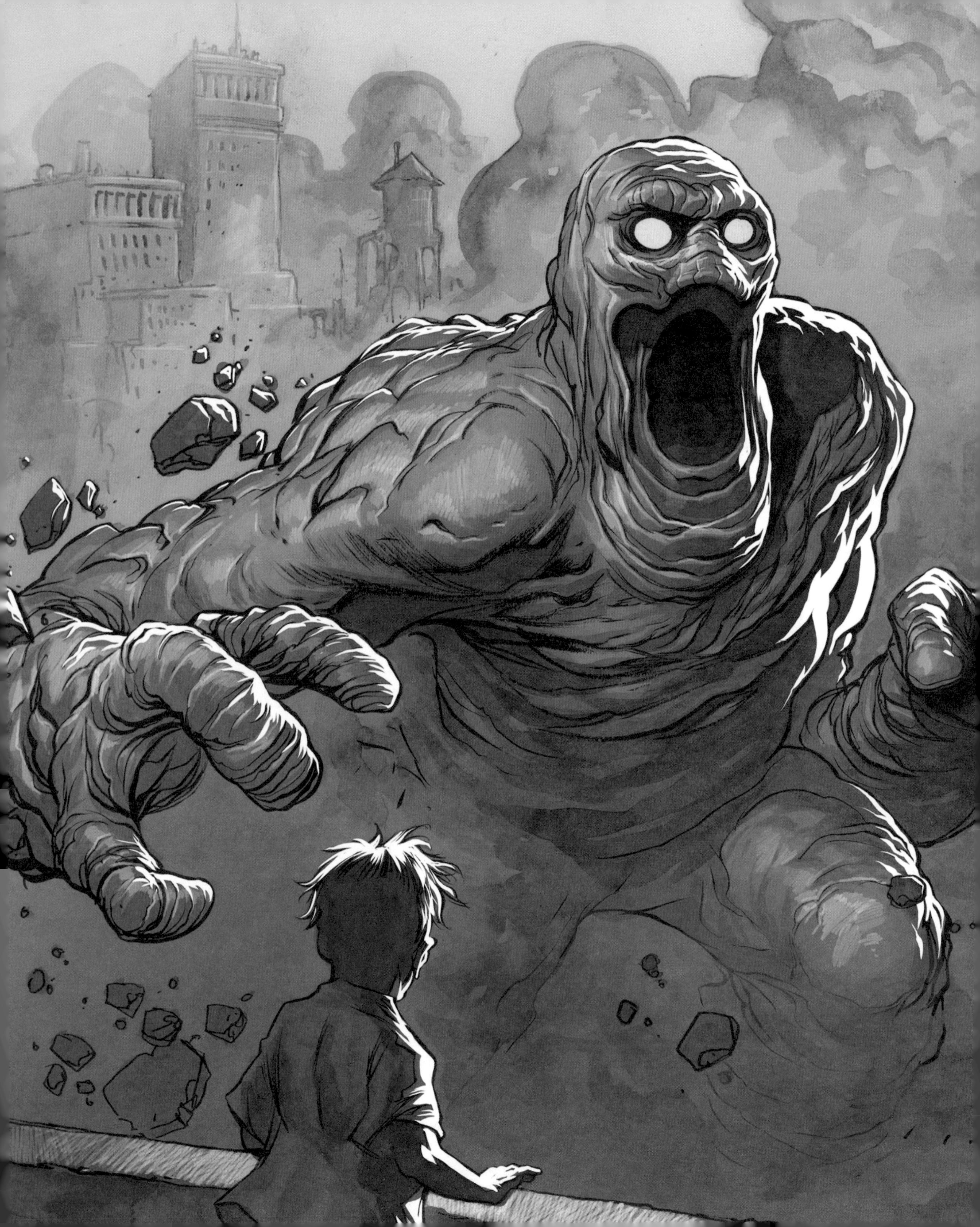

Height: Unknown **Weight:** Unknown **Origin:** Fourth Galaxy **Powers:** Massive size; advanced weapon technology; extrasensory perception

Rommbu

Sent by his warriorlike brethren with conquest in their sights, Rommbu's arrival on Earth caused great interest. However, humanity's excitement at meeting an alien soon turned to fear moments after the spaceship touched down and Rommbu revealed his true intentions.

Standing twice as tall as a human being, alien Rommbu's vastness, orange form, yellow, pupil-less eyes, and cavernous mouth make for an unnerving sight. As his first human witnesses could testify, he can also be unpredictably aggressive. Rommbu's vast power comes from his species' advanced technology—a mind probe, shrinking rays, metal disintegration rays, and powerful magnetic beams.

When Rommbu descended from his spaceship, he informed the assembled crowd that he was a scout who had traveled across the universe from the Fourth Galaxy. Earth had been chosen as the next target of his warlike people and the invaders would arrive soon.

To prove to his shocked audience that Earth should surrender, Rommbu showed off his weaponry. But as he returned to his spaceship to wait for the invasion, he sensed a presence aboard. A geologist-turned-robber named John Hunter had climbed inside the ship to escape the police guards who had been escorting him to jail. Intrigued at the stowaway's motives for hiding, Rommbu used a telepathy machine to reveal John's past. Assuming that such a criminal wouldn't be loyal to his own people, Rommbu concluded that John would not threaten the mission. He was wrong. Citing his geology expertise, John tricked Rommbu into landing his spaceship inside a volcano that was about to erupt. The ship, Rommbu, and John were seemingly destroyed in the explosion. The aliens, assuming the scout's defeat, halted the invasion.

Rommbu was later spotted as part of cosmic being the Collector's monster zoo. The alien answered the summons of Kei Kawade to defend the planet against Leviathon attack. He was last seen assisting the Guardians of the Galaxy.

First Appearance: *Tales to Astonish* #19 (1961) by Stan Lee, Larry Lieber, and Jack Kirby **Further Reading:** *Monsters Unleashed* #2 (2017)

Sole scout
Rommbu was the only one of his kind to make the trip to Earth. His scouting ship's destruction signalled the rest of the fleet to call off the attack.

Spragg, the Living Hill

When a large crack opened in the ground following trembling in Transylvania, a yellow, mountainous shape emerged from deep below—and opened its eyes. This monstrous mound is Spragg, the Living Hill, and he has come from beneath the Earth's surface with plans to conquer the planet.

American geologist Bob Robertson was working in Europe when he felt earth tremors. His curiosity piqued, Bob traveled to Transylvania to investigate the source of the quake. He soon discovered the locals there were acting strangely and evading his questions. Bob realized that they were all under the thrall of an alien entity named Spragg.

Also known as the Living Hill, Spragg has a body composed of rocks that resemble a large mound of crumbling earth, but he is also able to shape-shift into a semi-humanoid form. He has unsettling eyes and a chasmic, gaping mouth. Two billion years ago, Spragg was a spore in space. He was drawn to the core of the developing planet Earth, gaining intelligence and mental powers as he, and others like him, grew—but then become trapped beneath Earth's crust as it formed around him.

Spragg uses telekinesis to move the ground and create force fields. He has hypnotic abilities, which he employed to compel the villagers to build him a machine that would increase his power and prepare him for world domination. Bob, however, was able to resist Spragg's mind control and altered the machine to launch him back into space.

Thirty years later, the Living Hill was back on Earth. She-Hulk checked out a report of a moving mountain in Florida and met Bob, who suspected Spragg had returned. Deep underground, She-Hulk found Mole Man. The pair teamed up with Bob and others of Spragg's kind to defeat the malicious mountain, blasting him back into space.

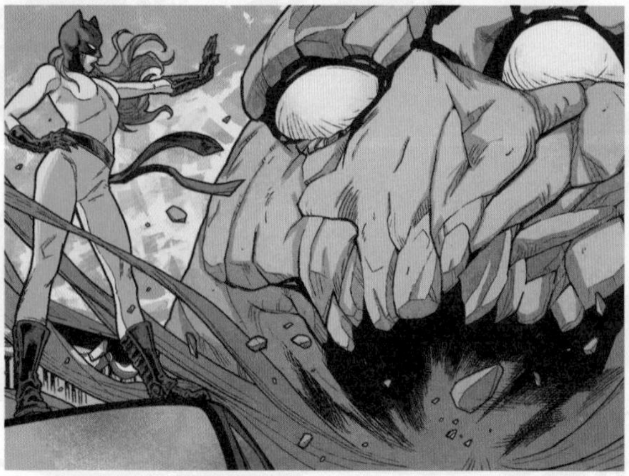

Lone hill creature
Spragg is a member of an ancient race called the Hill People, but became exiled from them and now operates alone.

First Appearance: *Journey Into Mystery* #68 (1961) by Stan Lee, Larry Lieber, and Jack Kirby **Further Reading:** *Sensational She-Hulk* #31-33 (1991)

Height: Unknown **Weight:** Unknown **Origin:** Space **Powers:** Mass hypnosis; force field creation; telekinesis

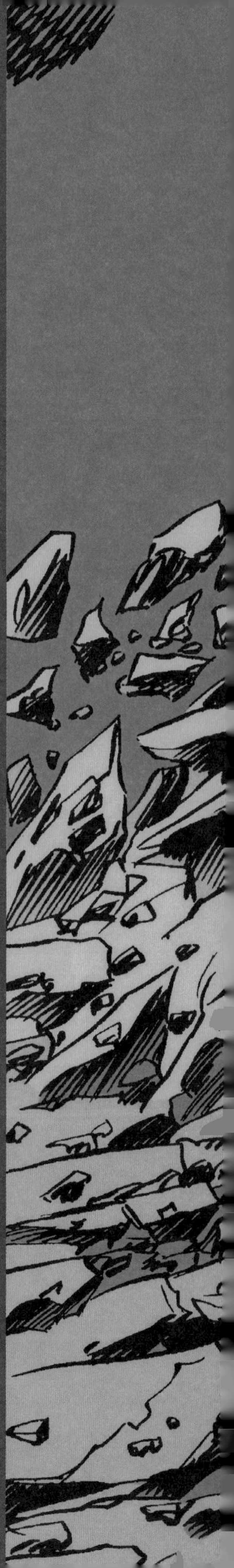

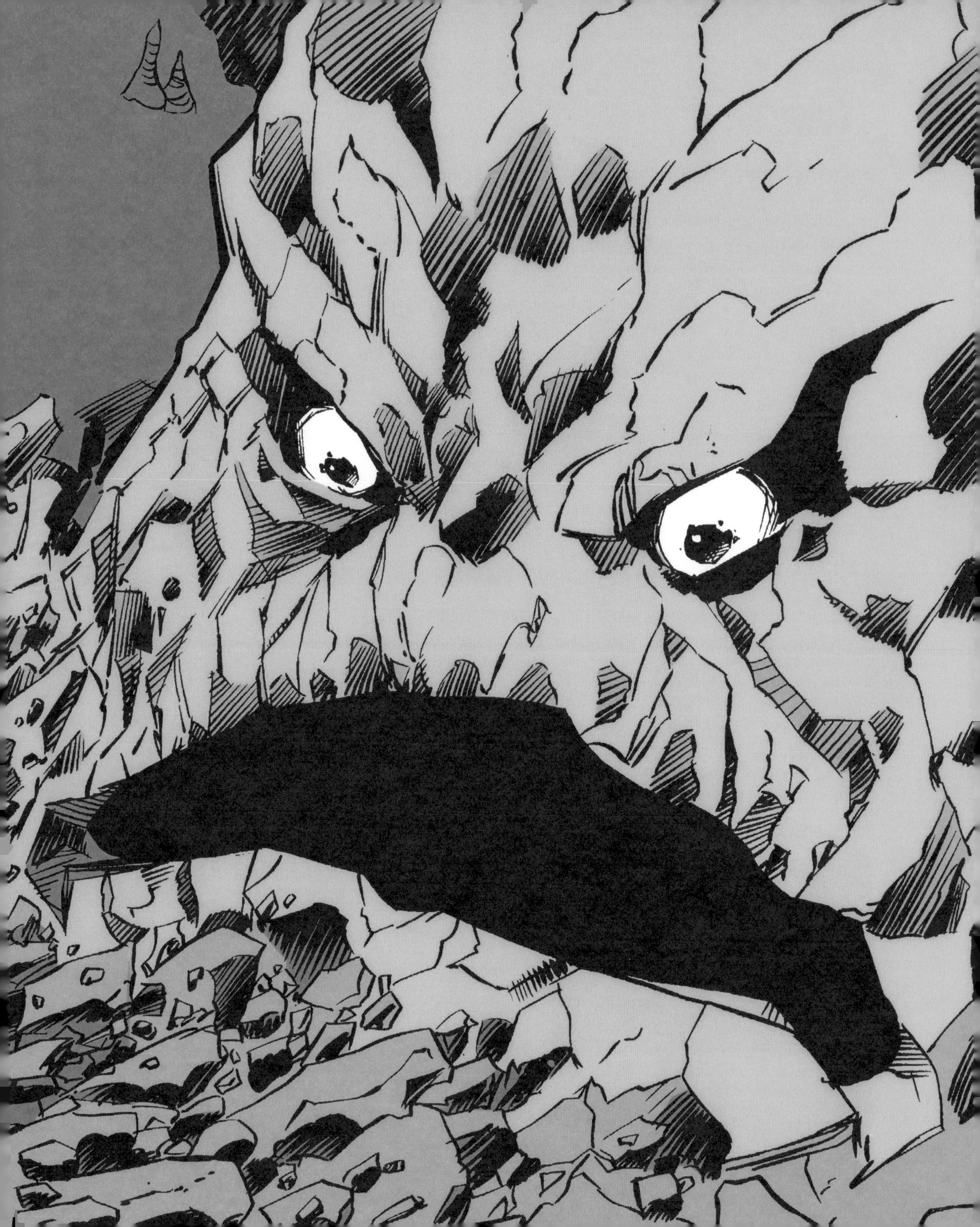

Kaa

From the distant Shadow Realm, a shape-changing, two-dimensional alien moves unseen among the shadows on Earth. This merciless commander of a legion of shape-shifting soldiers is Kaa, the Living Shadow, and his mission is to take over the world.

Arriving in their spaceships, the shape-shifting Shadow Soldiers, led by Kaa, prepared to attack, hoping to go unnoticed, by hiding in peoples' shadows. However, an author named Phillip Lawson discovered their plot. He warned the skeptical authorities about the "living shadows" and Kaa's Shadow Soldiers were soon captured. Kaa escaped in his flying saucer, threatening to one day return in his quest to take over the world.

Warlord Kaa and his soldiers can shape-shift into dark, shadowy, two-dimensional figures. Over time, they have learned how to possess human minds by inhabiting their shadows. Kaa and the Shadow Soldiers hail from the Shadow Realm—a planet opposite Earth on the other side of the sun—where advances in shape-shifting technology and spacefaring assist the inhabitants in their quest to conquer Earth.

Kaa kept his promise and came back to Earth, this time taking control of the Hulk's supersized shadow. Hulk and Kaa traded blows from sunrise to sunset. When it grew dark, the lights of a nearby oil field were switched on, and, exposed to the bright glow, Kaa seemingly disintegrated.

That was not the end of the Living Shadow, however. The warlord reformed his shape, contacted the Shadow Soldiers on his home planet, and assembled yet another invasion force. This time they attempted to control humans through their shadows—causing ranchers to riot in Arizona. Los Angeles hero team the Champions intervened. When Kaa commandeered Angel's shadow, the winged mutant soared skyward until the sunlight dissipated the alien's form, ending his mission.

Kaa and his warriors were last seen when alien scientist Yandroth summoned them to Earth to fight Canadian team Alpha Flight.

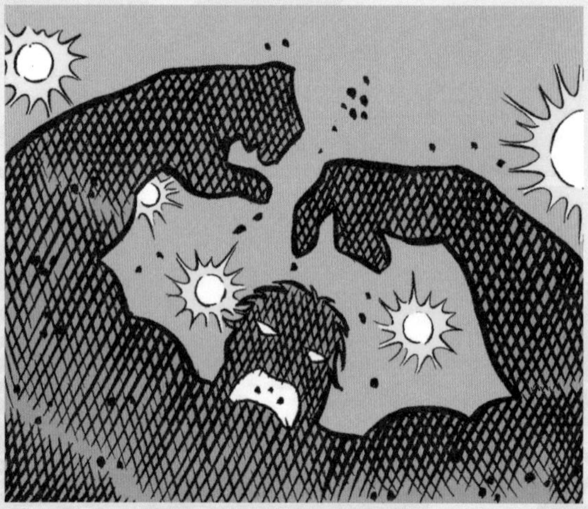

In the spotlight
Warlord Kaa might be strong enough to take on the Hulk, but he's powerless against the burning radiance of a bright light.

First Appearance: *Strange Tales* #79 (1960) by Stan Lee, Larry Lieber, and Jack Kirby **Further Reading:** *Incredible Hulk* #184 (1975)

Height: Variable **Weight:** Variable **Origin:** Shadow Realm **Powers:** Shape-shifting; space travel technology; human possession through shadows

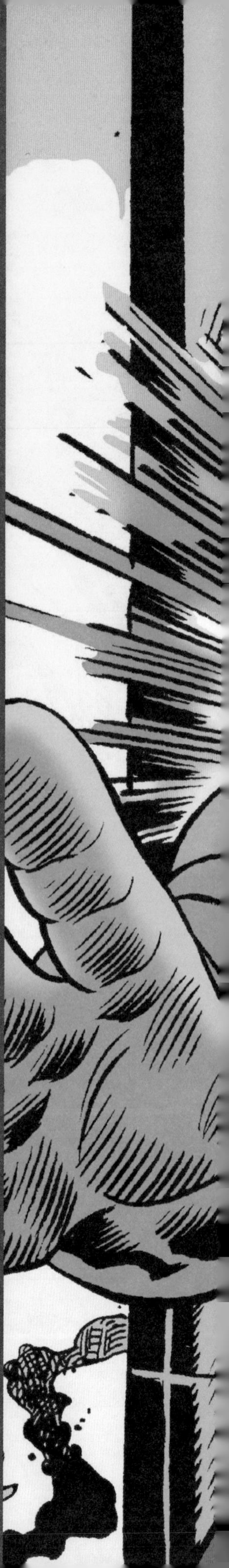

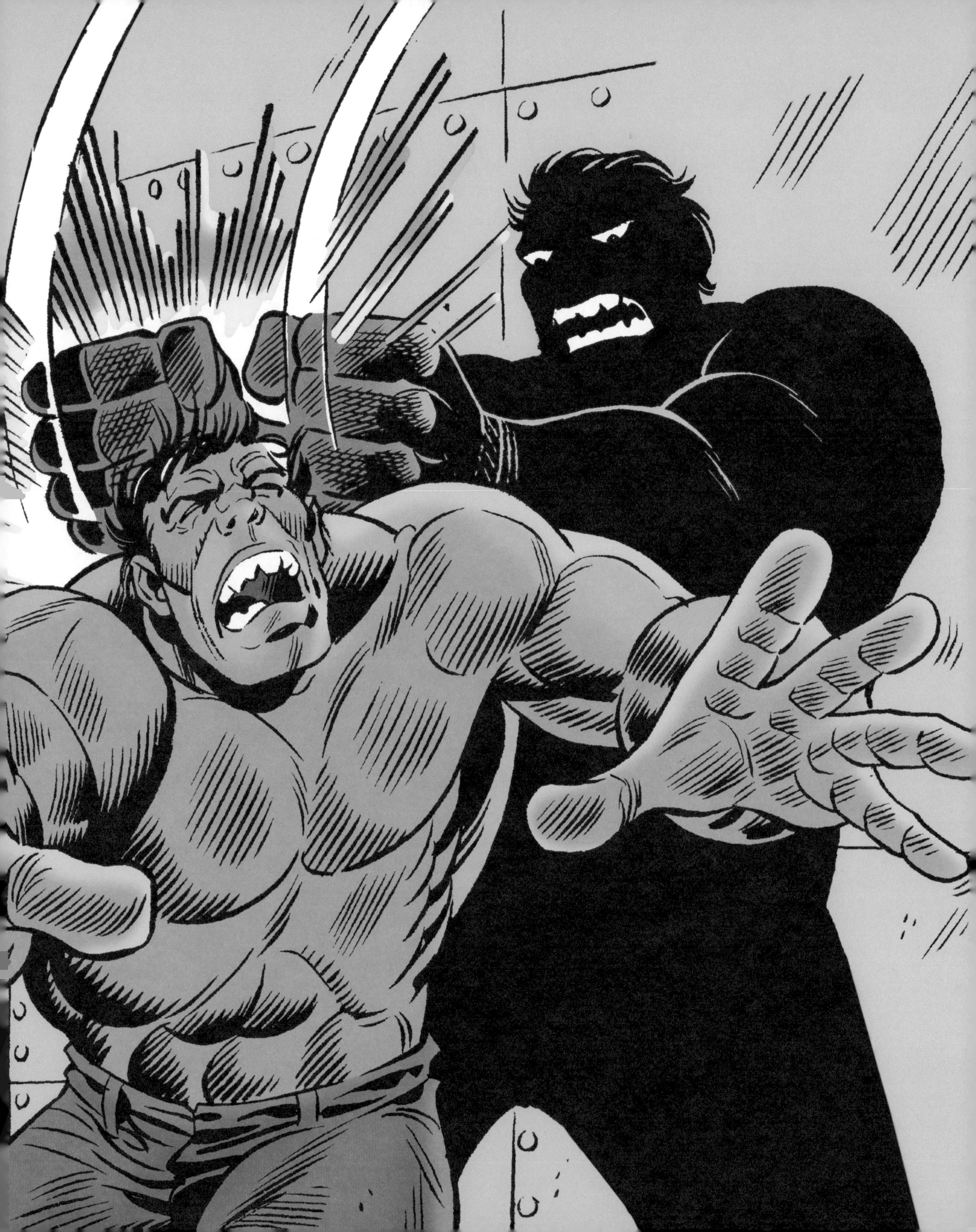

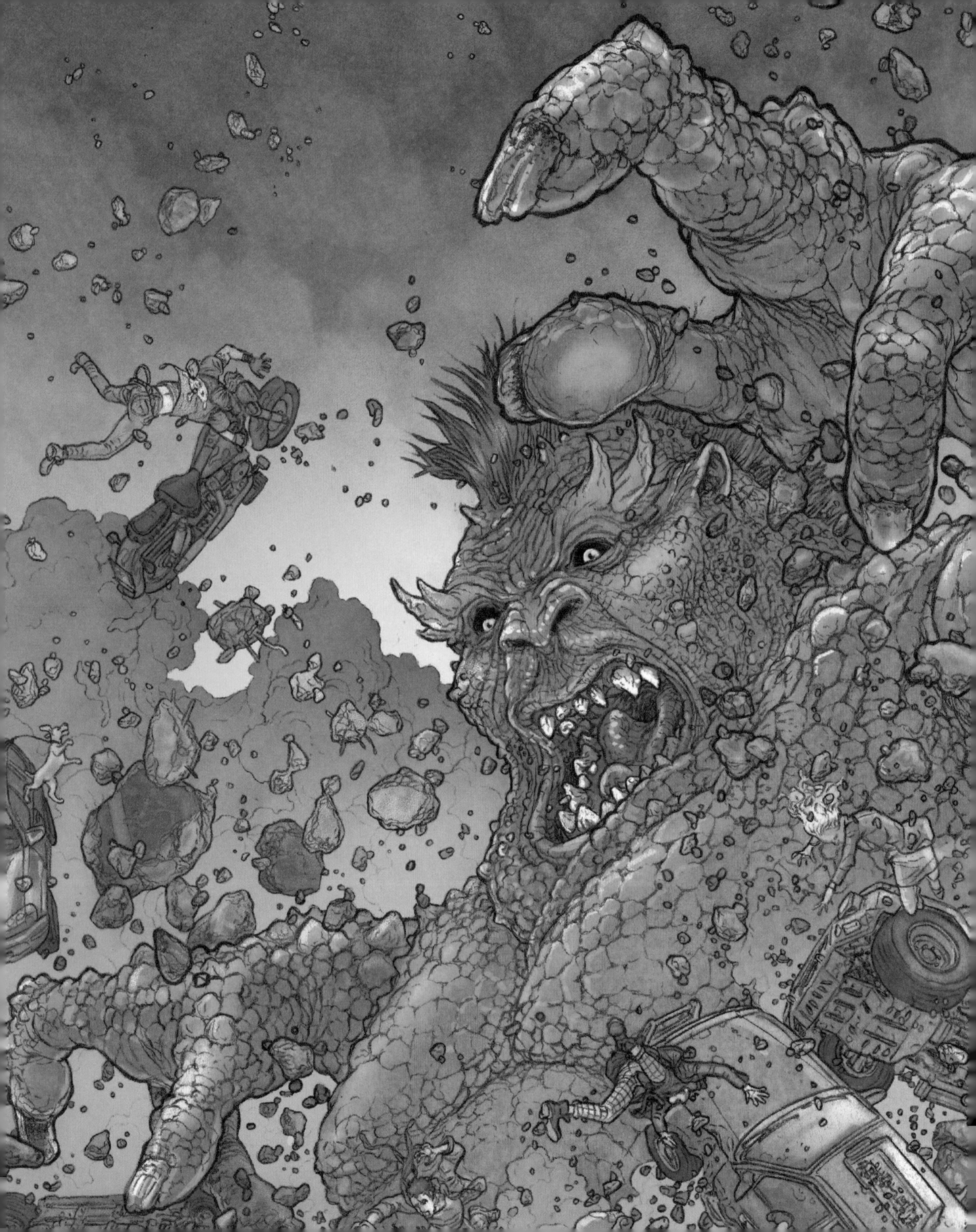

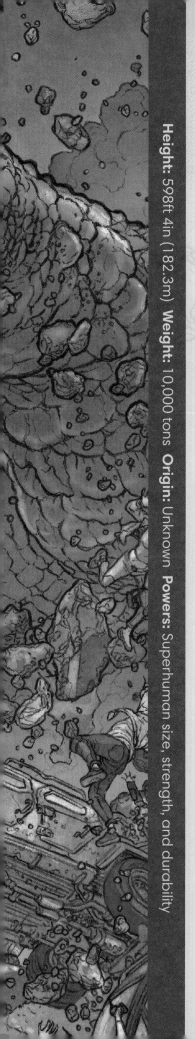

Monsteroso

When a seemingly dead alien suddenly awakens in a city museum, chaos ensues. The enormous creature smashes through its confines and rampages through the city streets in its confusion. Aptly named Monsteroso, the monster from space wreaks a large amount of havoc wherever he goes, but his intentions remain questionable.

Height: 598ft 4in (182.3m) **Weight:** 10,000 tons **Origin:** Unknown **Powers:** Superhuman size, strength, and durability

Most people dismissed news of an alien ship landing in an African jungle as a hoax, but an American circus owner named Phil decided to see for himself. He made the trek and found the massive, smoking wreck of a spaceship. Nearby, Phil made an even more incredible discovery: the body of a monstrous alien. Naming the colossus Monsteroso, the enterprising circus owner recruited local help to remove the body. Phil shipped the alien back to the U.S., where he sold the seemingly lifeless beast to a museum. Not long after, however, much to the surprise of onlookers, the extraterrestrial began to stir. Monsteroso was alive. He punched through the museum's walls and stumbled through the city.

Monsteroso is massive in size with strength to match, but exhibits great dexterity: using the three fingers on each hand to carefully pick up and examine creatures in a zoo, then gripping the sides of a tall building to ascend to its roof. His yellow-orange hide is thick, scaly, and impervious to bullets, and a distinctive tuft of hair sprouts from the top of his head.

The fact that Monsteroso caused great destruction was undeniable. However, the circus owner wondered if the alien actually meant any harm, as he seemed more inquisitive than intimidating. The authorities, ignoring Phil's concerns, assembled a giant syringe and deployed a sedative. Monsteroso plunged into the waters below, sleeping soundly. Then a spaceship carrying two gargantuan beings appeared—Monsteroso's parents, looking for their son. The young alien had accidentally crash-landed on Earth, and they were pleased to find him unharmed.

Many years later, the Inhuman Black Bolt saved Monsteroso from a cruel captor and reunited him once again with his family.

First Appearance: *Amazing Adventures* #5 (1961) by Stan Lee, Larry Lieber, and Jack Kirby **Further Reading:** *Black Bolt* #3 (2017)

Kidnapped
Once, Monsteroso was imprisoned by the Inhuman known as the Jailer, until fellow captive Black Bolt, king of the Inhumans, mounted a jailbreak. He was then again returned to his grateful parents.

Monsteroso Anatomy

Monsteroso is proof that appearances can be deceiving. While at first sight he seems like a violent fiend—due to his gigantic size and panicked movements—in reality, he is a bewildered and lost toddler from outer space.

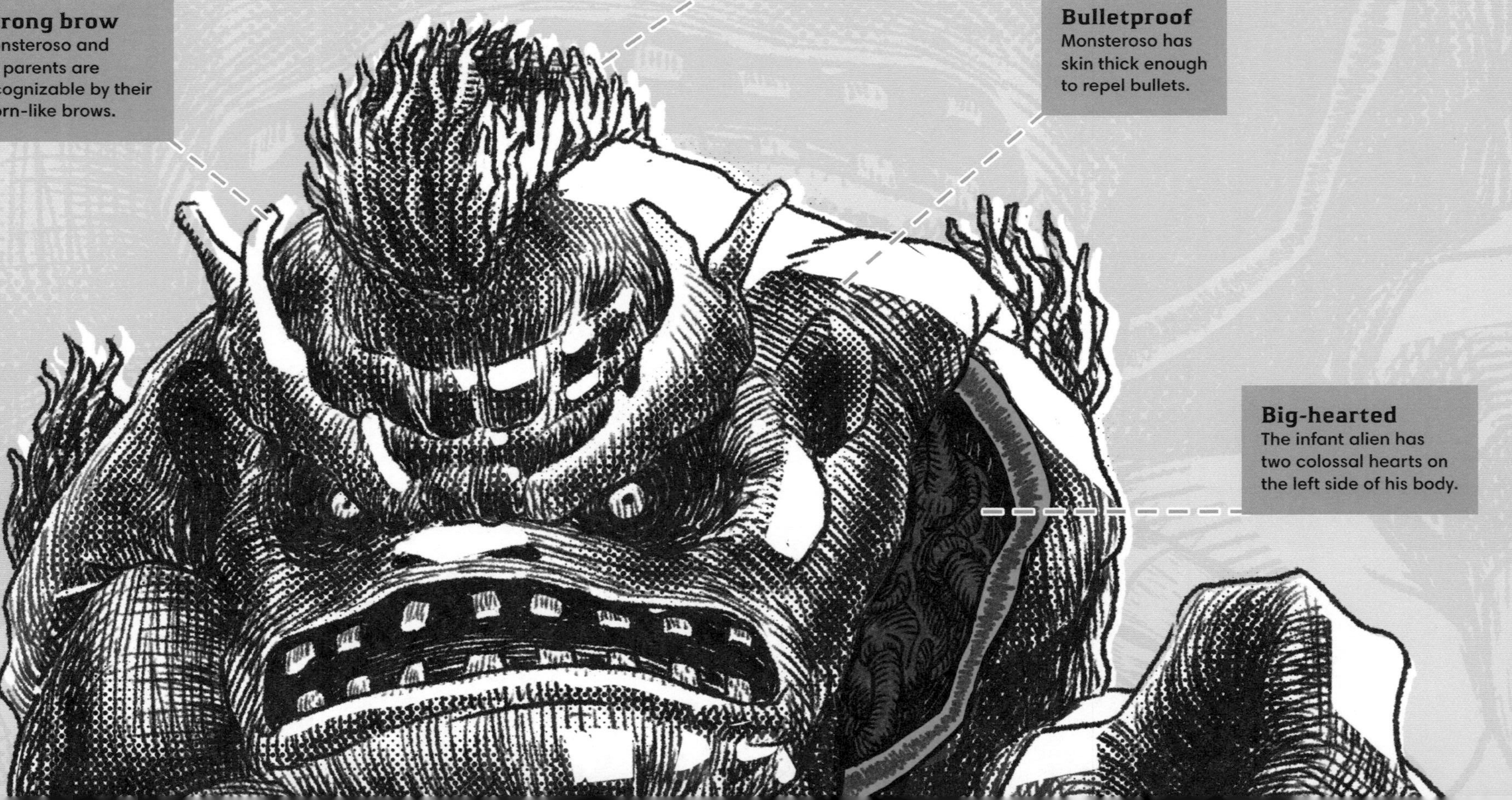
Strong brow
Monsteroso and his parents are recognizable by their thorn-like brows.
Spiky hair
Monsteroso's distinctive spiked hair is as strong as iron.
Bulletproof
Monsteroso has skin thick enough to repel bullets.
Big-hearted
The infant alien has two colossal hearts on the left side of his body.

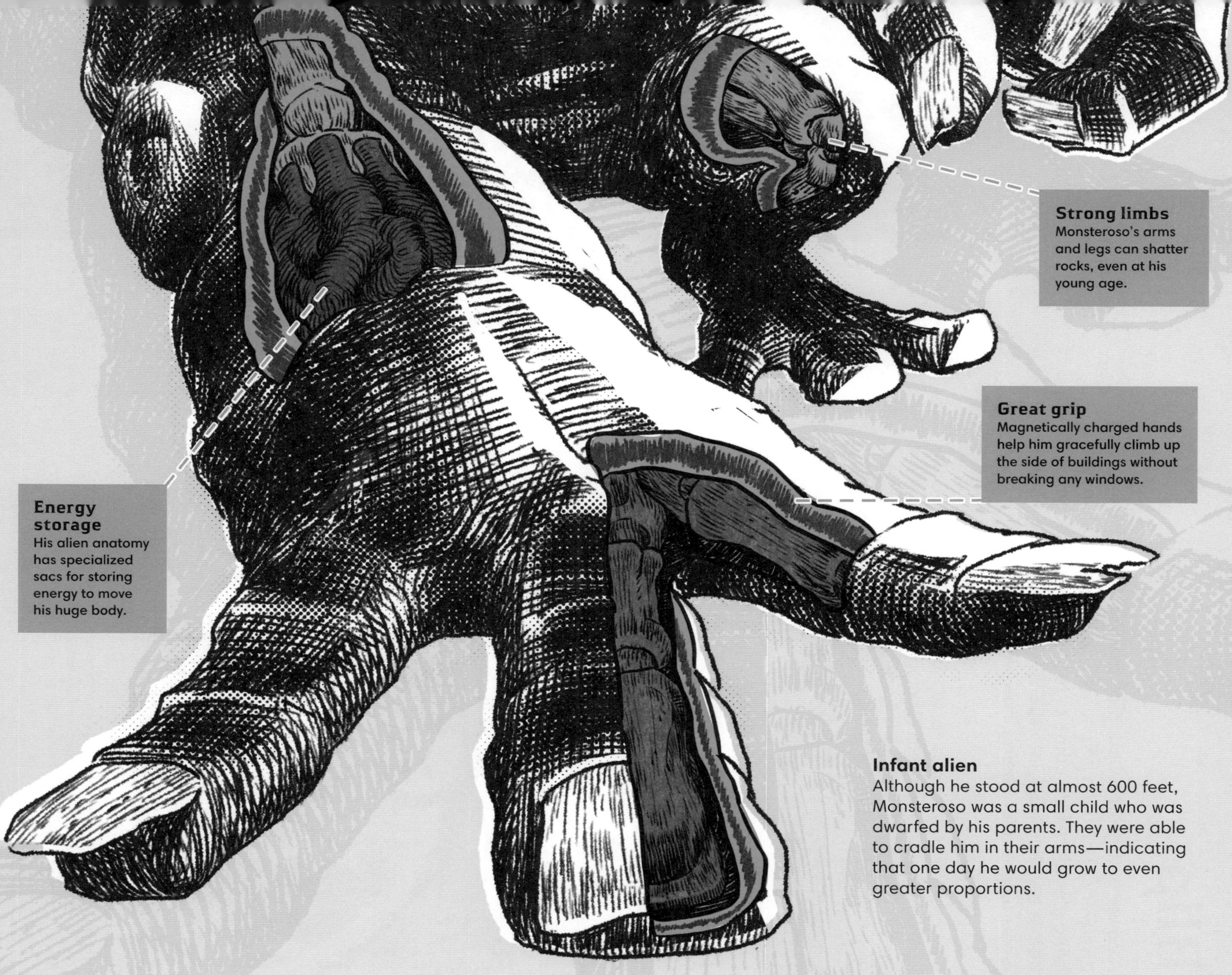
Strong limbs
Monsteroso's arms and legs can shatter rocks, even at his young age.
Great grip
Magnetically charged hands help him gracefully climb up the side of buildings without breaking any windows.
Energy storage
His alien anatomy has specialized sacs for storing energy to move his huge body.

Infant alien
Although he stood at almost 600 feet, Monsteroso was a small child who was dwarfed by his parents. They were able to cradle him in their arms—indicating that one day he would grow to even greater proportions.

Blip

A power outage in a Canadian town sparked the shocking discovery of an alien in a nearby cave. Dubbed Blip, the living electrical field came to rest on Earth to recharge itself before heading back into space. Not everyone believed it was a benevolent being, however.

One day, a radar operator noticed a strange blip on his screen. Shortly after, an entire town in the same area suffered a power outage. The radar operator set out to investigate. Using an electrometer, he traced the only electricity nearby to a dark cave. Inside, he came face-to-face with an alien entity, bristling with energy, from a race of electrical beings.

The Blip—as the man thought of it, although its name was later revealed to be Shzzzllzzzthzz—did not mean any harm and explained how it had arrived on Earth. It was an interstellar traveler who had become trapped in a space-and-time warp. Expending most of his energy to break free, the entity had come to Earth to rest and recharge—draining the town of its electricity in the process. As they talked, a group of men also looking for the source of the outage stumbled upon the Blip's hideout, and opened fire in their fear of the unknown. Their violent reaction angered the alien, and it fought back to protect the radar operator. The men were easily bested and left behind a dynamo that the Blip used to top up its power. As it departed, the Blip shared its hope with the humans that their next meeting would be more civilized.

Another of the species, named Phzzzrrzztlzzzz, faced off against heroic team the Fantastic Four years later. Also angered by its treatment at the hands of humans, the energetic alien attempted to drain the planet's electricity until it was stopped by Thing and the Human Torch.

The first Blip later returned to Earth and joined fellow monsters to defend the planet against the Leviathon invasion. An awe-inspiring ally, Blips can fly, drain electricity, and travel through space without need of a ship.

Intangible being
The Blip assumes a humanoid appearance, and is capable of expressions, although is otherwise without form as composed of electrical energy.

First Appearance: *Tales to Astonish* #15 (1961) by Stan Lee and Jack Kirby

Height: Unknown; variable **Weight:** Unknown **Origin:** Space **Powers:** Massive size; generates electric energy; resistant to physical damage; flight

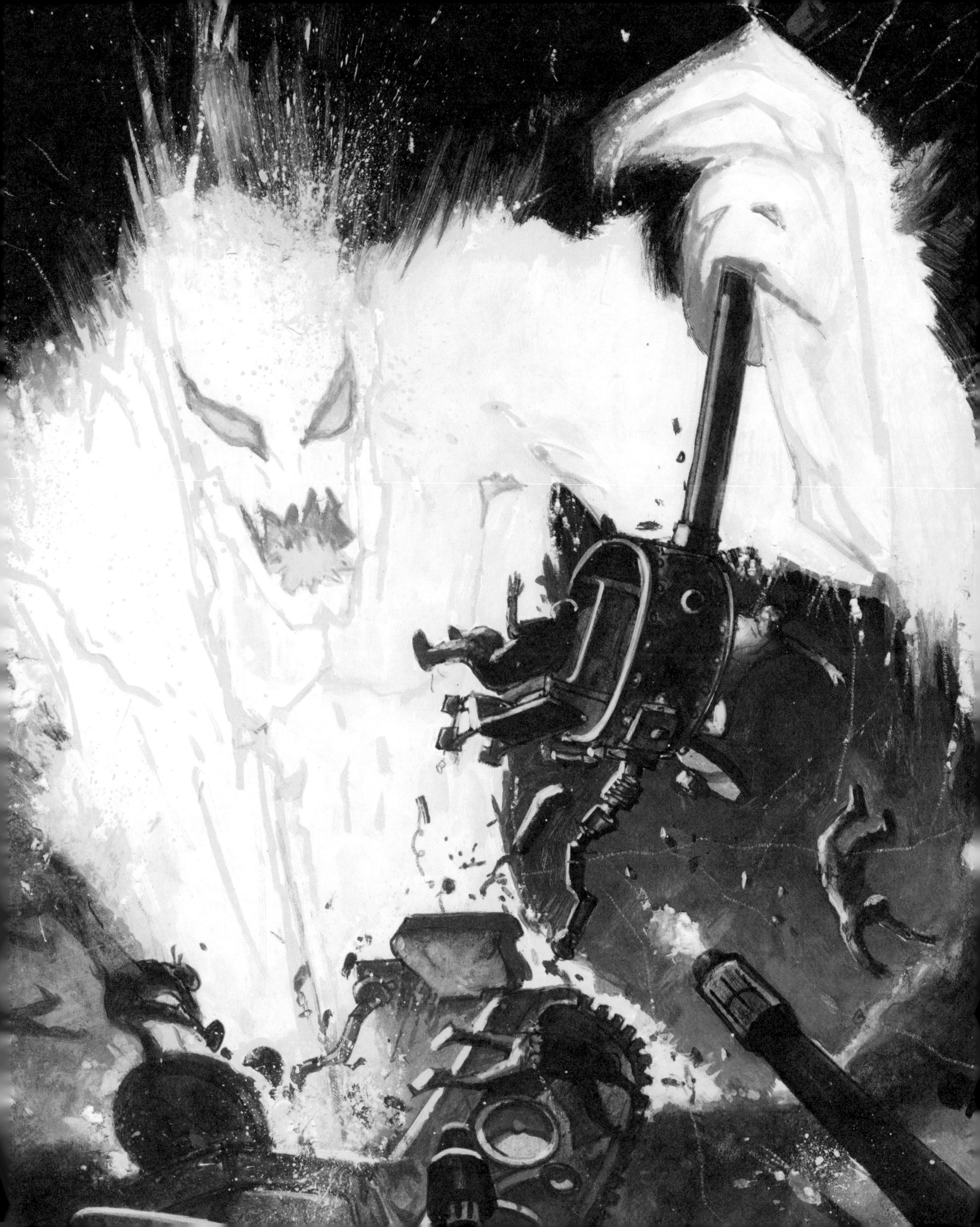

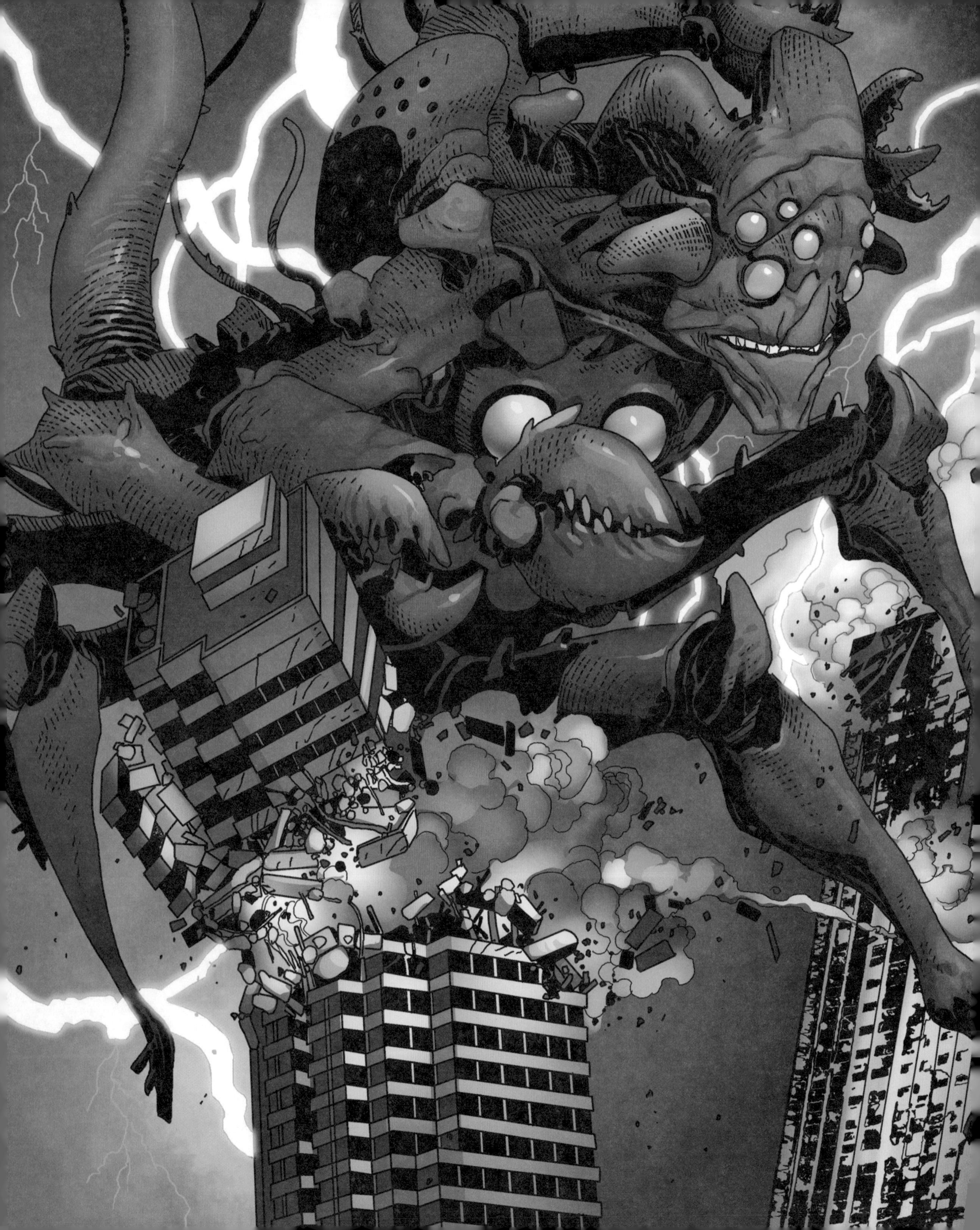

Height: Unknown Weight: Unknown Origin: Space Powers: Superhuman size, strength, and durability; command of brood

Leviathon Mother

The monstrous queen of the Leviathons commands lethal legions to raze planets in preparation for her nest-building. She is the Leviathon Mother, conqueror and destroyer of countless worlds. When her Leviathon Tide meets resistance on Earth, she takes matters into her own claws.

The Leviathon Mother, ruler of her kind, woke every few thousand years to find new worlds upon which she could build her nests. She destroyed and discarded an incalculable number of planets—annihilating all life-forms, bleeding the planets' magma cores dry, and nesting to increase her immense forces by birthing monstrous Leviathons and Leviathon Servitors. Sending a Leviathon Tide out from the Desecrated Nest, and able to see all that her Leviathons saw, the Leviathon Mother set her sights on claiming another planet.

The queen not only had hosts of huge creatures at her disposal, but also assassins to stop anyone who stood in her way. These hideous, human-sized Leviathon Servitors might have been smaller creatures, but they were no less vicious than their colossal counterparts. All of her brood were solely dedicated to a shared purpose—serving the Leviathon Mother.

A crimson-hued horror with green glowing eyes, colossal appendages, snapping pincers, and a prehensile tail, the Leviathon Mother made landfall when her Leviathons met with resistance from other monsters and hero teams on planet Earth. Dwarfing even the largest of her brood, she faced an Inhuman boy, Kei Kawade, who had used his super power to summon a battalion of monsters, dubbed Goliathons, from the pages of his sketchbook to defend the planet.

The Leviathon Mother finally met her match when Kei Kawade created and released six new monsters to attack her. Despite killing one—Fireclaw—she was felled by Smasher, the fused monster form of this young Inhuman and his companions. Immediately after she was killed, her immense corpse melted away into the streets of New York City.

First Appearance: *Monsters Unleashed* #3 (2017) by Cullen Bunn, Steve McNiven, and Leinil Francis Yu
Further Reading: *Monsters Unleashed* #1-5 (2017)

Stronger together
Only the combined might of Kid Kaiju's loyal team members could defeat the Leviathon Mother once and for all.

Monstrom

Spotted emerging from the Bayou is an enormous, orange monster bellowing in an alien tongue. This one-eyed, six-fingered extraterrestrial spent 1,000 years submerged in the murky depths of the Black Swamp and is now terrorizing humankind, albeit with seemingly misunderstood intentions.

A family on vacation in the Bayou had a shock when a slime-covered monster rose up from a nearby swamp. As he moved toward the father and son, mumbling and groaning, the frightened father fired his rifle in desperation. The bullets had no effect on the giant's thick hide, however. As the pair fled, the monster pursued them, crashing through the bushes and vines of the swampland. Eventually, he made his way to a nearby town.

Monstrom—as he later came to be known—smashed through the town's barricades and ignored all attempts to stop him in his tracks. The inhabitants were terrified. Suddenly, a stray lightning bolt struck some power lines close by. The creature's reaction to the flames gave the people the idea to threaten him with fire. Surrounded by a crowd carrying lit torches, the orange ogre gave an unearthly roar and fled back into the swampy depths where he had slept for hundreds of years.

An alien from a faraway world, Monstrom had simply sought the people's help in repairing his stranded ship, which was buried deep in the Black Swamp, but they were too scared to understand his pleas.

Monstrom's massive size grants him incredible strength, and he is able to smash through almost any obstacle placed in his way. His orange, folded skin is bulletproof and resistant to damage. He has a single eye, which perhaps contributes to his clumsy, stumbling gait, and two large horns protrude from the front of his head. Monstrom comes from a civilization with advanced space travel technology, and he hopes to return there.

Answering the call of the young Inhuman Kei Kawade, Monstrom resurfaced years later and helped defend Earth against the invasion of the Leviathon Tide. He was last sighted in Louisiana.

First Appearance: *Tales to Astonish* #11 (1960) by Stan Lee, Larry Lieber, and Jack Kirby
Further Reading: *Monsters Unleashed* (2017)

False appearances
Monstrom's size and inability to express himself in a manner humans can understand render him more monstrous than he is.

Height: 20ft (6m) **Weight:** Unknown **Origin:** Space **Powers:** Superhuman strength and durability

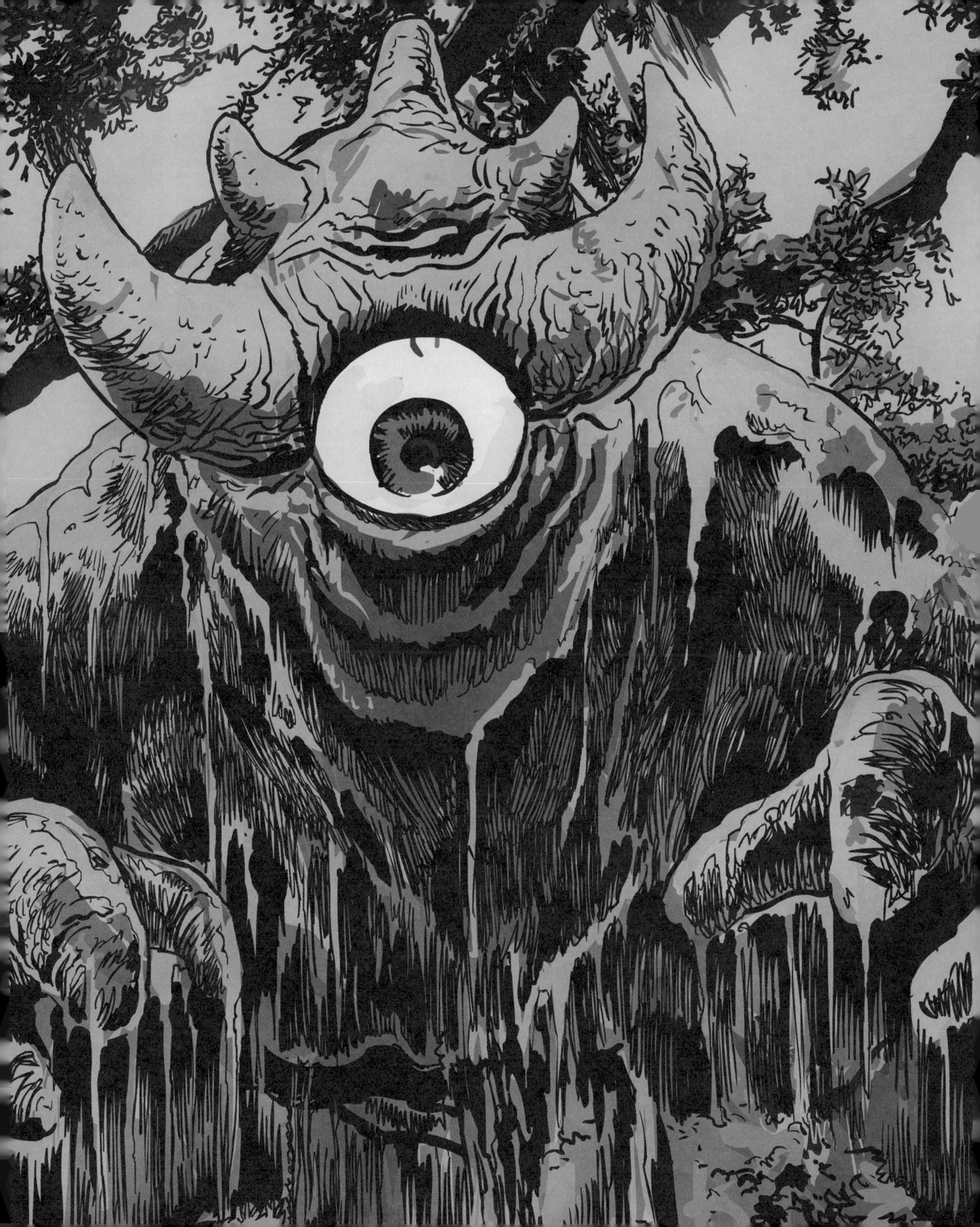

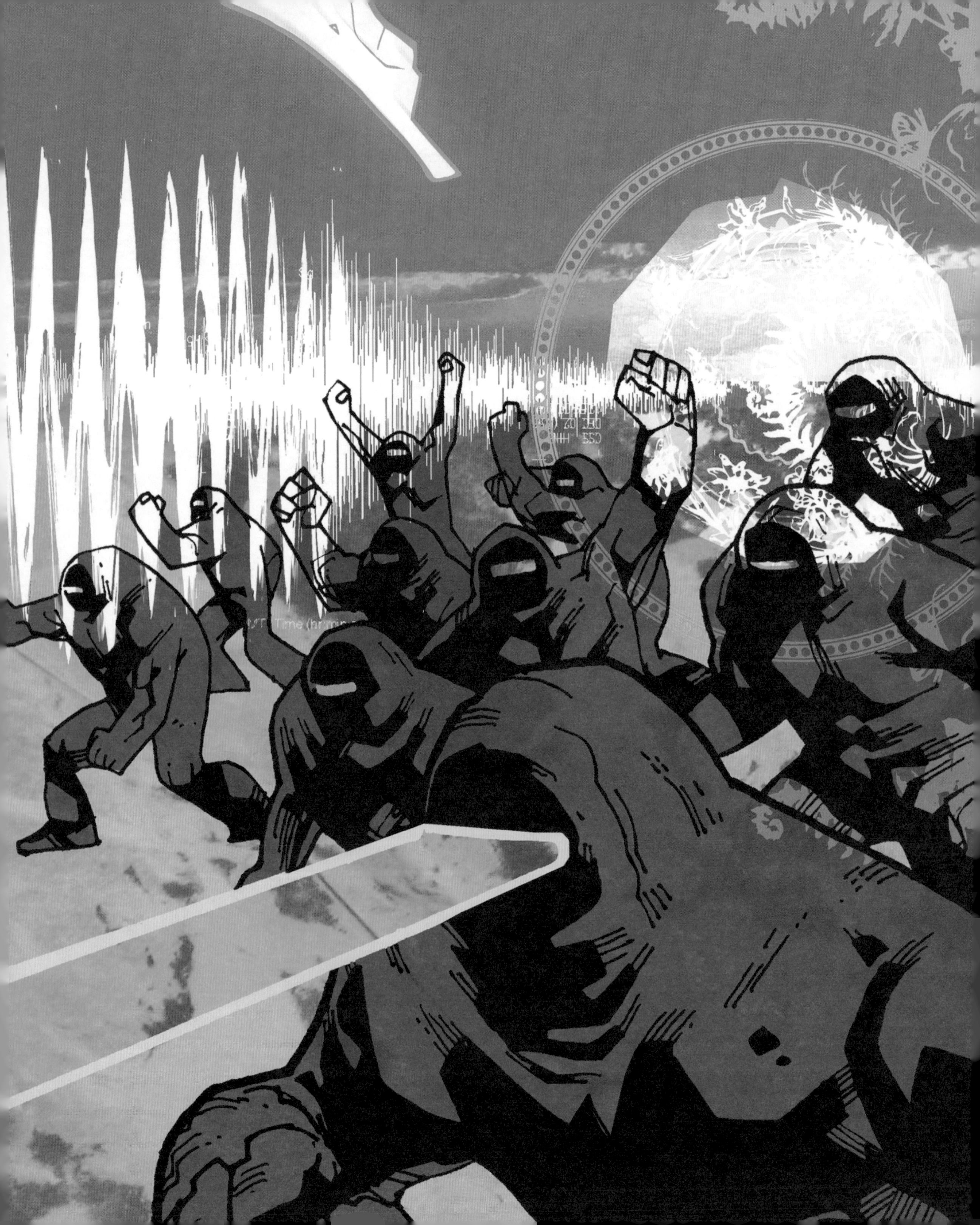

Height: Variable **Weight:** Variable **Origin:** Dark Dimension **Powers:** Superhuman strength; impervious to physical harm; energy blasts

Mindless Ones

They come from the far reaches of the mysterious Dark Dimension, exist to fight, and seek only destruction. Devoid of intelligence and emotion, the Mindless Ones are driven by instinct to attack using optic blasts. These soulless creatures are almost unstoppable.

The Mindless Ones are from the fringes of the Dark Dimension—a mystical place where dark forces exist. It is also where the powerful entity known as Dormammu was exiled and now rules. In order to trap and control the Mindless Monsters who lived there, Dormammu created a powerful, mystic shield that only he could maintain.

Standing taller than most men, the humanoid Mindless Ones are immediately recognizable by their muscled, hairless bodies. They can fire destructive energy beams from a single, red, cyclopean eye, and they fight with an unmatched ferocity. True to their name, the Mindless Ones have limited intelligence and are often summoned to carry out the nefarious orders of others.

The master of the dark domain—who wanted to extend his rule to Earth—summoned Sorcerer Supreme Doctor Strange to his dimension for a duel. Strange was at first reluctant to answer the challenge for fear that the Mindless Ones would escape if Dormammu was defeated. As the pair battled, the Mindless Ones sensed the barrier keeping them at bay was weakening, and they broke through. In a turn of events, Doctor Strange lent his power to Dormammu to stop the Mindless Ones from taking over the Dark Dimension and they were driven back. In exchange, the powerful entity agreed to leave Earth alone.

In time, the Mindless Ones would find a way out of the Dark Dimension on more than one occasion. These thoughtless minions have battled the Avengers, agents of S.H.I.E.L.D., Spider-Man, Namor, and many more of Earth's mightiest heroes, often set against them by Dormammu and other villains in need of their raw strength and unthinking commitment.

First Appearance: *Strange Tales* #127 (1964) by Stan Lee and Steve Ditko **Further Reading:** *Avengers* #118 (1973), *Amazing Spider-Man* #57-58 (2003)

From the Dark Dimension
Any time the Mindless Ones break through their dimension to rampage on Earth, it's all hands on deck to stop them.

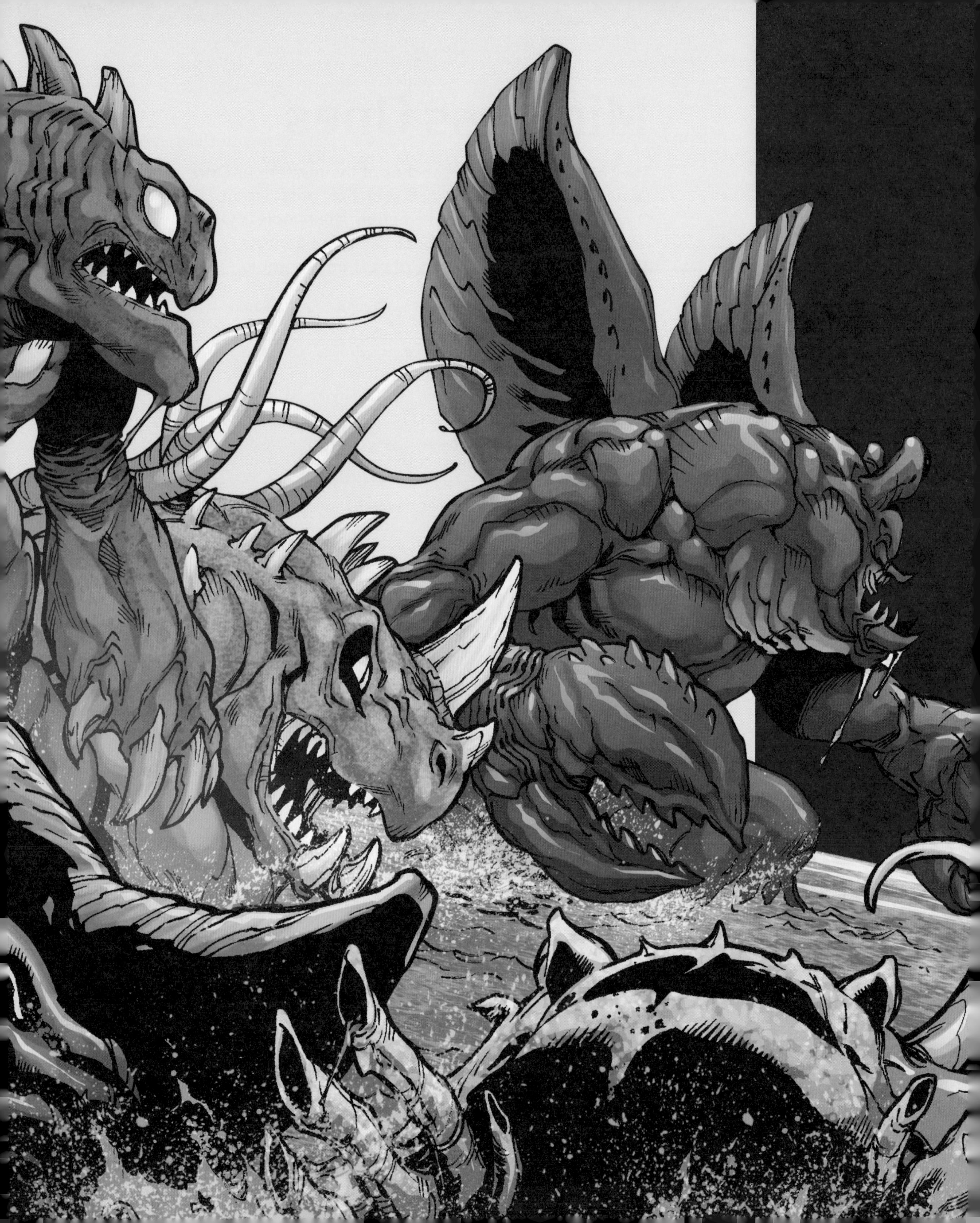

MONSTER TEAMS

Heroes that look like monsters and monsters that had once been heroes make up some of the most terrifying teams. The Howling Commandos, Legion of Monsters, Kid Kaiju and his monstrous allies, and the mighty Hulks seem like the stuff of nightmares, but all are dedicated to protecting the innocent.

Conversely, Marvel Zombies and the Undead Avengers may at first appear like the beloved heroes who have fought to defend Earth—until they step into the light to reveal themselves as ravenous, bloodthirsty, shambling creatures of the night.

There are groups of monsters so large that they are practically armies. The Leviathons from a distant galaxy and the creatures of Monster Isle all serve demanding rulers who command them in order to fulfill their own nefarious goals.

Gather your wits and get ready to meet these ghastly groups.

Monster Isle

This seemingly ordinary island is the literal stomping ground for some of the world's larger-than-life creatures. Located in the Sea of Japan, the tropical Monster Isle is dominated by an enormous mountain with a network of underground tunnels leading to the Earth's core.

Rising from the Pacific Ocean at longitude 136 degrees east, latitude 40 degrees north, Monster Isle is immediately identifiable by the craggy slope of its highest mountain, which seems to bear a grotesque face. The island is covered in a jungle of leafy trees and tangled vines, mostly untouched by human civilization, but teeming with other sorts of life.

The island was created by the Deviants, a technologically advanced race that preceded humankind; they also engineered some of the creatures that live there. Their secrets stayed hidden beneath the island's surface until the day the vilified scientist Mole Man stumbled upon Monster Isle's shores.

Mole Man claimed the island as his domain and deemed himself the master of the monsters living there. From his base, Mole Man plotted numerous attacks on the surface world. Although he was defeated by the Fantastic Four on one of their first outings as a Super Hero team, Mole Man continued to live in the island's vast underground caverns in his kingdom, called Subterranea. As the years passed, Mole Man rescued and recruited monsters for his ever-growing army. He also commanded the Moloids, a diminutive species created by the Deviants, as his minions.

Monster Isle later served as the place where the world-shaking Apocalypse Beast was finally defeated, thanks to the Moloids and the Deviant technology placed below ground in case of the monster's return to Earth.

Other individuals would go on to rule Monster Isle, such as Thing from the Fantastic Four and Latverian sorcerer and scientist Victor von Doom. However, Mole Man never gave up on his adopted home or lost his affection for its monstrous inhabitants.

First Appearance: *Fantastic Four #1* (1961) by Stan Lee and Jack Kirby **Further Reading:** *Uncanny X-Men #33* (2015), *Marvel 2-In-One #2* (2018)

Tourist trap
Monster Isle has had some notable visitors over the years, including the Fantastic Four, the Infinity Watch, members of the X-Men, and Victor von Doom.

Known Inhabitants: Mole Man, Moloids, Blip, Fin Fang Foom, Giganto, Gigantus, Googam, Tricephalous, Vandoom's Monster, Xemnu

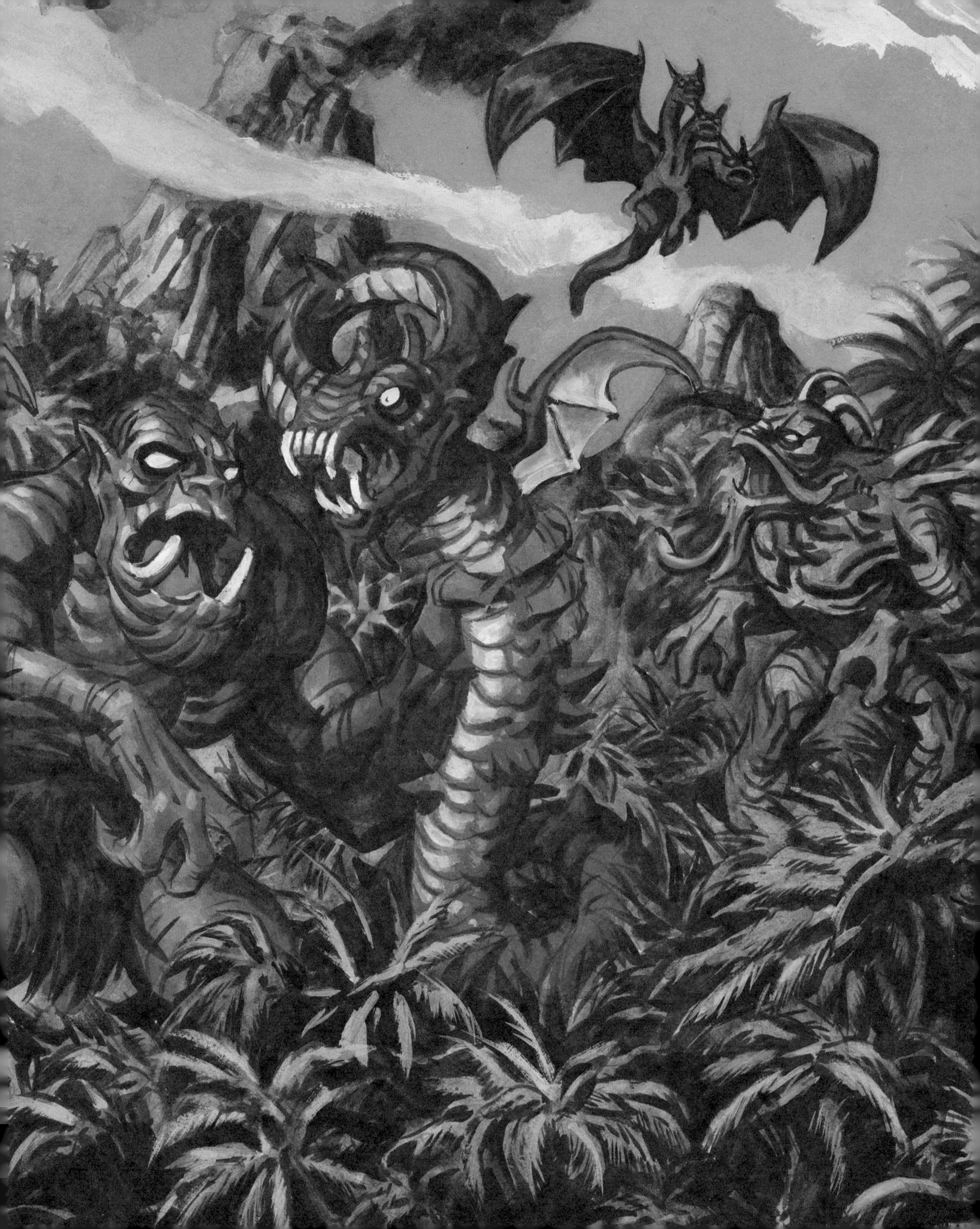

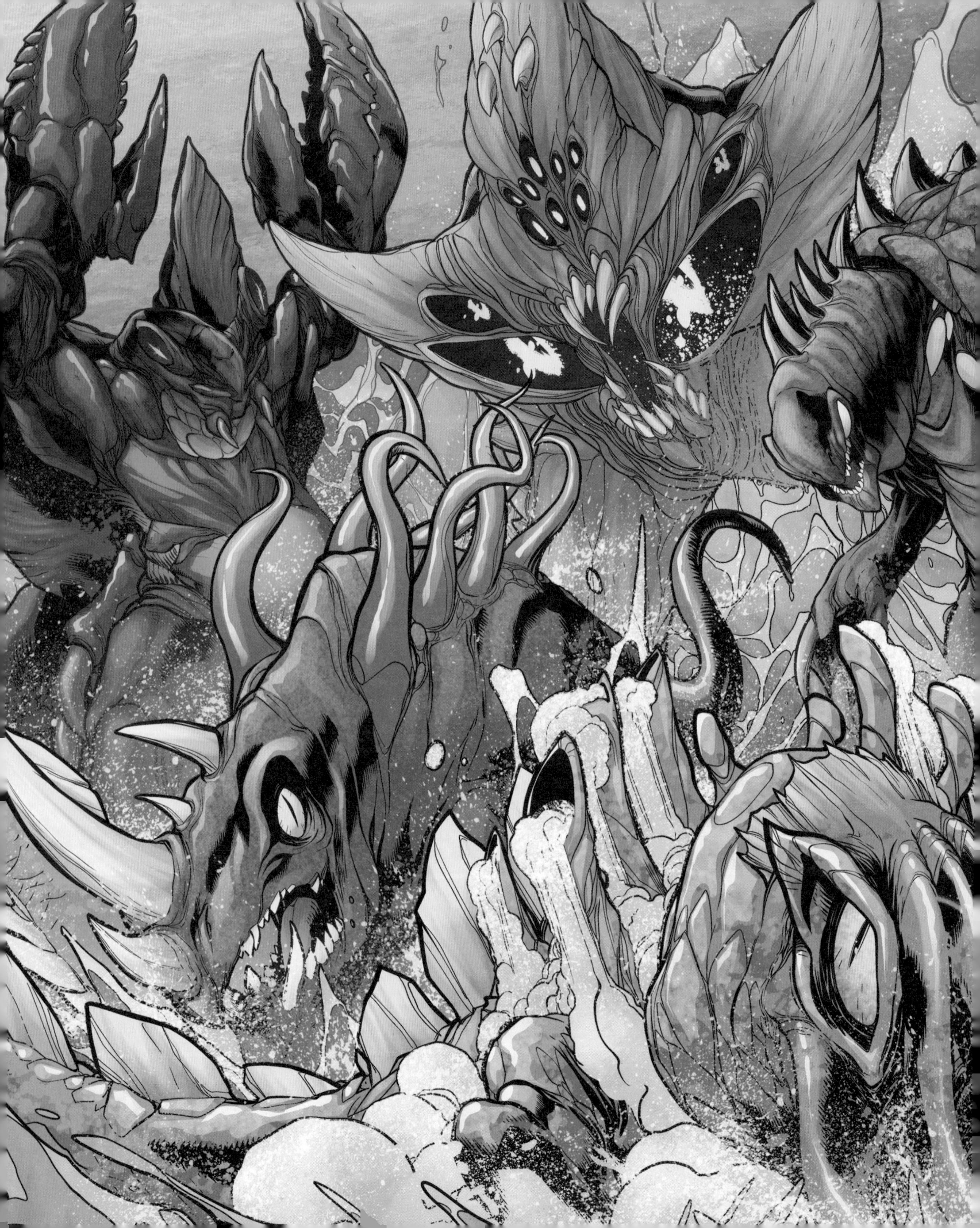

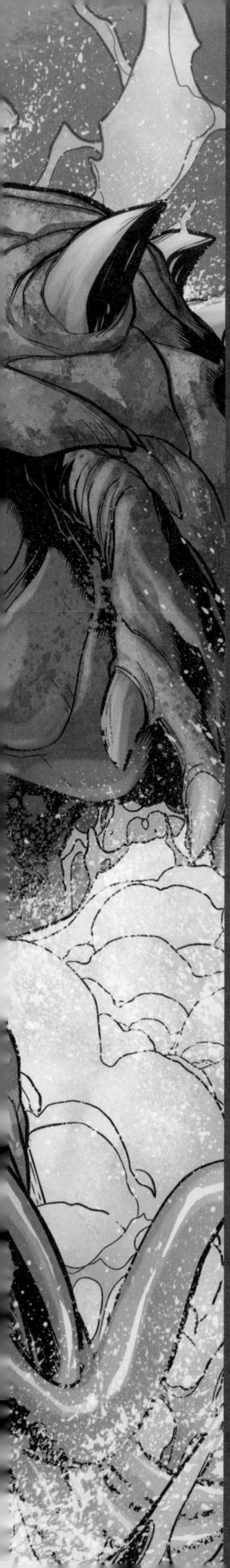

Leviathons

Every thousand years, a tide of assorted, massive, and misshapen monstrosities with gnashing teeth and slashing claws—the Leviathons—descends upon a planet. Their ultimate goal is complete annihilation. Earth is their next target, so some of the galaxy's greatest heroes prepare to battle the mighty force of these monsters and their queen.

Notable members: Leviathon Mother, Eggplant, Furnax, Giant Gorn, Glob-zilla, among others **Base of operations:** Desecrated Nest

Not from any one particular race or any one type of monster, each individual member of the Leviathons can unleash its own kind of horrifying, destructive attacks. Energy tentacles, super-heated magma flares, acidic blood, and impenetrable exteriors are just some of the weapons and defenses at the Leviathons' disposal.

The monstrous extraterrestrials began their invasion of Earth one-by-one, working in concert to destroy anything and anyone in their path. They communicated through unnatural shrieks and cries to coordinate their attacks. These alien invaders had been sent by the Leviathon Mother from a place called the Desecrated Nest in an unknown, distant galaxy. Their assault was just the first step in razing planet Earth to prepare it for the queen, so she could spawn there. On countless planets the Leviathons had wiped out all inhabitants and life-forms so that the Leviathon Mother could claim the remaining resources for a new nest.

It would take the combined might of an entire team of heroes to take down just one bizarre behemoth. Consequently, not even the united forces of the military, Avengers, Champions, X-Men, Guardians of the Galaxy, Alpha Flight, the Winter Guard, and the Inhumans could stop the unrelenting onslaught of the Leviathons. It wasn't until a young Inhuman named Kei Kawade and his cadre of monsters joined the fight that the tide finally started to turn. As her Leviathon forces retreated, the Leviathon Mother made landfall. The formidable eight-eyed, multi-limbed colossus faced-off against a combination of Kei Kawade's monsters. She was eventually defeated and melted away.

First Appearance: *Monsters Unleashed* #1 (2017) by Cullen Bunn and Steve McNiven **Further Reading:** *Monsters Unleashed* #2-5 (2017)

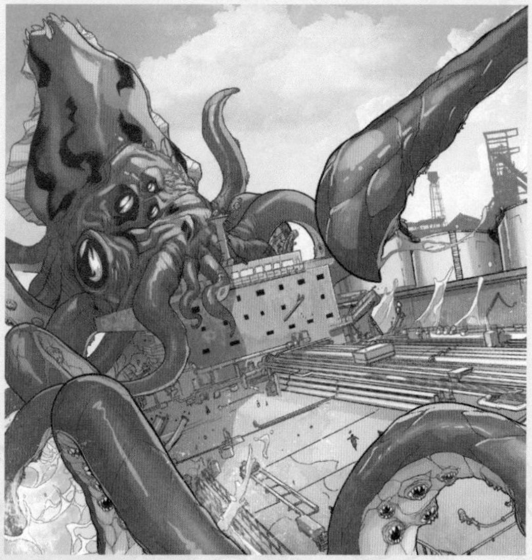

First invaders
One of the Leviathons resembles a giant squidlike creature and proceeds to launch its attack on Corpus Christi, Texas.

Kid Kaiju

With Earth facing the threat of annihilation from a Leviathon Tide, a team of monsters summoned by the young Kei Kawade (code name Kid Kaiju) is humanity's only hope. Imagined, and then drawn, by the 11-year-old Inhuman, this monster team is magically brought to life from the pages of Kei's sketchbook.

When Earth's Super Heroes assembled to discuss how to deal with the Leviathon invasion, the Inhumans shared an ancient prophecy declaring that only one of their kind could turn back the aliens. That hero was Kei Kawade. By drawing the monsters in his book, Kei called upon colossal creatures, some of whom who had once set their own sights on conquering the Earth, but now fought to save it. Blip, Fin Fang Foom, Goom, Googam, Rommbu, Tim Boom Ba, Zzutak, and more responded to his summons. They fought side by side with the Earth's greatest heroes and together managed to turn the Leviathon Tide.

However, when an even bigger threat—the Leviathon Mother—made landfall, Kei created and summoned new monsters to come to his aid. Named Fireclaw, Aegis, Hi-Vo, Scragg, Mekara, and Slizzik, each one had their own unique personality. Battling the Leviathon Mother, Fireclaw was killed. In response, Kei merged the other members of the team, creating a colossal sword-wielding warrior named Smasher, with Kei at the helm. Their combined strength defeated the matriarch. Her remaining brood fled, and Earth was saved.

Kei, his kaiju, and Kei's parents were relocated to the island of Mu where spy agency S.H.I.E.L.D. kept a close eye on them. Monster hunter Elsa Bloodstone served as his bodyguard and mentor. Kei even found a kindred spirit in Mole Man, who also had a soft spot for monsters that terrified everyone else.

Supported by family, mentors, and friends, Kei Kawade and the kind-hearted kaiju team face dangers that are too big for anyone else to handle.

First Appearance: *Monsters Unleashed* Vol. 2 #1 (2017) by Cullen Bunn and Steve McNiven **Further Reading:** *Monsters Unleashed* Vol. 3 (2017)

Monster talent
As the monsters' creator, Kei can summon his creations and communicate directly to them—even if his drawing is partial or incomplete.

Team: Kid Kaiju **Members:** Kei Kawade, Aegis, Hi-Vo, Mekara, Scragg, Slizzik, Smasher (merged form), Fireclaw

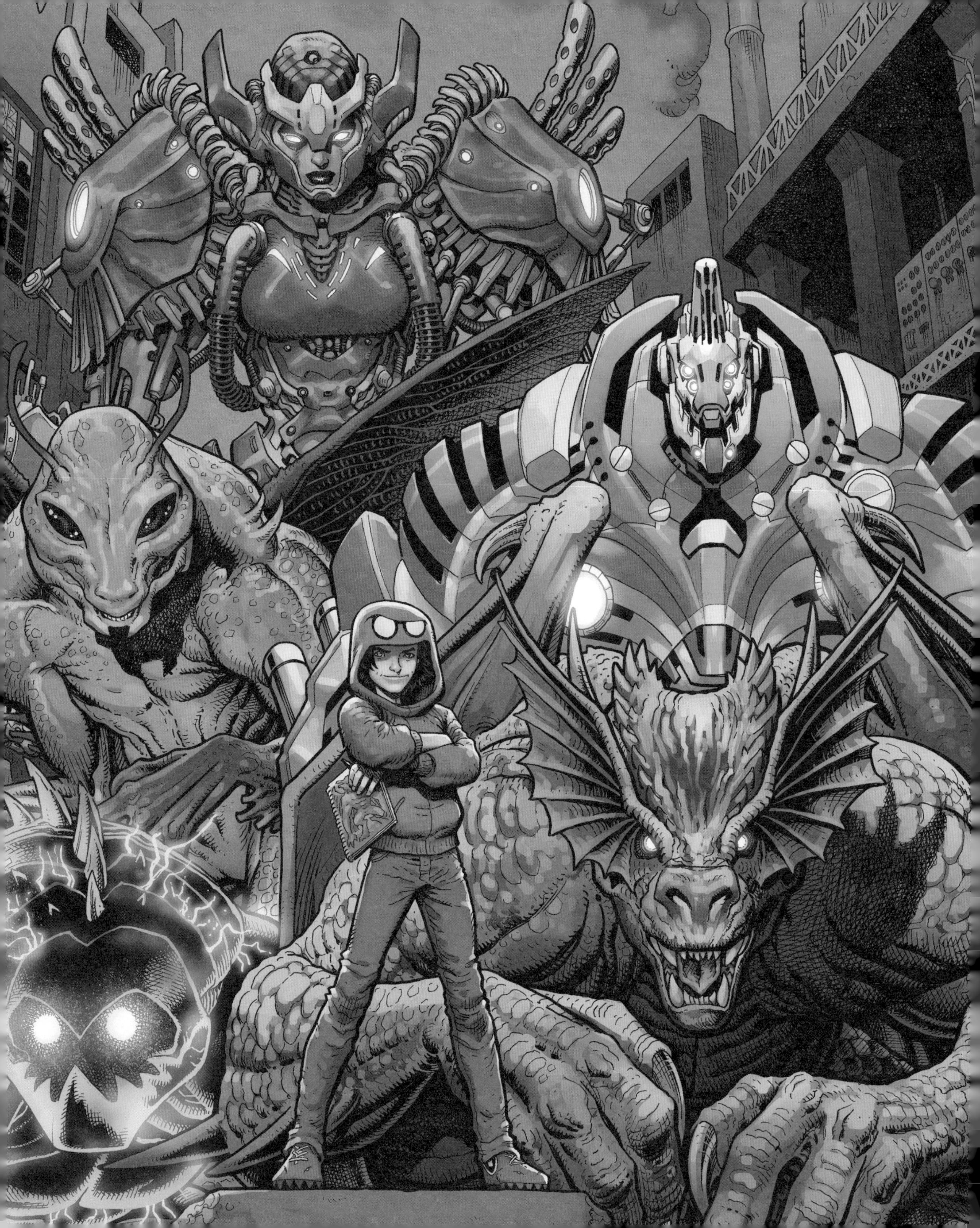

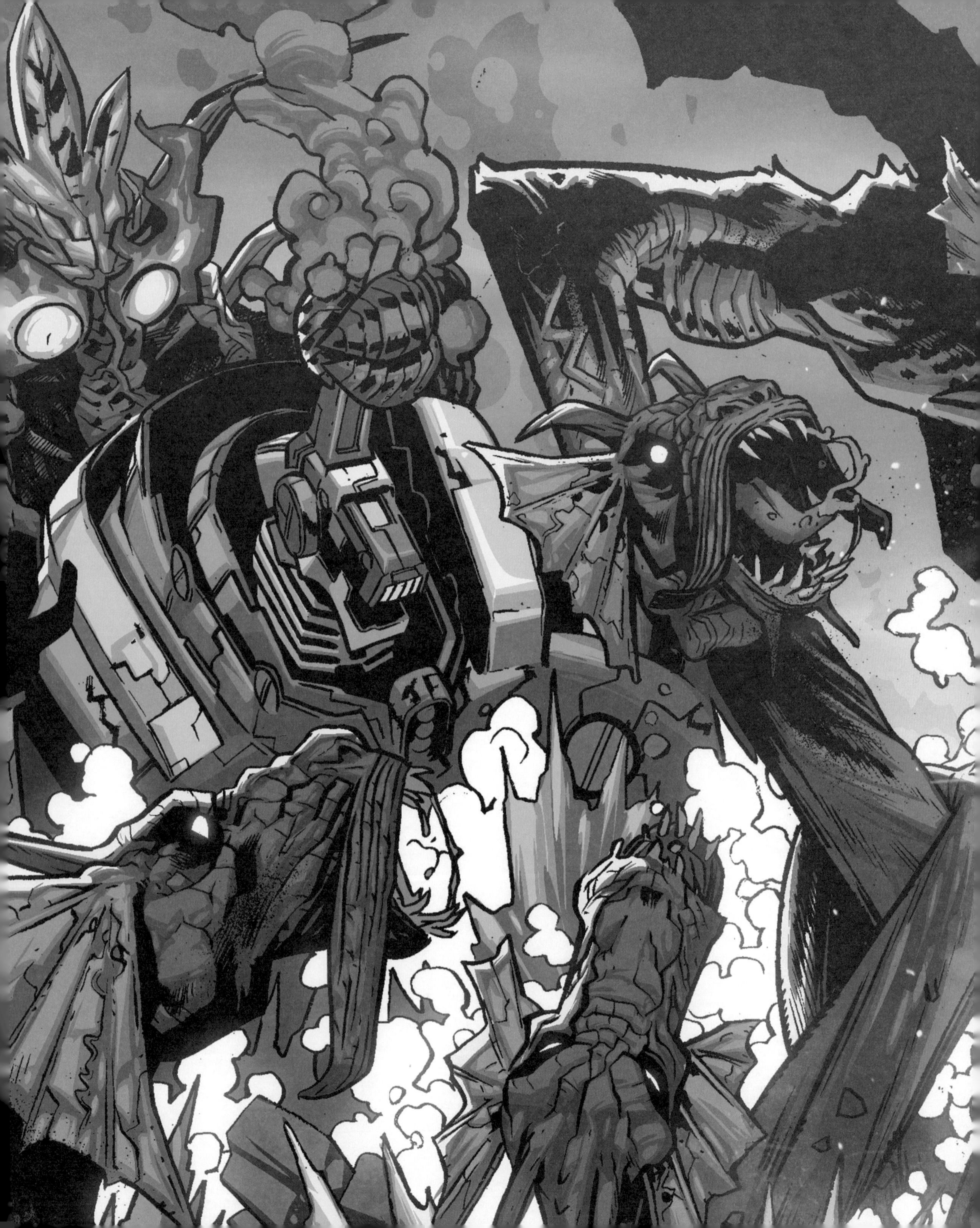

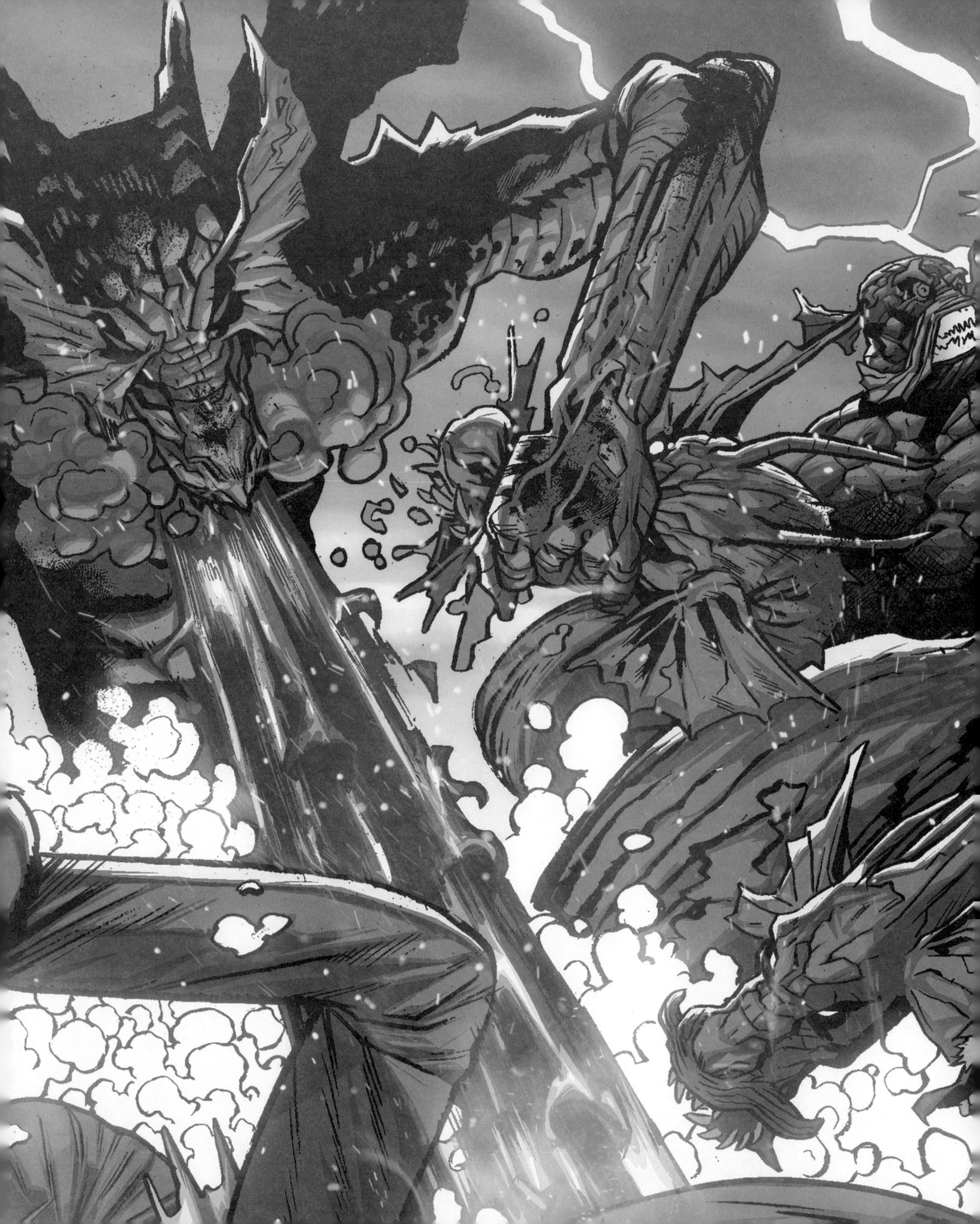

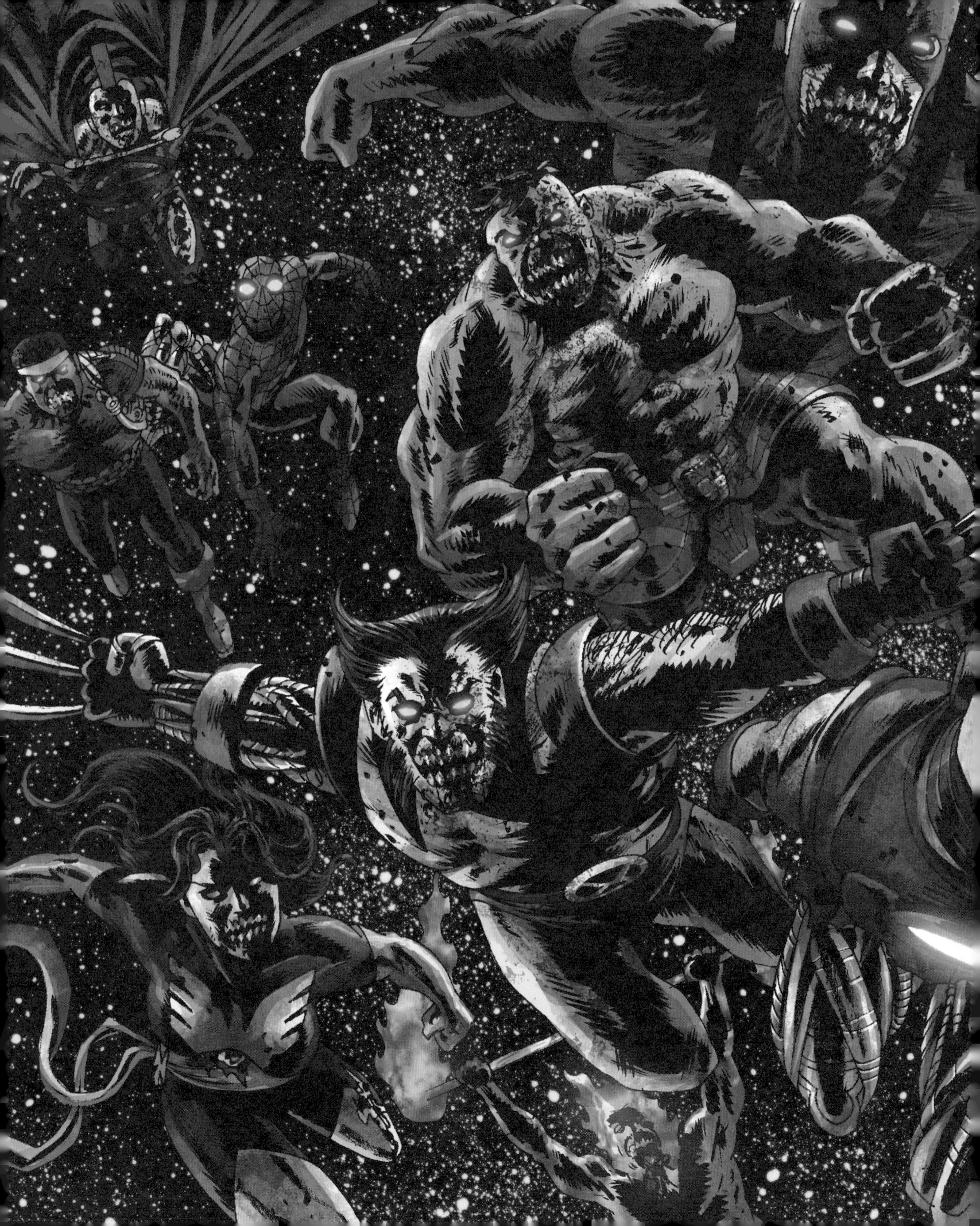

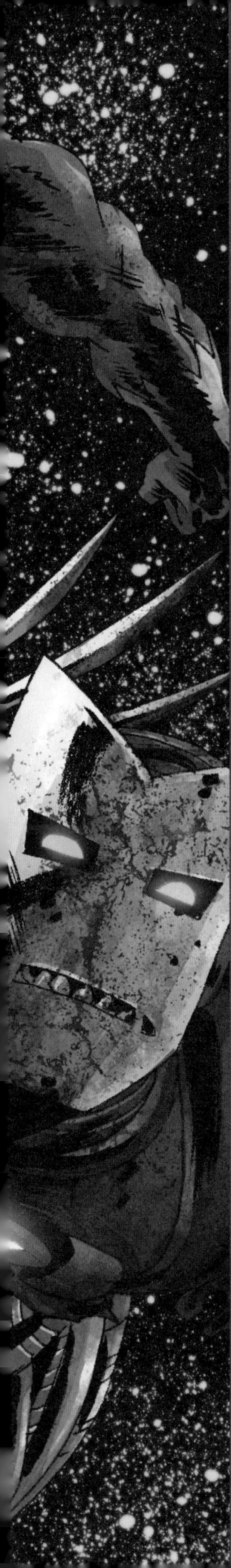

Members: All superpowered beings infected by the Hunger disease

Marvel Zombies

The living dead have overrun the Earth of another dimension. When a zombified hero falls from the stars to Earth-2149, an unstoppable virus in his body spreads like wildfire to the other Super Heroes. No one on any version of Earth is safe from the zombie Avengers, Fantastic Four, and X-Men.

Reed Richards of Earth-1610 was tricked into opening a portal to a zombie-overrun world. On that Earth and a thousand realities before it, the sentient infection targeted Super Heroes first so that it could spread and feed unopposed. The virus was transmitted to every powered being from that one single hero who hailed from an infected universe. The entire world fell to their insatiable hunger within 24 hours.

The infected superpowered creatures kept their abilities, along with most of their intellect and personalities, and coordinated attacks when searching for their next meal. No hero was left unturned. Only mutant Magneto remained uninfected. He helped save Reed and returned him to his Earth. However, the Master of Magnetism could not escape the cannibalistic horde, and he fell victim to their voracious appetites.

The shambling Super Heroes found their next meal in the Silver Surfer. After eating their fill, several individuals, including Colonel America—Earth-2149's version of Captain America Steve Rogers—found they were imbued with the Silver Surfer's Power Cosmic. Because of this, not even Galactus, wielder of the Power Cosmic, was safe. Colonel America, Luke Cage, Wolverine, Hulk, Spider-Man, Beast, and Giant-Man combined their Power Cosmic to take him down. Once the Devourer of Worlds was consumed, the zombie former Super Heroes took to the stars to find even more populations to feast on.

The Marvel Zombies' unending search for food would eventually bring the corpse of Galactus, and the ravenous zombie creatures inside it, to Earth-616. Having made a vow to keep humanity safe, it was left to Spider-Man to face the zombie hordes.

First Appearance: *Ultimate Fantastic Four* #21 (2005) by Mark Millar and Greg Land **Further Reading:** *Marvel Zombies* (2005), *Marvel Zombies: Resurrection* (2020)

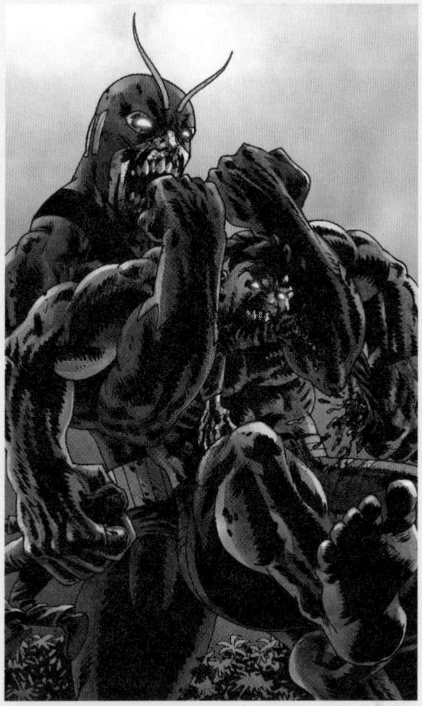

Fighting their instincts
Rather than battling villains, the undead heroes now struggle against their own ravenous impulses. The hunger always wins.

Legion of Monsters

A living vampire, a swamp monster, a motorcycle-riding demon, and a werewolf band together to become the Legion of Monsters. Some time later, other monsters join their mission to keep the innocent oddities and outcasts of Earth safe from persecution and harm.

The first Legion of Monsters was brought together when a mountain burst from the ground—right in the middle of Sunset Boulevard. As Morbius the Living Vampire, Ghost Rider, and Werewolf by Night raced toward it, Man-Thing was also urged toward a mysterious mountain that seemingly emerged from the muck of the Florida swamps. At its peak the foursome found a benevolent being called Starseed. The monsters could not help their natures, and they attacked. Unfortunately for Starseed, he did not survive. The cursed creatures went on their separate ways.

Years later, a new Legion of Monsters formally teamed up—this time without Ghost Rider. They were based in the dark tunnels beneath New York City. The Living Mummy and Manphibian joined their ranks as they fought to protect the hundreds of thousands of monsters seeking refuge in the subterranean city of Monster Metropolis. Not only did they handle unruly creatures in their own society, the Legion of Monsters faced ruthless attackers, such as the Hunter of Monster Special Force, a group hailing from Japan. To help counter these attacks, the Living Vampire Morbius gathered the pieces of the deceased Frank Castle, the Punisher—whose body parts had been tossed into the sewers—and reanimated him into the form of Franken-Castle.

Assisting his fellow monsters, this violent vigilante stopped the hunters and used the powerful artifact they sought to return to life.

Later, the Legion of Monsters assisted the Red Hulk in fighting off a dark entity and checked out a monster sighting with an appreciative Spider-Woman.

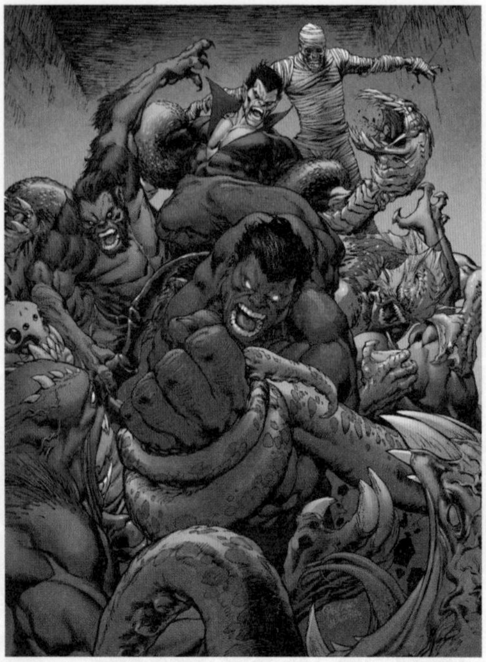

Terrifying team
The Legion of Monsters might be the most grotesque-looking Super Hero team of all, but every member is a hero on the inside.

First Appearance: *Marvel Premiere* #28 (1976) by Bill Mantlo and Frank Robbins **Further Reading:** *Legion of Monsters* (2011)

Original Members: Ghost Rider, Man-Thing, Morbius the Living Vampire, Werewolf by Night
Second Incarnation: Living Mummy, Manphibian, Man-Thing, Morbius, Werewolf by Night

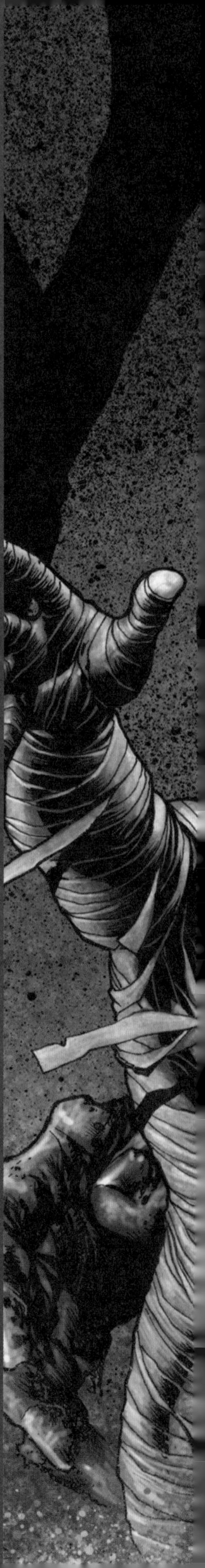

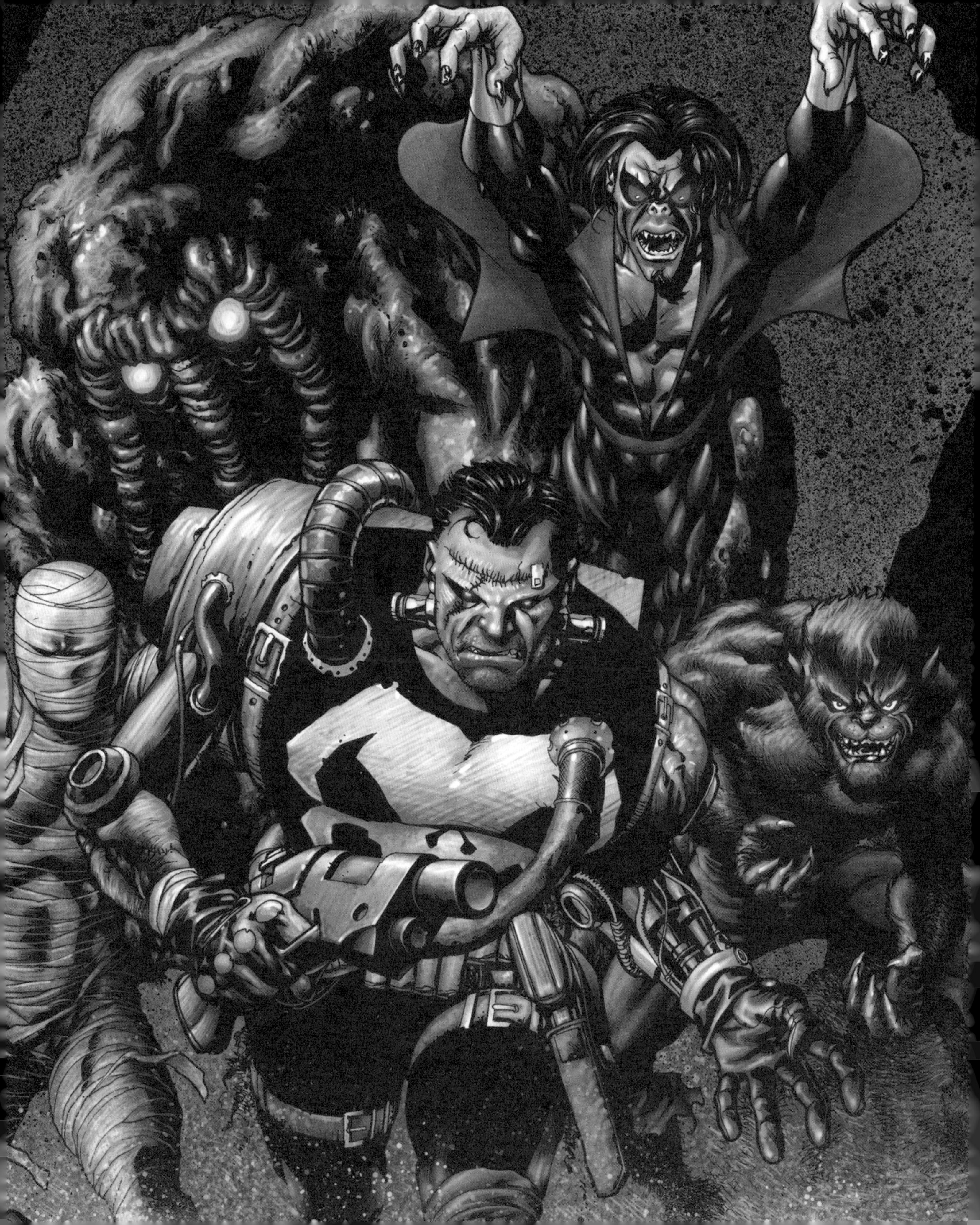

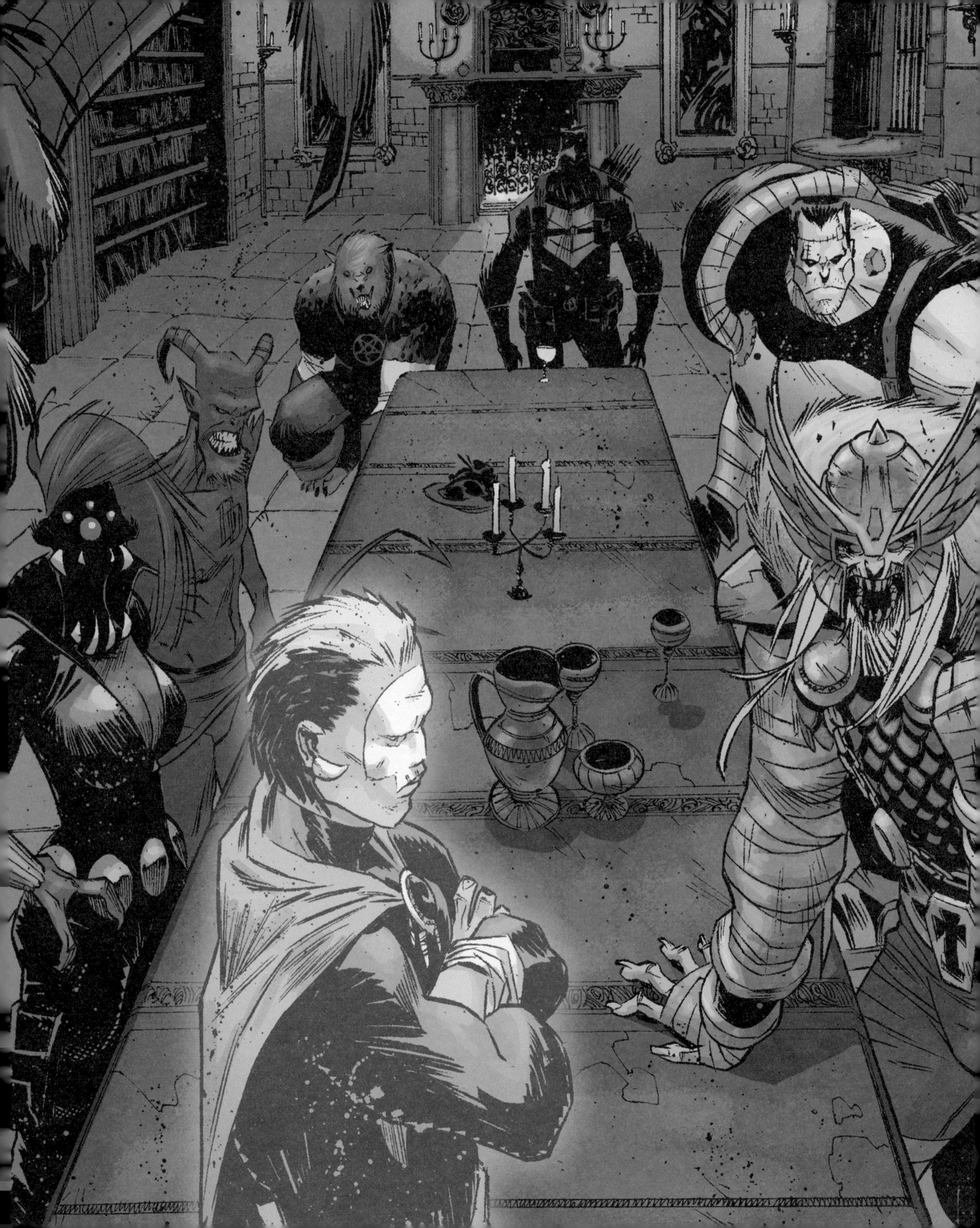

Members: Brother Voodoo (ghost), Steve Rogers (werewolf), Hawkeye (monster), Wolverine (vampire), Daredevil (demon), Franken-Castle (monster), Thor the Accursed (mummy), Black Widow (spider-monster), Spider-Man (spider-monster)

Undead Avengers

Earth-666 is a planet on which every inhabitant is undead. Werewolves, vampires, demons, monsters, and other horrors call this alternate universe home—and many of them were once the mightiest heroes of the Earth that we know. They are the Avengers of the Undead, and they serve death.

Twisted, cursed, and undead versions of venerable Super Heroes make up this terrifying team. Brother Voodoo is a green ghost and appears to be the spokesperson for the group. Captain America Steve Rogers goes by the name of Capwolf—a snarling werewolf complete with fangs, claws, and red eyes. Wolverine is a bloodthirsty vampire with three long Adamantium claws protruding from each wrist. Hawkeye has the head of a hawk. Dressed fully in red, Daredevil is an actual devil, and Spider-Man and Black Widow are monstrous half-human and half-spider creatures with multiple eyes. Thor the Accursed is an undead creature wrapped in tattered mummy bandages. The dead Asgardian brandishes Rinlojm— a malevolent hammer which drains magic and expels tendrils of dark energy. Finally, Franken-Castle (formerly the Punisher) is a stitched-together monster, similar to Frankenstein's legendary creation. The Undead Celestial is the god of this world of the midnight sun.

This unsavory team of Undead Avengers had little overlap with the Super Heroes of other worlds, until Captain Britain of Earth-616 hid the Orb of Necromancy—a mysterious artifact that had been used to give life to the beings the Descendants —with the unsavory group for safekeeping on Earth-666. However, the team was not willing to give it up when he came to retrieve it. The Undead Celestial and ghostly Brother Voodoo had plans to use the Orb to spread chaos and undeath across every universe and dimension.

In order to regain possession of the powerful talisman, Captain Britain, joined by Hawkeye and the mutant Beast, were forced to battle the undead former heroes before safely returning to their own version of Earth, horrified by what they had seen.

There have been no further reported sightings of the Undead Avengers, but it can be assumed the monster teammates continue to reside in Earth-666.

First Appearance: *Secret Avengers* #33 (2012) by Rick Remender and Andy Kuhn
Further Reading: *Secret Avengers* #34-36 (2013)

Changed inside and out
The Avengers on Earth-666 may look familiar, but they are nothing like their heroic counterparts. The Undead Avengers seek only death and chaos.

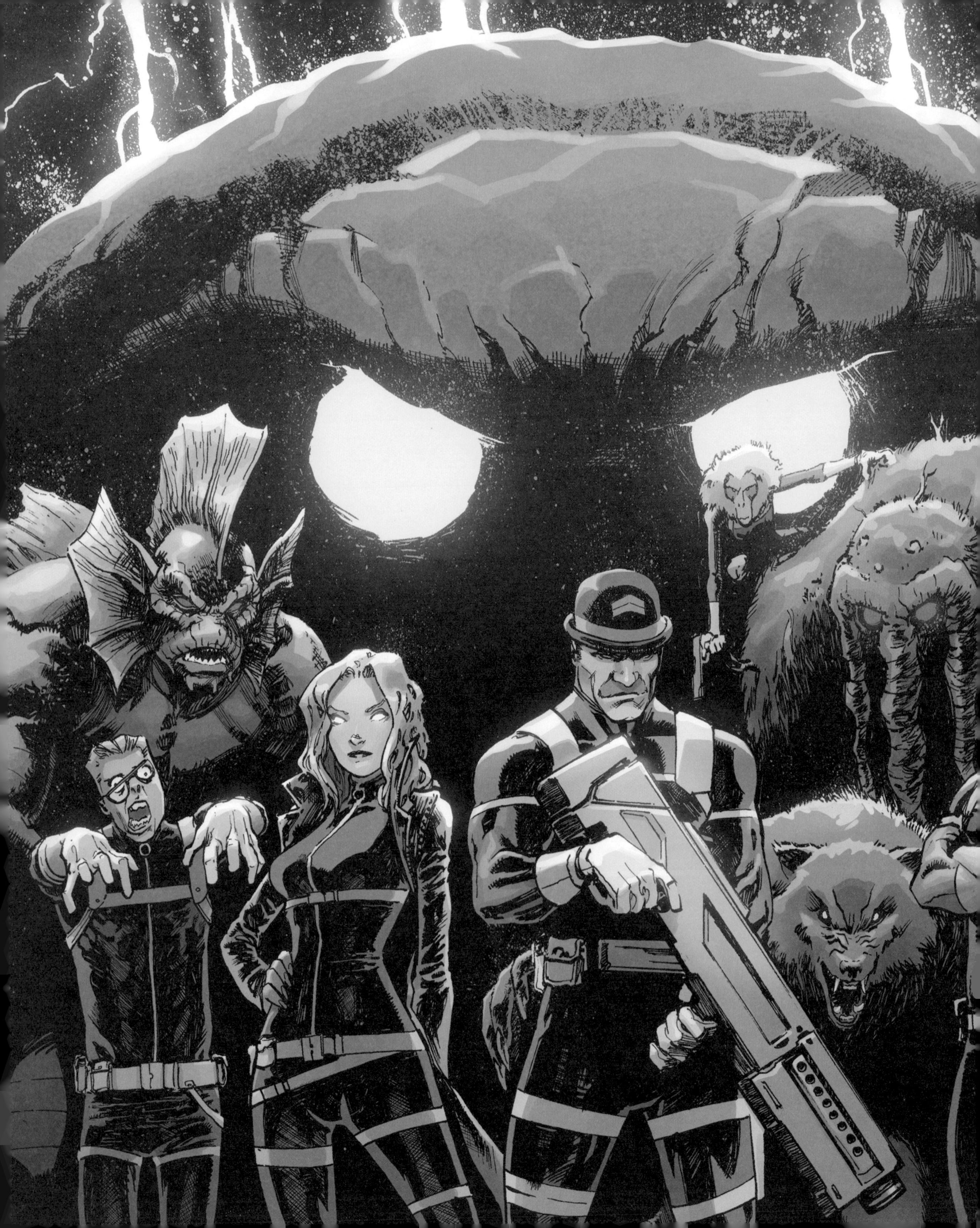

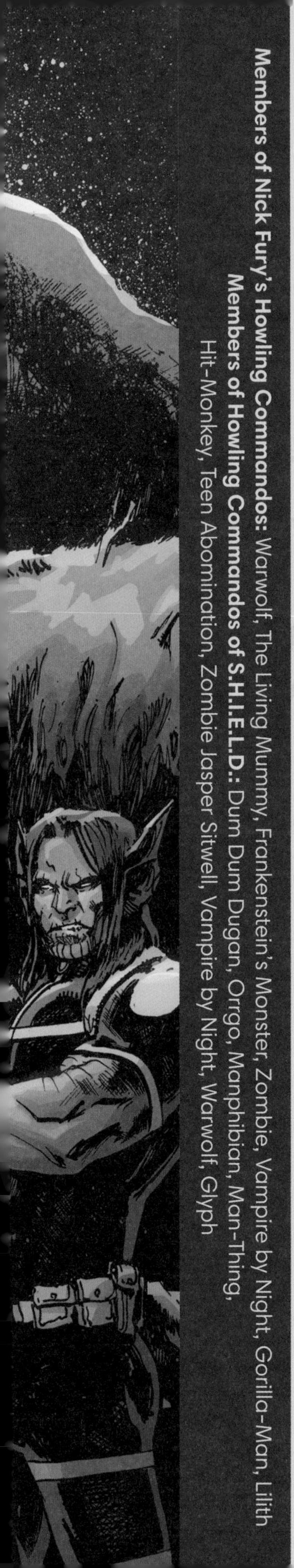

Members of Nick Fury's Howling Commandos: Warwolf, The Living Mummy, Frankenstein's Monster, Zombie, Vampire by Night, Gorilla-Man, Lilith
Members of Howling Commandos of S.H.I.E.L.D.: Dum Dum Dugan, Orrgo, Manphibian, Man-Thing, Hit-Monkey, Teen Abomination, Zombie Jasper Sitwell, Vampire by Night, Warwolf, Glyph

Howling Commandos

The namesake of this powerhouse team has a storied history, but the Howling Commandos make the name their own. The secret squad of monsters, helmed by some of the original team members, takes on the supernatural threats that are deemed too dangerous for ordinary heroes.

The Howling Commandos first fought in World War II under the command of Sgt. Nick Fury, going up against some of the Axis Powers' worst villains such as the Red Skull and Baron von Strucker.

Years after the war, Fury conscripted a group of macabre monsters to battle otherworldly threats. The "shock and awe" team was a part of S.H.I.E.L.D. and was unofficially dubbed Nick Fury's Howling Commandos. The motley crew consisted of mummies, zombies, vampires, and the like. They were based in Area 13 in New Jersey where S.H.I.E.L.D. ran its black ops program tackling supernatural threats. When a sorcerer claiming to be the legendary mage Merlin broke out of S.H.I.E.L.D. custody, the squad was dispatched to investigate. They followed "Merlin" to England, where they discovered he had turned the entire country into a fantasy realm. They were successful in stopping the mystical danger.

Some time later, a Life-Model Decoy of original Howling Commando Dum Dum Dugan was activated and used to head up a new incarnation of the team. The recruits comprised of a ragtag bunch of monsters—such as Man-Thing, Orrgo, Vampire by Night, and Manphibian. They were known as the Howling Commandos of S.H.I.E.L.D. As part of S.H.I.E.L.D.'s Supernatural Threat Analysis for Known Extranormalities (S.T.A.K.E.) division, the field team's mission was special threat assessment, containment, and recovery: taking on threats that were considered too dangerous for humans. Their adventures led them onto the *S.S. Chaney* where, thanks to Man-Thing, they defeated its crew who had been mutated by the Earth idol of Golthana.

A later mission saw them recruit teenager Nadeen Hassan aka Glyph, who struggled to control her ancient mystical powers as they successfully battled her possessed brother and the Sphinx. The team's current status is unknown.

First Appearance: *Nick Fury's Howling Commandos* #1 (2005) by Keith Giffen and Eduardo Francisco **Further Reading:** *Howling Commandos of S.H.I.E.L.D.* #1 (2015)

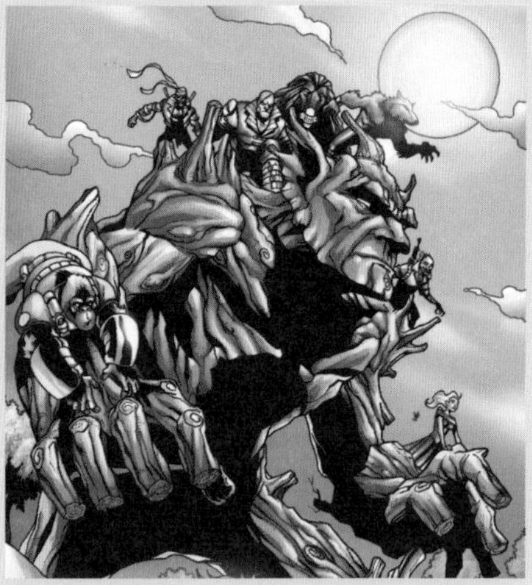

Found family
No matter the members of the team, the monsters who fight for the Howling Commandos quickly find kindred spirits among its ranks.

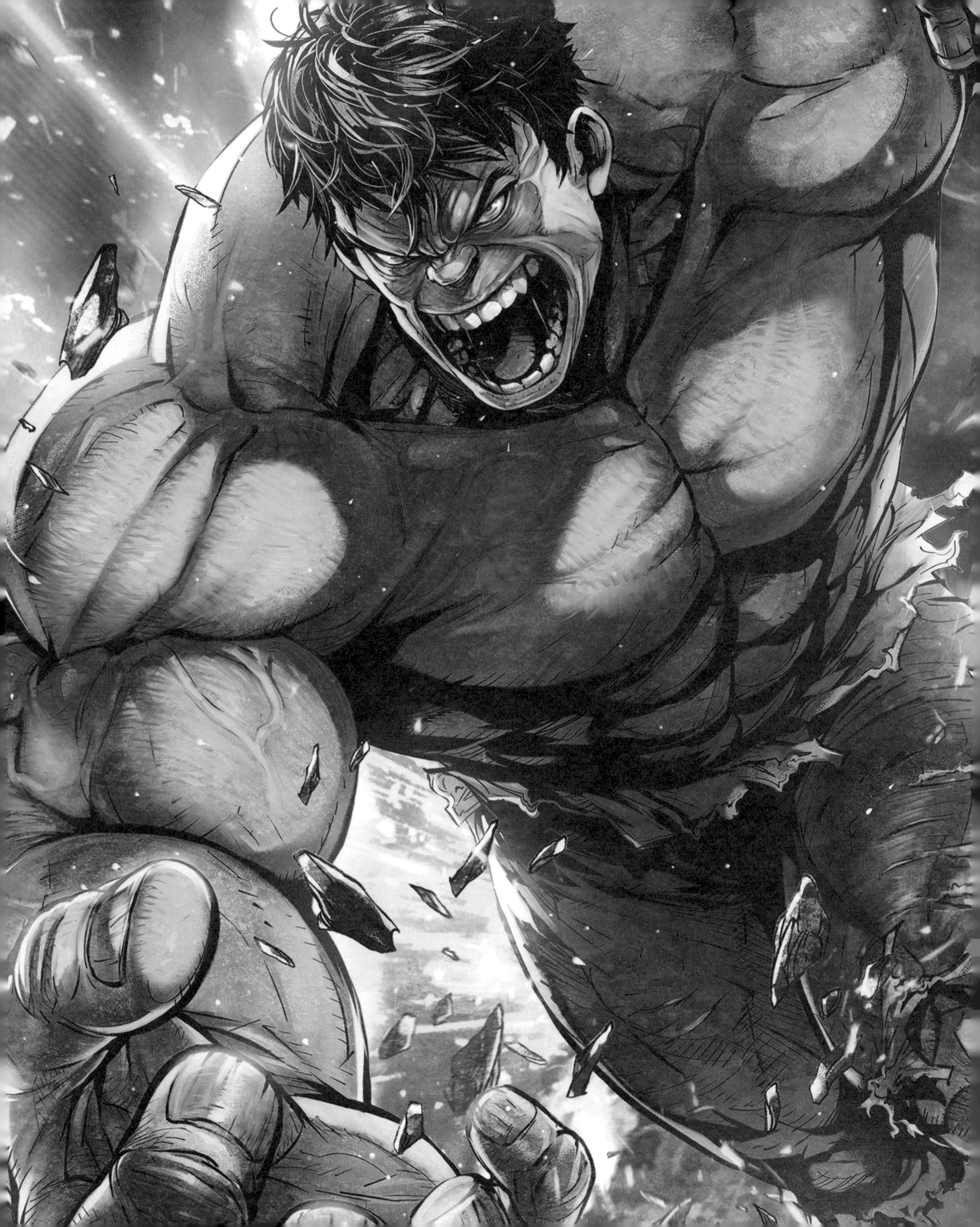

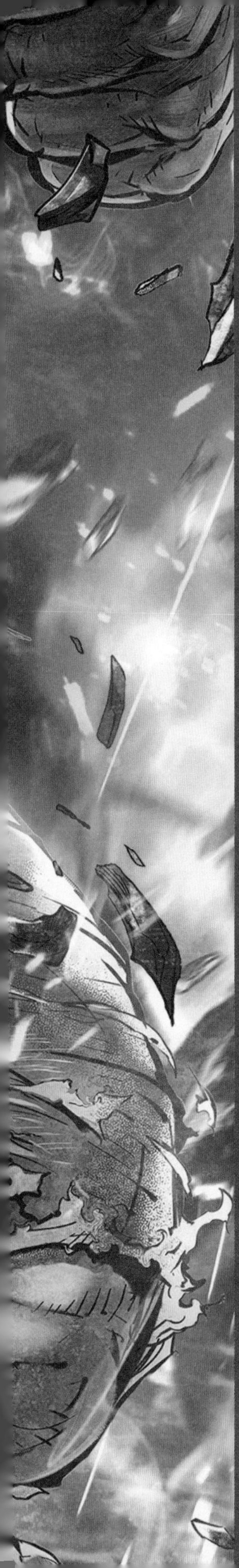

Hulks: Hulk (Bruce Banner), Totally Awesome Hulk (Amadeus Cho), She-Hulk (Jennifer Walters), Red Hulk (Thaddeus Ross), Red She-Hulk (Betty Ross)

Hulk

Many creatures have gone by the name of Hulk. Monstrous in size and appearance, but mostly heroic in nature, even when rage overtakes reason, they fight to protect those who fear them. Banner, Cho, Ross, and Walters—they are the Hulk!

Bruce Banner became the first incredible Hulk after an accident on a military testing site bombarded him with gamma radiation. The incident unleashed a monster. At night Bruce transformed into an unstoppable green-skinned behemoth capable of complete destruction. In time his metamorphosis would be involuntarily triggered by stress, fear, or anger, all of which drove the Hulk to destroy. But he also fought to protect and save innocent people. As the Hulk, Bruce has gone from an original member of the Avengers to savage leader of a war-torn planet.

When Bruce's cousin Jennifer Walters was attacked by criminals, Bruce gave her a blood transfusion. Not only did it save her life, it gave her the gamma-powered strength he had as well. She became the sensational She-Hulk. While she typically retained her intellect as a green giantess, trauma transformed her for a time into a more powerful but less rational Hulk. She practiced law and served with the Avengers and Fantastic Four.

Young genius Amadeus Cho took the mantle of Hulk when he used nanites to absorb excess gamma radiation from Bruce. He saved Bruce and transferred the radiation to his own body, creating the Totally Awesome Hulk. Amadeus struggled with arrogance, rage, and the darker side of his persona. In time the gamma radiation in the nanobots was depowered, and he learned to accept himself. Amadeus renamed himself Brawn.

General Thaddeus Ross, longtime opponent of Bruce Banner, became the monster he hated with the assistance of smart villains. As Red Hulk, Ross sought to even the playing field and finally defeat the Hulk. The goliath was conscripted into joining the Avengers after his own attempted takeover of the U.S. He found redemption as a hero.

His daughter, Betty Ross, was the love of Bruce Banner's life. As a result, she was often targeted by Hulk's enemies. She was kidnapped and transformed into the hideous, winged Harpy before Banner cured her. Later, she seemingly died, but had in fact been turned into the Red She-Hulk. The two fought side by side. In time, Betty's body again transformed into a horrific fusion of both Red She-Hulk and Harpy.

First Appearance: *Incredible Hulk* #1 (1962) by Stan Lee and Jack Kirby

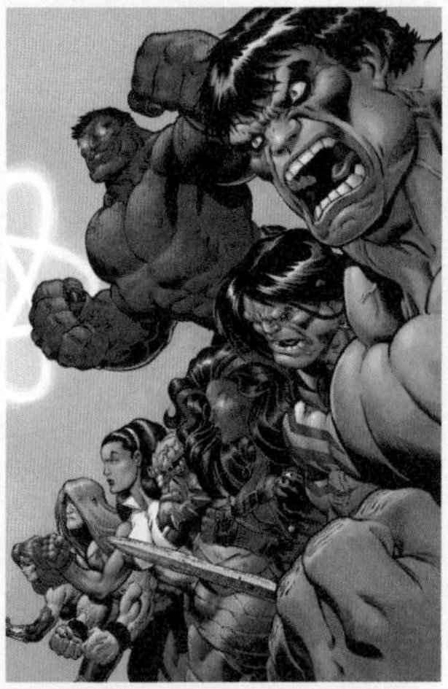

Incredible family
The extended Hulk family is a gamma-powered collection of heroes who are very strong and very angry. A-Bomb, Doc Samson, Skaar, and Lyra are often counted among their ranks.

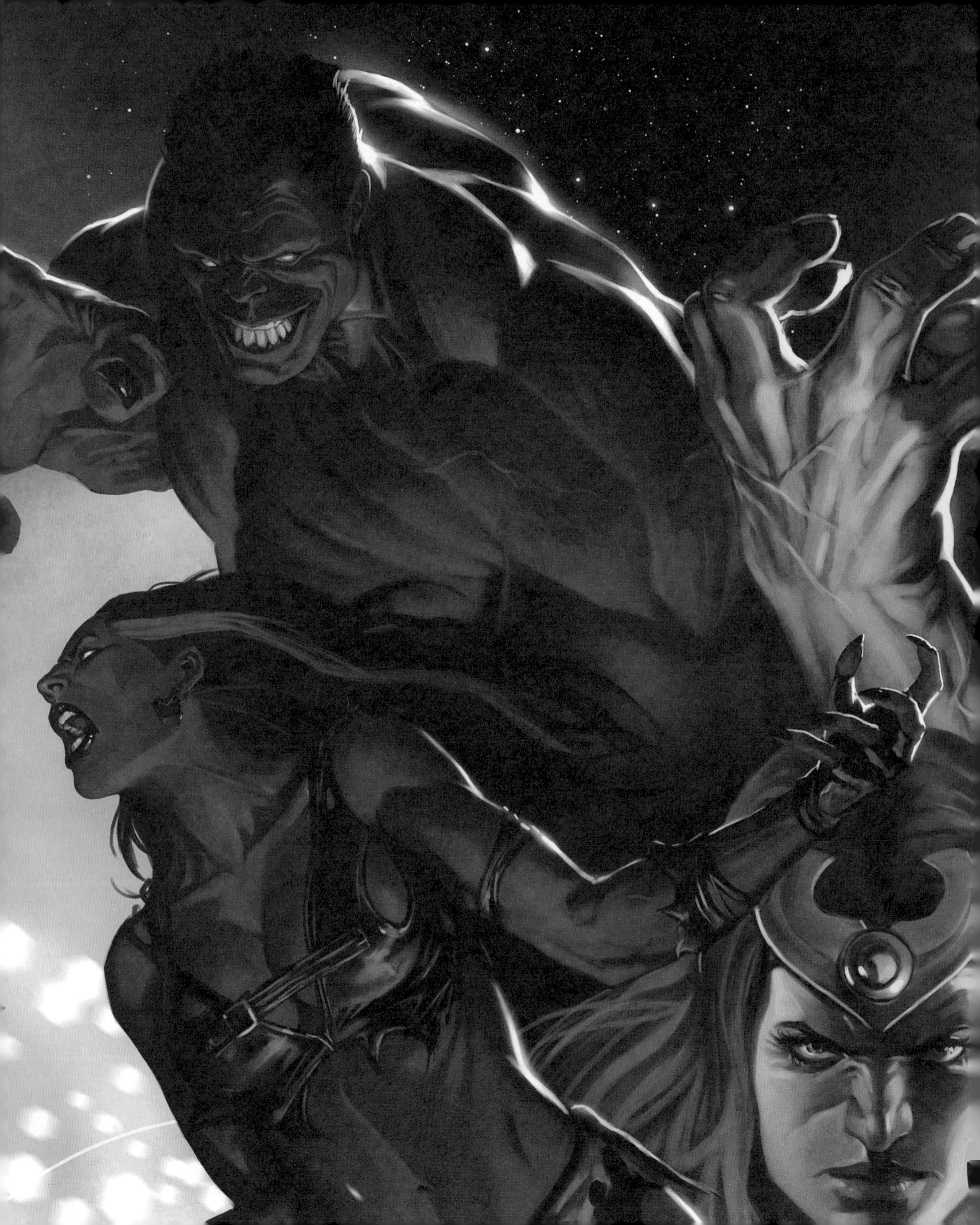

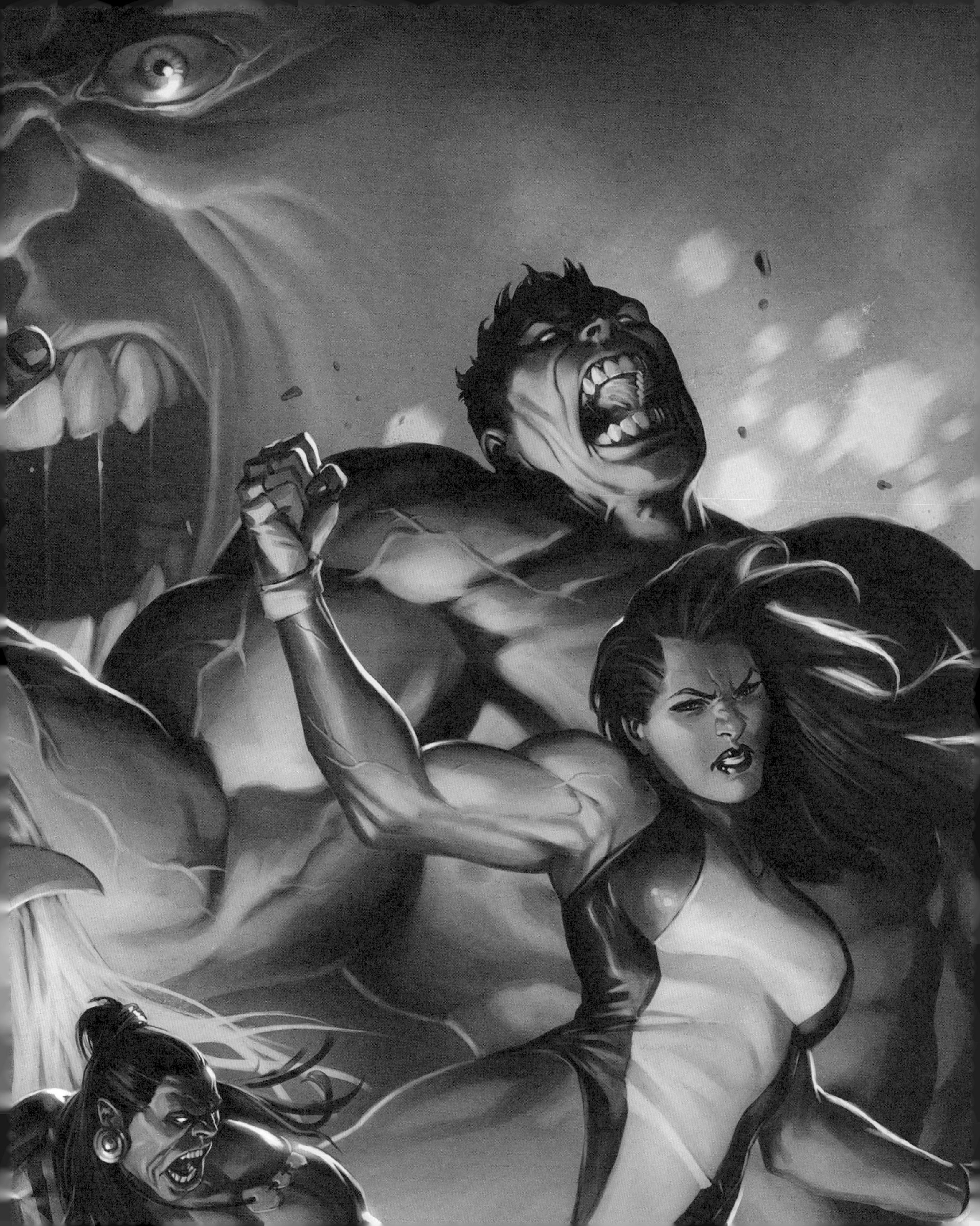

Index

Page numbers in *italics* refer to illustrations

T

U

V

W

X

Y

Z

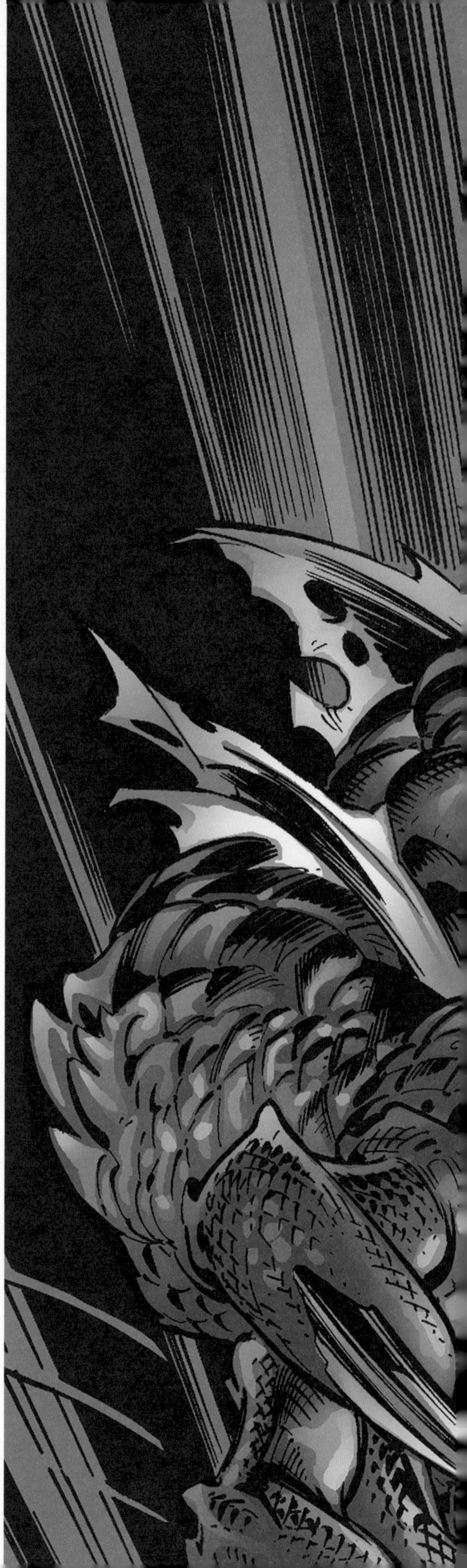

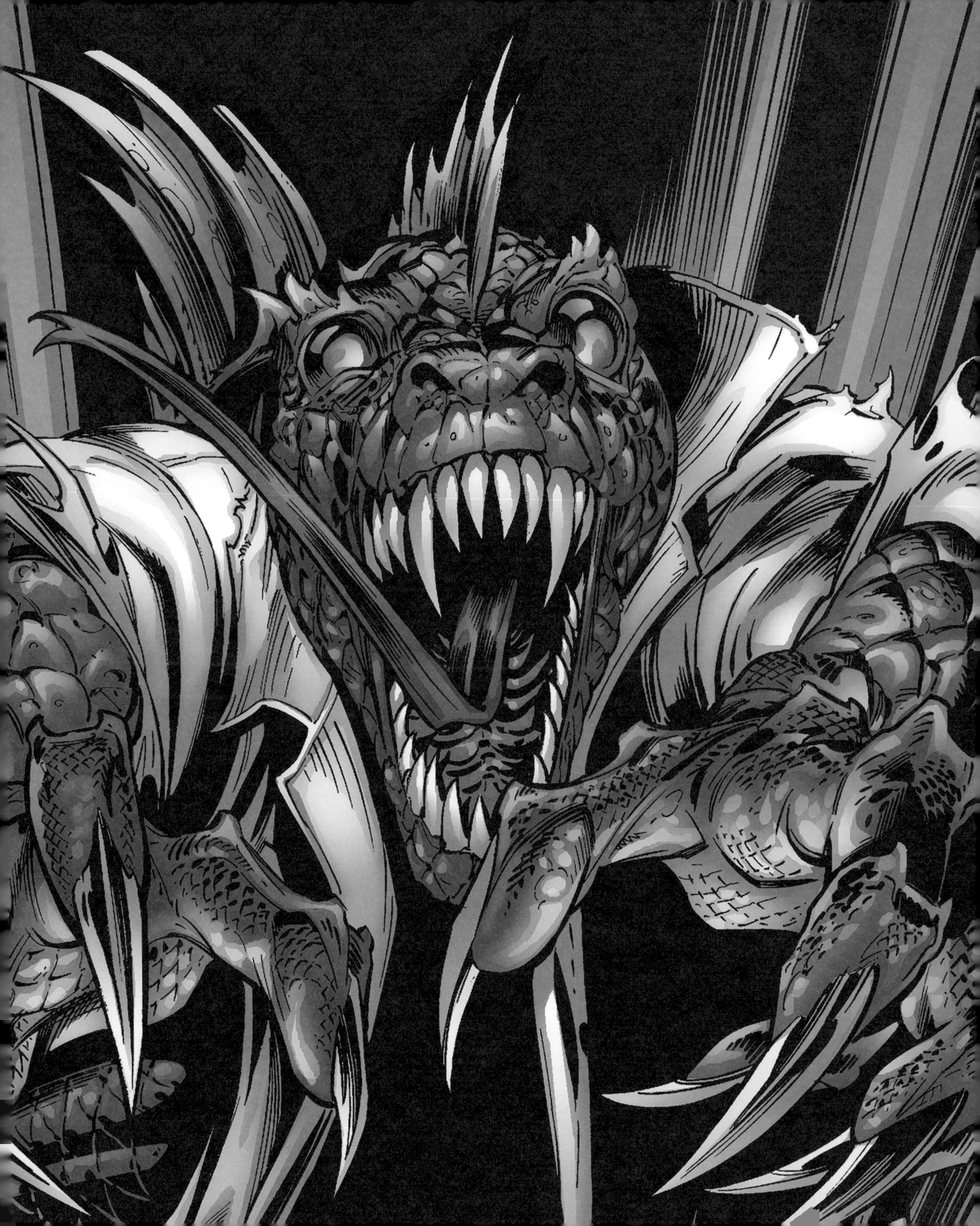

Senior Editor Emma Grange
Senior Art Editor Clive Savage
Designer Rosamund Bird
Editor Kathryn Hill
Senior Production Editor Jennifer Murray
Senior Production Controller Louise Minihane
Managing Editor Sarah Harland
Managing Art Editor Vicky Short
Publishing Director Mark Searle

First American Edition, 2021
Published in the United States by DK Publishing
1450 Broadway, Suite 801, New York, NY 10018

Page design copyright © 2021 Dorling Kindersley Limited
DK, a Division of Penguin Random House LLC
21 22 23 24 10 9 8 7 6 5 4 3 2 1
001–321874–Jul/2021

© 2021 MARVEL

A catalog record for this book is available from the Library of Congress.
ISBN 978-0-7440-2862-1

DK books are available at special discounts when purchased in bulk
for sales promotions, premiums, fund-raising, or educational use.
For details, contact: DK Publishing Special Markets,
1450 Broadway, Suite 801, New York, NY 10018
SpecialSales@dk.com

Printed in China

ACKNOWLEDGMENTS

DK would like to thank Kelly Knox for her text and input; Chelsea Alon at Disney,
Brian Overton, Caitlin O'Connell, Jeff Youngquist, and Joe Hochstein at Marvel;
Julie Ferris and Lisa Lanzarini; Matt Jones for editorial help; and Vanessa Bird for the index.

The author would like to thank Bianca, Brian, and Maddy for their unwavering support.

For the curious

www.dk.com
www.marvel.com

This book is made from
Forest Stewardship Council™
certified paper—one small
step in DK's commitment
to a sustainable future.

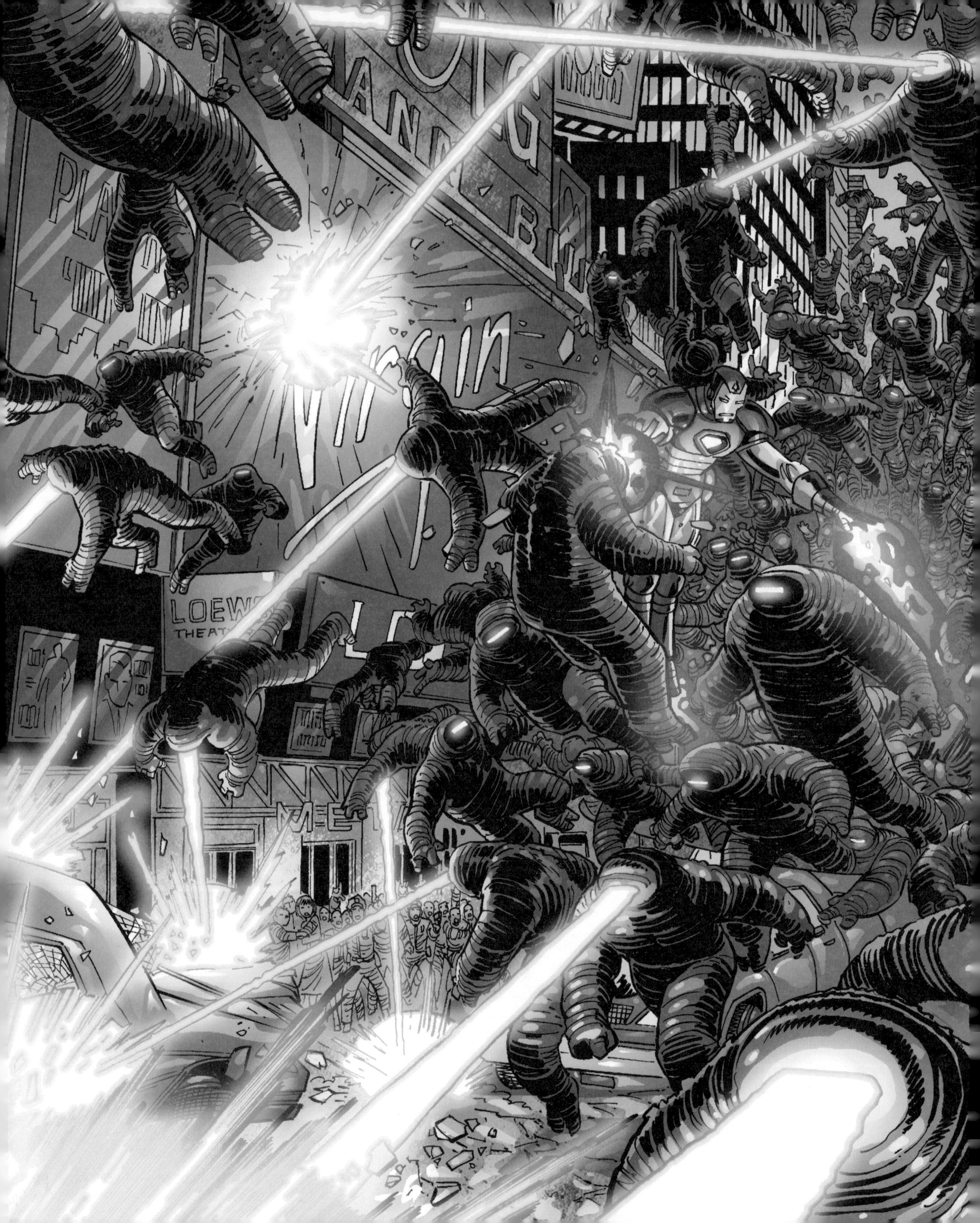